THE HOUSE OF GRINS

Books by Donald Levin

The Detroit Series

The Ghosts of Detroit
The Arsenal of Deceit
Savage City

The Martin Preuss Series

In the House of Night
Cold Dark Lies
An Uncertain Accomplice
The Forgotten Child
Guilt in Hiding
The Baker's Men
Crimes of Love

Poetry

Are You Listening? Selected Poetry
New Year's Tangerine
In Praise of Old Photographs

Dystopian Fiction

The Exile
Postcards from the Future: A Triptych on Humanity's End
(with Andrew Lark and Wendy Thomson)

THE HOUSE

OF

GRINS

A NOVEL

Donald Levin

Poison Toe Press

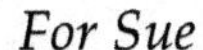

For Sue

"There is a kind of sadness that comes from knowing too much, from seeing the world as it truly is. It is the sadness of understanding that life is not a grand adventure, but a series of small, insignificant moments, that love is not a fairy tale, but a fragile, fleeting emotion, that happiness is not a permanent state, but a rare, fleeting glimpse of something we can never hold onto. And in that understanding, there is a profound loneliness, a sense of being cut off from the world, from other people, from oneself."

—Virginia Woolf

THE HOUSE OF GRINS

Space and light in every direction: this first impression does it.

Standing in the entrance foyer with the real estate agent, he sees ten-foot ceilings in the keeping room off to the left, a torrent of spring sunlight pouring through the leaded glass windows in the living room to the right, a seeming acre of golden oak floors with a new satin finish leading straight back to the dining room, kitchen, mud porch. From the front of the house, he can see all the way through to the back yard and the garage, with old-fashioned sliding wooden doors and room for four cars.

Of all the houses he has seen, only this, with its airy first floor and huge interior, has the room and charm to contain Robert Fitzgerald's outsized vision of the life he wants to create, and this alone persuades him.

He examines the rest of the house. He asks the usual questions— How old is the furnace? The roof? The wiring? The plumbing? He walks from room to room, up and down stairs, second floor bedrooms to dusty attic, down to the damp stone cellar (there are twelve squeaking steps from the second floor to the first, he notes with amusement). He runs his hands along walls thick with layers of painted-over wallpaper, bowed out by the substantial weight of years but still intact as the legacy of the people who have lived here, adding to and moving on, to death or other houses, passing this old thing into others' hands, others' lives. Robert Fitzgerald's. To do with as he wishes, project his own life upon the premises, along with the lives of the others who would join him here. Whomever they might be.

Only when he surveys the house again from the outside, convinced it is exactly what he wants, does he zero in on the wooden face looking out from the pediment over the front door. He laughs out loud. Painted brown against a white background is a man's face, a vegetable god with eyebrows, cheeks, and beard of stylized oak leaves. The bulging lunatic eyes of this amazing face roll heavenward on either side of a boxer's thick nose, and its mouth hangs agape in a wild flabbergasted grin above a sinuous bed of flowers like an exaggerated bowtie.

"Neat, eh?" the agent says, following Robert's eye.

Robert nods agreement. From the street he takes it all in. Three overgrown junipers with trunks thick as veiny arms partly obscure the white wooden porch spindles that run the width of the front of the house. Wooden columns on the railing support two full upper levels shingled with cedar shakes stained brown and two tiers of pitched roofs that rise to peaks along gingerbread woodwork. And of course, that wonderful face, setting this place apart from the other sedate homes on the tree-lined block. They must date from the early years of the twentieth century, these solid old things, their green manicured lawns sloping gently upward like the middle-class aspirations that caused them to be built. And built well: back then they had an eye for the constructional intricacies, the ornamentation and silhouettes at sunset, that make a home a joy to look at as well as live in.

That house is definitely more than neat, he reflects on the way back to the real estate office. Like that great face, it is funny, charming, teasing, taunting, exciting, providential, and entirely, ironically, appropriate . . . He turns these words over with pleasure like chunks of velvety bitter chocolate on his tongue.

"Owner's anxious to sell," the agent reminds him.

Good, Robert thinks. Buyer's anxious to buy.

CHAPTER ONE

1

Lined up on the counter with compulsive care are a cream-colored one-inch bristle brush, a newly sharpened No. 2 pencil, a brand-new roll of tan masking tape, a long pair of scissors with orange plastic handles, a short stack of this week's newspapers, unopened bottles of poster paint in red and yellow and blue, a torn tee shirt to wipe spills, and a cottage cheese tub of water for the rinse.

Am I organized or what? he thinks, and turns his attention to the floor.

There on his knees he tapes sections of the *Buckingham Press & Sun Bulletin* together (pleased finally to have found a useful purpose for the local rag, which is certainly no good for the news) and affixes it all to the linoleum with masking tape. He sweeps a long brown sheet of butcher's paper from a roll on the floor and reaches into the cupboard beneath the sink for something heavy to hold the loose end. He comes up with a box of Grand Union Automatic Dish Washer Detergent that he lays on its side to stay the paper's curling ends.

Robert Fitzgerald, sign painter's son, cuts a perfectly straight line across the paper near the roll and scampers monkey-like from one end to the other on cracking knees, unrolling tape down the lengths of the brown paper, attaching it to the newspapers underneath. His father labored mightily to make a sign painter out of him in the old days, but Robert had no desire to either learn the trade or please his father. Eventually the old man gave up and tried with his younger son, who had the will but not the talent, and then his daughter, who had the talent but not the patience. In the end nobody carried on the business the old man worked so hard to create and it died when he did. He never forgave any of them, not brother Tommy, who became a department manager at Saks' Detroit store, nor sister Lenore, who became head of the Math Department at Birmingham Groves high school in Michigan, and most especially not Robert, who set the bad example for the rest of them to follow. In this, as in everything.

Robert smooths the coarse paper of the sign he would never paint for his father. Gordon, Gordon, he says to the old man, dead fifteen years, if you had just lived long enough you would have seen me paint a sign after all. And it would have done you proud. This will be a great sign, an aesthetically pleasing and functional sign, a welcoming sign for the guests to my housewarming party tomorrow night, easy to read and with just the right touch of childhood gaiety tempered with adult irony.

In fact (he continues to his dad, already having a longer talk with him than they ever had in life, conscious he follows in the old bird's footsteps this night as he once swore he never would), if you'd lived long enough you would have seen me come around in any number of ways. The army, school, career, general craziness, marriage, all sorted themselves out with time. (Maybe not marriage. No, Robert considers on short reflection, definitely not marriage.) But you didn't wait long enough. And even before you died, you had turned your grim ram's head away from me forever, shoving your sweaty tangled hair in my face to kiss instead of your cheek on your death bed.

Well, who could blame you? Too many disappointments on both sides, too many hardened attitudes, too much bad feeling bred over the years between father and son. Nope, can't blame you, Robert thinks. Can't forgive you for turning away, of course, but can't blame you either.

Robert stands, forms a gestalt of the long canvas he prepared for himself, takes up the pencil, and begins.

He sketches round, festive letters that spell out "HERE'S THE PARTY!" then ovaloid balloons with squiggly tails hanging down like huge mutant sperm. He opens the bottle of red paint and fills in every third letter. The paper bubbles and absorbs the color. The edges of the letters blur.

He hears a familiar thrumming and before he can stop it Howard the cat pads into the middle of his poster and steps daintily into the first painted letter.

The cat stops and flicks his paw, in the process flinging drips and stamping pawprints over the poster. Then Howard neatly eludes Robert's outstretched hand that wants to scoop him up. Howard leaps up to the counter where, paw still raised, he dumps the tub of water and scatters the materials Robert laid out so anal-retentively.

"You stinker," Robert says (though in truth he loves the little bugger). Howard glares back at him with slitted yellow eyes, deep-chested, long-haired black body tensed for fight or flight. "Don't you be looking at me like that," Robert cautions. He shakes his brush at the defiant beast.

Howard's owner appears in the doorway. Tall and boney in a black tee shirt that says "Shit Happens" in white script. "What's going on?"

"Would you speak to your animal companion, please?"

"What's the matter?"

"Look what he did to my sign. He's on a search-and-destroy mission here."

"Well, just a second. How do I know those are his tracks?"

"I saw him do it."

Dennis Parker sticks his long nose right up to Howard's black leather snout and says, "Uh-oh. Caught in the act, pal." Howard swipes his cheek on Dennis's chin with a sneer aimed at Robert.

Dennis picks the cat up and examines the paint on his forefoot. "I think he's got you there, Howie." Dennis tears off a length of paper towel from the dispenser under the cabinets, wets it in the sink, and wipes the cat's paw.

Howard squirms lethally and Dennis has to toss him out the back door before the animal shreds him with his claws. The cat scampers off the mud porch with tail obscenely high, like a middle finger.

Dennis closes the door on his pet and turns to Robert. "Is that for the party?"

"Yeah."

"Did he really ruin it?"

"No. I just wanted him to think he did. Actually those pawprints look kind of nice."

"He's an artistic little guy, don't you think?"

Dennis takes a carton of Grand Union orange juice from the fridge and pours himself a glass. He folds his thin body into a kitchen chair, hunched as though already expecting Robert's disapproval over what he is about to say. "So, Robert. About this party, man. I'm not sure I can make it. No, really. Look, I'm an incredibly busy guy, my super-playboy-lifestyle social calendar is chock full, and I just don't know if I can fit it in."

"Dennis."

"I know what you're going to say, but—."

"Don't even try. I don't want to argue about this. It's going to be a good party. You'll have fun."

"What if I don't?"

"You'll have to move."

"Come on, man, I'm serious. I hate parties. I never have a good time."

"This is a party for the people who live in this house. You live in this house. Ergo, it's a party for you. It'll be fun by definition."

"But I really don't like parties. I mean, like, really."

"You're starting to whine."

"I'm serious, man."

"Tell you what. You're an adult. You don't want to come? Fine. Your decision. Stay in your room. I don't want to hear you complain about how lonely you are."

Dennis stares dispiritedly at the sign on the floor. "I thought you were a compassionate guy. Are you this tough on your clients?"

"My clients listen to me. They trust my wisdom."

Dennis pouts, has no response. After a while he sighs, "Oh man," and shuffles into the living room.

Robert finishes his poster after one a.m. He leaves it to dry on the floor, where it will be safe as long as Howard spends the night outside.

Dennis went upstairs an hour ago, still petulant from their run-in. Not that anyone was forcing him to come to this thing, for all Robert's cajoling. Dennis, a jangly twenty-five-year-old, makes his own decisions. That was part of the bargain when he moved in. It's not something he needs to be reminded of constantly.

Robert prepares a cup of instant decaf and carries it through the darkened downstairs. Out the window of the keeping room, the big brick house across the street looms ghostly blue from the streetlamp at the corner. The gloomy, silent street still glistens from the fall rainstorm that swept through earlier.

It's a good night to be inside. Robert, content burgher, sips his coffee.

At this late hour, with no distractions, the day's work well over, his contentment expands, fills every corner in the house, his house, where upstairs the rest of his new family, such as it is, lie asleep.

The pleasures of domestic life . . .

In the peace and darkness, he reflects on a period that seems several lifetimes ago, when he was little older than Dennis but already had the accouterments of adulthood, a wife and two young kids, a tour in Viet Nam and a decade of hell-raising behind him. Up early on dark winters' Saturday mornings, hardwood floors icy under his bare feet in the tiny apartment he and Jeannie rented above the music store in Royal Oak outside Detroit, while she and the kids, Brian and Nora, still slept, he was on top of the world then.

Even now, so many years later, he remembers the satisfactions—though his memory is elegiac, shaded as it is by the years that proved his satisfactions so transient. The truth was, no more knowing how to be a husband than a father, he would single-handedly dismantle his own happiness. He was wild when he was young, and he left home too early to join the army at seventeen ever to learn how to act responsibly in a family. He certainly had role models; his parents were stable and steady and loved their children, in their own boring, insufficient way. Robert was too wild to learn from them, Gordon and Mary, too seduced by the world beyond the walls of their tiny bungalow on the west side of Detroit. Gordon's insistence that his children live the conventional, respectable life fueled Robert's revolt and brought father and son into constant conflict, most notably Sunday nights after Robert, barely sixteen, would return home from a weekend of carousing to his father's scathing displeasure and, occasionally, beatings. The rest of the family hid in their rooms, or, in summer, sat on the front porch so the neighbors wouldn't think Gordon was yelling at them, Tommy and Lenore at their mother's feet while Bobby was getting what came to him.

Now he knew he had only himself to blame for ruining both his early family life and his adult one. Years after it was too late to keep blaming his father, Robert precipitated his own divorce when his wife caught him on the sofa in their living room one day with a graduate student from his clinical psychology master's program. And what a scene it was, Robert and Maureen not in the act exactly but real close, Jeannie bursting in, face fire engine red, eyes bugging out, Maureen scrambling for throw pillows to cover her naked breasts, Jeannie screaming, crying, pummeling him, driving him out of the house . . . At the time he had glib and (even then) unbelievable excuses. It was the month after his father died, following so closely on his mother's death that Robert was still too beside himself with grief to be responsible for his behavior and refuse Maureen's attentions. Jeannie didn't buy any of it, of course. She knew the part about Maureen's attentions was a flat-out lie. In his confusion and grief over his father's death, he directed at his wife the anger he had borne toward his father. In his mind, Jeannie came to stand for the kinds of ironclad familial duties and values that his father tried to beat into him. And the form his anger took was pursuit of Maureen in the home his wife made for them.

Maureen, emotionally inaccessible Maureen, who had just gone through a messy divorce from her own husband, an alcoholic like her father. Maureen, coming off a lifetime of holding herself in and pretending she had no feelings, a bundle of humorless manic energy, incapable of seducing him but surrendering to his anger and aggression with surprising ease. And in any event, she was not the first woman he had slept with during his marriage, just the first he had had the inconsideration to bring into his home.

Poor Jeannie, furious and humiliated over what he did to her. Poor Robert, how much he lost when he drove her away. He suspected it then; he realized it more each year. Mourned for it, but didn't yearn to recapture it—not with Jeannie, anyway. It was over when it was over. He deserved to lose her.

After his divorce, he and Maureen stayed together for the year it took them to finish their studies. Then she moved to New York to start the doctoral social work program at Columbia. He moved west, to Seattle, to work in a substance abuse treatment clinic. After they split, they spoke on the phone every week, making plans to get together that never materialized. By then he had met Catherine. After he moved in with her, he never heard from Maureen again. And Catherine, well, she'll never contact him again, ever . . .

At the age of forty-three, with both parents dead, siblings scattered across the country, marriage long over, in touch with his grown children only by phone, alone, generally feeling pitiful and unloved, he made the decision to split, go back east, make another new start in another new city with another new job, begin again in another new life he would consciously choose for himself. Only this time he would learn from his mistakes, evolve, be responsible. Or so he hoped. He would gather another family around himself, this one of his own creation. Taking, as he told his clients, one slow day at a time. Easy does it. When you're trying to come back from the dead end of something in your life, those simple bumper sticker credos made a lot of sense.

He returns his cup to the kitchen, admires his sign again, worries that the damp butcher's paper would soak through the newspaper to stain his floor, then decides it's too late to be concerned and goes upstairs to join the other members of his newest family in sleep.

2

In the morning, Martina Vitale is all cheerful apologies. She's sorry she got there so late. Sorry she has to leave so early. Sorry she has time only for a quick cup of coffee before she has to go. She has a meeting at the hospital and must get to her desk beforehand to prepare some papers. Sorry.

"Not a problem," Robert assures her. He is tired from the previous late night but mentally clear. She is bracing anyway, this crisp young woman, breezy and confident, her apologies self-mocking though sincere. She brings into the diner where they meet an aura of cool fall morning air and citrus perfume that buoys him.

She folds her arms on the table and says, "So." She smiles brightly, a lean woman with lustrous brown shoulder length hair and thin features, the most arresting of which are her chocolate brown almond eyes. "Tell me about it."

"Rent is $200 a month, and we split utilities. All new appliances. I'm in the process of remodeling. It'll probably take me through the spring at least. There's no lease for residents. Three of us live there already. It has four large bedrooms."

"Must be a big house."

"Huge. We each have our own room and we share the common living space. Right now the three of us are men."

"Three men, eh?" She gives him a skeptical side-eye.

"Yeah, but we're *sensitive* men."

"How much privacy is there?"

"As much as you want. We each have our own life."

"Sounds like a commune."

"That's not really my model. That suggests more self-sufficiency than I have in mind for us. I see it as an alternative living arrangement somewhere between a rooming house and a family. I'm still not sure I've worked the paradigm out completely. Less impersonal than a rooming house, but without the traumas and strains of people bound together by blood and history. Ideally, we could rely on each other for support, but membership in this particular clan is voluntary. It's a way to offer connection to people who would otherwise be disconnected. We'll develop this set of relationships ourselves, and, I hope, enjoy it that much more."

"Everybody gets along?"

"Absolutely. I'm pleased so far. And surprised. I thought, okay, three guys, the best that would happen would be we'd tolerate each other in the beginning while we felt each other out and set up our own rhythms. Friendship and enjoyment in each other's company could grow, if they came at all, but weren't required. We might need a couple of tries with new people before the group gelled. But the funny thing is, we sort of discovered we were all fellow travelers. We still give each other a lot of space, but it's a good, friendly arrangement."

"No pissing contests?"

"No pissing contests."

"Sounds nice."

"It really is."

"The thing is, I'd like to see what I'm getting myself into."

"Sure. We're having a housewarming party tonight. Why don't you stop by?"

She brightens even more. "Great."

"Starts at eight. Come anytime."

"I'm anxious to find a place. My landlord wants me out because he needs the apartment for his mother."

"Move in as soon as you want. Leave whenever you feel you have to. It's fluid."

"Terrific."

She gathers up her coat and the briefcase from the bench beside her. "I'll call you if for some reason I can't make it."

"No problem. We can do it another time just as well."

"Except tonight I'll get to see you all on your best behavior. You can all show me how sensitive you are."

"We're especially delicate in the company of strangers."

With a smile she disappears into the ragtag crowd of teenagers outside the diner. Farther up Main Street is Buckingham High School. The youngsters smoke cigarettes and roughhouse, dawdling before the first bell. They mingle with short, obese, unhappy-looking white women trailing dirty-faced mixed-race kids, a constant sight on the street. The social service offices are across from the high school.

He orders another cup of coffee from the old waitress, with eggs over medium. She brings them immediately, runny in the middle and crinkly brown on the edges. Virtuoso eggs. He loves this place.

Martina will work out well, he is certain. She is a nursing clinical specialist in the Oncology Program at the hospital where he works, Buckingham General. She saw the card he placed on a hospital bulletin board, advertising a house to share. Smart woman. Pleasant. Nice looking. Now, maybe, living under his roof. To the old Robert, this happy congruence would have led to a mild expectation of some tasty fun with this dishy gal. Today's All-New, 1984 Version of Robert is a new man. Today's Robert has sworn off sex as being just one more thing he's addicted to, along with alcohol.

The addition of Martina will make his house complete. With his first roommates he has made a good start. He knew the first takers in his great experiment would form a kind of first draft that would revise itself as people moved in and out until they arrived at the right combination of temperaments, ages, and sexes. Creating a new life takes a while.

Chewing his toast thoughtfully, he gazes out finger-smeared windows at his new town. Across the street is a fish market that looks as if it used to be a gas station. It still has a broad apron in front where the pumps were, and two big bay doors in front of fish coolers and display cases. Despite his new celibacy (or maybe because of it), things have worked out remarkably well in the six months since he came to town. This is his second fresh start in a row. Already he has established a life here, routines he could count on, favorite places, like this diner: an old-style art deco Greek joint with good, cheap food and a foul-tempered cook. It has in addition mismatched cutlery, chipped plates and saucers that are as dingy as tobacco-stained teeth, and a bizarre cast of characters that includes the irascible waitress Helen, whom he has made it his business to charm, and the man who presently sits at the counter, thin as a nail and with a neurological problem (Robert guesses Huntington's disease) that prevents him from sitting still, sending his limbs, head, and mouth in a constant dance, perpetual writhing that makes it an effort to focus himself enough to shovel a forkful of scrambled eggs into his mouth after three or four tries, but whose hands are remarkable for their slender, masculine grace.

With this place and these people, strange as Zen metaphors where the tenor floats just out of reach below the surface of reason, who could ask for more? Catherine, who loved diners too, used to call them nouvelle-Greco cuisine. Every Saturday morning, they had breakfast in the Daytop Diner in Seattle. She would have loved this one: The Tallye-Ho.

He shakes his head and turns away from the thought of her, a practiced mental gesture, to concentrate instead on his day, which like Martina's is going to be a full one.

He takes another sip of coffee from the chipped cup and replaces it in its puddle of liquid in the saucer. He comforts himself with how much he loves this place.

Sometimes fresh starts do work out, after two or three shots at them.

3

Four of them sit around the table, four white guys in suits. At this moment the executive vice president is reminiscing about his experiences in Viet Nam. "It was during the Tet Offensive," James Fawcett says. "We were having steak au poivre in the Officers' Mess in Saigon and so on and so forth—."

Robert tunes out. He was there too, but his experience was different from Fawcett's, who was (or claims to have been; Robert distrusts the man's constant references to his war experiences; they remind him of a virgin's sexual boasts) in Intelligence and spent most of his war in circle jerks around tables like this one with men in different kinds of suits. Robert was in Combat Demolitions. He blew up bridges, the work of spiteful boys knocking down flimsy structures built by others, great blossoming flowers of splinters and smoke and explosions in the humid jungle. Fawcett never moved on, apparently. Now he talks to his staff in the same condescending tone Robert heard everywhere back then, officers who ordered the shitkickers out on the pointless, suicidal missions from which many would never return.

The tone sits poorly with Robert even today. He sits thinking about the stairway wall at home that needs papering, the storm windows that need recaulking, anything but what Fawcett is blathering about.

Robert tunes back in when the other man's monologue eddies toward Robert's program and the reason for the meeting.

"The patient count is unacceptably low," Fawcett says. "We have to goose it somehow." He is thin and balding and wears heavy rimmed glasses and a mustache as limp and characterless as the man himself. In speaking he stares at a point straight ahead of him where the nearest wall and ceiling came together. His idea of a meeting is gathering his vice presidents and program directors around him so he can tell them what he thinks about things, as he is doing now.

And they listen to what he says. They are Ted McCarthy, vice president for ambulatory services, and Sal Perullo, vice president for marketing. Robert's boss, another white guy named Dr. Featherstone, the vice president for medical affairs, is away today at one of the endless seminars on hospital marketing the vice presidents are always going to. Fawcett has been here only a little longer than Robert himself; Robert can tell from their attention that the other administrators are still trying to impress their boss. They scramble for position at these meetings as best they can, considering that Fawcett isn't interested in what they have to say. Robert, with no position to gain or lose in Fawcett's eyes, looks on bemused.

The gist of the meeting is that the alcohol treatment program called New Directions, which Robert has been hired to administer, needs more clients. Fawcett expected this to be one of Robert's first priorities, which was okay with Robert.

"The future of medical care lies in the ambulatory clinic," Fawcett says, apropos of nothing. "The future of this hospital lies in the ambulatory programs we offer the community."

Right. Fawcett does not tell any of the men sitting around this table anything they don't already know. The other three sit silently because this is what's expected of them. Perullo appears to listen closely; you can tell because his brow is furrowed; he is an ex-service man too. McCarthy, also an ex-army man, sits with a scowl, as if he were smelling something really bad.

During Robert's orientation interview, Fawcett, who like many voluble men with power was indiscreet, had let slip that he made up his mind that McCarthy would be the first administrator to be replaced in the coming executive purge.

After describing the impact of ambulatory services upon reimbursement practices in contemporary health care, Fawcett gets back to New Directions, which is a residential, not an ambulatory care, program. "What can we do to get more customers in?"

All three men recognize this as a rhetorical question.

"First," Fawcett goes on, knowing himself that his question was not meant to be answered, at least not by those whom it is his misfortune to have around him, "we need to do some extensive marketing."

Perullo rouses himself. His chain has been jerked. He is a bull of a man whose collars are perpetually too tight for his bulging neck. At his orientation with Robert, Perullo told him that when he was a Ranger in the army he once jumped out of an airplane without a parachute and broke every bone in his body except his head. Which must have been the body part he landed on, Robert thought at the time, listening to his inanities. Today he is certain.

Before Perullo can even begin to list the marketing alternatives open to them, Fawcett refocuses on the angle formed by the wall and the ceiling and expounds on the role of advertising in hospital marketing. He just got back from a seminar on the subject and now considers himself an expert.

After a while, he opines they need more advertising expertise than is available through the hospital public relations department. He tells Robert to approach local advertising agencies about working up a marketing campaign for the unit.

The other men readily agree, including Perullo, whose actual job title is marketing.

The meeting ends when Fawcett abruptly stands and returns to his desk on the other side of the room and asks his secretary to place a call.

Back in his office on his unit, Robert tasks his assistant with preparing a list of local ad agencies with their principals. For the next hour, he switches out of his administrator mode and becomes a counselor for an intake interview with a prospective client—a young man, solidly middle-class and not yet out of his teens, but already in the grip of a mature addiction to alcohol. The young man's hands shake. His voice quakes and his eyes fill with tears as he describes his long slow slide down to treatment. As usual, his addiction is the key to all of the other problems that will take longer than the program's twenty-eight days to resolve. Anger, hostility, self-loathing, alienation, isolation, feeling unloved, unworthy, inferior: they are all there. Robert would bet many, if not most, of these have their roots in the life this young man led in his family of origin. And will manifest themselves in the families he forms as an adult. Families, not solely individuals, are chemically dependent.

Family life. How often has he seen this in the substance abusing young—children produced with the genetic propensity toward addiction, then trained for it, programmed to self-destruct by their families through love withheld or confused, taught to hate themselves and sent out into the world, waiting for the right combination of events to set them off. How often was physical child abuse associated with the lower socioeconomic classes, but the middle-classes have their own form of abuse that is just as rampant. They are just sneakier. Their abuse is psychological, more subtle but no less destructive in the long run of the poor youngsters' lives.

4

Oh yeah. This party rocks and rolls.

By 9:30 that night, all the staff from Robert's program are there, as well as many of the others from the hospital with whom he has become friendly. He told Dennis and Gene to invite guests too, and there are faces he does not recognize. The house is full of people in their twenties and thirties and forties standing in groups of twos and threes in every corner and sitting on the sofas and bridge chairs and even on the floor with their backs propped against the walls. Mostly they have distributed themselves based on job function. Hanratty the head nurse roisters with her nursing crew Harper, Webster, and Ianaccone. Counselors DeGroot and Vanderbilt confer with each other. Gilchrist the medical director huddles with the only other physician in the room, who has come with one of the nurses. Dates and spouses mingle as best they can. Occasionally the groups reform across disciplines when people visit the kitchen for a handful of melting ice cubes from the bag in the sink and a refill of the cold sheet pizza and assorted baked goods and alcohol-free cider and soda that are tonight's fare. The local oldies station murmurs discreetly in the background.

This, Robert thinks, surveying from his vantage point both the living room to the left and the keeping room to the right, is turning into One Great Party.

He works the crowd happily, touching a shoulder here, an arm there, piecing the fragments of the party together, weaving the disparate bits of conversations together, creating a fabric of community this night in his house. He loves people together like this, especially when he is the center around which they constellate.

Dennis, he notes with pleasure, has joined the ensemble after all. He is not actually connected to any one group, but at least he is here, sort of. He wears Robert's blue Seattle Seahawks cap down low over dark glasses, part of things and not part at the same time. Robert sidles up beside him. "How's it going?"

Dennis turns his impenetrable dark orbs on Robert. "Oh, great." He forces his heartiness obviously. "Just great. This is fun, isn't it? I mean, the fun's actually started, hasn't it?"

"Doesn't get any more fun than this."

"Well, gosh, that's great. I had a feeling this is what fun felt like."

"Pretty close."

"Darn close."

"Follow me, smart ass."

Robert angles toward a group from the Social Services Department, but when he turns around Dennis is not behind him.

No matter. Dennis's presence here is progress enough for one night. Robert feels particularly responsible for Dennis, his first recruit. Dennis is under the care of a psychologist at the outpatient mental health clinic at the hospital. Robert's colleague brought them together, Dennis needing a place to live and Robert with space available. Even though Dennis himself made the decision to move out of his parents' house, his therapist felt Dennis needed a strong, supportive environment. To her, the arrangement seemed perfect.

Robert, too, thought this manufactured family might provide

Dennis with just what he needs, structure and support without the pressures of Mom and Dad. Dennis's therapist assured him that he functioned perfectly well, and in fact things have started off in a great way. Dennis keeps his job and regularly and cheerfully pays his rent and his share of the expenses. He's a little odd, it's true, but that fits in, too.

The second resident also seemed promising. Now in the thick of things, putting a heavy move on an attractive dark-haired woman by the stairs, Gene Anderson is a part-time social worker at the hospital, and can probably give Dennis some support too. Though Gene is a tad self-absorbed these days. Divorced from his wife, he had his own apartment until he decided to give up his full-time job as a supervisor at Broome County Social Services because it was too restrictive of what he has described to Robert as his search for the free and spiritual life. A job will do that, Robert responded. Looking for a cheaper place to live, he answered Robert's notice on the bulletin board and the three men hit it off.

Already his housemates seemed to strike a right note to Robert's ear, pitched high for this experiment in living. Fellow travelers, seekers, eschewers of the elusive average happy life are Dennis, who struggles with the aftermath of a breakdown, and Gene, the type that Robert's father used to call, and not admiringly, a "free spirit." Robert believes that living with them promises great things. These two eccentric men satisfy the part of him that rejects normalcy, even as he consciously sets out to create a new kind of family life for them all. When Dennis first took a look at the wooden face over the front door outside the house and said, "This must be a House of Grins," Robert said, "Of course," warming immediately to the rightness of it. A circuit had been closed: the enterprise had been given a name.

Now using his two housemates as guides to the progress of the party—lonely Dennis on the fringes, sociable Gene throwing his head back and laughing with his new lady friend—Robert finds this to be a House of Grins after all. He is pleased.

A blast of cool air from the front door announces Martina Vitale's arrival. Welcoming arms out, he heads toward her. She is standing in the living room, swiveling her head for him.

I can handle this very easily, Martina thinks as Robert takes her through the crowded rooms to meet his housemates.

They first find Gene, cuddling with a woman on the staircase. He has big teeth and when he smiles, which he does readily, his tongue lolls in his mouth like a dog's. Indeed, he is almost too easygoing, too laid-back and carefree. There is a vagueness about him, a lack of focus that puts her off slightly. Shouldn't a man of his age— late forties, she guesses, by the gray flecks in his beard and the wrinkles around his eyes—be more connected to the responsibilities of grownup life than Gene seems? Why is he living here? Why doesn't he have a life of his own, she wonders as he attempts to win her over with his smile and his personality. Shouldn't he have a place of his own instead of rooming here, a sleepwalker in another man's dream? Martina surely would, at his age.

Next Robert introduces her to Dennis, who interests her the least of the three men. Closest to her own age—she will be twenty-nine on New Year's Day—he appears the most juvenile, with his shades and baseball cap. An Alienated Young Man. He is the quietest, with the least sense of himself. Well, she does go for older men as a rule. The young are so . . . jejune. But look, she's not all to blame: he has few words to say to her, no apparent interest in her beyond mere politeness, and while it may be unfair to judge him from the briefest of meetings, the other two men almost knock her over with their enthusiasm. Dennis also seems uncomfortable with her attempts to win him over. Is he gay? Whatever his sexual orientation, he shows little personality to speak of, and she does not easily take to shy men. So she smiles at him and writes him off. Thinking, as she does, Poor Dennis; this is probably the story of his life.

Most fascinating is Robert, clearly the driving force here. Threading his way with her around his guests, showing her the dramatic peacock-hued half-moon pattern on the wallpaper he has put up in the dining room, the paint job in the living room, the plaster patch job upstairs in what would be her bedroom, describing the new wiring and copper plumbing, and finally, back in the kitchen, expounding on the plans he has drawn up for remodeling this room to make a large eating and food preparation area, he radiates a warmth that makes it a pleasure to wrap him around her finger, which she does handily, continuing the job she started at breakfast, oohing and aahing over this idea for a commune. Because that's what it is, she believes, no matter how he rationalizes it: a group of unrelated adults living together with a leader who has a vision of the life he wants to live sounds like a commune to her. No problem. To someone like herself, who has lived all her life in this town, the thought of being in this kind of arrangement is just outrageous enough to be attractive.

And overall, it's not a bad deal. The house is gorgeous, the men get along, the rent is excellent, and it may well be only for the short term anyway. She hasn't mentioned this to Robert, but her boyfriend is building a house that will be ready next fall and he has repeatedly asked her to marry him and move in, though not necessarily in that order. She has been putting him off with one concern or another: she's not sure she's ready to marry, not sure she's ready to be a stepmother to his two adolescent daughters, not ready for this, not ready for that. The point is really that she doesn't know if he's the one. He's so staid, so unimaginative, so conventional. This arrangement here with these men is so tempting because it will give her what may be her last chance to experience something other than the kind of sedate wedded life that will be in store for her with Max.

She stays for a drink, mingles a bit with some of the hospital people she knows, then says, "I have to get going."

"Why so soon?" Robert asks. "You're going to miss my performance. When I feel in the mood at these things, I haul out my guitar and start singing great songs of the '60s. And when I really get wired, I make them up myself."

"My boyfriend gets back to town tonight and I'm picking him up from the airport."

"Personally, I think my rendition of 'What a Day for a Daydream' is worth letting him cool his heels a little. But far be it from me to change your plan."

He walks her out to her Celica parked down the street. "I'm sure there'll be other times," she says.

"Does this mean you like what you saw?"

"If I passed the audition."

He waves away her concern. "I have to talk it over with them, but from what I saw you were a big hit with those two in there. As I knew you would be."

"Actually, I'm looking forward to this. I think it's going to be an interesting experience."

"I know it is."

"Sorry I'm going to miss that guitar."

"Me, too. Everything's right tonight: the crowd, the occasion, the moon, the stars. I can feel it, I can feel the creative power. It's going to be a rare and singular performance."

She says, "That's the breaks," and hooks his gaze with an ironic smile. Robert raises his head and offers a laugh up to the propitious night sky.

He really is in rare form. Before long he has broken down the distinctions that separate the different groups and collected everyone crowded around him, howling out approximations of the early Beatles and Stones under his direction, sitting, standing, swaying. He sits in the middle of the living room on a bridge chair with his ancient Martin twelve-string on his lap, strumming away as hard as he can, stomping his foot to "She Loves You," "Twist and Shout," "I Want 'to Hold Your Hand," "You've Got to Hide Your Love Away," "Satisfaction," and more. It is a joyful noise.

All that are left after his party are a sink overflowing with green plastic glasses and a kitchen filled with bulging black garbage bags stuffed with dirty paper plates and used plastic cutlery. Robert gathers the trash together and shoves it all into one of the bags, ties off the top, and stows it by the back door.

Gene enters the kitchen bearing a platter of half-eaten crudites, broccoli stems like small tree trunks and cauliflower bits like little brains. He is trailed by the woman he has been putting the make on all night. She carries what is left of the salad, wilted lettuce and crushed cherry tomatoes. "Robert," he says, "I want you to meet my friend, Sharon Krasner. Sharon, Robert Fitzgerald."

"Hi."

"Hi." She is a dark-haired beauty, with short thick hair in a boyish cut and brown eyes and olive skin freckled with tiny black points over apple cheeks. "Great party," she says.

"Thanks. Glad you could come. Thanks for helping out."

"My pleasure." She goes back out to the dining room to collect more plates.

"Dennis out there?" Robert asks.

"I think he's still downstairs somewhere," says Gene.

"Dennis?" Robert calls.

"Yeah?" From the living room.

"Time for a meeting."

Shortly Dennis pads into the kitchen. "What?"

"What did you guys think about Martina?"

"Well," Gene says, like an academic winding up for a gassy explanation, "I think . . . I think she'll work out fine."

"Dennis?"

Dennis shrugs. "Yeah, sure. Why not?"

"There's an unequivocal recommendation if ever I heard one," says Gene.

"What do you want me to say?"

"I want to hear if you have any reservations about her," says Robert. "She's going to live here, you know."

"How can I have reservations, I only talked to her for like five seconds? What can I know about her?"

"You must have formed some impressions," says Gene.

"No, no," says Robert, "he's given us his answer."

"And what did you think of her?" Gene asks Robert.

"I'm satisfied."

"There you go," Gene says. "Unanimously approved."

"Okay," says Robert. "She's in. I'll tell her tomorrow."

"So can I go now?" says Dennis.

Robert brings a clean plastic cup down like a gavel on the sink. "Meeting adjourned." He holds his hands out in benediction. "Go in peace." His housemates scatter.

"Dad? Is that you?"

The line crackles. Static surges over his son's voice. As always, the maturity of its colorations and timbre surprises him. "Yo, big guy."

"It's Dad," Brian says to someone there.

Nora gets on the extension. "Hi, Dad. This is a surprise."

"Two at once. What's the occasion?"

"We had dinner together," Brian says. "Tomorrow I'm off for my course."

"Good luck with it."

"Thanks."

Brian is starting a sales training course in the morning. "I dunno," Robert says. "My son's an IBM salesman. Where did I go right?"

"You did okay with me," Nora says. "I'm mostly unemployed."

She is a dancer for a modern dance troupe in Detroit but she's right: she rarely gets a regular paycheck.

"It's true. At least one of you understands the bourgeoise life as a sham and a travesty."

"So how are things going out there?" Nora asks.

"Good. Getting settled. I had a housewarming party tonight. Had some people from the hospital over."

"Was it a hot time?" she asks with a smile in her voice.

"I had to behave myself. Most of the people were from work. Too bad you two couldn't have hopped a plane in for the night."

"No way," Brian says. "I had to get ready for my trip."

"So when's your next vacation?"

"Christmas, maybe."

"Come then. Both of you."

"Can't," says Nora. "Christmas is a busy time for me. Lots of 'Nutcracker' performances."

"Ah. Of course."

"Can you come here?"

"Possibly."

"Though if we're both going to be busy, you might as well wait for a better time," Brian says.

"I suppose," Robert agrees. How did they get so sensible, these two? "I'll tell you what, though. It's hard being out here by myself."

"Have you made any friends there yet?"

"Nobody I'm really close with. You make it sound like I'm away at camp."

"What about the people you live with?"

"They're nice. So far I wouldn't call us friends. I'll make some soon. I'm a pretty cool guy."

"You are a cool guy," Nora agrees.

"Maybe we can get together for Easter."

"That'd be great," says Nora.

"Yeah, sure," Brian allows. Neither seem in any hurry to make reservations.

"Hey," he says. "I miss you guys."

"We miss you, too," they say automatically, in unison.

CHAPTER TWO

1

You bastard," Harry's brother says. He is not angry.

"Come on," Harry says, "who knew it was going to go in? First I thought I sliced it. I thought, there it goes, into the trees, that's the end of us. That's what I thought. Until it went in. I couldn't believe it!"

Harry McGuire talks quickly, rolling his head from one side of the street to the other behind the wheel of his Seville. Today he shot his first ever hole-in-one. He shot it while playing in the Pro-Am Tournament of the annual PGA circus that rolls into town every fall. Harry got the chance to play in the Pro-Am because he owns the ad agency that promotes the tour locally and because he went to high school with the president of the golf club where they play, not for any skill he might have at the sport. No matter, as he says; he'll take it. Just like he took the hole-in-one. It was a fluke, and he knows it. Harry is not that good a player. No matter. He'll take it.

Harry takes a lot. Lucky stars, Midas touches, charmed lives: Harry's wife has thought more than once during the six years of their marriage that her husband proves these things do exist. Some people, her husband for one, are favored in all they set their hands to. He is Fortune's Golden Haired Boy, is Harry McGuire.

Reclining in the cushy back seat of his new car, borne quickly through the darkening early autumn streets, listening to him recount the story of his latest piece of good luck, Brooke McGuire is reminded again of this fact of Harry's life: where he is concerned, everything comes up aces. The ad agency he owns is flourishing. The condo he and his brother own in South Carolina has a year-long waiting list for vacation rentals. Harry's college friend who lives in New York City feeds him happy little tips on the stock market from time to time, definitely illegal, no killings but enough to allow him to pay cash for the teal Alliance he gave Brooke for her last birthday, at a great price from his friend the AMC dealer. Today is but the latest example of his good fortune, which he wears lightly on his broad shoulders.

Brooke knows that when fortune smiles upon Harry, it smiles on her, too. And fortune positively beams upon Harry McGuire.

Sharing the Seville on this night are Harry's brother Michael in the front seat and Michael's wife Joyce next to Brooke in the back. Their mood is heady. They are off to celebrate Harry's luck on the golf course and what may be the beginning of yet another successful business venture. Harry drives quickly, though it seems to Brooke a bit too recklessly through the wet streets, buoyed by his excitement on the links.

Harry has had his Seville only a week. The car is serious machinery, complex as a spaceship, plush as down. The digital instrument panel winks and glows in the darkness with the promise of great sleek power; it throws a ghostly amber light on Harry and Michael. The new car smell wars with the heavy musk of Joyce McGuire's perfume. The close quarters give Brooke a sharp pain behind her eyes. She does not like confinement in small spaces. She longs for a breath of fresh chilly air but does not feel like opening the window in the climate-controlled automobile and listening to Harry complain, however good-naturedly.

Ground fog hugs the damp street in curlicue wisps. The car swerves slightly as it roars over squashed piles of sodden leaves. Brooke must brace herself sharply on Joyce's elbow, then against the door as her husband speeds into the turn onto the skeletal steel bridge that separates the north and south sides of town.

"Harry!" she cries finally.

"What?"

"Slow down!"

"I'm not going fast."

"You are!"

The overpowering "ooommm" of the tires on the steel bridge betrays his speed. Obligingly he cuts back.

Off the bridge to the left is the implacable blackness of the Susquehanna, one of the rivers that flow through town; to the right, in the hills in the distance, scattered lights of the communities that surround Brooke's adopted hometown of Buckingham in the Southern Tier of New York State glow as cozy and warm as lights in a toy village at Christmas.

"Have you seen this place?" Brooke asks her sister-in-law.

"No. You?"

"No."

The women exchange a knowing look and cackle, naughty schoolgirls, at what they know is coming. Their husbands will soon have a new toy. Honestly, if they weren't so successful, these guys, they'd be just as bad as kids.

2

Their destination is the Oasis, a bar downtown near the Arena, dark and smoky and noisy and full of young adults having fun. The smell of beer is strong and sharp as cat pee. It adds to Brooke's headache. Harry does not notice. He and Michael are busy counting the house.

The two couples pick their way past the bar, crowded four deep with young bodies. At thirty, Brooke is the youngest of her party, but even she is over the hill here, older than most of the patrons by a half dozen years at least. She has not been in a bar like this since her college days.

This reminds her, in fact, of the rough-hewn college pub where she used to hang out, the same one where she and Harry first met. She was with a group of her friends, he with his, all blowing off steam after final exams at Syracuse University. He picked her up with a line about her hands, then as now mottled with ink from her graphic design work. They went back to his place together, and she stayed the night. It was something she did a lot with guys she had just met. This time was different from the usual in-and-out. She and Harry both knew it. Afterwards she felt as though she had fallen into place. Click! went Brooke, who until then would often lament with her girlfriends that they couldn't find a guy who wasn't a jerk. To her amazement, she found in this pickup artist the non-jerk of all time. Harry was brainy and ambitious, two years ahead of her in the advertising program, and even then (she believes today) she realized that life would dump endless shitloads of good luck (and the money you used to keep score with) on his darkly handsome head.

She remembers how captivated she was by his goals and ambitions as he explained them to her that first night. They were, she realized later, nothing unusual except in the ways in which they crooked their finger at her by way of invitation to the happy, prosperous life, the ultimate worth of which she and her friends discussed so critically in those post-Liberation days of the mid-seventies, but which none of them would have turned down had it been offered. Brooke found her ticket to it in this bar smoothy from out of the blue. How mathematically simple it was: she suffered in her early life, and Harry was her reward. It was a scenario worthy of Harry himself.

And she was his reward too, she hoped, an attractive, bright woman whose innate levelheadedness held her artistic talent firmly in check. She had been a gifted design student; already her work had appeared on programs in the Syracuse University Theatre Department and in the alumni magazine.

How long ago, how important everything had seemed then, how close to the hot source of things she had felt . . . And how much closer to it she is today, at least as far as this town is concerned. The proof is the table that magically appears for them in the back room of this dive, as if they were celebrities. This happens often with Harry; doors open for him, tables appear, opportunities materialize.

As soon as they are seated, a young woman with heavy dark raccoon rings around her eyes and orange hair moussed in an outrageously slutty cascade takes their order. "Well?" Harry shouts, leather-lunged through the din. "It's a gold mine!" He is beaming and high-colored. Perspiration dots his forehead. In his eye is the look of heightened expectation he gets in the presence of a Chance.

"This is great," Michael screams back. He shakes his big head in admiration. He is Harry's older brother, manager of a Computerland at the mall, but when it comes to understanding money and the Deal, Harry is his elder.

"This can't possibly lose money," Harry says. "It can't. Look at this crowd!"

Obediently, Brooke does. It's true, the place is packed. It probably is a gold mine. "Why are they selling it if it does so well?" she asks.

"The owner's retiring to Florida," Harry says.

Their drinks arrive at the same time as the Steens, Polly and Lee, who sit at two chairs that have appeared and been made to fit the table. They travel in the same social circles, both McGuire couples and the Steens. Lee is another young entrepreneur, like Harry and Michael. Only he makes his killings by developing the small office plazas and condos that sprout around town like mushrooms after a summer rain. He also was the one who turned the building next to the bar from a decrepit old cigar factory into a trendy mini-mall with elegant red brick front stores and art galleries. His wife Polly is an interior designer whose business, as luck would have it, consists largely of office plazas and condo units.

This is not a social occasion, entirely. Tonight Polly is working. Harry and Michael have brought her in to consult on what can be done with this place. "Well," says Michael, after the Steens have their drinks, "what do you think?"

She looks around, measuring and judging. She wears her sleek brown hair drawn tightly back from fine features and restrained with an elaborate lavender bow. "Looks very promising," says Polly. "Very sound."

"I thought we could keep the layout pretty much as it is," Harry says, "but bring it up to date."

"I like this brick," Michael says of the bare red brick walls. "Don't you like the brick?"

"Definitely appealing," says Polly.

"I think it's gonna be great," Harry shouts.

"Harry," Brooke says, "you're talking like you already bought this thing."

"If they take what I'm going to offer," he says, "it's a done deal."

"How did you hear about it?" Polly asks.

"From Herbie." His accountant. "He does the taxes of the guys who own it now. One of them wants to move to Florida. His partner doesn't want to run it by himself, so they're both selling out. Excellent price, too, just excellent," Harry allows.

Polly pulls a square floral spiral notebook from her purse and begins to write and sketch. She gazes around the crowded bar with narrowed eyes.

"Harry," Lee says, "how'd it go on the golf course today?"

Later, Harry and Michael gaze up and down the street outside the bar. They calculate the distance from the arena that hosts concerts and minor league hockey games. They figure parking strategies and judge traffic patterns. They smoke cigars and rock on their heels, then stroll with easy proprietary grace down the street to Harry's car.

As they reach it Polly says, "Oh, wait a minute, I think I dropped my keys in the bar."

"Oh, Polly," says Lee. "Leave it to you."

"I'll just run back and get them. Won't be a sec."

When she does not return immediately, Brooke says, "I may as well go to the bathroom while we're waiting."

Everybody moans. "It's the beer," she protests, and hurries back, this time giving the front of the bar a more careful once-over, the blue and red neon glowing rhomboid Genesee and Rolling Rock and Miller signs, the steady flow of customers in and out, the importunate beat of music that escapes every time the door opens. Soon, Brooke now is certain, this will swell the list of Harry's ventures. The boy's roll continues. He's irrepressible.

The ladies' room is off a darkened, recessed foyer beside a pay phone—over which Polly Steen is bent.

She has pressed herself into the corner with the telephone. Brooke maneuvers by without the other woman noticing. Mercifully, both stalls in the tiny lav are free. She has to pee with urgency.

The place stinks of industrial strength deodorizer. This'll have to change, she thinks, and washes her hands at the sink when the door swings out and a young woman with a porcupine's head of heavily moussed hair squeezes in. She holds the door wide open for a friend trailing behind her, and Brooke hears Polly, now not three feet away, say clearly, as though the din in the bar ceases long enough for her words to float through dead quiet into the ladies' lav, "I can't tonight, I'm with my husband. We can't see each other till Tuesday."

Brooke freezes, hunched over the sink. Her eyes crawl up the dingy tile of the sink backsplash to the mirror to confront her own embarrassment.

The lav is pretty tight with three women. But she waits a few minutes more and edges the door open. Another woman is now whispering into the phone. Busy night for furtive calls.

She walks out and loses herself in the crowd at the bar, searching for Polly by the door. A tall man with a closely trimmed red beard gazes down happily at this chick who has thrown her body against his. Brooke smiles up nervously. She spots Polly making her way out the door. When Polly is safely gone, Brooke disentangles herself from the man's long arms, which have snaked around her shoulders—"Wait!" he cries after her—and tears herself from this place.

Outside, plumes of white smoke stutter out of the tailpipe of Harry's Seville down the street. When she joins them standing by the car, Polly gives her a tight smile, which Brooke returns.

The three couples go off to a late dinner at Chez Nous, the only French restaurant in town. It is owned by another of Harry's friends, who greets them all with great extravagance and ushers them through the packed dove-gray dining room to the lone empty table in the place, reserved especially for them. This is definitely the McGuires' town.

3

Rising and falling, breathing in and breathing out, Harry's hairy torso moves gently in sleep, vulnerable as a sleeping child's. Beside him, head braced on her elbow, Brooke watches him in the room's silvery-gray moonlight.

He lies in bed, bare to the waist where the sheets are wound tightly around his hips. The blankets bunch at the foot of the bed, where he has kicked them. Lately he sleeps poorly, grunting and snuffling like a pig.

He claims he loves their life, but he's under a lot of pressure. If he's not careful in another ten years he'll wind up the same way as a friend of his who owned one of the other agencies in town. One minute with a client, the next minute dead, splat, face down on the desk, heart saying, *I quit*. Tough business, advertising. Only the strong survive.

Rising, falling . . . Her husband is strong. The man who died was overweight and a chain smoker, as well as your classic Type A. Heart attack waiting to happen. Harry is fit and healthy, his body thick with muscle from his workouts at the Y three times a week.

Still, these would not protect him from sudden death, not from cardiac disease, anyway. Weightlifting is not an aerobic exercise, and besides he is more concerned with the aesthetics of his body than the efficiency of its inner workings. His knees are bad. He can't run or cycle. He hates swimming. Golf is as close as he gets to outdoor exercise, a game she can't stand. He concentrates on making himself look good. Well, he's vain, she has to admit it. He wears contact lenses and smokes cigars.

Of course, he has a lot to be vain about. Harry is a handsome man, dark and firm-jawed with intense brown eyes. People have said he looks like a young Burt Reynolds. Usually just before they said how lucky she was to have him.

Breathing in, breathing out . . .

Tangled mats of monkey fur cover all his skin she can see, from furry epaulets on his shoulders to rivulets of hair down the gully of his chest to the fuzzy goblet of his navel. There is even hair on his face, a thick black mustache. Except for the chain of coarse twisted gold around his neck, he is all hair, black hairs that leave wee wavy impressions on her own bare skin whenever he lies upon her, as he had less than an hour ago, engorged with the eroticism of acquisition. He was wired, too. Normally he is a slow and tender lover, bringing her off with long, languid, slow strokes. Tonight, in his enthusiasm over the bar he was wild, pounding, crashing into her like surf.

He has already made up his mind. This bar will be another "iron in his fire." That's good; it makes him happy. True, it will take up more of his time and attention, like the monthly business trips he makes to service his industrial clients in little towns in Pennsylvania, or the jaunts to Hilton Head with Michael to inspect the condo periodically, or his trips to New York City to wine and dine his friend Jay who gives him stock tips. She knows these are necessary. They make their life possible. And while she misses him when he goes, she has enough to do in her own life to keep herself busy. And sometimes she goes with him to New York, which she loves to do.

She has the best of both worlds, a comfortable small town day-to-day life, and access to the glittering big city a few hours' drive away. She loves to go with Harry and get dressed up in the fashionable clothes she buys at Bloomie's and Lord and Taylor's, and bask in his pride in her. His occasional absences are small enough prices to pay.

Prices to pay. Her thoughts wind around to Lee and Polly. What prices do they pay for their lives? What will they be doing tonight? Will they make love when they get home, too? Will Polly be thinking of her husband, or of another man, someone she would rather be with but will have to wait until Tuesday to see? She thinks of Polly with a mixture of admiration for her courage and envy for the worldliness that Brooke, who has never been with another man since the day she met Harry, believes adultery confers upon those who practice it.

Could she, Brooke, handle something like that? Had she the nerve? What if Lee had come to check on her search for the keys? How would Polly have explained the call? Just checking with the sitter, honey. Would she have had to explain? Could Lee possibly know? Brooke does not know either of them well enough even to make a guess. And what of the other man? How does he cope with his lover's life apart from himself? The Other Man, like the Other Woman. Nobody thinks of their problems.

She blows delicately on her husband's chest. His hairy forest quavers. Brooke loves her husband. And loves the life they lead together. She has never been tempted by another man. None of the men she knows attract her in the least.

Anyway, most of the men she knows are Harry's friends, or know him from some business connection or other. Harry knows practically everyone in town. Every so often one of them makes a boozy pass at her, which she turns aside with as much grace as the situation requires. It is her charm that keeps things from getting too awkward afterward.

It is 2:30 by the dim red numbers of the digital clock on the nightstand, beside her slender Rolex and her rings, her heavy diamond engagement ring and wedding ring with thick intertwining coils of white and yellow gold. They are substantial, even ostentatious pieces of jewelry, and she loves them. Harry got them for her in New York.

Harry smacks his lips. Her bladder aches. Can't stay in bed any longer. She slips away and pads into the bathroom.

Before she sits, she catches sight of herself. Her tousled shoulder length hair falls coyly over dark green, almost brown eyes. She lightens her hair's natural auburn color with Miss Clairol because Harry likes her to. It is a nice contrast with his black Irish good looks.

Before she stands, she wipes off his sticky effluences and tosses the paper into the toilet with a plop. Bye-bye, Junior. She flushes away this residue of their latest attempt to have the child he wants so badly and that she is trying so hard to conceive. She gets up, examines her face in the mirror again, twists her hair upon her head as she does for work during the week. Brooke McGuire, blowsy after sex, bloated before sleep, face creased from the pillow and chest red from her husband. She gives herself a sassy, sex kitten pout.

"Hi, sailor," Harry says. He stands in the doorway behind her, puffy-eyed himself.

She turns her pouty face on him. He braces himself against the wall over the toilet and lets loose a firehose of pee into the bowl. Gazes down tenderly at what can send out a stream that strong.

He pees and pees. His pee, like his lovemaking, is endless. When he finishes, he knocks the drops off the end and looks at her with dreamy eyes, says, "Maybe this time." He enfolds her in a hairy hug.

She lets herself be squeezed. He hardens slightly between her thighs. His body is warm and moist and at once hard with muscle and soft with monkey fur in a combination that tickles her. He has a sweetish salty smell. He squeezes her breath away, then lets her go. "See you in the sack," he says.

As she herself would be the first to admit, Brooke's is a life of glorious privilege. She has, she believes, all the gifts a woman could be favored with in the mid-1980s: a loving husband, all the money she could want, and a good job as art director of the region's largest insurance company. She also teaches a course in graphic design at the community college on Wednesday nights.

She believes she is fortunate to live such a life.

She also periodically dreams of suffocating.

While she was growing up, and as recently as the first years of her marriage, the dreams came almost monthly. Over the past three years they have all but disappeared, those vivid dreams of being enclosed, encaged, choking. Now they return only very occasionally, dreams in which she struggles to free herself from dark prisons, boxes whose lids she cannot budge, airless closets, suffocating damp caves. When they come, they bring her awake gasping and sweat-drenched beside Harry, who sleeps through her travails peacefully. As far as she can remember, he does not appear in any of these, in any form she can identify. (Unless he is the boxes themselves? She puts the idea out of her mind.) After their marriage she never talked with him about her dreams. He would think he was the cause of them, and she does not want to worry him.

She has only talked about them once with anyone else in this town. She mentioned one to her sister-in-law Joyce during lunch on a Saturday shopping trip. They ate at T. Moneybags, a chic eatery downtown in a defunct bank building. The previous night Brooke had a particularly vivid dream that stayed with her all day. Today she has forgotten its images; then it distracted her so much she dropped her guard and described to Joyce the sickening feeling of oppression, the panic of not being able to breathe.

"Maybe it's your creative self," Joyce suggested. Joyce at that time had just begun her job as a sales clerk at Discount Floorcoverings. "Maybe it means you feel stifled."

"I don't think so," said Brooke with a touch of defensive indignation to attractive, blonde, earnest Joyce. "I'm perfectly happy."

"Maybe you should do more drawing or painting or something."

"Why? I never did any of that. Besides, my jobs are creative. Designing an annual report is every bit as creative as painting a picture of dead flowers."

"They're your dreams. I'm just trying to help."

"My dreams aren't about being unhappy. I don't think they are," she amended, not to seem to contradict Joyce too openly. "I'm not unhappy. I have a wonderful life. A wonderful husband, a beautiful home . . ."

"Just a thought. What do I know? I sell rugs. I'm not a shrink."

They never spoke about the subject again.

In her heart, Brooke knows that she has her dreams not because she is unhappy. She believes she has her dreams because there is a streak of craziness in her. And not a good craziness, either. It is a bona fide hereditary insanity that comes to her through her mother.

She remembers the exact date when she first became aware something was wrong with her mother: her fourth birthday party, July 30, 1958. It was late in the afternoon. They had just finished with lunch, hot dogs and potato chips. To this day she remembers perfectly how all at once her mother took after her brother Len with the knife she was using to cut the birthday cake. She chased him— he was then seven—around the rumpus room with the knife still full of cake, billows of pink and white frosting clinging to the blade. It was no joke. Her mother was serious. Brooke remembered her conviction that her mother would have killed Lenny if she had caught him. Her mother screamed, though her exact words Brooke has forgotten over the years. Lenny, three years older and light years wiser, didn't even bother shouting. Zooming around the room, his crazy mother chasing him with a knife covered with birthday cake, he concentrated on escape. He finally ran out of the room and that was that. As if nothing had happened, her mother turned her attention to doling out the rest of the birthday cake to the party guests, children from the neighborhood who—at first frightened— then laughed and clapped at the show she and her son had put on for them.

Neither of her parents ever mentioned the incident, and their mother never tried to hurt either of them again. But Brooke believes this was the key event in Lenny's childhood that warped his development and set him on the way to being the social misfit he is today.

It didn't help that as the two children grew, their mother's antic nature turned inward and she took her own self, her own body, as the object of her aggression, and fell down stairs, and gave herself second degree burns with the steam iron, and became prisoner to deep, desperate depressions. Brooke believes she has escaped only by a stern force of will that has enabled her to distance herself from these goings-on and that today keeps any sign of her family's looniness under firm emotional lock and key. Except in her dreams.

After her lunch with Joyce, she never talked about her dreams with anyone, not even Harry. Which left exactly no one with whom she could discuss the scariest thing in her life, her incipient insanity. She has few female friends anymore, and none who are not connected in some way with Harry. She sometimes has tea with the old widow who lives by herself down the street, but Brooke only listens to the woman's own tales and reminiscences of her carefree early life, which is what the woman needs from her. Brooke is friendly with women at the office, but she does not see them socially. In fact, she would just as soon keep away from them. Though she does not think of herself as a snob, she knows she is connected to a different social set than they are. Through Harry she is part of the primo social circle in her town, the men and women who are the new generation of business and community leaders. Harry knows and socializes with them all, the lawyers, the architects, the businessmen, the promoters of cultural programs, and their wives who raise children and serve on the Hospital Auxiliary and do socially useful volunteer work. Through him Brooke is connected with the town in a way unusual for an outsider.

This gives her great pleasure. She is from Pittsford, a neat, prosperous suburb of Rochester in upstate New York. Her father moved the family there from Cincinnati when he took a job as design engineer for Kodak, and Brooke never did feel like part of the rich and complex history of the area around her home. Harry, on the other hand, is a native here. He has roots in this town where Indians once lived. (The remains of a longhouse were discovered at the site of the golf course where Harry shot his hole-in-one today. The Cultural Center for which Brooke designs the annual calendar has an exhibit of indigenous Indian artifacts and relics.) The town was active during the industrial revolution, with cigar and shoe factories where Harry's grandparents worked in the nineteenth century.

Now, after years of decline, things are stirring to life again thanks to an influx of high-tech defense contractors. Many of them, jobbers for IBM and General Electric, use Harry's agency. Harry believes his—and the town's—recent prosperity is due to President Reagan's economic and defense policies. He voted for Reagan last time and will vote for him again in the November election. Brooke will, too.

Still, for all her connections, for all the parties they attend, for all her proximity to the social heart of the town, she has no one to tell about her dreams. This would be an overt admission that everything is not perfect in the life that she has labored so hard to make appear so. And it is sort of perfect, she knows—except for the craziness that sits awaiting her, rocking in its chair patiently with her mother's face and all the time in the world.

4

As they do every week during the warm weather, Brooke and Harry spend Sunday at his parents' house for a cookout. Besides his virtues as a husband, Harry is a devoted son, a loving brother, a doting uncle. Michael and Joyce are there with their six-year-old Maggie. Brooke and Harry see Harry's father, an electronic assembly foreman retired from IBM, and his mother, a housewife, at least once a week, either at a midweek dinner, on these Sunday afternoons, at picnics, miniature golf outings, or any of the other events that let them spend time together. Brooke sees her parents barely three times a year, at Christmas, on her mother's birthday in September, and in early spring, for her father's birthday. And even these come around too often. Harry's family has gladly adopted her, and she them.

"What are you going to do with a bar?" Harry's mother asks him when he tells her what he and his brother are planning.

"I've always wanted to own a bar."

"Since when? You never told me."

"I thought I did."

"Never."

"Now you know. It's going to be a blast," he says, and means, it's going to be profitable. Nobody in this family has any doubts about that.

"Well," his mother cautions, "don't drink up the profits."

"Mom," Brooke protests, "Harry's not a drinker!"

"Mommie!" Maggie bounds across the yard to bring a stiff sheet of construction paper over to her mother Joyce and Auntie Brooke. "Look what I made!"

She shows the two women the drawing she has made with a pin scratched into the paper layered with colors and covered with black crayon. "Oh," says Brooke, "that's really good!"

"I drew it myself!"

"I know you did." Brooke holds it up to show Joyce. "Look at this, Mom. Isn't that good?"

"It sure is."

"Are you going to use it in your magazine?" the little one asks.

"Know what?" says Brooke. "This is much too good for my magazine. This is so good I think I should frame it so your Mommie can hang it on the wall in your house. Don't you think so, Mom?"

"I think that's a great idea."

"Yeah!" Maggie agrees. She runs off happily to show her father, who stands talking with Harry at the smoking grill. Harry scoops his niece into his arms with a holler and smothers the giggling, squealing girl with scratchy, mustachioed kisses.

"They sure like each other," Joyce says.

"They sure do. Harry loves kids."

"I know. How's your, um, project coming along?"

Brooke raises her shoulders. Joyce pats her arm.

"Matter of time," Brooke says. The two exchange wan smiles, and Maggie squirms out of her uncle's arms and chases after a squirrel.

CHAPTER THREE

1

G ot a minute?"
Without waiting for her answer, the program manager of the Oncology Department at Buckingham General Hospital breezes into Martina Vitale's office and drops into the chair across from her desk. He jumps into an involved question about how they can use funds from a federal grant earmarked for developing nursing clinical protocols. He wants to use the money to make a pricey videotape promo of their program instead. Martina Vitale's eyes glaze over in no time. He has that effect on her, as, she thinks, on many people around the hospital.

His name is Larry Kowalski. He has the heavy-jowled face of a basset hound entering middle age with great reluctance. He has just traded in his horn-rims for contact lenses, which give him an exophthalmic pop-eyed look as if he has a thyroid problem or is on drugs, which he may well be; he is altering his lifestyle fairly radically. He is trying to dress with what he pathetically considers to be a greater attention to style, less like the rumpled bureaucrat that he is. Now his ties are red striped and wide instead of brown striped and wide; his droopy pants are pleated. While his wife minds the two kids out in the boonies where they live beside a lake, he is looking around for a woman in town, ideally here at the hospital, with whom he can have a discreet affair. To this end he has propositioned Martina so many times, and she has turned him down so often, that his lechery has become a joke between them—as far as he is concerned, anyway. From her point of view, Larry makes her skin crawl.

"Larry," she says when he is finished describing his scheme, "why are you bothering me with this?"

"Who else should I bother? Nobody else knows the answer."

"Are you asking me for my permission?"

"Sure. I want somebody to share the blame with me."

"If you were smart, and I know that's an awfully big if, you'd know you can't use the money for anything other than what it's earmarked for: developing nursing protocols. It's against the terms of the agreement. You'll never get the people in the grants office to go for it."

"I will if you say it's okay with you. See, the thing is, the proposal for this videotape won't get reviewed until after the San Francisco conference. And we want to make a tape to take with us."

"I thought you were going to take the protocols with you."

"No, the protocols we want to take to the Paris conference. That's later. Those we can develop with the money we get for the video. Don't you see? It's like borrowing from Peter to pay Paul."

"More like stealing from Peter to pay Paul. What if you don't get any money for the videotape?"

"Then we'll steal it from someplace else." His mouth forms a vulpine grin.

Martina buries her face in her hands. "Whose idea is this?"

"Mine."

"Why am I not surprised?"

"What's the matter, don't you think I can have an idea?"

"No, I don't think you can have a *good* idea."

"I think this is a good idea. And I think we should find a way to do it. And what's more important, Gerard agrees with me. And he's going to be pissed you're standing in the way."

She picks her head up. "I'm not standing in the way. The federal government is standing in the way. Larry, watch my lips: You. Can't. Do. This."

"Thanks for nothing. Next time I'll show you something to do with your lips that's much more fun."

"I'd rather drink boiling Drano."

He leaves her office as fast as he has come in, and she stares dispiritedly at the stacks of paper on her desk, her research notes for the protocols that it is her responsibility to develop in time for San Francisco, despite what Larry said. Unless Gerard changed his mind without telling her. Which is a definite possibility.

The sorry thing is, of course, that Larry's right. Once they take the money for the nursing protocols and use it all up on a videotape, they will certainly be able to replace it with money from someplace else. This program is like Bowling for Grant Money. This is Cancer Program as grant scam to build empires and fund junkets to exotic vacation spots for the staff's enjoyment. And the patients? Oh, yeah, them. Well, they get the finest care anywhere, don't they? Regional Cancer Center, caring through every season, high tech-high touch type thing? That's what the PR crap says, so it must be true, right?

She has no doubt that Larry wants to make a videotape to satisfy the raging ego of the director of Oncology, who loves nothing better than to see himself on TV. The videotape will surely focus on Gerard, and will certainly be made in time for San Francisco. Larry, brown nose supreme, will find a way.

Her phone rings. Expecting it to be Larry again she is sharp in her hello. Instead it is Deirdre, her boyfriend Max's oldest daughter. She is home from school, wanting to know if she can be excused from the dinner her father has planned for them all tonight in his pathetic attempts to ease their transition into family life. Deirdre says she wants to have dinner at her girlfriend's before they go to the library. Her father told her to ask Martina. Martina agrees, doubly annoyed at Max for foisting this decision off on her and at Deirdre because she knows the girl is lying. Instead of going to the library she will party by the river. Martina knows because this is what she used to do at Deirdre's age. Her own adolescence was largely a series of increasingly extravagant lies to keep her mother from finding out about her intimacy with sex, drugs, and rock and roll. Her introduction to these came early, and she renewed her acquaintance at every opportunity. That both of her parents worked gave her ample opportunities indeed.

Martina knows that the essence of adolescence is lies and rebellion. Deirdre, fourteen, will grow out of it; Max's other daughter, eight, hasn't yet begun.

Max is ten years older than Martina. If they get married (big, big If), it will be the second marriage for both of them. She divorced her first husband when he decided, after she finished her master's in nursing, that what he really wanted out of life was to play tennis all day long, which was incompatible with working for a living, as well as the more upscale kind of life Martina had in mind. Her ex has since moved to Florida, where he can indulge himself all year long.

She is not anxious to jump into marriage again, especially not into a ready-made family.

When she hangs up from Deirdre, she closes her door and settles in for some serious work. Soon somebody knocks. She sighs, calls, "Come in!"

Lydia Dunaway enters. The small feisty woman who is the program's administrative director flashes Martina a brittle, insincere smile and says, "I wanted you to hear this from me. I'm leaving."

"No."

"My husband's being transferred to New Jersey. I gave my resignation today."

"Wow." Before she can rein it in, her mind gallops along a track of career advancement into Lydia's slot.

"What did Gerard say?"

"What could he say? 'Good luck.' It's about all he can muster."

Martina rouses herself and shakes Lydia's hand. "Best of luck. Do you know what you're going to do when you get there?"

"I want to take some time off before I look for work. I wanted to let you know I was going," Lydia says, "because I think you should apply for my job."

"Think I'd have a chance?"

"They'll have to post the job and do a search and all that. But I think you have a good shot at it. Except I'll tell you right now who your biggest rival is going to be. Inhouse, anyway. Larry."

"I'm so much better than he is, it isn't funny."

"Yeah, but his pointy little nose is so much farther up Gerard's ass."

"This," Martina reflects, "is a true fact."

2

When the candidate for county executive enters the offices of McGuire Marshall Concepts trailed by his two campaign managers, things start to happen. John Marshall, Harry McGuire's partner, looms up to escort them into the conference room, where comforts materialize: black coffee for the candidate, tea with lemon for his aides, a plate of the sweet rolls the candidate enjoys. The candidate is this fall's Big Client.

He and his managers have a meeting with Harry and John to let the admen know what should happen during the next stage of their campaign. The candidate is a tall, bony lawyer with the slow gait and molasses speech of an emaciated Jimmy Stewart. If he wins the upcoming primary election, which he is convinced he will, his ascension to the office is all but assured; Republicans have held this particular post for the last sixty years.

Harry sweeps into the conference room and shakes their hands with great warmth. Harry knows how to show his sincerity, even—especially—when he doesn't feel sincere.

As the candidate settles himself in this cozy room with framed posters of paneling and plumbing supplies (Harry's other clients) on the walls, John says, "Excuse us just a second?" in his husky booming voice and steers Harry by the arm into a corner outside the conference room door, where the four young graphic designers slave away at their light tables, sad heads bowed under the enormous pressure Harry puts on them to produce.

"Before we get started here, I wanted to let you know we just got a call from one of the program directors over at General. He wants an appointment to talk about getting some work done."

"That's great. Which program?"

"Alcohol rehabilitation."

John is a big man, a faded athlete, defensive lineman in high school, weightlifter in college, racquetball devotee in his middle age. If only his muscles were brains, Harry often thinks.

"That's good," Harry says. "Have Dorothy set up a lunch appointment at the Downtown Club."

"Sounds like a small job."

"Maybe, but it's a way to get our foot in the door over there. Why don't you tell Dorothy and I'll start out with these guys."

John lumbers off and Harry goes in to start with the candidate. "Sorry for the interruption, guys."

"We were just about to take our business elsewhere," one of the candidate's men says.

"Ah, ha ha ha!"

As he settles into some preliminary schmoozing with his clients, Harry of the Midas touch thinks: Perfectly, perfectly right. It's raining business. He does nothing in the way of advertising for his own firm, yet his client list just gets bigger and bigger. Perfectly right.

If you play your cards right, Harry believes, life in this latter part of the twentieth century is fundamentally good. Harry's cards always come up aces, even when his mind isn't on the game.

3

Dennis Parker turns into the cul-de-sac—after first enjoying the NO EXIT sign on the corner—even the universe is giving me hints, he thinks—and drives slowly toward the turnaround at the end of the street. He peers at the tumbledown houses along the road through his rain-streaked and dirt-spattered windshield, the window washer pump having long since failed. The last thing they need around here is a visit from him. A nasty thought, even a case of bad vibes, could send these puppies crashing down all over the place, leaving only the chimneys standing, shaky towers of crooked brick among the rubble.

He turns the Pinto off and pockets the key. Pulls his appointment book out and checks the address and the time. Right on both counts.

He sits back and sighs, which steams up the windows slightly on this humid fall day. (The ventilation fan is also kaput.) Leaning porches, broken stoops, plastic sheets nailed half over windows and flapping in the breeze, front yards strewn with tires and empty bulbous milk containers, driveways cluttered with dilapidated cars, grow indistinct. Why should this make any more sense than anything else?

Before getting out of the car, he checks his book again. Only slightly compulsive. I don't really need to; I'll just make sure. His book is supplied by the company, his only perk. His only perk. It is a Senior Pocket Day-Timer. Alligator pigskin. (Interesting combination.) Made in Canada. Two pages per day. Divided into pockets for Tasks to be Done Today, Diary Record Notes and Memos, Appointments and Scheduled Events, and Expense and Reimbursement Record.

It also comes complete with a phone directory, a work organizer, a six-year planner, a credit card holder, a handbook on How to Use Your 5-in-1 Pocket Day-Timer Personal Management System, a brochure on How to Manage Your Time Effectively, and a handful of lined cards that give you the chance to list your time management goals, your goals with your company, your personal life goals, your questions for prioritizing a daily action list, and some other good stuff Dennis can't remember because he has left them all back in the box in his desk in the office, having not gotten around to finish reading the instruction manual.

Anyway, he has no real use for all this. He has no life goals, no goals with his company, no time management goals. Daily action list? Get serious. Dennis uses this thing to carry some spare cash around and keep a perfunctory schedule of his extremely infrequent sales appointments.

Though his Senior Pocket Day-Timer is also useful for orienting himself to time, place, and person. Great phrase. It posits the personality at the intersection of the mental (time) and the physical (place). As if the center of the universe resided in each of us, in some insubstantial effusion of the pineal. How New Age. Have to mention this to Gene back at the House of Grins.

Time, place, and person. He heard the phrase during his brief yet memorable stay in the Andrew T. Southworth Infirmary of Hampford College in Vermont. Where are you? What year is it? Who's the President? Who are you? When Dennis was in his last year at Hampford he suffered a breakdown, nothing big, just a wee tiny one, though serious enough to bring his mother and father up to drag him back home after he had to be physically restrained from throwing himself off the roof of his dorm. Twice.

Small breakdown. And everybody made such a big deal about it! You'd think nobody ever went bonkers at that place before. It was a small college where misfit children, mostly of the wealthy (though some, like Dennis, were on scholarships), could get a liberal arts education, if they were sober long enough. Few were, Dennis included, though most graduated anyway. Every semester, a few students would try to do themselves in, and every so often somebody would succeed. Most of those who were messed up enough to try were too messed up to pull it off.

But hey, there was Dennis, one morning after breakfast, up on the roof of Edgar Hall, crying his eyes out and teetering on the brink of nonexistence, one step away from the Big Zero. A crowd gathered below him, he remembers, deathly quiet. A thin twisting column of smoke rose from the dorm across the quad. The campus shrink saved him by talking him back onto the roof, where Dr. MacDonald threw his tweedy arms around him and hauled him in.

They didn't have to look very far for reasons: he was doing poorly in his classes, he was terribly lonely, miserable, alienated, he had tried to find a girlfriend, any girlfriend, and couldn't even get a date out of anyone, let alone someone to care for his pitiful self . . . etc., etc. MacDonald was satisfied, but to Dennis these weren't causes but symptoms of something else that he seemed to wake up with one morning, like a flu that could only be cured by killing the patient.

The second time he tried it he surprised even himself. It was in the middle of the night and everybody was asleep except Dennis and his roommate. Dennis tried to express his compulsion to do away with himself, become nonexistent, but couldn't find the words and struggled past his roommate to reach the roof again. His roommate saved him by calling the campus cops, who called the campus shrink, who talked Dennis down again. "Dennis," MacDonald said as the police led him away to the Infirmary where they said he would be safe (translation: restrained), "you just can't make this a habit."

They sent him home; his family wasn't rich enough to justify the aggravation he was causing. Dr. Bertoni worked with him as an outpatient at Buckingham General. That was almost a year and a half ago. He is well along the road to recovery, as motherly Dr. Bertoni says, or used to say during their weekly appointments, which had been suspended over the summer. Dennis reminds himself to write a note in his Day-Timer to make a new appointment now that fall is here.

He still does have some problems, however, including a serious one with motivation. If he doesn't go through with this call, what will he say to his boss, the repulsive Sid Baumgartner, he of the bald freckled head and polyester sport shirt and hairy arms, when he gets back to the office?

This thought forces Dennis out of the car.

He collects his binder and display samples from the back seat and hitches the whole load under his arm. He walks up to the door of the house where his appointment is. Rings the bell, which of course is out of order. He knocks.

No response.

He waits, deciding how much of an omen to make of this, when he hears footsteps behind the door. Too late to run.

Well, not too late exactly, but too rude. I mean, here I am, and the door is opening and all, and how fast can I really move, laden down with this junk

Behind the door is the tallest man Dennis has ever seen. But at the same time the skinniest, most skeletal man Dennis has seen in all his years on Planet Earth. God, if you're there, what a funny guy you are, to make people so tall and yet so thin, so cadaverous between the chest and the crotch . . . And then to send people like me around to meet them and try to sell them triple-paned thermal insulated windows to put on their houses that couldn't even survive the installation process! God, what a merry prankster you really are.

"Yeah?" says the guy at the door.

Dennis is so sick he almost drops his armful of samples right there and sucks in his cheeks and holds out his arms and stomps zombie-like around the crummy porch in an unbelievably cruel mockery of this poor rail-thin man. Oh, he is cruel, all right, but not that cruel. No, instead he looks this boney guy right in the eye, thinks, God, you are too, too much, and jumps into his pitch. "Mr. Warnicki?" he begins. With a straight face, even. "I'm Dennis Parker? From WonderWindows?"

Dennis holds out his business card between the first two fingers of his right hand, the only ones free. "You called our office for a free WonderWindows energy audit? I'm here to do it, right on time." And place and person.

"Yeah?" says Mr. Warnicki. "Well, I didn't make no call. I dunno who called. Wasn't me. I dunno who called."

"Maybe your wife?" Can this man have a wife?

"Yeah. Maybe it was her." He has a wife! "I didn't call. You want to wait here, I'll get her."

"Fine."

"Want to wait inside?"

"I'll wait here, thanks."

"Suit yourself."

Mr. Warnicki stork-walks away. Dennis holds a quick debate with the devil and the angel perched on his shoulders. Go. Stay. Go. Stay.

He sets his samples down, the better to run away. And yet . . . If he shows up at the main office without his samples, Baumgartner will kill him with his bare hands.

And in fact the more he thinks about it, the more the angel on his shoulder wins. Walking away from this appointment would be tantamount to quitting. Much as that would have given him immense pleasure, Dennis knows he cannot do it. He has not made a sale yet this month. He has to eat. He has to pay rent. He has to have gas money. He has to see to all those basic needs before he can move on to satisfying his more sophisticated personal needs, probably the most important of which is figuring out what exactly those are. So he can write them on the Senior Pocket Made-in-Canada alligator-pigskin Day-Timer cards and study them for the next six years.

Or not. The bad angel triumphs. He picks his samples up and hurries down the crooked front walk to his Pinto.

Back at headquarters, Baumgartner is out. Good news for Dennis. Headquarters is an old car dealership remodeled with aluminum siding and imitation hardboard paneling. And, of course, triple-thickness WonderWindows in all the window frames.

As he hopes and fears, Jackie is at the desk in the outer area. She is the new receptionist. She is a pert young woman, maybe nineteen, with long, shapely legs and the sweetest bum that kind of swoops down like the back of a Saab, and a small, tasty bosom and long, crinkled, artificially highlighted blonde hair with a topknot tied with a red ribbon like a poodle. Her face is heart-shaped with plump red lips that smile at Dennis whenever he is around. Her good nature and friendliness amaze poor Dennis, who is used to being ignored and disdained by women as good-looking as this one. He lingers by her desk. "Hi," she says. She raises a slim hand in greeting. Her smile is entirely charming. Her canines are slightly crooked, as are her center bottom teeth. Her mouth is moist and luscious and apple-like. Succulent red lips, gleaming white teeth. Even her fingernails on the hand she holds up are carefully tended and tempting enough to suck on like tender crab legs.

"Hi." Dennis holds his sample case and pretends to examine the bulletin board where Baumgartner posts his threatening memos to the sales force.

"Make any big sales today?" she asks.

"Nope."

"I guess they don't know a good salesman when they see one."

"Or maybe they do."

She smiles. "Better luck next time."

"Thanks."

One of the window installers comes in, a dirty muscular young roughneck in filthy jeans and plaid shirt with the sleeves rolled up to the crosses tattooed on his biceps. His name is Dave. Low on the socioeconomic—and, if his crude swagger is any indication, the evolutionary—scales, is Dave. But with his curly blond hair and skeptical blue eyes and muscles, he is the kind of guy that Dennis Parker naturally assumes Jackie would be more attracted to than she would be to him, wimpy crazy Dennis. Dave seems to know this. Ignoring Dennis, he leans a hip on her desk and chats her up. Dennis has heard the other installers in the big garage that is the company workshop talk about what they would like to do to her. Which has all crossed his own mind more than once. Probably old Dave actually does all that.

Exhausted and disconsolate, Dennis drifts away. She does not call after him with any kind of goodbye.

Knowing he is beaten out of any chance with her (he is pre-beaten, having never had a chance), he wanders into the inner office to dump his samples in a pile beside his desk, next to the big display model of a triple-glazed WonderWindow. The kind that doesn't let anything in or out, not heat nor cold nor dust nor air. Nor hopes. Nor dreams. Nor screams. Nor bodies anxious to plunge to the ground.

Back home, he has dinner alone. Gene comes in to change his clothes and let Dennis know he will be eating out tonight. Robert has already left the same message on the answering machine. Dennis makes his old standby, tuna noodle casserole with peas and cream of mushroom soup, and scarfs it down in front of "Family Feud." Is this all there is to my life? he asks himself.

'Fraid so.

Good answer!

4

The boy on the bed is fragile and brown-skinned, his face angelic in peaceful repose and sweetness. His dark-brown, almond-shaped eyes stare off into nowhere; his limbs are slender and graceful except for one leg in bulky plaster. He holds his thin arms together with his hands clasped as though in prayer. Beside the bed a woman straightens his hospital pajamas, fluffs his pillow, holds a cup of water to his face and gently inserts the bent straw in his mouth.

"Mrs. Williams?"

The woman looks up to see stout, tallish, round-faced, Caucasian Gene Anderson standing in the doorway. "Yes?"

He introduces himself. "I'm from the hospital's Social Services Department. This is Derrick?"

"Yes."

Gene leans over the boy. "Hi, Derrick. My name's Gene. How are you feeling?"

Derrick turns his head slowly and dreamily in Gene's direction. His eyes do not focus.

"Leg okay?"

When the boy does not respond, his mother says, "He doesn't talk."

Gene says to her, "Your doctor told us he was admitted after the accident. I just wanted to look in and make sure you have everything you need."

"Everything's fine so far." She is short and thin, with the same almond-shaped eyes as her son behind overlarge glasses that slip down on her nose. Her cheeks are prominent and rounded and her lips are full. Her skin is the color of milk chocolate. "Everyone's been very nice." Her voice is low and silken.

Not often caught off-guard by women, Gene finds himself flustered by her. He covers his discomfort by checking the notes on his clipboard.

He worries he is being officious and obnoxious. "They told you they're just going to keep him overnight to make sure everything's okay?"

"That's what his doctor said."

"His leg has a slight fracture, and it looks like he had a seizure in the ER."

"He takes medicine for his seizures, and they're pretty much under control. I think he was just scared. When he doesn't know where he is, he has one sometimes."

"The doctor's just playing it safe. The bus was going to the Developmental Center?"

"They were coming home. The police told me the man who ran into them was drunk."

"Any other kids on the bus?"

"Yeah, but they were all belted in their car seats. Or in wheelchairs. They're all okay. Derrick was sitting right where the car hit the van, and that's why his leg got hurt so bad."

Gene shakes his head sadly. He imagines the intoxicated driver accelerating down the street toward the yellow van nosing cautiously out of the driveway with its cargo of crippled children strapped into wheelchairs. All our societal delusions of greed, speed, death, and entropy converged on this one little handicapped boy.

His mother strokes Derrick's close-cropped head. Her fingers are long and slender as pencil points. They end in purple nails. She has an aura, green and peaceful, like a tropical bird.

"Does he have a social worker or therapist at the Developmental Center you want me to call?"

"I called his social worker right after I got here. She's going to stay with him later on when I have to go to work."

"That's nice of her."

"Yeah, she's really great."

"Where do you work?"

"I sing at Suspenders."

Gene has trouble taking his eyes off her. "You're a singer?"

"Yes."

"What kind of music?"

"All kinds. Mostly pop."

To cover his mounting agitation, he says, "Well, as long as Derrick seems to be doing okay for now, I should be moving on. Goodbye, Derrick," he says. The boy's gaze drifts over but never quite makes it to him. Gene reaches for the mother's hand and is conscious of its cool dry weight while they shake. "Mrs. Williams. Please let me know if there's anything you need."

"It's Crystal."

"I'm Gene. It was a pleasure to meet you."

"Likewise."

"Maybe I'll catch your show some time."

"I'm there every night but Monday," she says, and smiles. She nudges her glasses up with the point of an index finger.

Wow, a voice in his head goes. He moves off toward the elevator and his next visit inflated by the energy he has absorbed from her. The elevator door slides open like the sudden path illuminated by this woman and her radiance. *Wow.*

Tonight is his night with his youngest son, who lives with his ex-wife. Jason is fourteen. Gene has another son, Danny, who is nine years older and lives in San Diego with his girlfriend.

"Leslie," he says, standing on what used to be his doorstep, shoulders hunched against the cold, "how are you?"

"You're late," his ex-wife answers.

He does not fall into the trap of arguing with her, even though she does not step aside to let him in. "Jason ready?" he asks instead.

"You were supposed to pick him up at six. It's already quarter to seven."

"Sorry. I got tied up at the hospital."

"Meantime, Jason's sitting here hungry."

"If he's ready, we'll go now."

With great reluctance she turns aside. "Jason. Your father's here." To Gene: "You'll bring him home by ten, I presume."

"Sure."

"Not ten-thirty."

"Got it."

"This is a school night."

"Work night, too."

"As if you had a job."

Jason appears behind his mother. He is a gangly kid and looms over her. He wears his Buckingham Middle School Patriot's baseball jacket. His high-top laces flop untied. Every time he sees the boy Gene is more amazed at how his son is turning into himself. As it should be, he thinks; aren't I becoming my father?

"That's not warm enough," Leslie says. "Go change your jacket. It's cold out."

"It's warm enough."

"It will not be warm enough. Go change."

Jason looks to Gene for support. Gene keeps out of it and Jason fades away to get a heavier coat.

At dinner, his talk with Jason is desultory. Leslie's animosity toward him has stung and quieted them both. Gene talks about his clients at the hospital, about the importance of knowing oneself, about his own efforts to get back in touch with his real feelings, so deeply buried under decades of social conditioning. "These are important things, Jas. I only wish my father had told me about them. I had to discover them on my own. I lost a lot of time. Too much time."

Jason is mostly silent. Under his father's prodding, Jason talks about soccer team practice at the middle school. Gene asks him about girls; Jason defers with discomfort.

They have gone to El Cholo's for Mexican food. Midway through the meal Jason claims he no longer likes this kind of food.

Gene has him home by ten sharp. They embrace, or rather Gene embraces his son, who lets himself be wrapped in his father's arms but does not respond.

"I'm losing touch with my son," he murmurs later on. "We had dinner tonight and neither one of us could think of a thing to say."

He is silent, then says, "Once we could go out to eat and have so much to talk about, we'd forget about eating. Our food would get cold before we'd get around to it. And now we have no meaningful communication at all."

Gene stares into the ceiling light fixture, a flat round plate held up by three nuts in a triangle. It gazes down on them like a face empty of thought.

Sharon Krasner, the woman Gene met at the house party, lays a hand on his atop the kitchen table. "Must be hard for you."

"It's very painful. I keep wondering what I can do differently, how I can get back in touch with him."

"It's not necessarily anything you did, you know. This is a tough time for him. He's a teenager. They go through changes. You should know that."

"I do."

"So don't take it so personally. Didn't you go through it with your other son?"

"Danny never had a word to say to me after he hit fifteen."

"All right then. And you're okay with him now, aren't you?"

"Things could be better. But that's as much my fault as his. I wanted things to be different with Jason. You're lucky you have girls."

"Jason doesn't have to talk to you if he doesn't want to. He just needs to know you're there for him if he needs you."

"I guess."

"In the meantime, give him some space."

"I keep thinking Leslie's turning him against me."

Sharon shifts in her chair, takes a sip of coffee. Though they have been seeing each other only a short time, it turns out she and his ex-wife went to high school together and were friendly at one time. This was long before Leslie married Gene, and he became a Methodist minister until he had the spiritual crisis that caused him to abandon church and family. Sharon's husband left her for another woman two years before the Andersons were divorced. Her three girls are now ten, eleven, and twelve, spending the night at their grandparents'. This was to be her night alone with Gene, but she seems to be spending it with Leslie and Jason as well as Gene.

"Is she turning him against me?" Gene wonders aloud.

Sharon is silent. She has seen this all before, from the woman's point of view, left with sole responsibility for the children while the father has the luxury of doing what he likes, which includes feeling sorry for himself and the situation he has caused. She has no doubt her own ex has more than once thought she was turning the girls against him when it was really his own stupidity and self-centeredness.

"Jason's getting so old," Gene says finally, and means, I'm getting so old myself.

Abruptly he straightens. "I should go. It's late. I have to be up early."

Sharon says nothing. He comes to her for comfort, she knows, but she can't make him feel better about the boy, which means assuaging his guilt. All she would be able to do is take his mind off the boy for a while. She knows the small comfort she could get from him wouldn't be worth keeping him here till dawn. She walks him out. He doesn't even kiss her goodbye.

CHAPTER FOUR

1

"Many hands make light work," says Robert Fitzgerald.

"Oh no," Martina protests, "I couldn't impose. Really."

They stand out on the front porch. It is a mild evening with the sweet scent of wood stoves in the air.

"You're not. You live here now, remember?"

Beaming, Martina directs her friend Max to back his Blazer up the driveway so Robert, Gene, and Dennis in Robert's Seahawks cap and dark glasses can help her unload. Most of what she has to move is clothing, and there is not much of that, just her seasonal coats, sweaters, blouses, skirts. She stashed the rest of it at her mother's. If she gets married, she will move it all to her new home; if not, Mom will keep it.

"Guys," she says when her stuff is unloaded, "I really can't tell you how welcome this makes me feel."

"No trouble at all," says Robert.

"These jamocas made me feel the same way when I came," Gene says. "It's our duty to pass it on."

They are all together in the hallway at the top of the stairs. Martina's friend Max is the only one not sharing in the general good feelings here. This living situation seems a bit too much for him to grasp. He has his suspicious eye on Robert, giving him a once-over from head to toe. Max is a big, paunchy guy with frigid blue eyes and high forehead. He seems older than Martina by as much as a decade, Robert guesses. He puts his arm around Martina with conspicuous possessiveness. As they talk about how nice this house is, Max inches her backwards toward her room, anxious to mark out his territory in this new and confusing arrangement.

The others are happy to withdraw. They reassemble in the kitchen to compare notes. "What do we think so far," says Robert, group facilitator.

"I like her," says Gene. "I think she's neat. I did the first time we met her."

"Dennis?"

Wan Dennis shrugs. "Yeah, sure. Why not."

"Ever the enthusiast," Robert says, and Dennis manages a wan smile before going into the living room.

Robert and Gene exchange a look. "Problem?" Robert asks.

"Has he said anything to you?"

"Nope."

"Not to me, either."

"Something's wrong."

Robert goes out to sit beside Dennis on the couch. He puts his feet up next to Dennis's scuffed Nikes on the coffee table. One of the baseball playoffs is on TV. Dennis wears Robert's cap turned around, like a catcher. For a few minutes neither speaks. Then Robert says, 'What's the score?"

"Something to something. I think somebody's winning."

"So an interesting game?"

"Whatever."

At the commercial break Robert says, "So you don't seem to be all right about this."

"The game's okay."

"I mean Martina."

"Why shouldn't I be all right?"

"You seem disturbed."

"I'm all right. I'm all right." Then he says, "It's just—." He searches around the room's high ceilings for words, shakes his head and gives up when he can find none.

"Aren't you comfortable with a woman in the house?" Robert prompts. "Lots of room for embarrassment."

"No. It's not that. I just . . . I dunno. I guess I was hoping this could be like a refuge from the world."

"That's what it's supposed to be."

"It's not any more. For me, anyway."

"Because of Martina?"

"Yeah."

"What's different now?"

"I never have any luck with women. I always feel like they're comparing me to other guys and I'm losing. Now, to have a woman in our house . . . I dunno. I feel like she's constantly gonna judge me."

Robert considers that. From upstairs comes a shout of male laughter, then the unmistakable bouncing of a bedframe. Great timing, you guys.

"Oh, swell," Dennis says. "That didn't take long." He holds the remote out like a gun and blasts through the channels with it. News shows and sitcoms and movies of the week and blue fields of empty channel air and black and white "Honeymooners" and "Leave It To Beaver" blink past. "Is that going to be her stay here? One fuck after another? You've heard of 'Endless Summer'? This is going to be 'Endless Screwing.'"

The young man's anger takes Robert aback. "It's a bit early to say that."

Dennis is silent. "I think we should give it a chance," Robert says. Dennis lets the comment pass.

"Though if it turns out you're right, and it really is a problem for you, we can talk about it, and we can talk with Martina and see if we can come to some kind of mutually acceptable resolution."

"Jesus, you're so reasonable." Dennis stops the channelflipping on the baseball game again.

"I agree this should be a refuge for us all. But it's a new arrangement now. Things are going to be a little different. We can adjust. You adjusted when Gene came. Remember the party? You had reservations about that, and that didn't turn out so bad, did it?"

Dennis stares in mounting fury at the television. He despises being condescended to.

"Let's give this a try and see what happens. You might like having her around."

"Right."

"Did you have any sisters when you were growing up?"

"Look, don't try and psych me out, okay? In fact, why don't you just fuck off altogether? Okay? I got enough problems without you doing therapy with me. Unless I have to put up with that here, too."

"Okay, okay. Sorry I asked."

"This is supposed to be my home, not a residential mental health center."

"I said all right, Dennis."

"I'm tired of you doing this shit with me all the time. Who do you think you are, my father?"

Now Robert is shaken. "I'm sorry, Dennis. I won't do it again."

"Yeah, well, you do this about every goddam thing. And I'm pretty sick of it."

He tosses the remote clattering on the marble top of the coffee table and bolts from the sofa. "I'm going for a walk."

"Dennis, I'm not going to get on your case anymore. But I don't want to leave it like this."

"I'll adjust, okay? You were right about the party and I'm sure you'll be right about this. Okay? Are you satisfied? I'll adjust."

And he is gone.

Nice work, counselor.

Robert finds Gene in the garage. He is moving U-Haul boxes out of the center of the floor and stacking them against the wall. "Get it straightened out with him?" Gene asks.

"I tried to get him to give it a shot, at the exact moment they picked to start getting it on upstairs. Dennis freaked. And I screwed up."

"Tough luck. He still in there?"

"Well, no, he left kind of suddenly."

"Going to be a problem?"

"I hope not. I hope he'll come around."

"What makes you think he will?"

"I guess because I hope he will."

"Sounds like a vain hope to me. I thought you were a more practical man."

"Maybe it's a good sign, he walked out."

"Yeah, right. Maybe if the Pope got married, he'd have kids."

"No, really. He told me to leave him alone. Maybe he's starting to stand up for himself. That's a good sign, I think. Maybe the best thing to do is leave him alone."

"Doesn't sound like he gave you much choice."

"No. What are you doing?"

"Now there's another body in the house I thought I'd clear some space so we could keep a couple cars in here when it starts to snow."

"That's a great idea."

"I appreciate your saying so."

"Gimme a break."

"No, really. I'm serious. I do."

He stacks the last box in the corner. "I also wanted to get away and do some thinking."

"Aha. Well, I've already made a balls of one encounter today, so why don't I just slink away and leave you to your thoughts."

"No, no. Stay. I just have to sort some things out. The thing is, I met this woman a few days ago. I was doing a room visit at the hospital. Her son was in an accident. Kid's multiply handicapped. She's been on my mind a lot."

"You're seeing somebody, aren't you?"

"Yeah. I am. Was. Whatever."

"I see, said the blind man."

"The other thing is, there's my son. I feel like I'm not part of his life anymore."

"Yeah, I hear that. That's a hazard of divorce. How old is he?"

"Fourteen."

"Bad age. When my son was fourteen, he got in a shitload of trouble with the law. Hell, when *I* was fourteen . . . "

"What happened with your son?"

"He straightened out, but we had some bad times. He's twenty-three now. Your basic yuppie-in-training. Got the bad stuff out of his system. Just like I did, when I was his age. Only it took me a lot longer. In fact, I don't think I've quite gotten it all out yet, now that I think about it."

"Were you there for him?"

"His mother and I were divorced. I lived in another city. I had another life. It was hard, with both my kids. It's one of my big regrets."

"See, that's the trouble. Jason's right here, practically around the corner. I want to be more a part of his life than I am. Or than he'll let me be. Maybe I do need a change in my life. Maybe it's good I met somebody."

Gene takes a broom from against the wall and starts sweeping a pile of broken glass and dead leaves into the center of the garage floor. "She's a singer at a bar around town," he says. "This woman I met. One of these nights maybe I'll catch her act."

"Let me know if you want company."

"Yeah, thanks."

"Well," Robert says, "time to quit while I'm behind. More lives await my healing touch in the morning."

"And time for you to lighten up, pal."

"Sure."

He does, and he is rewarded. Upstairs, Martina's room is quiet. Dennis's door is closed.

2

"Mrs. McGuire, what a pleasure to see you again," the small Egyptian says.

He is a darkly handsome man with delicate features and glossy black hair and thick eyebrows that set off the soulfulness of his black eyes. He is elegant even in his white lab coat over a plump-knotted plum silk foulard tie and custom-made, richly woven white shirt that she has a desire to touch. "When was your last period?"

"The fourteenth," Brooke says. This is her fifth visit to him in the last year. She is used to his abruptness. Once a week, he travels from Upstate Medical Center in Syracuse to consult at the local fertility clinic; he has no time for pleasantries with his clipped accent. His waiting room is always jammed with the barren and the hopeful, who come from miles to be healed, made fruitful. Brooke included.

"Mmm," Dr. El-hakim says. He studies her chart. "Any trouble with the medication?"

"No. Though my flow seemed heavier than usual last time."

"Mmm." A scowl brings his oaken features together. "No spotting?"

"No."

"No headaches, flashing lights, visual problems at all? Stomach pain?"

"Nope."

"Nervousness? Anxiety?"

"No more than usual." She forces a smile.

"Your husband's health is good?"

"Yes."

He lays her chart on the desk and looks over at her. She returns his scrutiny with a sheepish smile.

Harry did some checking when they started seeing him and found out he was reputed to be the best reproductive specialist outside New York City. She has willingly put herself in his care—though she has not told him of the bittersweet mixture of disappointment and relief that overtakes her each month when her menstrual blood begins to flow. This is her secret, one she keeps from both El-hakim and her husband, who considers each month's bloody pads with disappointment and, she increasingly believes, disapproval, though he would never admit to this.

Dr. El-hakim had them both tested. Everything seemed to be in good physical working order with both of them. Dr. El-hakim's diagnosis was unexplained infertility. For this he prescribed medication for her, Clomid 50 mg. a day for five days each week, then up to 100 mg., little white pills she keeps in the medicine cabinet.

"Getting discouraged?" he asks.

"A little. I think Harry's getting impatient."

"Of course."

"He's usually very patient. It's just that we've been waiting so long, and he's so anxious to have a child."

"Of course." The physician takes a deep breath, exhales it in a sour and exotic current of air. The spices of the Nile pass over her. "As I told you," he says, "medical therapy is the preferred course of treatment at this point. And it is slow. But enough women in your situation respond to make me want to reserve the other alternatives as last resorts. By no means are we there yet. You understand me, Mrs. McGuire?"

"Of course."

The other alternatives begin at artificial insemination, where, as he explains it, they sort of squirt Harry's sperm into her, and from there in vitro fertilization that includes surgery and a technological procedure that she cannot get her mind around. As the Egyptian has explained the methods to her, they are physically, emotionally, and financially demanding, and he is perfectly happy to put them off for as long as possible.

"If you want me to repeat this to your husband, have him give me a call."

"No. I can explain it to him."

"We haven't exhausted our medical armamentarium." The last

word flows out in a proud and complicated rhythm of trills and hums. "You understand me?"

"Yes."

"Good. Let's keep the dosage where it is, and when you come see me next time we'll see about putting it up to 150. Yes?"

"Yes."

"Good. And don't get discouraged, will you?"

"No."

"In two months, then. Keep trying, eh?"

3

Harry McGuire's overnight case awaits him on the parquet floor in their front hall. A gift from Brooke on his last birthday, the case is glove-soft black leather, with his initials, HPM (P for Phillip), embossed on a mock American Express Gold Card luggage tag, also a gift from Brooke. It is packed for his weekend trip to New York City. Harry is on the phone in the den, giving last minute instructions to his partner for the breakfast meeting the next day with their candidate and his campaign staff. Harry tells John exactly what to do and say, even what to order, a detail made necessary by his opinion of John's level of intelligence. Brooke sits on a stool at the bar, watching him.

When he hangs up, she says, "You're doing this on purpose." She smiles to show she is teasing.

"I am not," he says testily. "I told you, he just found out about it himself."

He is referring to Jay, his friend in New York City, the one who feeds him stock tips. Jay called him the night before about a deal he has going that he wants Harry in on. Jay always has a deal going, and Harry is always ready.

"He couldn't talk about it over the phone?"

"No. He wants me to meet these guys who are only going to be in town tonight and tomorrow. Look," Harry says, "I'm sorry I can't go with you this weekend, but this is a last-minute business thing."

"I know," she says. *A business thing* excuses everything. "I'm sorry. I'm just on edge."

"Well, I'm uncomfortable about you going up there by yourself."

"Harry, it's my family, remember? I grew up with them. I can face them alone for one night. I'm coming home tomorrow."

She follows him up the short flight of stairs to the hallway.

"They weren't as crazy when they raised you as they are now. Just don't get in any fights with anybody," he says.

"I won't."

"I'll call you tomorrow morning."

"I'll be fine. Don't worry about it. They won't do anything to me they haven't already tried a hundred times before."

Her father is waiting for her on the front stoop of their house, one of many split-level ranches on the curving street in Pittsfield, outside Rochester. He is smiling, but the smile is the familiar tense one. The knot in her stomach tightens. She was last here at Christmas, when her mother had been in the hospital. It was the time she had slipped on the ice in the driveway. Or that's what her father had told Brooke at the time. Nothing seriously wrong with her, her father assured her. Your mother's just being held for observation in case she hit her head or something. According to her father, nothing was ever seriously wrong.

That was the time her mother had not allowed Brooke into the room to see her. She claimed it was because she did not want her daughter to see her in such bad shape in the hospital. Brooke suspected at the time her mother just didn't want to see her. As her mother ages, she has become more and more hostile. It reveals itself in little things, a harsh word, a sneer that showed itself before she can replace it with a softer, more maternal—and more consciously composed—expression. But Brooke has seen the disapproval in the curled lip and said nothing. She doesn't see her mother often enough to make it an issue. She believes she best serves her mother and their relationship by playing the dutiful daughter only occasionally.

Now the driveway is filled with cars. Good sign. Except for the battered old Jeep, which can only belong to her brother. If Lenny is here, things will automatically be worse. Though in Lenny, at least, she will have an ally who knows what their mother's eccentricities really are.

She catches herself. "Eccentricities" is her father's word for his wife's behavior. Others use harsher words to describe what she does. Lenny openly refers to their mother as crazy, which in part explains why their father never wants to see him. Brooke believes her mother is crazy, but doesn't ever say it out loud. Lenny doesn't care. For this he is often the lightning rod for much of the family's anger and confusion.

Brooke's father hugs her tightly, then pushes her away. Since the last time she saw him, he has aged noticeably. Though he's only in his early sixties, the lines at the corners of his mouth, which once distinguished his face with craggy strength, are now etched too deeply, set in channels of sorrow. His shoulders have begun to sag. Worry has stolen her father's good looks, as mental problems stole her mother's. Decrepitude, physical as well as mental, is making its way slowly but surely through this family. And whenever she comes back it reaches out to her too, the sole truly welcoming arms in the house. And she must do all she can to avoid them.

"Come inside and say hello to your mother," her father says. He turns and shoulders silently past Lenny inside the doorway. Her breath flutters in anxiety at the sight of her brother. He is as tall as their father but much heavier, fatter, their mother's fine oval face buried in bloat, their father's coarse hair long and greasy as ever, scholarly and owlish in his dark-rimmed glasses. They do not hug. As usual, his body odor is strong.

They are completely out of touch, except for these rare meetings. "Hey, babe," he says.

"Hey."

"Welcome home." His mouth twists with bitter irony.

"Thanks."

"Where's the yuppie?"

"If you're referring to my husband, he's away on business."

"You mean he's using the excuse of making money to avoid having to visit your family?"

She bites off her sharp reply. Lenny just might be right.

They walk into the living room together. "Sometimes it's hard to tell when you're kidding," she says.

"Who's kidding?"

Their mother is lying on the sofa with a damp cloth on her head and her arm thrown across her eyes. The shape her mother is in explains her father's tense smile.

Lenny pulls Brooke forward. "Hey, Ma," he says with too much enthusiasm, "look who's here. Your favorite child."

Her mother moves her arm just enough to spy Brooke. Her skin is pale and dry, like flakey pastry. Her dull brown and gray hair is combed straight back from her forehead, and sticks up here and there in hopeless spikes against the pillow.

"Hi, Mom," Brooke says. Her mother drops her arm and sighs heavily.

"She's overjoyed to see you," Lenny says to Brooke *sotto voce*. "She can't find the words."

Brooke ignores him and leans over to kiss her mother, who offers the merest patch of parchment-thin cheek. Brooke tries to encircle her mother in a hug, but the old woman remains too stiff and unyielding. Instead, Brooke works her hand beneath the pillow under her mother's head and settles for an awkward squeeze of her fragile body. Mrs. Cooper smells faintly of lavender, which Brooke knows her father has dabbed on her to cover the old woman smell. "How are you feeling?" Brooke says. She speaks loudly, as though talking to a child. Her mother brushes off the question with a shake of her head.

Her father steps into this scene. "Marjorie," he says in a loud, phony-cheerful voice, "looks like you've got your whole family around you this time!"

She makes no reply beyond the pained expression when she moves her arm to readjust the cloth on her forehead.

Brooke carries her suitcase up to the room that used to be hers, now redone as a den. She sits on the bed, stares around at the walls that were once filled with her sketches and paintings, now covered with some characterless beige discount wallpaper and sofa art done by one of her father's colleagues at Kodak who specializes in kitschy water scenes. Her old digs are neutral as a motel room. She left this room for good, except for summer and Christmas, when she went to college. Now it bears no trace of her under her father's attempts to reconstruct the past.

The hallway steps creak. Her brother heaves his bulk into the doorway. "Hey," he says.

"Hey."

He comes in and sits beside her on the bed.

"Lenny," she says, "what are you doing here?"

"What, I can't visit my parents? My family? My flesh and blood?"

She is conscious of a vibration, a continuing shudder in the bed beneath her. Its origin is his big soft body.

"*Your* family?" he continues. "This is your family, too."

"Come off it. The last one of her birthdays you came back for ended in a fight." Like every other family event for the past two decades.

"What are you saying, I'm going to ruin this one?"

"Probably." Now she begins to shiver at the same frequency as his body. She amends: "I hope not."

"The old man wanted me to tell you lunch is ready," he says. He stands, and the shudder is gone from the bed. But not from her insides.

Brooke spends the day with her mother, talking about Harry, about her job, about their life together, about their plans for a baby, all of which she thinks her mother may be interested in. As usual, her mother all but ignores her, interrupting her monologue only to demand that she straighten her pillow or make some tea. Brooke does these, glad to be of some use.

Dinner is another matter. At dinner, after her nap, attended by Easter, their housekeeper, her mother is a changed woman. Her face is flushed and she carries herself at the table with an uncharacteristic lightness. She opens presents with whoops of joy, tosses the wrapping paper onto the floor without care, and lets the Waterford bowls that her husband and daughter have bought jointly wobble drunkenly around the tabletop. By the end of dinner, she is in a state of advanced excitation that leaves her glassy-eyed and the rest of the family solicitous. Privately, each worries lest this fragile and unnatural atmosphere of familial joy will disappear instantly with one sudden shift of her mood, or, more probably, one wrong word from Lenny.

Astoundingly, it doesn't. After dessert, over coffee, Brooke's mother is almost normal—not for her, of course, but for any other woman whose family has thrown her a birthday party. Her excitement passes, leaving her tired but lucid, grateful her family has gathered to celebrate her birthday against every expectation of a good time. "My husband," she says, holding out her thin arms, "my children, Brooke, Lenny my son, thank you all so much. So much." She shakes her head at the good fortune that has brought them all into her life, and given her the clarity of thought to realize it. Her eyes glisten.

In that moment, Brooke believes they are all glad they came—even Lenny, defiant, nihilist Lenny, who has learned to scorn the bourgeoise trappings of family and home through too many scenes like this one that ended not in love but hatred, not quiet gratitude for gifts received but angry shouts about unappreciative children and parents who never deserved to be treated so poorly, not lucidity but sheer craziness on the part of a mother whose connection with reality was fleeting at best and a father whose sole desire was for the peace and quiet that yearly withered in the emotional barrenness of marriage to a woman old before her time and lost somewhere in the space behind her eyes. The children's father pretended that things were otherwise, and blamed instead his fat and disrespectful son for the sins against such a fragile peace that he knew, secretly in his heart, were committed not by his son but by his wife.

With her mother retired for the night, and her father reading the paper with the television on in the living room, Brooke throws on her coat and says, "I'm going for a late walk." Lenny says, "I'll go with you," and their father, who is about to respond to Brooke, says nothing after Lenny gets up. He turns his attention back to his newspaper.

The night is warm, almost springlike, with the humid smell of rain in the air. The subdivision continues aging gracefully, the trees fuller and older, the houses themselves settling into a character they were only just beginning to assume when Brooke left for college. When Lenny left home years before, the neighborhood was even less mature, like an early sketch for a painting. There are still no sidewalks. They stroll down the side of the road, past the houses of their neighbors that glow brightly in solid contentment.

"Old man's a pisser, ain't he?" Lenny says. "Won't even give me the time of day."

"How long are you staying?"

"Leaving tomorrow. You?"

"Same. I don't want to press my luck."

"I hear that."

They walk on in silence. "Lenny," she says, "you look pretty good."

"Yeah, well, last time you saw me I was in bad shape."

"When was the last time I saw you?"

"Who knows."

"I'm proud of you," she says.

He snorts. "Right."

"No. Really. I am. You don't know it, because you never bother keeping in touch with me, but I care how you're doing."

They walk on. "This wasn't so bad," she says. "Tonight was actually sort of pleasant, compared to some other times I can think of. Right?"

"It was unpleasant enough."

"Why, what happened?"

He gives her a searching look, and by way of answering says, "I hate those two back there."

"So what are you doing here if that's how you feel?"

"I came to see you."

The answer surprises her. "You could have visited me away from here. At my house in Buckingham."

"Wouldn't have been the same. Your husband thinks less of me than those two. If that's possible. Anyway," he continues to shut off her protest, "I wouldn't feel comfortable there."

"I could visit you."

"Then you wouldn't feel comfortable."

"Yes, I would."

"No, you wouldn't. Trust me on this one."

"I didn't come all the way up here to argue with you," she says with a sudden yet controlled fury that makes her uncomfortable.

"Look." He stops and folds her in his bearlike, smelly embrace. "I don't want to argue. I really did come to see you. You're the only one in this shitty family I care about."

She returns his hug. "You never told me that before."

"I'm going to this counselor. In a drug program."

"That's great."

"Yeah. Trying to get it together. She told me I need to ask forgiveness of the people I've hurt. I thought I'd start with you, see how it went."

"Oh, Lenny."

"Remember that time we were little and she chased me around the room with a knife?" They start to laugh about it, softly at first, giving in reluctantly to the absurd family they share. "Problem with staying straight is that all this shit comes back to you," Lenny says.

Before long she is overtaken by a mix of feelings, sadness at his anger, regret for the past, resentment over the dream of happy family life that never materialized for them and yet never left them either. Her laughter turns to sobs. Shortly her brother is pressing his face into the back of her neck and weeping along with her. For a long while they stand there in the road in their old neighborhood clinging to each other and crying like a couple of real crazies, bitter fruit from their mother's tree.

When she gets up in the morning, Lenny is already gone. She leaves soon after lunch. Her mother is back to her old self. Neither parent has much to say to Brooke. Even before she drives off, they withdraw into their own world again, shutting her out of the unit they have formed of themselves, without children. They say goodbye to her coldly, and she remembers again why she doesn't make it up here more often.

CHAPTER FIVE

1

The man holds his head down and murmurs something Robert Fitzgerald cannot hear. "I'm sorry?" Robert says.

The client clears his throat. "I said I don't know how it happened. I wish I did.

He is a chunky blond in his late thirties. He has two days of stubble on his handsome, full-boned face. "I was on my way up the ladder at the Glendale IBM Lab, when the drinking just started to get the better of me."

"Is drinking all you do?"

"What do you mean?"

"Do you use any other substances?"

"Maybe I smoke a little grass," the client admits. "Used to drive my wife crazy, too. She could cope with the drinking, but not the grass."

"How much did you smoke?"

"Couple joints a week. Nothing heavy. Occasionally, you know?"

Robert says nothing.

"I used to think," the client begins again, "I could control it. The drinking, I mean. Then when it started to get out of hand, I used to think, okay, I took a drink every once in a while because I was frustrated at work. I had a different job, or lived someplace else, I'd stop and everything'd be okay."

"Do you still feel that way?"

"I guess not. I don't know. Maybe a little."

"Why do you think it's taken so long to figure out?"

The client shakes his lowered head again. The moment stretches, pulls apart, and Robert knows he has lost him for now. The chemistry in the air is changed. He is too far inward to come out right now. It is almost time to stop anyway. The client's focus will come again.

All that remains of the session is talk from the young man about how low he has fallen and how much he has lost. Useful, but not as significant as the insights he needs, that he can't control his drinking, that he has to learn how to stop.

The young man shuffles back to his room, shoulders bowed under the weight of the ruins of his life. Robert sits a minute after he goes. Like many of his colleagues, Robert ultimately feels uplifted by his work because he feels he is helping people with their problems, is making however small a dent in the huge piles of suffering in the world. Yet he hasn't quite hit on how to be a conduit for the pain instead of a receptacle.

A salmon-colored phone message waits for him at his secretary's desk. James Fawcett wants to see him.

The executive vice president sits in his shirtsleeves with his big wingtips up on the desk. He wears black thick-and-thin socks. He shouts into the phone. He is one of those bores who do not acknowledge people who come into their offices and stand uncomfortably in front of their desks. Robert sits in the chair across from him and positions himself so that Fawcett's oversized brogans prevent the two men from making eye contact.

After Fawcett hangs up, he turns in his chair, feet still on the desk, and gazes out the window, squeezing the fleshy tip of his nose between thumb and first finger. He feigns distraction. Heavy hangs the head that wears the crown. As much of a pain in the ass as this guy can be, he is drolly predictable.

Fawcett reaches into a drawer for a paper clip. He bends a prong out so he can clean his fingernails.

He takes his sweet time about this. Doesn't bother Robert, who knows he will leave precisely five minutes before his next client appointment regardless what this guy is doing.

Finally, Fawcett says, "That McCarthy is a real piece of work." He moves his feet on the desk so Robert can see that he is not looking at him. He is talking about Ted McCarthy, vice president for ambulatory services. "I've asked him for six months to get the sign in front of Ambulatory Care fixed and he still hasn't done anything about it."

Robert says nothing. He does not want to be this man's confidant.

Fawcett thrusts his lower lip out, shakes his head. "Well," says Fawcett, "my problem, not yours." When he at last looks Robert in the eye, it is with a blank gaze, as though trying to remember Robert's name. "How are things going?"

"Good."

"How's the ad campaign coming along? Up and running?" He must know it couldn't be; it's only been two weeks since their meeting about it.

Robert returns his blank gaze. "No," he says pleasantly. Refuses to be either bullied or lumped in with McCarthy as a do-nothing. "I'm still interviewing agencies. I have an appointment with one this afternoon. Supposed to be the best in town."

"We have to jump on this. I want to see some positive results before the month is out."

"Moving as fast as possible."

"Here. This came across my desk. Thought you'd be interested."

He hands Robert a letter from the town's Retired Senior Volunteer Program. It invites Fawcett to address them on a health care topic of his choice in two weeks.

"I want you to do that in my place," Fawcett says. "Talk about the clinic. Substance abuse, alcoholism and the elderly, and so on and so forth. I've already accepted, but I'm sure they'll take a substitute. Besides whatever you come up with on this ad campaign thing, I want you to start keeping a higher profile around town. Set up some speaking engagements and so on and so forth. Best thing in the world in a place like this for spreading the news about something. Be good for you, too. Get you out in the community. See what's on people's minds."

"Fine. In the same vein, you might be interested to know I've been asked to take over as editor for a year of the *Journal of Alcohol and Other Drug Abuse Prevention*. It's put out by one of my old professors at Wayne State University in Detroit."

"If you want to take up your time with it, it's up to you. My main concern is it's not going to do much for us locally. When I was vice president at Bethesda Hospital in Cincinnati . . ."

This is Robert's cue to tune out. His attention, a frisky dog, slips its leash. He reads the diplomas on the wall announcing Fawcett's degrees and associations, and examines the framed black and white photos of the exterior of the hospital during different stages of its evolution, as it grew along with its neighborhood, the town, the century. Fawcett does not even notice. He drones on. Robert flings a not-so-subtle look at his watch.

2

Brooke McGuire and Edith Markowitz sit in the office of Ron Selby, director of corporate communications at the National Life Insurance Company, for their weekly meeting. The women do not speak, though Edith, middle-aged chain smoker, wheezes. Selby is on the phone with his co-campaign manager for the candidate for the county executive, who happens to be one of Harry's clients. Selby reclines in his chair with his back to them, showing his perfectly round bald spot on the back of his head as he stares out the window at what passes for the small city's skyline. He is head of the County Republican Committee.

When he hangs up, he spins in his chair to face the two women. He wears a dull striped brown tie with a sloppy knot loose at the open neck of his white shirt. Brooke hates boring ties with sloppy knots. It's okay with her if men choose to wear their collars open, but she distrusts ones who can't tie a decent knot. It is something she absorbed from her father, who is always meticulous about his clothing. His life may have fallen in around his head (and often did), but his tie was always picture perfect.

Selby's desk is empty of anything except the proof of this month's *Reporter*, the company's house organ. Before the phone interrupted him, he had handed out all his other assignments and papers to Edith, director of public affairs and managing editor of the *Reporter*. She in turn will dump them on her hapless editorial assistant at their own meeting after lunch.

Selby shoves the proof across the desk. "Final approval. Couple last minute changes, which I've flagged. Otherwise, it's ready to go."

"Great," Edith says. "We'll get it to the printer right away."

"I especially liked the changes in the layout," says Selby.

Brooke beams. They are her changes.

"Oh, great," Edith says. "We worked pretty hard on them."

Brooke's head swivels on her neck in Edith's direction, like a gun turret.

"Well, you did good," says Selby. "Now if there's nothing else?"

Back in her office, Brooke spreads the proof on her light table and spends the next few minutes channeling her frustration with Edith into straightening her desk. Her office is sparse and corporate utilitarian, with a company issue metal desk, a comfortless plastic chair, a light table with strips of type spread out over opaque glass, and a low flat beige metal cabinet for art supplies. National Insurance does not allow its employees to decorate their offices. Management believes it has paid too much to have the offices professionally decorated to allow its employees to muck up the decor with pictures of children on the walls. Brooke gets around this rule by festooning her workspace with bold geometric pastel posters announcing design contests that she changes frequently; as a member of the "creative staff," she is allowed some leeway in corporate rules.

Edith sticks her head in the doorway. Her hair is messed up, as usual, as if she combs it mornings with an egg beater. She is a pasty-faced woman who has plucked her brows to a fine line but wears no makeup, which draws as much attention to her plain looks as too much would. "Ready for lunch?" she asks with insincere brightness.

3

The Caddies in the parking lot of the Downtown Club let Robert know this is not your average lunch joint. He meets Harry McGuire in the second floor lobby, which he reaches via a cramped elevator. Harry has reserved a table for their luncheon meeting in the cavernous dining room. Harry is a young and vigorous man, Robert notes, younger than himself and quite handsome in the Black Irish way, with bright gray eyes and long eyelashes and a full black mustache that gives him a pirate's dash. He is in marked contrast to the desiccated old-money farts who slump in rumpled suits at tables in the big, drab room.

The maître d' greets Harry with great obsequiousness and shows the two men to their table. Harry leads Robert through a gamut of greetings from the elderly gentlemen taking lunch. Harry recognizes them with princely nods. Robert catches Harry watching him out of the corner of his eye, making sure he is duly impressed by this show of respect. Robert is more amused than amazed. Harry doesn't know that he is hardly ever impressed by people who try.

"Have any trouble finding the place?" Harry asks.

"Nope."

"Been here before?"

"No. I've only been in town since the summer, actually. Haven't had a chance to get around much."

"I'll have to give you a guided tour."

"Great."

Harry asks him where he comes from, and they talk about the midwest and the west. Harry says he has been all up and down the west coast and the east coast, but does not know the midwest at all. Robert tells him about Michigan, its flat farmlands, its margins of water.

Harry is an interested listener and an easy talker. They ask each other questions and make appropriate replies. Sniffing butts, as Robert calls this interplay between newly-met men. Where do you live? Are you married? Do you play tennis/racquetball/golf? Do you jog?

"My partner's a real jock. Lifts weights and plays racquetball," says Harry. "I work out at the Y, but all that other stuff, all that racquetball shit, all that seems too much like work for me. My game's golf. I have bad legs, anyway. Play golf?"

"Hardly ever."

"Too bad. Great game, golf. Do a lot of business on the golf course."

"My work is mostly indoors."

"There's a nice country club in town. You might want to check it out. I shot a hole-in-one there a couple weeks ago. My first."

"Really."

"Yeah. Big thrill. Made my day."

"I had an exercise bike once. Came in handy."

"They do."

"I could hang a lot of clothes on the handlebars."

"Ah, ha ha ha ha ha ha ha."

"I had a rowing machine once but I gave it away. Couldn't hang any clothes on it. Too low."

Harry throws his head back, laughs silently.

Abruptly he stands, taps Robert on the arm, says, "Excuse me," and starts out for the lobby. A middle-aged woman has just walked in followed by a younger couple. Harry strides up to the group and they all greet him. He separates the younger woman and talks with her in the lobby while the others in her party continue on.

She looks in Robert's direction. She is smiling broadly. She wears a forest green suit cut close at the waist, accenting her bust and hips. From across the room Robert is struck by her big eyes and broad smile.

Shortly Harry returns and the woman joins her companions. "My wife," he says. "And the people she works with. Every month when they get their approvals for the magazine they put out, her boss takes them to lunch here. I forgot today was her day."

"Is she a writer?"

"No, she's the art director for National Life Insurance."

"Where are they going?"

"There's a smaller room off to the side. That's where the women sit."

"Excuse me?"

Harry manages a crooked smile. "Women members aren't allowed in the main dining room. At one time, women weren't allowed in here at all. Then—it was only within the last couple years, when the financial picture started to dim and a lot of private clubs around the country started to be sued to admit women—the Board of Directors decided women could join. And could even eat here. But they drew the line at sitting in the big room. They have to eat in the little rooms at the side."

"Sounds like discrimination to me, Harry."

"Well, I admit it's ridiculous, in this day and age. But it's not as bad as it sounds. This is an old town. It's backward in a lot of ways. And in a lot of ways, it's progressive. I'm certain this last rule will change too, before long."

"I hope so. Can men eat in the smaller room?"

"Of course."

"Why aren't we eating there?"

Harry shrugs. "This is my usual table."

Edith and her assistant, a round-shouldered mousy young man named Dave, are already at their table in the other room when Brooke joins them.

"How's Harry?" Edith asks.

"Good. He's here with a new client."

Edith chuckles, which Brooke can't interpret, and turns her gaze back on the menu. A glance is all it takes: this club is short on good food. The fare is sandwiches, small and served with a pitiful handful of potato chips. Edith and her husband are members. She likes the exclusivity of it, the sense of belonging it gives her; like Brooke, she is from out of town. Unlike Brooke, she has a husband who is not a native, so she has no built-in connection with this town and its fussy old society.

Edith makes many strange noises, small cooing sounds as she looks at the daily specials. Brooke knows them all already, the noises and dishes, roast beef sandwiches that will arrive ice cold and tough as airplane food, broccoli quiche that will show up as a dappled dried egg triangle. Dave makes no noises, nor does he say much of anything. Mostly he smiles in bemusement at the appropriate moment. Which is not a bad talent to have.

At the table behind them sit a group of older ladies, widows in handbags and pearls, the geriatric moneyed set of this town, the set that Edith will never in a million years crack. The set that Brooke belongs to by virtue of her husband Harry, who sits wining and dining a new client in the next room with the rest of the men who mean something around here. Some day when Harry kicks off, Brooke will sit around these same tables with other older ladies. Edith thinks she is introducing her two minions to the high life, but Brooke has been a member of this club since she and Harry were married, and has, in addition, been in any number of finer spots with Harry in other parts of the country. So there.

Like Dave, Brooke is silent during the course of this meal, uncharacteristically for her. The conversational ball, such as it is, is borne singularly by Edith, who does not even seem to notice, let alone mind, that she is the only one prattling on. And how Edith prattles—about the magnificent dinner she made last night, about the chance she missed years ago to write a microwave cookbook and scoop the entire cookbook industry at that time, about her husband's alma mater Dartmouth, about her experiences as Richard Nixon's upstate campaign coordinator, all of which she has told these two countless times before, in this very room. It is the kind of shameless self-promotion that Brooke has come to associate with this woman, and with public affairs in general.

Edith talks and talks, and coos and wheezes, and Brooke barely listens. Her thoughts are elsewhere. With her work for the afternoon, with their plans for the weekend, with Harry and his client in the other room.

What was that guy's name again?

He told her and she tries to remember, but she cannot. Damn: he is sitting not fifty yards from them. If she listens carefully, she can probably even hear his laughter at Harry's endless supply of jokes. And good jokes they are, too. Harry has a way with a joke. And he learns hundreds from the men he hangs around with. And she can think of the punchline to literally dozens. Harry tapping his head and slyly saying, "Kidneys"; Harry saying, "I dunno, but the pig's in the wheelbarrow"; Harry holding his hands out like a penguin and singing, "I love a parade"; Harry saying, "Are you Dunne? Whyn't you call your mother?"

But what is that guy's name?

This is it. The first tickle of her mother's inheritance. The old lady in the rocking chair in the corner of her mind stops, waits, listens. The chill of mortality creeps up her back.

With Edith's sharp voice in the background, talking about who knows what, Brooke has an exhilarating rush of relief. The man's name comes to her: Bob. Bob Something. Bob Irish Name.

Bob Fitzgerald. The creaking of the rocker starts up again. Rock on, Mamma.

"Don't you?" says Edith, apropos of what Brooke has no idea. Brooke smiles along with Dave. "Of course," she says, knowing by now that the right answer is agreement with Edith, no matter the question. Edith smiles too, with great satisfaction.

At meal's end, on their way out, Brooke pauses briefly at the archway to the men's side. The room has mostly cleared out. In the far corner she sees Harry and his client dawdle over coffee. Harry, facing in her direction, spies her in the doorway and waves. Brooke waves back. Bob Fitzgerald turns in his chair. She and Dave and Edith file into the tiny elevator that brings them down to the ground floor from the upper reaches of the town's society and back to work. "When I won the Fontaine Award for a Special Public Relations Event," Edith starts to say, and the rest of her words to this familiar story are lost as she sails out the entrance door to lead the way out to the parking lot on her tiny clattering feet.

4

At lunch Harry makes a singularly poor impression on Robert Fitzgerald.

It isn't that Robert actively dislikes him. But there is something about Harry that goes over badly with Robert once Harry goes into his song and dance over coffee, something bothersome behind the white teeth and preening mustache. Robert pegs Harry as someone who will say whatever he thinks his listener wants to hear. This talent may be the secret of an adman's success, but to a substance abuse counselor it gets old fast. As their lunch crawls to a close and they are left in the big room with only the young waitresses cleaning tables for company (women are allowed in there for purposes of service, evidently), Robert cuts off Harry's pitch to get back to the clinic. He has had enough of this guy.

Back to the phone book. Robert makes appointments with heads of the two other agencies in town. (There were three, he finds out, but the head of the third recently passed away and the company is not taking on new clients till things settle down.) The first one he sees is an aggressive sharpy who sashays into Robert's office and proceeds to push his own company by dropping snide remarks about the town's other agencies. Maybe they are as lame as he paints them, but Robert doubts that every project this man's agency handles is Major, the focus of every campaign National, the response uniformly Fabulous. Robert doesn't know much about advertising but knows the samples this man peddles are second-rate and as ridden with cliches as his speech. "My artists are brilliant young designers," he says to Robert in parting forever, bearded, bloated, red-headed.

The other agency head is a long-faced woman with artificial golden hair who shows him more mediocre samples and drops the name of her husband, one of the area's more prominent politicos. This, of course, is exactly the wrong tack to take with Robert, who has heard of the man and considers him a crook and a jerk, in that order. "When can we look forward to starting?" the woman says when he stands up to conclude their brief interview. "I'll call you," says Robert, knowing he never will.

In the end, he is left with the choice of bringing in out-of-town agencies, or relying upon Harry McGuire after all; Harry's samples were superior. Robert's time to get this campaign going is short; he chooses Harry. He will have to give him especially close guidance, that's all. He hasn't had a chance to discuss the particulars of the campaign, but he wants it aimed at the general public, with special mailings to physicians and counselors. Robert knows he can guide Harry's hand, and he will be, after all, the Client, the Father with the power to approve or disapprove, love or withhold love, the stern figure whom Harry and his group must strive to serve, to please, and to curry favor with. He, Robert, will be in control of this. Considering who he'll be working with, this suits Robert fine.

5

We got the hospital account," Harry tells Brooke.

"That's great!"

They are both in a rush, she to finish the dinner dishes before she goes to teach her course, he to get out to the bar. This is his first week of ownership. He has been at Harry and Mike's every night, hurrying off right after dinner or going right from work, eating something there.

"See you later," says Harry, out the door.

He comes right back. "Hey," he says.

"Hey you."

"The open house is on for a week from Saturday, did I tell you?"

"No."

"It is. You're still going to do the art for the announcements, right?"

"Sure."

"Great. Talk about them when I get home?"

"Harry," she says, "when you get home, I'll have been asleep for quite some time."

He kisses her cheek. "I know, kid. Listen, I'm sorry. But this is my new toy. I'm excited about it."

"I know."

"I'll chill out soon enough."

"I know that, too."

In fact, Brooke barely notices the difference between Harry at the bar or Harry working late at the office, or Harry at any of his boards of directors' meetings for the community organizations he has been tapped to join as a businessman of some smarts, sophistication, and success. He is on the boards of the YMCA, the St. Vincent's Hospital Foundation, the local chapters of the American Red Cross and the New York Lung Association, Catholic Charities, the Buckingham Symphony Foundation, the Junior Chamber of Commerce, the County Young Business Owners for Reagan Committee, and Brooke cannot remember what all besides. Often she is asleep by the time he gets home from these, just as she has lately been asleep when he gets home from the bar.

That reminds her—the Symphony Foundation's annual dinner is coming up soon. When? As soon as next month? A panic seizes her. She must find out. She and Harry of course will be seated at one of the head tables. She must arrange things for this: examine her evening dress and Harry's tux to make sure they're cleaned, check the tickets for the date, clear their own schedules . . .

Waiting at a traffic light in her Alliance on her way to school, she pulls a notebook from her purse and makes a list of the things she must do in connection with this affair. Among all her other gifts, Brooke has a genius for organization.

In the small mustard-colored office behind the bar, Harry opens his leather briefcase and removes his phone book, a frayed workhorse filled with slips of paper held together with a rubber band. Reeboks up on the desk, he makes his calls.

He phones his friends, his business associates, his acquaintances in the local media, his vendors, his clients, and anybody else he can think of who might help him along.

"Hey," he says, "it's Harry McGuire. Listen, my brother and I just bought a bar. Yeah, I know, right? Always something new. So, we're having a sort of party to kick things off a week from Saturday night. We'd like you to be our guest and look the place over, and have a good time for a couple hours."

"You own a bar?" says Robert Fitzgerald the substance abuse counselor when it is his turn to be called. "A bar?"

"Yep. Come on down and check the place out."

"I'll definitely do that, Harry."

"Notice," Brooke says, "the force of the line in this design? See how it comes in off center but pulls your eye across?"

Brooke stands facing the screen with her back to the class. She feels as if she absorbs the power in the image and demonstrates it physically for the students, clenching her fists and pulling hard, pantomiming a tug. She tries to keep herself out of the beam of light thrown by the slide projector at the rear of the studio, but in her enthusiasm she fails. The image of the slide she is talking about—an airline ad with a single silver arrow of airplane and the words, "Phoenix, Phast," underneath—plays over her body. A line of inch thick red letters wavers over her bare forearms like a living web.

The art studio in the basement of the Fine Arts Building on the Broome Community College campus is a darkened, windowless square of cement block walls and corky suspended ceiling, its air a head-spinning perfume of oil paint and turpentine. In the silence following her question Brooke hears the whir of the slide projector, watches smoke curl lazily in the cone of light. Students are not supposed to smoke, but they ignore the prohibition. Artists are supposed to be rule-breakers, aren't they?

Here and there her dozen students sit cross-legged on the floor, recline on the crosspieces of artist's benches, lay casually pulling on cigarettes in the stiff folds of a tarp pushed against the wall. They are tough kids, working class community college students as arty types in torn black Levis, black leather jackets heavy with zippers and studs, black tights with white skin peeking through jagged holes, shapeless bodies in black dresses, black sweaters, jet black dyed hair with shaved temples. They cop creative attitudes with each other, and occasionally with her, not knowing she is not impressed by moody and temperamental artist-children. And this isn't fine arts, as she explained to them that first night, heart pounding and hands trembling, this is graphic design, a practical application of what they learn in their other art classes. Brooke with her Vanderbilt jeans, rounded womanly hips, tinted hair, settled job, successful advertising executive husband, luxury cars, understandably feels apart from them, at once feels benevolent in her mission to bring the real-life side of the working artist to them and slightly resentful of their aspirations and pretentions and the holy light of possibility in the future that still warms them, tough as these children are. Which light flickers lower and lower in her own life, to be swallowed up eventually by the lengthening shadows of her age, her work, her family.

Still, though she may feel out of place among them, she has taken to this situation better than she feared she would. It is a chance to expound, to perform, and finally to realize how much she knows and how competent she is in her field, unexpected rewards indeed from this job she took because Harry arranged it for her. A different Brooke McGuire has evolved in the lidded gazes of these kids than began the course. She will miss this class when it ends.

"What makes this thing work," says Brooke now in her loud teacher voice, standing off to the side, "is that great action quality it has. And that comes from the way the form moves in its space. And that's the message too, isn't it? That we get you there fast?"

Nobody answers. She turns on all the lights in the room, says, "Next time, I want you to design a print ad for this school. You can take the school itself, or this program, or any other program or part of the school you want. Just remember to make your design simple, and make it mean something. I want you to get started on it tonight. I'll be coming around to help you out and answer questions when I grade your assignments from last week." The students bestir themselves with little energy.

"Leave your assignments for tonight out where I can see them," she says.

When the dozen students finally get going, Brooke moves among them judging their homework, the redesigned logos for the companies and businesses they work for, or someone in their families works for. They began these in class last time and were supposed to finish them at home for this week. "How's it coming," she says to each, sharp to the scrape of bench and scratch of pencil and felt-tip pen around her, and to the emotional effect (or lack of it) of the too-precise geometric logos, many of which she knows are pale versions of the symbols that the companies around town already use. It's her job to know what's going on.

Brooke goes from student to student, a bee from flower to flower. "I like that."

"Needs a little punch."

"Coming along."

She pauses at the bench of Claudia McKinney. The logo is an arrow-type arrangement for the financial services company Claudia works for during the day. It is remarkably similar to the company's actual logo, which Brooke herself designed two years ago. Brooke feels a rush of pleasure at the imitation.

Claudia keeps her head down. Her long shapeless dull brown hair obscures her face. "How are you doing?" Brooke says.

"Okay." Claudia is a serious young woman in her early twenties who reminds Brooke of herself, only in a different life, with different pressures, maybe fewer options, different frightening demons to overcome.

"Looks good," Brooke says. "Lots of strength there. Inspires confidence."

"Thanks."

"Looks kind of familiar, though."

"Yeah, well, I guess it looks a little like the one they already have."

"A little. What makes it different from the one they use?"

'The real one has this kind of like forward lean, like it's just been shot out of a gun?"

"I know just what you mean. Great description. So what does this do that the other doesn't?"

Claudia, embarrassed by the attention, smooths her long hair with a delicate hand soiled with ink, shrugs both shoulders, keeps them raised. She is a younger version of me, all right, Brooke thinks, down to the dirty hands. "I'll give you a tip: Even if you don't know, sometimes you have to make something up on the spot," Brooke says. "A lot of times that's what you have to do in the real world. It doesn't matter if it's true, it just has to sound good. For this one, I'd talk about how solid and trustworthy the typestyle is. How it's meant to inspire confidence."

This brings a slight smile to Claudia's grim thin lips. Brooke kneels, dashes off in rough red crayon on the lower right corner of the paper the five-pointed star of an A.

The grade pries a broad grin out of Claudia.

Brooke has momentarily duped all the forces controlling this student's life, brought them into a weighty convergence and then suddenly shifted them, made them, with a deft jujitsu of the will, grant this young woman permission to do something completely outrageous. Like feel good about herself. Like smile.

She moves on to the next student.

6

Tonight the turnout at the monthly Retired Senior Volunteer Program spaghetti dinner is disappointing. The icy rain that began around four o'clock has kept the crowd small. The Senior Center hall is packed with tables set for eight people each, yet not even two tables are full as Robert Fitzgerald meets his host for the evening, a short, sharp-eyed old guy with a round head and a Jimmy Durante nose. He introduces himself as Curt Flaubert (which he pronounces "*Flaw*-bert") and apologizes right off for the showing.

"No problem," says Robert. "I don't have a formal speech anyway."

"Good thing," says Flaubert. "Saved yourself some trouble." There are so few people attending that Robert decides to bag even the brief notes he has made and sit at one of the tables and eat his spaghetti and discuss his program informally. They are a lively group of socially aware oldsters, predominantly women—but he wishes there were more of them. Particularly since a television news crew is here to shoot some tape for a feature on health care and social services for the area's seniors. Somehow this fact had escaped the attention of Fawcett, whose idea it was to dovetail Robert's talk with a little marketing ploy.

The reporter is a young woman in a shapeless burgundy blazer with shining blond hair that falls softly about her shoulders and frames a forceful face. Her nose and chin are sharp as the prow of a ship. "No speech?" she says when Flaubert tells her of the change in plans. "I would have appreciated somebody letting me know earlier."

"Didn't know earlier," says Flaubert. "Low turnout, you know. Weather kept 'em away."

Unhappily she directs her cameraman to shoot Robert talking with the old folks. She sits at the next table with her steno pad beside the plate of spaghetti she has been graciously provided. She leaves it untouched. That she is an attractive if stern and supercilious woman is not lost on Robert.

"The thing is," says one man at Robert's table, his mouth and chin orange from tomato sauce, "government don't do nothing for us." "You said it," says another man. "And what it does do is wrongheaded. And I'm not just talking about these national politicians. The problem is just as bad with these local guys."

"What do you think about the mayor giving that developer money for building that parking garage?" says Flaubert. "That Kolata crook." He peers at Robert sitting beside him. "That's just wrong, that's all that is."

"I don't follow you," says Robert.

"The mayor's giving this crook Al Kolata the taxpayer's money so he can build a garage downtown without risking a buck of his own," Flaubert says. "While Six-Pack Jimmy's got a towing program going on, of all the goddamn things, so we'll think we need a parking garage to reduce congestion downtown when it's nothing but a sham to smooth the way for his crony. And no doubt line his own pocket."

"Who's Six-Pack Jimmy?" Robert asks.

"Jimmy Schultz," says Flaubert. "The mayor. People call him Six-Pack because when the blizzard of '78 hit, the city services were overwhelmed. Streets didn't get cleared and nobody could get out of their houses. He told everybody to just grab a six-pack and hunker down at home. He's a Republican," Flaubert says, as if this explains everything. "He's up for reelection against the daughter of an old Democratic ward heeler, and he's mighty worried, believe you me. He can feel her breathing down his neck."

"Not that she's any great shakes either," says another old guy. "The taxpayer's paying the tab," a man at the next table says.

"That's who's always footing the bill. The taxpayer."

A woman asks the reporter, "You're not writing this down, are you?"

"Course she is," Flaubert says. "And write this down too. Jimmy gave Kolata a present once before. Remember? It was the contract to redo the streets and sidewalks on Court Street. Ran way over budget, took a year longer than it was supposed to, upset bus schedules all over town—and by the time it was done, the big stores along the strip they renovated closed because their customers stopped coming downtown because it was so inconvenient. Penny's closed, Jacobson's closed. They just went to the mall instead. Which Kolata also developed. This guy's getting rich while the whole town sinks into the mud. This isn't the free enterprise system," Flaubert continues, "this is just corruption between the fat cats at the expense of the little guy."

He turns to the seniors sitting at his table. "It's a scandal," Flaubert says. He scrapes his mouth with his napkin. "This don't have nothing to do with health care," he says to the reporter at the next table. "But it's an example of the kind of government we have 'helping' old folks."

They all agree these are not the kind of leaders they want to live under.

After the dinner ends, Robert moves over to the reporter's table as the seniors help clean the tables. She is scrawling some notes in her pad. "You never did hear much about health care and social services tonight," he says.

"No," she says, unsmiling. "But what I did hear I can use." Her voice is carefully modulated, low and urgent, an imitation of the network news stars. When he hears it, Robert remembers that he has seen her on the pitiful local news, with a cheesy backdrop and sound quality so hollow it could be shot in somebody's basement. Covering small stories at a small station in a small market, paying her dues with spots on traffic accidents and school board disputes so she can move on to someplace with more visibility. Like Binghamton.

"When is it going to be on?"

"Sometime in the next month." She folds her notebook and shoves it into her voluminous purse at her feet. "Excuse me."

She goes to corner Curt Flaubert, who clearly welcomes her attention. Robert watches her across the hall. She is one serious and intense reporter.

When she finishes with Flaubert, she shakes his hand and, still without having cracked a smile, returns to the table where Robert is sitting. She picks up the plum-colored down coat she has thrown over the back of her chair. Her prow of a chin cuts the air. She runs her fingers through her blonde hair, pushing it back over her head with the crisp, dismissive gesture that Robert knows so well.

What she says is, "Actually, I was going to grab a cup of coffee and sort through my notes. You're welcome to join me."

He considers briefly, says, "Thanks. But I'm going to get going. Been a long day."

"Well, good night then," she says, and pushes through the doors of the center without so much as a glance back.

CHAPTER SIX

1

In her office on Saturday morning for a few hours to finish up personnel evaluations, Martina Vitale lifts her head from the piles of forms in front of her. The director of the Oncology Program stands in her doorway. "I thought I saw you come in," he says.

"Dr. Gerard. Hi."

"When you have a minute, bring your coffee down to my office?"

"Sure. I can come now."

She follows his narrow back down the hall. "Close the door," he says to her. She obeys and sits in the chair facing him across his desk, piled as high as hers with papers, forms, manila folders, patient charts, journals.

"Burning the weekend oil," he says, and grins. He has awful teeth, long and twisted and yellow. He is a homely man in his late forties, with bad skin and a boney jaw and brown hair that is curly but that he blows dry so that it lies across his head in stiff waves, looking too phony to be false.

"Here." He hands her a draft of a nursing protocol he has reviewed. "I made some notes. Some points I think need clarifying."

"Great. Thanks."

He leans forward on his elbows, his thumbs touching and tapping the papers on his desk. His thumbs are short, with slender nails and huge halfmoons. "How's it going?"

"Good," she says, pleased he has seen her working on the weekend.

"I just wanted you to know I have your application for Lydia's job. You're one of the top candidates.

"Great."

"It's going to be a hard choice."

"When do you expect to decide?"

"I want somebody in place when Lydia goes."

"Great."

"You know Larry also put his name in?"

"I know."

"Going to be a tough choice. You're both good."

"I don't see it as such a difficult choice," Martina says with a smile, which he returns. With his bad teeth, it is not a pretty sight.

"I want to do the best for the program," says Dr. Gerard. "That's going to be my primary criterion. Beyond that, there are all kinds of other considerations."

"Such as?"

"Oh, educational background, work experience, that kind of thing. And," he says pointedly, "maybe some other things we could chat about. I just wanted you to know your candidacy is right up there."

"Thanks. I'm glad to hear that."

"I thought you would be."

"Any time you want to talk about those other things," she says, summoning up her courage, "I'm ready."

Dr. Gerard's thumbs tap twice. "Why don't we talk about it over coffee in the cafeteria?" he asks with his ghastly smile.

2

Dennis Parker wanders from room to room downstairs, not looking for anything, nor even particularly restless. He's home alone. He walks, living room to dining room to kitchen to keeping room to front hall to living room, with his head down, step measured, lost in his thoughts.

He has no sales calls scheduled for today. He has no errands to run. No plans with none of the friends he doesn't have anymore, nothing to occupy his time or while away the long, long hours that separate him from Monday morning. Saturday afternoon, then Saturday night (the worst), then all day Sunday, morning, noon, and night. Time like an empty bottle to be filled with the plain, tepid water of his life.

As usual, everyone else has something to do. Gene is off in Ithaca attending a New Age concert, some group of Wasps from Minnesota who play ancient Indonesian instruments and hum. Robert is at the hardware store buying materials to make a new storm window. (Dennis can't even make a WonderWindows sale in his own house.) Martina is just away, mercifully, most likely shaking the walls in her boyfriend's apartment for a change. When they are here, the pounding upstairs is continuous. They must do it not only on the bed but in the chair, on the enormous desk Dennis helped struggle up the stairs, against the walls, swinging from the light fixture on the ceiling . . .

Well, maybe it's just Dennis's imagination. Maybe all they are really doing is moving furniture, and Dennis, with his morbid fear of everyone else having more fun than he is (yeah, right: any fun at all would fit that bill, anything this side of acupuncture with scimitars dipped in pig shit), has simply made up the rest, hears passion where there is only innocent exertion, hears unhuman, never-ending fornication where there is only the attempt to locate the desk in a spot that gets the most sun. It would not be the first time Dennis imagines things that are not.

From room to room, he travels through yellow sunlight, itself unusual at this time of year. Robert suggested he give this new arrangement a chance. But if it is going to be this way, with Dennis feeling so uncomfortable that he hears the echoes of their lovemaking even when they aren't home, then there would have to be a change made somewhere.

Dennis paces. He follows the lines of the creaking oak flooring below his feet. In the keeping room he gazes out the window. Neighbors work on their lawns, rake last spring's dead flower beds, cut back mums to spikey stumps, gather the last of this season's leaves into huge shiny trash bags, clear newspapers the wind has swept into their shrubbery, prepare for winter. They move through their average happy lives while Dennis stays inside, hiding from the sun, from his neighbors, from his new housemate. From life.

The sight of the guy across the street with a fringe of hair on his bald head makes him think about the look Martina's balding boyfriend gave him when they were introduced. How wary! It tickles him (though not enough to cheer him up, nor force a grin). Is there anywhere in this world anyone less of a threat to Martina's boyfriend than Dennis? Anyone anywhere less likely to steal Martina away from him, or any woman from any man, seduce any babe with his charms (wait, his what?), sweep anyone off her feet? Anybody with less going for him than Dennis?

Get real.

Ba-boom, ba-boom, ba-boom: when they are up there, the noise spreads throughout the house, pursues Dennis through the walls, the floor, chases him outside, like the tell-tale beating of a heart in a Poe story.

Even now, when they are someplace else, the thought of it pushes him from room to room and finally expels him. He grabs his coat and Seahawks cap from the coatrack on the mud porch at the back of the kitchen and sprints out to his car as though pursued. With no place else to go, he drives to work, trembling at having been forced out of the empty house by his own anger.

He parks in the lot beside the building. Through the front door, which he faces, and a little to the left, which he can't see, sits Jackie Veninski, the receptionist. Poor Dennis. He is so friendless that this young girl who takes the trouble to speak to him is the closest he has to an emotional relationship. The innocent questions she asks, the light bantering that he returns in his heavy-footed way, are what have drawn him to this despicable low building on his day off. And he knows how pathetic it is, to have driven all the way over here on his day off and parked outside the room where she sits answering her telephones, being as pleasant to perfect strangers who call for window installations as she is to pitiful Dennis Parker, weirdo loon who takes her impersonal cheerfulness too much to heart. Friendless Dennis. Despairing, desiring Dennis, who daily sprays his bed with the sticky seeds of his ache for her. For anyone.

He goes inside.

He sees Baumgartner looking out at him from his desk in the office behind her. Has this vulgar merchant the sensitivity and acumen to pierce to his most secret heart and intuit how vulnerable Dennis must be to be drawn here today by Jackie? Surely Baumgartner, with a heart the size of a flea's nuts, can sense how ridiculous a figure Dennis feels himself to be, and how little chance such a ragged, friendless creature such as Dennis Parker actually has with a dish like Jackie.

What Baumgartner says to him is this: "Parker! Why the fuck ain't you working today?"

"I came to get my call schedule for next week." He and Jackie share a conspiratorial smile. His spirits somersault.

"You work every goddam day, that's what your schedule is," says Baumgartner. "Maybe if you worked every day you'd sell some product for once in your life, you miserable excuse for a human being."

Dennis and Jackie lock eyes and he cannot bring himself to either answer Baumgartner or turn his head away. Jackie is no rocket scientist, understand, and Dennis would probably be the first to admit that she has no interest in him whatsoever. Still, they are sharing a moment of some kind, and that is good enough for Dennis. He could die happy right about now. Jackie has acknowledged his existence again.

Because that's really what drew him here, isn't it? This woman is one of the few in Dennis's life who is willing to acknowledge that he is more than just a human garden slug on the primrose path of life, to be ignored at best, squashed at worst. That he is not a miserable excuse for a human being.

Will Dennis do what he really wants to do—ask her out?

Well, let's not get carried away here. He not only won't ask her out, he won't even admit to her she's the reason he's here today.

Certain beyond any doubt that she will reject him outright the first time he tries a pass at her, he enjoys her company for the brief time he can force himself to stay around her (less than a minute; he doesn't even know how to make small talk with her) before he believes she'll start to put two and two together and figure out the real reason for his visit. And then tell him she thinks he's a nice guy, but she really doesn't want to get involved or go on a date or have dinner or let him buy her some coffee or spend any more time in idle and harmless (except to him) flirtation.

And thus he drags himself away and goes off to the corner in the back room where they keep his humble desk to pick up his pitifully abbreviated list of calls. He stays longer than necessary because he doesn't know how to bring this charade to a close, or go by her again on the way out.

When at last he readies himself to face her, she is gone from her seat. With great reluctance and unbearable relief, he leaves the building.

He hunkers down behind the steering wheel so he can keep an eye on the front door.

Two hours later her trim figure steps into the early evening darkness. She walks quickly to her car, arms across her sweet bosom, shoulders hunched against the gathering cold in the black leather jacket belted around her waist, where Dennis's arms should be. Dennis slips down deeper behind the wheel.

He follows her back to her apartment complex. He pulls in and idles around the parking lot until she is inside her building. Then he pulls the car into a space where he can watch her door and begins another wait. But he does not know which apartment is hers. He watches every window for a sign of light, but sees none.

In an hour and a half, she has not come out but a succession of others have—young men, couples, older women. Realizing the futility of yet another activity, Dennis gives up and goes home to spend the rest of his Saturday at the empty house reliving every aspect of this miserable experience that will culminate in an orgy of baby lotion and Kleenex.

3

Cosmetic changes have made Harry and Mike's a remarkably different place than the bar it used to be. Gone are the garish neon beer signs from the front windows, replaced by a thin golden circle around the name of the bar in old fashioned serif lettering, and beige cafe curtains hung from a brass curtain rod, tastefully pleasant yet not chichi enough to scare off the regular clientele. Inside, Harry has replaced the round scarred rough-hewn tables with tastefully pleasant square blond wooden ones. He had the scuffed floors stripped and polyurethaned. The hopelessly tacky beer plaques are gone, replaced by tastefully pleasant framed posters of floral watercolor art exhibits from cities like Denver and Minneapolis. The nerve-jarring heavy metal music is gone too, in favor of more middle-of-the-road fare for the older crowd Harry has invited tonight.

Shrewd changes, these, Brooke reflects. Most are Polly Steen's doing. They will bring the lunch-time crowd from downtown offices during weekdays and still draw the sports crowd at night, who wouldn't notice the cafe curtains or the shape of the tables as long as a pitcher of beer fits on them and is replenished periodically by a woman with a short skirt and large breasts that bob in their faces.

Tonight there will be a mixture of crowds, the Saturday night regulars mingling with Harry and Michael's invited guests, plus the walk-ins who saw the ads Harry placed in the newspapers (Harry's idea, Brooke's art) who just want to check a new place out. The bouncer is still at the door, except now he's called a Greeter (Harry's idea) and he's ditched the sweatshirt in favor of a green cotton sweater with a tiny "Harry and Mike's" logo on the breast (Harry's idea, Brooke's art). The Greeter gives everyone who comes in a little green and yellow card that says "This card good for two free drinks" (Harry's idea, Brooke's art), with two little boxes for the bartenders to check off.

He's giving out lots of cards: by nine o'clock the joint is jumping. Every table is full and the bar is even more crowded than it was the night Brooke made her first visit. Now she wears her own Harry and Mike's sweater and her best hostess smile as she stands at the steam table and doles out Swedish meatballs, Buffalo chicken wings, and peppers and sausage to all comers. The boss's dutiful wife.

Some visitors she knows, some she doesn't. Those whom she knows kiss her on the cheek and congratulate her, as if she had anything to do with all this. Periodically she catches sight of Harry, glad-handing somebody or having his back slapped by one of the hundreds of people he knows in this town, many of them early middle aged, narrow shouldered, and balding with black mustaches and pastel cotton sweaters over open-necked shirts with gold chains peeking out among graying chest hair and pleated slacks and brightly shined tasseled loafers.

And there is brother Michael in his Harry and Mike's sweater behind the bar, Mr. Inside to Harry's Mr. Outside, smoking one of his big cigars in between drawing draft after draft for the sea of faces around him. And there is Joyce, free-floating hostess, standing by a table filled with some of the legion of men and women with whom the McGuires socialize.

One of these couples is Alphonse and Louise Kolata. Alphonse kisses Brooke on the lips. Louise plants one in the air beside her cheek. They have often had Brooke and Harry as guests at their estate, to swim in their pool and ride horses from their stable. Alphonse is the town's leading real estate developer; Louise, his second wife, is your basic social butterfly, freed from having to take a job by Alphonse's wealth and her own lack of interest in working, freed from housework by the housekeeper they maintain, freed from motherly duties by their childlessness. All Louise has to do is play and shop and have lunch. And love every minute of it. Alphonse indulges his wife, as he indulges Harry and Brooke with the fatherly kindness and generosity he shows only to his intimates, reserving his tougher self for business.

Also hugging Brooke is Polly Steen, here with her husband Lee. When they separate, Brooke takes with her the perfumed dead body smell of Polly's face power. Lee kisses Brooke full on the lips. Tonight she has heard a rumor that Lee's cigar factory mall next door might be going belly up and he is getting ready to default on his bank loans. "The place looks wonderful," says Brooke to Polly.

"It turned out great," says Polly. "And this is a great crowd."

"Harry's out of his mind about it. He's like a kid at Christmas." She laughs. Polly and Lee laugh and move away with their food held before them like offerings.

The bar gets even more crowded. After a while cigarette smoke drives her into the ladies' room, which has also been remodeled, though it has not been made much larger. Waiting for a stall, she remembers her first night here, Polly's hunched shoulders in the hall outside the bathroom, the man with the red beard in whose arms Brooke threw herself. Polly is not my problem, she tells herself as she hikes her skirt and lowers her pantyhose and underpants. She changes her pad, tosses the monthly symbol of her continuing failure to conceive into the pail thoughtfully provided by management.

When she steps out of the bathroom, she sees Joyce McGuire has replaced her on the food line. Brooke takes the opportunity to mingle. She works her way through the crowd, touching arms, receiving kisses. The noise level has risen.

She sees Harry standing at the end of the bar, talking with a man she recognizes as the man he had lunch with that day at the club. Several other men stand around Harry in a half-circle. Harry's client spots her as soon as she spots him. He holds her gaze and she averts her eye.

She continues working the room, making her way slowly back

to the food table. By the time she gets there, Robert Fitzgerald is there, talking with Joyce.

"Do you two know each other?" Joyce says. She is not shouting exactly, but talking loud enough to be heard over the happy uninhibited buzz of the crowd around them.

"No," says Brooke, adopting the same volume. "Hello."

"Hello," says Robert. "I've seen you from a distance. Nice to meet you close up." He is smiling. His eyes are slits and he has strong yellow teeth. He is dressed in a thick handmade ecru ropey Irish sweater over khakis. He offers Brooke his hand. "Are you back to take over?" says Joyce.

"Sure," says Brooke.

"Good, because I have to talk to somebody over there." Joyce heads off toward the bar.

Brooke turns her attention to Robert. Joyce has not served him yet. "Would you like some food?"

"Please."

"What can I get you?"

He examines the food, and moves closer to her so he doesn't have to shout his answer. "Just some meatballs, I think," he says, close to her ear. He has no smell, unlike Harry and the rest of the men who bathe in cologne.

"That's all?"

"That's all."

"On a diet?"

"Not yet. Though I'm working up to it."

"No."

"It's true."

"But you're thin as a rail," says Brooke with great sincerity. Then she gives him a bright smile and a laugh and reaches out automatically to lay a hand lightly on his forearm to show she's really kidding. Will he figure that out? Her hand rests for a moment before dropping away.

"I'm fatter than I was when I moved here."

She serves him and hands the plate to him. It is a real plate. No paper stuff for this occasion.

Unlike the others, who move away as soon as they are served, he stands there. "All I do is eat."

"Same thing happened to me when I moved here. I gained ten pounds in the first six months."

"Where are you from?"

"Suburban Rochester. You?"

"Most recently from Seattle. Originally Michigan."

"I've never been to Washington. I hear it's nice."

"If you like rain. How long have you lived here?"

"Going on nine years."

"You're almost a native."

"Not around here. You're not a native unless your family goes back four generations. Harry's the native in the family." She gives him another bright smile.

"Are all the people here your friends?" he asks.

"Most of them are people Harry knows."

"He must know a lot of people."

"That's for sure."

"I was surprised when he invited me. I don't know him all that well."

"Harry knows how to launch a public relations campaign," she says. "As I'm sure you must know." Another quick smile, another quick hand flitting on his arm, out and back, another laugh.

"Do you think it's a conflict of interest if a guy who owns a bar also has a substance abuse program as a client for his advertising agency?"

"I don't know. Interesting question."

"That's actually why I came tonight."

"Check the place out, eh?"

"See for myself what goes on here. Talk to Harry about it."

"What did you two have to say?"

"At first, I was upset by the thought of him being a bar owner. Then I realized, what better place to campaign against substance abuse than where it's happening?"

People in the line behind him begin to crowd him. "Well," says Robert, "I guess I'll do some mingling. Nice meeting you."

She holds out her hand to shake his. After a tricky maneuver to balance his plate of food in his left hand, he takes her hand and gives it a quick squeeze before letting go and moving on. "Nice talking with you," she says after him. She watches him disappear into the crowd, twists her ostentatious wedding ring around on its finger, ladles up some meatballs for the next one in line, Harry's local printer.

4

Across the river on the south side of town, Suspenders is a subterranean lounge beneath a massive red brick building that was a firehouse before being converted to a restaurant with a lounge in the basement. Gene Anderson sits by himself at a tiny table in the rear of a close, low-ceilinged cabaret.

On the bandstand at the end of a tunnel-like room, in red and white light a trio, organist, bassist, and drummer, make music that throbs against Gene's forehead. They play a slow shuffle with a heavy bass line. It fills the room with sound, overpowering the noise from the bar and the few tables occupied primarily by black couples, an unusual sight for this upstate town. The drummer is a curly-headed and bearded white man who plays as though transported somewhere beyond this plane of existence. His eyes and mouth are closed, his eyebrows are raised, his head vibrates as his hands, wrists crossed, snap the sticks out and back. The bassist is a young black man with a round face and cookie duster goatee. The organist is a black woman in a flowing dress that appears purple under the lights. A kerchief is tied around her throat. Crystal Williams's straightened hair is fastened at the back of her head with a huge beaded band.

The bass player and the drummer back off and Crystal works the keyboard by herself. This is met with a wave of light applause from the crowd. She sits at a thin Yamaha with slender steel legs. Her hands dart over the keyboard, opening up the melodic line of the song. The notes embellish a tune that Gene cannot quite identify.

The bass and drum join in and Crystal leans close to the mike that snakes over the side of the keyboard and sings:

> *Have you ever loved a man*
> *Who was another woman's man?*
> *Have you ever loved a man*
> *Who was another woman's man?*
> *When you can't leave that man alone,*
> *People, you can't leave that man alone*

Then all you do is cry
Like I cry, cry, cry.
All the time I cry for you.

Her voice is soft and restrained and sounds like the way warm honey drizzling down the back of the throat might feel.

The song goes on for fifteen more minutes, each musician taking a turn with licks that bring shouts of approval from the crowd. They do six or seven more songs with varied rhythms and increasingly more complicated chord changes, each of which has long instrumental breaks. Crystal gives a little introduction before each number. At last, she leans into the mike and says, "We're going to take a short break now. Don't go 'way."

They disengage from their instruments to applause and regroup at a table off to the side. A waitress appears with a pitcher of beer.

Gene makes his way over to them. "Hi," he says, mostly to Crystal.

"Hi," she says back. The other two look at him with curiosity.

"Gene Anderson? I met you at the hospital the other day when your son was in."

"Sure," she says, "I remember you. Did you hear the set?"

"I loved it."

"All right!" the drummer shouts. He gets up and helps Gene into a chair. "Sit right down there, my man."

"This is McGoo Blumenthal," Crystal says. "And Tony Watson."

Gene shakes hands with them. "McGoo?"

"Really Mickey," says the drummer.

"Whatever. Pleasure," Gene says.

"Okay," says McGoo.

"S'up?" says Tony.

"I don't want to interrupt. I just wanted to say hello. How's your son doing?"

"Really good. He stayed in the hospital another day and then came home. He hasn't started back to school yet."

"I'm glad he's okay."

"Me, too."

"I really enjoyed your music," he says.

"Thanks. We appreciate it."

He leans closer to her. McGoo and Tony take the hint and drift away with their beers. "Do you work every weekend?"

"Pretty much."

"What do you do afterwards?"

"Mostly I go home to Derrick."

"Some night during the week I'd like to take you to dinner. If you're free." Her hand goes to the kerchief at her neck. It is a large paisley print. She watches him with ironic brown eyes softened by flattery.

"That'd be nice." She writes her phone number on a napkin. "Give me a call during the week and we'll work something out."

"Great," he says. "I'll like that."

"Ditto."

During the next set she glances out at the room more than she did before. When she spots him, she directs many of the remaining songs toward the back of the room where he sits. At the next break, the musicians' table is surrounded by friends who have come in during the set. Gene catches Crystal's eye, and they nod to each other as he makes his way to the exit.

5

I'd say this was a successful beginning," says Michael McGuire. They all slump at a table in the rear of the bar. It is after two in the morning. The staff has finished cleaning and setting up for lunch for the day shift. The two brothers and their wives are exhausted. Even Harry is no longer hyper.

They sit for another few minutes, then drag themselves outside, where they part. Things have an almost engraved clarity: the haloed streetlights, the skeletal parking garage across the street, the looming early twentieth century buildings, the sparkling sidewalks—all are limned with an exquisite sharpness of detail. Michael and Joyce, parked across the street from the bar, get on their way at once. Brooke and Harry walk arm in arm farther down the block to where he left his Seville.

"How'd things go, boss?" she asks.

"Great. Super."

"Looks like it's going to be a big hit."

"Hope so. I hope they come back when the drinks aren't free."

She climbs into the car and settles back in her seat with a deep, tired sigh.

"Almost everybody I invited came," he says.

"I know."

"The Kolatas were here."

"I saw them."

"And the Steens."

"Them too."

"Even my new client came. Fitzgerald. Did you see him?"

"Yeah. We chatted a bit."

"Nice guy. I feel kind of sorry for the guy. New in town, doesn't know anybody."

"Uh-huh."

"Must be tough."

They drive in silence. The client was nice, she has to admit. She does not usually get to know her husband's clients. Must be something special about this one for Harry to include him. Nice-looking, too. Though not physically attractive in the way she likes her men. Not a tall man, nor a husky, muscular one like Harry. There is something about physical men that attracts her, much as she imagines men are attracted by physically striking women. In fact, plain was the first word that sprang to mind when she met Robert Fitzgerald. A plain and wiry man, with kind gray eyes and a ruddy complexion and worry lines in his forehead, as if he took on other people's problems too easily. Sharp nose and thin lips. Taller than she is, but then she is a short woman. His hand was warm and tender, as Harry's tends to be. In his physique he reminds her of some of the men she sees at the Y whenever she waits for Harry. She imagines him with lean shanks and legs and strong arms with a vein running down his biceps.

After a few minutes, Harry says, "I was thinking, maybe we'll have him over to dinner some night. Would that be okay with you?"

"I guess."

"Maybe we can fix him up with one of your single girlfriends."

"Maybe."

"Think about who we can introduce him to. We'll do it in a couple weeks. What do you think? Sound like fun?"

"Sounds great," says Brooke, who is too intent upon getting home and going to bed to think much about anything, especially one of Harry's clients.

6

The tea scalds the roof of his mouth. Robert grimaces and half-swallows to get past the pain, which unfortunately only keeps the hot liquid suspended in his throat, where it does more damage. Finally, he forces his unwilling muscles to gulp and feels the warmth travel down to his belly. He sets the cup on the table beside him in the living room and lolls his mouth open to air out his poor hurt tissues.

His clothes stink of cigarette smoke. Too late to run up and change, and he is unwilling to lounge around the drafty living room in his nightshirt. So he can put up with the smell until *The Third Man* on the VCR relaxes him enough to get sleepy and go upstairs and dump his clothes in the hamper in his room and finish off this day. He needs to do his wash again tomorrow anyway.

He picks up the warm mug again and blows across the steaming lip. This is his favorite movie. Dirty doings unfold in Vienna to the sweetly sinister zither, in the oblique angles of a camera that is slightly off center, symbolic of the skewed morals of the postwar world of the movie. And poor dumb Holly, a victim of his own innocence.

What people won't do for money. Like the Swiss clocks Harry Lime talks about in the Ferris wheel, Robert's mind steadily moves over the events of this night. All orchestrated by Harry McGuire. Who seems like he may do if not anything for money (Robert can't imagine him watering penicillin; the booze, maybe), then at least a great deal in terms of separating a sucker from his wages, which Robert concludes not solely on the basis of his success in advertising, but because only someone who would do a lot for money would want to be an ad executive in the first place. A subtle yet meaningful distinction. And Robert never did get an answer to his question about a conflict of interest from this bar owner.

Still, he seems to have the world by the short hairs, Harry does. And he has an awfully attractive wife, Robert has to give him that. Flirty thing, too, with all those pats to his arm and leaning close to him with big smiles. Well, why not? What does she have to lose?

Attractive, sparky personality, stylishly turned out, handsome and successful husband. Those would do a lot for anybody's self-esteem. She can afford to flirt.

And yet, she does not seem fundamentally to be a confident woman. Robert knows the type well. He has met, and been involved with, too, some real nasty types, some hard types who are prisoners of some wicked wants. She is not one of those. Something vague and unfocused about her keeps her from that, something unformed about her keeps this woman transparent. Some desire to please and be liked keeps her from being the complacent suburbanette with a houseful of kids and a housekeeper that would clearly be her fate with this husband, at the top of such heap as there is in this glum little town. Though with time what sets her apart from the others may fade, and she may well become one of the rest, one of the pod people. A podette. Petty bourgeoise life conquers all: nothing stands in its way.

He falls asleep to the sound of scurrying footsteps, the sight of giant menacing shadows projected on the walls of postwar Europe, gunfire echoing in the sewers. He dreams of his father selling alcohol in the bombed-out ruins of old Vienna, and of himself chasing after, knee-deep in fetid tunnels, the skewed shadow always just around the next bend.

He jerks awake to Gene's touch.

"Sorry," says Gene. "Thought you might want to finish the night in bed."

Robert gazes around, blinking. Gene has turned the television off. A residual electron glow illuminates the screen. "What time is it?"

"Quarter after two."

"Oh," Robert says. "Late." Groggy.

Gene sits on the sofa next to him, rubs his hands over his eyes.

"How was your date?"

"Oh," Gene says, "it wasn't a date."

"Thought it was."

"No. I just went to see this woman perform at a bar. She's a singer. Plays keyboards too."

"How was she?"

"Pretty goddam good. Does bluesy kind of stuff. I only got to talk to her for a couple minutes, between one of the sets."

"Going to see her again?"

"No doubt." Then: "When I left the bar I went to see my other friend. Sharon."

"You're floating in women. And how was she?"

"She's okay. Felt kind of funny, though. Going over there right after seeing Crystal."

"So why do it?"

Gene shrugs. "She's a good woman. But Crystal, man. I can't stop thinking about her."

"Does the one know about the other?"

"God, no."

"Going to tell them?"

"Not if I can help it."

"Don't think they'll find out sooner or later?"

"I think I'll cross that bridge when I come to it."

"Or double-cross it, as the case may be."

Gene sighs. "Things were so much easier when I was married."

"Freedom is the proliferation of mutually exclusive options."

"I don't think you can ever have too many options."

"I do."

"Not me. I also think you can love two women at the same time."

"Good luck with that. I've always had enough trouble loving one."

"I think you can love two. Not with the possessiveness we usually think of when we think about love. I don't think you can love even one person that way. But if you think of love as a celebration of other people, you can love many."

"You think love is a celebration?"

"Sure. A total celebration, emotional, physical, intellectual, the works. Marriage used to be a celebration. The sacrament of cosmic intermingling. Not any more. Marriage today is too restrictive. It says you're only supposed to celebrate one other person, till death do you part. It's impractical. It's repressive. I think you have to go through your whole life celebrating. When you stop celebrating people, you're dead."

"Bop till you drop," Robert says.

"There you go. Marriage is celebration according to the white guy in a starched minster's collar who's afraid of living. And who has a rather large two-by-four stuck up his ass."

Gene smiles so broadly he clenches his teeth. "Like I used to have."

"No."

"Yep. I was a Methodist minister. Two-by-four and all."

"What happened?"

"Oh, I started to see my real life's work lay in another direction. I started to see the starched collar and the good life as restricting my freedom, rather than as agents for the actualization of my freedom. Or others'. I began to see my life in terms of an evolutionary destiny that I had been denying myself."

"In other words, you screwed a parishioner and got cashiered."

"In fact, I did have an affair with a woman from my church. But that wasn't what did it. Although I must say the buildup to it caused me a lot of guilt. Lot of guilt. You know, the flirtations, the whole chess game that goes into a relationship. We were both bundles of mutually raw needs. We each found in the other a possible way to meet those needs. A forbidden way, which made the whole thing tastier."

"What happened?"

"I decided the only way to assuage the guilt was to plunge through to the other side of it. We went to a motel in the middle of the day once to get it over with. And the strangest thing happened. We were in bed together, it was after we made love, and I thought to myself: This is good. I mean, I thought, this is so good, so unbelievably good, how could it be bad? How could organized religion possibly deem this kind of complete satisfaction sinful? How could the Ten Commandments prohibit adultery when there I was, committing adultery, a man of the cloth, no less, and absolutely loving it?"

"These are usually questions we ask as younger men."

"Very tactfully put. You're a true counselor. Another man would have called me juvenile. Jejune."

"Gene, I don't think I'd ever call you jejune."

"But it's true: I was a case of arrested development. That day was a watershed in my life. I felt like I met myself for the first time inside her. She freaked, of course, and broke it off immediately. We never saw each other again like that. But I knew by then my marriage was over, despite the fact that I never stopped loving my wife. And I knew my days as a starched collar minister with a two-by-four up his ass were over too. Can we love more than one person at the same time? Yeah, I think so. I think I want to try. I loved one person for so long, I think I want to love as many as I can from here on out. I want to meet myself in as many others as I possibly can."

The two men are silent.

"What about you?" Gene asks, unwilling to let his volubility go.

"What about me?"

"What's the story of your life and loves?"

"Just one damn thing after another."

"No, really."

"Look, I don't know if you know this about me, but I'm a pretty cynical guy. I believe love is a sickness. A mental illness. I've been in love a few times, too, so I know whereof I speak. People say, 'Care for me,' and you do, and you're hooked. You start to care about someone else's happiness, and pretty soon that's all you think about. And you start to believe you're responsible for it. And necessary for it. And really, you can do so little for another person's happiness, when it comes right down to it, that you're doomed to fail. Love is failure."

"Sounds bitter to me."

"I'm a bitter man."

"Bullshit. Mr. Counselor of the Western world. You're the one who opened your house to us. You didn't do that out of bitterness."

"Jesus, I don't love you people. I tolerate you so you can pay my house payment for me."

"You're full of shit."

"Okay, maybe that part is wrong. But I'm serious, man. Love is upset. Love is disequilibrium. Heartbreak and false yearning. Stay away from it, that's my advice."

"I wish I could. I'd be a lot better off."

"Do it. Make up your mind. Turn off the love switch. It's easy."

"You're a pretty depressing guy at this time of night, you know that?"

"You asked."

"I'm sorry I woke you up. Go back to sleep. Speaking of depression, how's our compadre upstairs?"

"Now there's an unhappy camper."

"I worry about that one. Is it just Martina, do you think?"

"I'm sure it's more than her. He's so hard to reach, though. Doesn't want to talk about anything, ever, says this isn't a residential therapy program. And he's right. So I don't want to push too hard. But I know he needs somebody to talk to. I'm trying to let him know he can talk to me if he wants to, but I'm not getting through."

"He can talk to me too."

"He doesn't lack people to talk to. But he needs to feel safe doing it, away from shrinks and parents."

"That sort of lets us out."

"I feel bad about the effect Martina's having on him."

"But hey: she has her rights too. And he has to take responsibility for coming to terms with them."

"At the same time, we have the responsibility for making sure he has a supportive environment here. And she has too, for that matter."

"Is she home now?"

"Don't think so. Unless she snuck by me while I was asleep."

"Well, there you go. He has some respite. It's not like they're screwing on the sofa every night."

"No. They screw upstairs often enough."

Gene stands and combs his fingers through his hair. "He's a grownup. Has to take responsibility for himself. How was your night? Didn't you go out too?"

"Yeah. The guy who's running my ad campaign I now find out owns a bar. He had an open house. I went to check it out."

"Meet anybody?" Gene asks.

"No."

"You will," Gene says.

"Gene, I don't think you've been listening."

"I've been listening. I just haven't believed it." He yawns hugely. "Well, not that I haven't enjoyed this little chat. We should do this more often."

"We can go out and get looped at my ad agency's bar."

Gene gives Robert, still seated, a pat on the shoulder as he passes behind him. "I'm for bed."

"Goodnight," Robert says, then sits for another minute staring without a clear thought into the blank eye of the television.

Did he really believe what he told Gene about love? On his darkest days, maybe . . . but wasn't that really just the cynicism of a failed romantic? If he fell for someone who also fell for him, wouldn't all that go out the window in a minute? Gene was right to call bullshit; Robert knows this in his secret heart.

CHAPTER SEVEN

1

The rambling Parker house by the river on the west side is down a side street off Riverside Drive in a cul-de-sac not fifty yards from the water, a drafty twelve-room house with a stone foundation. Every few years, when the river rises exceptionally high in the spring, the back yard, which slopes downward from the house, disappears under several feet of water and the drain in the basement gushes sludge. Dampness moves in for weeks.

Standing on the front porch before entering the house, Dennis Parker listens for the river. The Susquehanna. Old friend, it murmurs to him behind the bare branches of the trees that surround the house. Beneath the river sounds he hears human voices. Some kids play on the rocks by the opposite shore in the twilight gloom. They jump from one rock to another, shouting, he realizes with an ache of sadness, obscenities across the water. Dennis has done this himself, in years past, with friends he no longer has, freed by youth from fear of the rush of the waters. Now he's landlocked. They call him sometimes, his ex-friends, but he can't bring himself to keep the dates they shame him into making. They are now stereotypically successful young lawyers, doctors, stockbrokers, shop owners. He feels he has nothing to offer them but his unhappiness.

He steps into the warm odors of a turkey dinner, the familiar sight of a family tableau: his father, his mother, his brother, his two sisters, and his older sister's husband in the living room on the sofa, on two chairs, on a dining room chair, and on the floor, along with their red setter Mike. The television is tuned to a Jets game. Your basic Sunday afternoon dinner at home. The Brady Bunch East.

All welcome Dennis. Except his father, whose eyes never leave the TV. "Dennis," his mother says, "just in time to make the potatoes. Come on." She pulls herself up from the sofa and waves him into the kitchen with her.

She is a tall thin woman with gangly arms and limp, thinning, baby-fine hair. Dennis takes after her, not his father, who is short and round with great garbageman muscles.

The airy country kitchen is in its usual dinnertime disarray, dirty pans everywhere, everywhere a dusting of flour and sugar like light snow. On the stove a chipped white enamel pot of boiled potatoes awaits him. His job at these family get-togethers, when he bothers to come, is mashing the potatoes. As a youngster he would insist on having mashed potatoes even when no one else wanted them. So he took over their preparation, and now it remains his adult job. He would be just in time to make the potatoes no matter when he arrived; his mother always kept them till the last, in the event he showed.

The electric hand mixer awaits him, too, an antique Sunbeam poised on its handle with prongs attached like a pathetic puppy showing off. He goes through the steps, adding milk, plopping in a half stick of butter, a sprinkle of pepper (no salt: his mother is not allowed), a pinch of sugar, squeezing the beaters through the heavy undulating clots of potato. Sunday dinner at home.

Dennis has an open invitation to his parents', especially to this weekly occasion, but can only force himself to come once a month, if that. He can stand just so many of these family sights, family sounds, family smells. Not that his family's life never changes, not that it is caught in amber some time back in his early adolescence (as Dennis feels himself to be). No, he knows his family in fact is evolving quite nicely, as a group and individually. His mother has gone back to work after raising her family, opening her own antique business in a small shopping plaza nearby. His brother is in his final year of high school and will begin Broome Community College next year, much to the family's joy at his having overcome the learning disabilities that dogged his early years and led his parents and teachers to fear he might be retarded. One of Dennis's sisters is married and expecting a baby, the other is about to wed.

Even Dennis's father is changing, that bastard, though not necessarily for the better where Dennis is concerned. Sessions with his shrink have made Dennis understand these changes (while disproving the psychiatric truism that the truth shall set him free; on the contrary, the truth swelled him with bloated paralytic rage the way lies never could). Once proud of his intelligent, sensitive son, Dennis's father, like many parents whose expectations for themselves were lower than their children's (Mr. Parker drives a sanitation truck for the city, proudly but with no illusions about the status his job imparts), has gradually become alienated from his son because of the accomplishments of that very intelligence that was once a source of pride. Then too, as Dennis's way in life grew more and more muddled, his father found it harder to reconcile his son's squandering his obvious gifts where the younger boy Billy worked so hard to overcome disabilities that left him, on the surface, at least, seeming less intelligent than Dennis. Dennis could have had it all, has always thrown away every opportunity, just as he pissed away his chance at college by having that breakdown. Billy has always had to struggle for the limited success he has been able to achieve, which makes Billy a success and Dennis lazy, ungrateful, and fundamentally a disappointment—so thinks Dennis's father (so thinks Dennis).

Not that his old man could ever tell Dennis any of this. Confronting his son with his disappointment would be much too painful for both of them. So the taciturn man has kept it inside—as if this would be any less painful for his son, who interprets keen disappointment as dislike and disinterest.

Dennis's perception is largely responsible for his own lack of self-confidence, to say nothing of his ability to function in the world as an entirely too sensitive young man.

The mixer blades clatter against the sides of the pot. He sticks a finger in for a taste test. More butter. He adds what he knows is the appropriate amount. Say what you will about me, he thinks, I make mean mashed potatoes. Not much of a career, but it does come in handy.

When the football game ends and the family reassembles around the dinner table, Dennis's father becomes a real talker, passing dishes right and left, filling in the two eldest (excluding Dennis, to whom he addresses none of his remarks) on what has been happening on their street since the last dinner, especially the sale of the house next to theirs. He has much speculation upon the color and religion of the new buyers.

It falls to Dennis's mother and sisters, the family peacekeepers, to bring the sensitive elder brother in on the conversation. They ask him how work is. (Lousy, he thinks but does not say. He has not made a sale in over three weeks. Baumgartner is furious.) How his love life is. (Lousy. He hasn't been laid since—well, since never, and has no realistic prospects for the foreseeable future. This question in particular makes him squirm, so relevant is it to the actual unhappy circumstances of his life.) How his housemates are treating him. (Good, though not great. The two men are good to him. His feelings are still too confused about his female housemate.) When they get to how his car is working, he knows they are running out of things to ask about. And he runs out of monosyllabic answers anyway.

When he leaves, his mother gives him a CARE package of turkey and mashed potatoes and stuffing. She plants a wet one on his cheek and sends him back into the world of grown-up responsibilities, where mashed potato making is not considered a crucial skill.

Couples: On his way back to the House of Grins, Dennis sees couples everywhere he looks. He sees them walking hand in hand across the bridge. He sees them pressing their bodies against each other on corners, unconcerned for who might be watching. He sees young men with long hair and bandanas tied around the thighs of greasy tattered Levis walking with strong, possessive arms around the shoulders of their girlfriends as if holding them in custody. Nature adores a couple. He sees young couples in the bloom of youth, frail old couples hobbling along on canes, and overripe middle-aged couples motivating along in station wagons with the kids in the back. He even sees a pair tool down the sidewalk in electric wheelchairs, holding hands: crippled couples. Each couple he sees is another two people in the world who couldn't care less about Dennis Parker and his troubles.

At the house he finds Robert standing at the counter in the kitchen with the Sunday paper open in front of him. Robert is by himself, but this doesn't help Dennis, because the kitchen is redolent with the homey smell of a cake baking in the oven. The scene mocks Dennis's alienation. His anger flares briefly before he brings it under control. It is not Robert's fault, though Robert seems to bring this out in him.

Even the big smile Robert greets him with doesn't help. Dennis is in bad shape today.

"How was dinner?" Robert asks.

"Great."

"Really?"

"Really. Couldn't have been better. Everybody was there. It was family life in its finest shining hour."

"Families are good," says Robert, determined to see behind the bitter irony that is Dennis's constant face to the world. "Got room for dessert?"

"Oh, no." Dennis pats his full belly. "Stuffed. Really. Mom had turkey and everything. Pumpkin pie to top it off. Whipped cream. The works.

"Cake'll be done in another couple minutes, if you change your mind."

"Thanks. But I'm going upstairs."

"Okay. Hey," Robert says, "you really all right?"

"Fine and dandy." Robert nods, disbelieving. Dennis passes him, thinking, *He can smell my lies*.

Upstairs Dennis sits on his bed, his mind a blank. Howie meows pitifully outside the door, struts inside when Dennis lets him in. He jumps onto the bed and curls into an adorable black ball. Dennis sweeps his hand over the animal's thick silken fur. Howie sighs with enormous contentment and purrs obtrusively.

Dennis takes the hallway phone into his room. He sits with it on his bed next to the cat for ten more minutes. Clearing his mind like a commando before a mission. Howie ignores him until he picks up the receiver and quickly punches in the numbers. Then the cat gives him a stern, reproachful look.

"Shaddup," says Dennis.

The phone gets picked up on the second ring. "Hello?"

Here we go.

"Jackie? It's Dennis Parker. From work?"

"Oh, hi, Dennis. I know who you are." A note of surprise and—dare he think it—pleasure in her voice? "Hi."

"Hi. How are you doing?"

"Just fine. I'm finally getting around to cleaning up my kitchen. How are you?"

"I'm okay."

"That's good. Ready to start the week?"

"Never."

She laughs. Tinkling bells.

Big pause.

"So Jackie, I was wondering if you'd like to meet me for a drink or something tonight?"

'Tonight?"

"Yeah. I know it's last minute. But I thought you might want to, you know, nothing special, just like have a drink, maybe a sandwich, cup of coffee type thing. If you're free."

"Oh, Dennis, I'd love to."

"Great!"

"Except I have these like plans for later on?"

"Oh, okay."

"It's really great of you to ask, though."

"Sure. I know it's short notice. I just thought you might not have anything planned. Sunday night and all."

"Oh, no problem. Listen, I got to go now, okay? I'll see you at the office tomorrow."

"Sure thing. Talk to you then."

"Bye, Dennis. Thanks for calling!"

Dennis takes the phone back to its table in the upstairs hall. The stairs creak under the heavy tread of Martina's boyfriend. "Hi, there," says Max, and beats Dennis into the bathroom. As he faces the closed door, another rush of anger like the one he experienced with Robert in the kitchen grips him. He shakes with it. Martina has the bad fortune to bound up the stairs at that moment in a cloud of perfume, singing, "Hi-ee!"

"Jesus Christ!" Dennis explodes. It catches her up on the way into her room. "Isn't there a goddam bathroom downstairs? Why's he have to use this one?"

"Robert's in the one downstairs. Max's going to be right out, Dennis."

"Well, I'd like to have a little privacy up here, you know," he screams. "If I don't have to listen to you two fucking like bunnies all the time, I have to fight you to use the bathroom in my own house. Fucking hell, this is working out great!"

Furious, mortally ashamed of himself, he retreats to his bedroom and slams the door behind him.

Max opens the bathroom door. Sticks his big head out. It wears a quizzical look. "What's going on?"

Martina shakes her head in frustration.

"Should I go?" Max asks.

"Let's go downstairs. All of a sudden I'm out of the mood."

Later Dennis goes down and apologizes. Max is gone. Martina sits reading a *Country Living* magazine in the living room. Robert is nowhere around. "Dennis," Martina says icily behind the magazine, not giving him the satisfaction of looking at him, "I don't 'fuck like a bunny all the time.' I really resent your saying that. Especially in front of my guest."

"I'm sorry."

"I can't help it if you're unhappy or disturbed about something. That doesn't give you the right to insult me. Or my friend. And I'm not going to put up with it."

"I know. I'm sorry. I'm sorry I lost my temper. There's no excuse for it."

"No, there isn't. I'm furious with you," she says, as if he couldn't figure that out.

He hangs his head. He feels terrible.

She shuts him out with her magazine.

When neither one says anything else, Dennis returns to his room.

He goes to bed early, mortally ashamed of himself.

2

How about Janine?" Harry asks.

"She just met a man," Brooke says. "I don't think she'd be interested."

They talk on the phone from their offices. Brooke treats herself to an afternoon cup of tea. Her office looks out on the impressive nineteenth century courthouse across the street with its verdigris dome with clocks facing each of the four directions. It is vacant, its functions moved to the state office building in the new government plaza nearby. Al Kolata owns the building and is thinking about turning the courthouse into a luxury hotel. Harry and Brooke were at a party at his house last month when he talked about the plan.

Harry thought it was a great idea. He wanted in on it.

Now Harry goes through the list of women whom he thinks might be suitable for the occasion. He believes them to be Brooke's friends. In truth they are his friends from school, his relatives' friends, his buddies' wives' friends. They are her acquaintances at best. She has lost touch with all her close girlfriends in Rochester.

"What about Marsha?" Harry asks.

"Engaged."

"Since when?"

"Since the beginning of the year. They haven't set the date yet. She thinks it's going to be in January."

"I didn't know that."

"Now you do."

"I didn't think she'd ever find anybody good enough for her."

"She still hasn't. She's anxious to settle down. So she stopped being as picky as she used to be."

"Good for her."

"I guess."

"So who else is there?"

"Not many," Brooke says.

"What about Lorraine?"

"Sworn off men."

"What!?"

"Those are her words. She can't take the bullshit anymore."

"What bullshit?"

"The male-female bullshit. Don't you remember what it was like?"

"No."

"Well, trust me: Lorraine's out."

"Isn't there anybody at work who might be okay?"

"Can't think of anybody."

"It's just a dinner, babe. It isn't a lifetime commitment. There must be a single woman in this city who has a free night. What about Debby Saunders?"

"Harry, Debby Saunders is not this guy's type."

"How do you know what his type is?"

"I just know."

"What's wrong with her? She's single, she's bright, she's built like a brick shithouse . . ."

"She's what my mother would call a floozy. She's not going to be right for him. I know. And he's not her type, either."

"I think she's perfect. She's even a social worker. Look, we don't know this guy. We don't know what he's like. Maybe he's a real trouser snake."

"Maybe."

"What's her number? I'll call her."

She gives in, finally, and after she hangs up from Harry, gets Debby Saunders's number from directory assistance and calls her herself. Debby accepts with pleasure. She has just ended a long-term relationship, she says, and is "at large." Brooke calls Harry back to let him know it's okay to invite Bob Fitzgerald.

Harry says he already has.

On the day of their dinner, Debby arrives early to help prepare the meal of Cornish hens, wild rice, and an elaborate dessert of spiced pears in chocolate and vanilla sauce with ice cream. While they cook the food, Harry is upstairs showering after his workout at the Y.

Robert arrives precisely at the appointed time. He bears an armful of cut flowers. To Brooke's surprise—and dismay—he and Debby hit it off at once. Debby has an easy, breezy manner that fits perfectly with his, which initially comes across as reserve, then gradually he shows himself to be an enjoyable, and enjoying, man. (Though he does introduce himself as Robert and not Bob.) Debby turns the strength of her personality upon him with the force of a spotlight, and in the bright light of their connection, Brooke sees him as lively, vigorous, and interesting.

At each juncture of the evening she learns more about him, from the thoughtful and, to her mind, original gift of flowers instead of wine; to the choice of seltzer with a twist during cocktails, an honest choice for a substance abuse counselor (Harry drinks a vodka tonic, Debby a white wine, Brooke a blush); to his conversation during the early part of the night (why the government has the right to subsidize the growing of tobacco when cigarette smoking is responsible for 360,000 deaths every year, which Robert graphically describes as the equivalent of two fully-loaded jumbo jets crashing and killing everyone on board every day of the year); to his eager drawing out from Debby during dinner the details of her background (master's in social work, long-ago divorce), her job (casework supervisor for the County Department of Social Services) and how she feels about it (loves it), all done so skillfully that even Brooke is forced to reconsider Debby in a new light; to his relaxed and good-humored description over dessert of the not-so-subtle ways in which Americans are bamboozled by double messages over drugs in the name of moneymaking, citing the example of the *Time* issue on the McGuires' coffee table which has a front cover story on "The War Against Drugs," and on the back cover a slick ad for Seagram's. Robert rises from the table to get the magazine and hold it open for them to appreciate the juxtaposition.

Harry, bar owner, advertising executive, says, "But you're not really being fair, are you? I mean, on the front page you have an informational, journalistic image, and on the back a persuasive one. The two have completely different purposes."

"Maybe," Robert says. "But what's the purpose of a cover story? Isn't it to persuade a customer to buy the magazine? My point is that one image plays to our rational sense that drugs are bad and should be avoided, and the other plays to our need to indulge in just the behavior the first impulse decries. And we're being manipulated both ways. Both images make us consumers. One tries to sell us on repudiating what the other image tries to make us buy."

"If it weren't for the ads, we wouldn't even get what passes for news," Harry says, not sure himself whose point he is making. He chews on that one as Brooke pours them all more coffee. Harry finally says, "But advertising doesn't create the need. It's just a vehicle to allow the consumer to satisfy a need that already exists."

"Oh, take a look at the bottle in this ad, Harry," says Debby. "You don't think that isn't a subliminal message? Something long and slender and dewy and hard?"

"I don't believe in subliminal advertising. What I do believe is that this isn't creating a need for the product as much as trying to raise brand awareness among people who already drink."

"Yeah, that's what the tobacco industry wants us to believe, too, with their propaganda," Robert says. "Did you ever see those old ads that stood up some old men in white coats and called them doctors and had them talk about how healthy cigarettes are? How healthy they are! Can you imagine anything more irresponsible? Did you ever see the ad years ago with Reagan hawking some cigarette brand?"

Harry starts to squirm and repeats his theory of brand awareness. Even Brooke wants to tell him to stifle it. Yet how unthreateningly does Robert make his points . . . How low his voice, how soft his chuckle, how ironic and rueful his grin. Of course he is right; the whole purpose of all these images is to sell: as an advertising professional herself she knows how a powerful emotional image can contradict the most reasonable message.

As the talk shifts to the role of the mass media in determining the quality of American life, Brooke realizes she feels comfortable in Robert's presence and trusts his manner in a way that never happens when she entertains Harry's clients, who are mostly boors and jerks even though they help pay the bills. This guy is different. Well, he's a counselor, not a salesman or a manufacturer of war accoutrements. He must be a wonderful counselor. Brooke is mesmerized. What's worse, so is Debby.

Brooke does not have to be a mind reader to predict what's in store for these two once they leave: A little parallel parking between the sheets for this slender gracious man and this strong-bodied woman. After their goodbyes, she sees them off together with a pang of regret. On one hand, she wishes he could stay so she could continue to enjoy the vibrations he gives off, his peaceful aura. On the other, she wishes she had not brought him together with Debby.

There is a third hand, too: the ache of the futility of either emotion as she crawls into bed beside Harry after she cleans up the kitchen. She is attracted to Robert, no doubt, but it is a pointless and vain attraction, a flutter of emotion that arises from nowhere and will soon subside, that will not come to anything under any circumstances that she can foresee (or could admit to). A momentary reminder of feelings from a former stage of her life, that's all, now safely buried beneath layers of custom and habit. Likewise, her jealousy is a wasteful and unnecessary thing; given the futility of any attraction to him, why should she feel angry or betrayed that he had (through her own offices, no less) found someone who could please him, who obviously liked him, and who was a tasty enough number to earn his attention? If, as she believes, love and happiness are deserved, doesn't he deserve a little?

Does he, indeed. On these three pinions—her positive attraction, negative jealousy, withdrawal from the former two—does the ending of her night turn. Harry, being tired, gloats over his matchmaking abilities only a short while before slipping into sleep.

So does she, finally, give herself up to relief from her conflicting feelings—surprised, even at the end, in the twilight of drowsiness, at the power of these emotions to stir her, indeed at their presence at this time in her life at all.

As the lights go off in the McGuires' home, Robert and Debby stand talking by her car parked on the street.

She rests her broad hips against the fender. She is a robust, buxom woman with a head full of tawny shoulder-length hair. A trench coat hangs open, falls away from her great rounded breasts, flat stomach, shapely legs sturdy as tree trunks. Robert stands beside her, arms folded. They face Harry and Brooke's split-level. The house is now dark, along with most of the other houses on the block in this damp, overcast night.

"Bedtime for Harry and Brooke," Debby says. "How long have you known them?"

"Couple weeks. I'm actually Harry's client on a job he's doing for me. We're not so much friends. You?"

"Fifteen years."

"Long time."

"I used to be married to one of Harry's cousins."

"So what does that make you to him?"

"Somebody he tried to make a move on at a party once."

"Get out."

"I shit you not."

"When was this?"

"Couple years ago. Just after my divorce. I guess he was drunk, I dunno. I was a little stewed myself. Not one of my happier moments."

"So what happened?"

"Nothing, really. Oh, he sidled up beside me and felt me up a little and stuck his tongue down my throat and tried to lick my tonsils till I spit him out. I didn't like him that much."

"You've stayed friends with them," Robert points out.

"I'd see them at family things until we all drifted pretty much out of touch. I assume they called me tonight because they couldn't think of anybody else for you."

"Did you ever say anything to him about it?"

"He never brought it up, and I didn't either. I just never got near him again. And I never mentioned it to Brooke."

He watches her in the faint blue luminescence of the night. "That was another time," she says. She looks away at the curve of the thick black hill nearby, then begins to fuss through her purse for her keys. "Well. Time to get going, I guess."

"I had a good time tonight," Robert says. "Regardless of why they called you."

"Thanks. I did, too."

A long look passes between them that ends in a clinch. Her face close to his, she exhales a breath full of sweet wine and strong coffee.

Finally she pulls away. She stares at the collar of his shirt. "I better get going," she says. "I have an early morning. I'll see you again, I hope." Her eyes narrow.

He follows her brake lights down the hilly winding streets of the McGuires' subdivision. At the highway she goes west, he east.

She is probably right, he thinks on the way home, about calling her because all their other women friends were busy or taken. It was probably Harry's idea too, not Brooke's.

Brooke. Hostess Brooke, quiet, soft-spoken Brooke. So different in her domestic life from her flashy public pose. Remaining calm, or trying to, anyway, in the midst of Harry's demands, well-meaning yet relentless. Get this, bring this, pass this, Brooke there's no butter on the table, Brooke pour Robert more soda. And she complying without anger or resentment, happy to be of service to her husband and his client from work and his cousin's ex-wife on whom he tried to put a heavy move once some years back.

Did she know? Does Harry make a habit out of this kind of thing? At best, Robert has had only a nodding acquaintance with fidelity, and anyway who hasn't tried something like that in moments of weakness or inebriation? But at least he had the consideration for his ex-wife never to carry on with a relative. (Though there was that time on the sofa with Maureen . . .)

Yet again he is unimpressed with Harry. McGuire, you are a jerk: Robert sends this message winding telepathically back through the labyrinthine streets to find the self-satisfied Harry asleep next to Brooke in their dark home on Sweethaven Drive. I only hope you are a competent jerk when it comes to doing the job I hired you to do. Fortunately, the subject you are unleashing your slimy advertising talents on is socially responsible. Not that you would necessarily care.

3

Harry McGuire calls him at the hospital the next morning. It is a weird feeling, picking up the phone and hearing Harry say, "I just wanted to let you know how much we enjoyed having you over." Harry has in fact been much in his thoughts this morning by virtue of his connection with Brooke, who has been the true center of Robert's scattered musings. Puttering around the house before leaving for work, getting organized at the office, meeting with the head of nursing to argue for more staff for his clinic, through all the business of his brief day he has kept as the focus of his thoughts the dinner with Brooke, their brief conversations, the look in her eye more intense and searching than it should be for one of hubby's clients—all in all her sudden, and not altogether welcome, appearance in his life.

And now here's old Harry himself on the phone. Robert half expects to hear him say, "Hey—stop thinking about my wife!"

But of course Harry's purpose is entirely different. And his perceptions entirely wrong.

"I also wanted to make sure you got home okay last night," he continues.

"Why wouldn't I?"

"Oh, I just thought you might have gotten sidetracked."

"By what?"

"Your dinner companion, for one thing."

The salacious tone of Harry's adman voice makes Robert spitefully glad that nothing happened with Debby last night.

His dominance over his wife, his come-on to Debby, now this. They do nothing to raise Robert's opinion of him. Strikes eight and nine against poor Harry.

But Harry's batting average is more than Robert wants to discuss with him right now. "It was a very pleasant evening," he says instead. "Your wife's an excellent cook."

"She is indeed. We'll have to do it again soon."

Then, because Robert has not yet picked up on his reference to

Debby, Harry says, "I'm sure we can get Debby in on it too. Brooke tells me you two really hit it off. Tell you the truth, I knew you would too."

"You did."

"Yepper. I just knew."

"And how did your wife know?"

"She just knew, too. She could tell."

"You must be a very insightful couple."

"Yeah, there isn't much Brooke misses. Hey, she's an artist, what can I say? They're different than we are."

"Mmm."

"We talked about it over breakfast. She said she could tell there was something going on between the two of you. Maybe we could all meet for dinner at the Downtown Club some night. We could get together at the Y for a workout first, if you want, then meet the girls for dinner."

"Right. Actually," Robert says (time to jerk this guy's chains), "I'm glad you called. I want to make an appointment to start going over your work on my campaign. How soon can you get something together?"

"As early as next week. How does Friday sound?"

"Not as good as Wednesday."

"Great. We'll make it Wednesday. Shall we say ten?"

"Let's say eleven."

"Great. We can go over the proposals and then have lunch at the Club."

"Maybe we can just go over the proposals and save lunch for another time." This advertising foolishness has its moments. It's fun when you hold all the cards.

"Sounds good to me," Harry says.

"Okay. Call me if there's any change. Otherwise, I'll see you then."

"Great," Harry says, but Robert has already hung up and forgotten about the adman and gotten back to thinking about the adman's wife. I've sworn off sex, he reminds himself—but there is something about this woman that draws him. Not just her outward attractiveness, but the looks that passed between them. They were charged with something, some promise of connection.

Whatever it was, he knew he had lacked it in his life for a while now. The residents of the House of Grins took care of part of it, but not Robert's need for intimacy. Maybe that's what he picked up from Brooke McGuire—a spark of connection. If he blew on it, would he extinguish it, or turn it into a tiny blaze that might burn through the ice that he believed kept part of them both frozen?

Thinking about her, he hatched a plan to test out that question. He was due to take over as editor of one of his professional journals, and he had been thinking about getting it redesigned. Maybe that project is something Brooke might be interested in taking on. And that would be the chance to bring them closer.

Whatever might—or might not—happen between them, the idea of seeing her again cheered him.

4

Brooke takes the call on the first ring. "Hi," says Debby Saunders. "Are you on a deadline or anything right now?"

"Well, I'm always on sort of a deadline." She is standing over her light table, shaping up a board for a page of the next *Reporter*. She balances the phone between her shoulder and her ear. Debby is not among those people to whom she most wants to speak this morning.

"Okay," Debby says, "I won't keep you. I just wanted to touch base about last night. I had a wonderful time."

"That's good. We're glad you could make it." She makes herself sound gracious.

She almost means it, too. She had awakened in the morning as though from a sleep following a migraine, drained but purged. I'm my old self, she told her reflection in the mirror as her early morning habits closed in on her. Her shower, her trooping back and forth over the familiar traffic pattern in the bedroom as she dressed, the coffee she made for Harry, the blue bowl of Honey Nut Cheerios she slipped on the table for him with perfect timing as he rolled into the kitchen, these convinced her that her life was the same as it ever was. Her attraction and jealousy, her light and dark, resolved in the coming of dawn into the background of her life. With Harry, in the home they share, the child they are trying to create—that's where the true center of her life lies. And she has worked mighty hard to make it so. She has an outlet for her love (her husband) and her creativity (her work), and what happens outside of this closed system, the linkings and pairings and couplings of other people, is not her concern. Especially when they were as frivolous as a meaningless attraction to a strange man.

"Robert and I got on fabulously," Debby says.

"I thought you did. Seems like an awfully nice guy."

As she speaks, Brooke picks up a column of type and runs it through the electric waxer. It comes out of the whirring machine tacky on one side and yellowed and ribbed on the other.

"I know. There aren't many of them around. That's kind of what I called about. I was wondering how well you knew him."

"I don't know him well at all. Harry's the one who knows him."

"I was hoping to find out something about him."

"Anything in particular?"

"Oh, what's he's like, what he's done, that kind of thing."

"Last night was only the second or third time I met him, and the first time I spent any time at all with him."

"Oh."

"Sorry."

"No problem. I'll just have to find out for myself."

Brooke is reminded she and Debby are not good friends after all.

"I'll tell Harry you're interested. I'm sure he'll be glad, too."

"Right. Well, I won't take any more of your time. I'll let you know how things work out."

"Do."

"Bye."

Brooke drops the phone onto the receiver and studies the piece of copy she holds. Her mood is dropping precipitously. She is working on the "People" section of the *Reporter*. It lists employees whom Brooke has never heard of and their Births, Graduations, Marriages, Promotions, Retirements, and Deaths.

That's about it, folks, she thinks to herself, measuring the copy for the slot she has in mind for it, trimming off three lines and running them over to another column. The milestones of life. The beginning and the end and everything in between reduced to six easy-to-remember steps.

Just like baking a cake, really. Birth is assembling the ingredients. School is mixing them all together and beating for four years. Marriage is—well, sometimes marriage is the perfect finishing of it, but also sometimes like sticking it inside a dry, hot, airless oven and baking all the juices out of it. Promotion is frosting it, retirement is separating one piece away from the whole, and death is gobbling it down until there is nothing left but the empty plate and a crumb or two to remind you of what used to be there.

These six steps make a life. Though she has taken part in four of the six, she sometimes believes the real enjoyment of them is reserved for other people. In her own life, they often just mark time: four down, two to go.

"Know who I talked to today?" Harry asks that night in bed.

"No."

"Bob Fitzgerald. My client? I called him to see what kind of a time he had last night."

"You certainly are fascinated with that guy."

"I think he's interesting. Don't you?"

"Not that interesting."

"I think he is. Know what we talked about?"

"No idea."

"Debby Saunders. I think this may be the beginning of something between them."

"I talked to her today, too. She called me."

"There you go. It's starting."

"What's starting?"

"Them. Their thing. What did she want?"

"Find out more about him."

"Like what?"

"I dunno, Harry. I told her I didn't know him very well. I told her she should ask you."

"What did she say?"

"She said she'd find out by herself."

"There you go."

"What?"

"Told you they were right for each other."

She sighs. "Yes, dear."

After dinner at Harry's parents' that week, Brooke and Joyce find themselves alone in the kitchen, cleaning up the dishes and putting away the food. "What's wrong," Joyce asks. "You down?"

"I think I'm depressed."

"Something happen at work?"

"No."

"Everything okay with Harry?"

"Sure."

"So what's the matter?"

"I don't know. I just feel lousy."

"Maybe you're coming down with something. There's some kind of bug going around."

"Maybe."

"How'd your dinner go the other night?"

"Just fine."

"Why do you say it like that?"

"Debby Saunders did everything but rape that poor man at the table."

"I'm sure that came later."

"I'm sure."

"Harry say anything about it?"

"Harry thinks it's the greatest thing in the world. I, on the other hand, feel like I helped throw him to the sharks."

"Is that what you're down about?"

Brooke shrugs.

"Guy's a grownup," Joy says. "I'm sure he can take care of himself in the clinches. Of which I'm also sure there were many."

"I'm sure there were," says Brooke. "I have no doubt of that at all."

5

Robert pauses in the living room with his briefcase still in his hand. "We have a problem," Gene says.

Before he gets out another word, Robert knows. "Dennis?"

"He won't come out of his room. He didn't go to work today. Didn't even get out of bed."

"Is he sick?"

"He has some kind of problem. He won't tell me. He looks bad.

He sounds bad."

Upstairs, Robert taps on Dennis's door. There is no response and he tries the knob. It does not turn. "Dennis? It's me. Can I come in?"

No answer.

"Dennis, Gene tells me you're not feeling well. Do you want me to call a doctor? Will you open the door please, so we can talk?"

When there is still no answer, Robert goes down to the kitchen to retrieve a skeleton key from a drawer. Back upstairs, he tells Dennis through the door, "Dennis, I'm going to try this key in the door, okay? I want to come in because I'm worried about you."

The key will not go all the way into the lock. "Dennis, is there a key in the door already? Will you take it out so I can open the door? Dennis? Will you take the key out, please?"

Still no response from inside the room. Robert puts his ear to the door and hears nothing. Knocks again. "Dennis? Will you let me in?"

No answer.

Robert decides to let him have more time. Over dinner that night he asks Gene, "Have you seen him at all?"

"He came out to go the bathroom."

"Has he had any run-ins with Martina lately?"

"If he has, he hasn't mentioned it to me. Not that he mentions anything to me. I haven't even seen her since this morning."

"Her friend hasn't been staying overnight, has he?"

"No. She was up early, in fact. By herself."

Later he taps on Dennis's door again. Still no response. "Will you try to get his therapist on the phone?" he asks Gene in the kitchen. "Her name's Edna Bertoni. The number's in my phone book. Let me know and I'll take it upstairs."

Gene calls from the bottom of the stairs. "She's on the line."

Robert picks up the phone in the hallway. He takes it partway down the stairs. "Edna? It's Robert Fitzgerald. Hi. Listen, I'm sorry to trouble you, but Dennis Parker is having a little problem here."

"I know," the woman says. "He called me this afternoon. He didn't sound very good."

"Well, I'm afraid he isn't very good now. He's locked the door to his room and he won't open it or talk to me. Did he say what this is about?"

"Just that he's depressed about something. He wouldn't tell me what it was."

"I'm concerned I can't make any contact with him. I thought

maybe he'd want to talk to you."

"I already spoke with him once today. I can try again."

Robert taps on Dennis's door again. "Dennis. Edna Bertoni is on the phone. She wants to talk to you."

There is a stirring behind the door. Robert hears the shuffle of feet, then a fiddling with the door handle. Then more fiddling. Then Dennis's voice says, "I can't get the door open."

"Is there a key in the lock?" Robert asks.

"Yes."

"Can you take it out?"

"Yeah, but it isn't opening the door."

"Just take it out and I'll try and get it open from this side." Robert pushes and pulls and tries his own key, but can't get it open.

He winds up taking the door off the hinges while Dennis's shrink waits patiently on the line. Howard the Cat tears out of Dennis's room and scrambles down the stairs. Dennis is haggard and rumpled in his bathrobe and smells like stale burnt coffee grounds. He looks at Robert with dazed and confused eyes.

Robert hands him the telephone, which he takes into the bathroom and then closes that door after him. Robert pulls the lock out of Dennis's door and examines it. Broken spring. He sits with the mechanism on the top step of the staircase, trying not to listen but keeping alert for the steady murmur from the bathroom.

In a while the toilet flushes and the door opens and Dennis comes out to put the phone back on the table. Dennis comes over and sits beside Robert on the landing.

"Bad time?"

"I guess."

"Did you eat anything today?"

"No."

"If you get cleaned up, I'll make you some dinner."

"Not hungry."

"You'll feel better. Okay, okay. I'll fix your lock tonight. I'll take a lock set out of one of the doors in the basement."

'Thanks."

"You scared the shit out of me, you know that, don't you?"

"Must have," Dennis says. "You called in the heavy artillery. When in doubt, bring in the shrink."

"It got you out of your room."

Dennis gets up and pads into the bathroom again and closes the door behind him.

"Well?" Gene asks downstairs.

"He's out. Doesn't want to talk about it, needless to say."

"The immediate crisis is over, anyway."

"I wish I knew what the problem was. And what his counselor said to him."

"Ask him."

"He won't talk about it."

"Ask her."

"If he doesn't want to talk about it, I have to respect that. I'm sure we'll find out sooner or later."

6

Robert comes out of a meeting with the executive vice president and the nursing director in a much better mood than he has been in recently. They have all agreed that one more full-time nurse would be appropriate, considering the push to build the clinic's census. Robert and the nursing director even part smiling, he back to the clinic and she off to another meeting, this time with the director of ambulatory services, who will also need more nurses. He will try, stupidly, to bully her. With him she will be more militant than she was with Robert.

"If the docs just treated 'em right in the first place, they'd have enough to go around," she shouts down the Administration Wing hallway. "Those guys ruin everything!"

He finds a message from Debby Saunders stuck on the message board on his door. He folds it in half and pockets it. He will not call her now. He may decide to call her later, but not now. He wants to call someone else first.

"Brooke? Hi. It's Robert Fitzgerald."

"Oh. Hello."

"Did I catch you at a bad time?"

"Tell you the truth, I'm swamped with work."

"I won't keep you. I just want to thank you for a lovely dinner."

"You're very welcome. It was a pleasure. Harry and I both had a good time."

"I know. He called me."

"He told me. I also heard from Debby. She said she had a nice time, too."

"Then it's unanimous. Are you confidantes, you and she?"

"Not really. But she did ask me what Robert Fitzgerald is 'really like.'"

"And what did you tell her?"

"I said I didn't know you very well. I told her if she wanted a better answer, she should ask my husband. He knows you better."

"Not much."

"Better than I do. Anyway, she told me she was going to find out for herself. Consider yourself warned. Now I hope you aren't going to ask me what *she's* really like."

"Actually, no. I'm calling for another reason. I was wondering if you'd be free for lunch tomorrow."

"Tomorrow?"

"I'd like to talk to you about doing some freelance work for me."

"Freelance work?"

"At your standard fee, of course."

"Well, I'm flattered. But what about Harry?"

"This is a completely different kind of project. It's for me personally, not the hospital. And I'm not sure Harry would want to handle it. I'd like you to do it. For reasons I'll explain at lunch."

"I appreciate your thinking of me, but I'm not sure I have the time for freelance work just now."

"I might not need a full-fledged project. Maybe more of a design consultation. Maybe after we talk, you'll have a better sense of how much time it would take."

"I guess that would be all right. The problem is, I teach a course tomorrow night, and I usually prepare my class during lunch."

"What kind of course?"

"A class in design at the community college. Nothing big."

"You're too modest. How about the day after?"

"I think that would work."

"Terrific. Now, I have to ask you to recommend a suitable place to eat."

"Have you ever been to T. Moneybags? That's where I used to meet clients when I was freelancing."

"Sounds good to me. Shall we say twelve-thirty?"

"Twelve-thirty it is."

7

The instant she hangs up, before she can even think about what just happened, Edith sticks her eggbeaten head in the door. "Busy?" she says in her annoyingly ingratiating way.

"Kind of."

"This won't take a sec. The boss just handed me this."

She lays a manuscript on Brooke's light table. It is the text of testimony presented before joint hearings of the State Assembly and Senate Insurance Committees by the Chairman of the Board and CEO of the company. The head reads: Chairman Urges Regulatory Reform. Edith's assistant Dave wrote it.

"He wants this to go in the next issue. Got room?"

"We'll make room," says Brooke. "Where's he want it to go?

"Front page. Don't look at me. Orders from the top."

Brooke shrugs. "Front page it is."

"Gotta scoot."

She is gone in a flurry of clipped footsteps. Brooke's eye skims over the editorial without comprehending anything. It is filled with short paragraphs and section numbers from the state insurance law. It will have to run with a picture of the chairman, in all his gray-haired, bland, nimbused respectability.

She lays aside the editorial and stares at the board on the light table. The two-page spread, an article bylined by the Salesman of the Year describing his techniques and written by Dave, is almost composed. She just needs to do a little straightening, then maybe add filler or art to the square on the lower right, and she's done. Maybe she can find an inspirational message. Something she herself would be ashamed to say usually goes over big.

She moves away from the table to gaze out the smoky window across the downtown's low skyline of stately late Victorian buildings. She can see all the way down Court Street, the main street, to where it curves off over the bridge across the Chenango River. Traffic is characteristically heavy in this part of the afternoon.

Thickening, like sauce. Confused, like her thoughts.

She is not so concerned about why Robert Fitzgerald called her, actually. She is willing to take his explanation at face value. There could not be anything more involved than that, she is certain, unless it is a ruse to get her to talk about Debby Saunders, which she doubts. She is more concerned about getting control over her own feelings about the call. For the thought of meeting him again, alone, sends her sailing over the congested city streets.

Down, girl!

After all, isn't she a designer? And didn't he say he needed a design consultation?

So what's the big deal? A business associate of your husband calls you to talk about throwing some business your way. Isn't that basically how things work in this town? Doesn't that account for your mark being everywhere, on logos for bars, on menus in restaurants, on the bookmarks given out at the library, even? All through Harry's contacts? So get yourself under control, girl. This man couldn't be interested in you for anything other than just what he said: design consultation. Don't make more of it. Don't, especially, let yourself believe that any of the designs he needs consultation on are for you.

Of course, if they do happen to center more on her than on her talent . . . well then. Brooke smiles. She lets herself consider that she may be in for an interesting lunch after all.

8

Martina doodles and thinks.

She is meeting with Larry Kowalski and several of the hospital administrators. It does not involve her total attention. Or even one-quarter of it. Larry dominates the discussion, as usual, and as usual there is little of substance in what he has to say. His bray intrudes upon her thoughts and leaves her annoyed. And jealous.

Larry's prattle has gotten him far in this hospital, and listening to the drone of his voice she is becoming more convinced that it will take him farther yet. He is a visible, albeit obnoxious, character, and his visibility has gotten him assigned to personnel grievance committees, bioethical committees, and ad hoc committees to consider everything from a potential hazard in Radiation Therapy to the placement of a helicopter landing pad in the parking lot. Larry has brown-nosed himself into important places all around the hospital, while Martina's considerable (to her mind, anyway) nursing and administrative skills have not gotten her any visibility or committee assignments. Except the social event planning committee, whose responsibilities include picking the day for the annual staff clambake each summer. Anybody with an employee ID badge is eligible for that one. Big whoop.

She is burned that she has been so consistently taken for granted and ignored. She has tried to talk this over with Max, but he's no help at all. He would be happiest if she quit work and married him, which she has said time and again she will not do. Not that he listens.

Even to get this stupid promotion she has to compete with Larry Kowalski, of all people. She has struggled to get to this point, and will have to struggle to get to the next point—a struggle that she is not confident she will win. For a variety of reasons, the prime one being that he is a practiced and prized ass-kisser, Martina believes that Larry will get the job.

And so she is jealous that her career will be stalled while Larry's will be moving forward again because his line of bullshit goes down so easy with the jerks who run this place, from the head jerk on down. Unless Martina does something drastic, Larry Kowalski, the dumbest jerk of them all, will become her new boss.

By the time the meeting breaks up, Martina has made her decision. She returns to her office and closes the door. She calls Dr. Gerard and tells him she would like to continue their last conversation. They agree to meet at his office at eight that evening to talk things over.

That's that, she tells herself when she hangs up. I won't take this lying down.

She smiles a bitter little smile.

Which turns out to be an even unfunnier joke than she could have imagined.

After the initial small talk, during which Dr. Gerard tells her how qualified he believes her to be for this job, but what a strong candidate Larry is, he works his way around the desk to sit in one of the chairs beside the one she sits in. He draws it closer to hers.

Say what you will about his abilities as a physician, she thinks, the man has rotten teeth. You'd think a man with his money and vanity would at least have had them capped.

"I want you to know something else," he says. "It's rather personal."

She tightens her grip on the chair.

"Since the first day you started here, I've found you exceptionally attractive."

Well, the pitifulness of the line would be funny, if it weren't happening to her. For an instant, she is immeasurably saddened at having gotten herself into this spot. But then Gerard leans into her and his putrid breath washes over her face and he fastens his lips on hers, and insinuates his tongue into her mouth.

When he takes it out, she begins, "Dr. Gerard." But he says, "No. Don't say anything."

He stands and pulls her from her chair and wraps his thin arms around her. He grinds his hips into hers and buries his head in her neck. She feels a singular lack of anything resembling an erection.

"So beautiful," he says when he comes up for air.

There is a plush velour sofa in his office. He leads her to it. Her lack of feeling for him makes the entire episode more like a clinical exam than a seduction. Martina suspects that she is supposed to take a more active role, but cannot bring herself to.

He begins undoing her blouse and she realizes she can't go through with this. "Wait," she says, more sharply now, and grabs his hands. "Wait! Don't. Please."

"I thought you wanted this."

She can only shake her head; she can't muster a response that fully captures how much she doesn't want this.

To his credit, he stops immediately.

"Sorry," she says (and hates that she feels like she has to apologize), "but I can't do this."

He straightens his lab coat. "Yes," he says. "Of course."

For some reason she cannot figure, she feels the tiniest degree of something—besides repulsion, of course; is it pity?—for this skinny, homely, unpleasant man.

She retreats to her own office, where she sits until she hears his door close and his footsteps fade away. Then she closes up her office and leaves.

CHAPTER EIGHT

1

When he arrives for the eight-thirty a.m. staff meeting, Robert learns that during the night one of the patients in the clinic smacked another patient, who happened to be blind, in the face. The night charge nurse had just finished talking to the blind man, and when somebody hit him in the face, he assumed it was the nurse and began shouting, "Help! Help! The nurse hit me!" Chaos ensued. Hospital security was called, and came, and lost control of the situation at once. The man who hit the blind guy raged up and down the hallway and pulled a fire alarm, which sent the Code Red bells ringing all over the hospital. The blind man passed out and an inexperienced security guard called a Code Blue, which sent a public address announcement echoing through the sleeping building. Within three minutes, the city police and fire departments showed up with sirens blasting in the middle of the night to join the hospital fire brigade and the Code Blue crash cart team milling testily around the unit hallway out of breath. Some fun.

Before Robert arrived, the blind man's daughter already called the Legal Aid Society for help in filing assault charges against the nurse whom he thinks punched him. He also wants to sue the hospital for failing to protect his safety. The nurse who has been wrongly accused has her own call in to the representative of the local nurses' union that is trying to organize the hospital. This puts the fear of God into executive vice president Fawcett, who already has six calls in to Robert. The director of nursing is on her way over. The director of risk management is already here, parked on Robert's doorstep popping Tums. Everyone looks to Robert for deliverance.

Solomonic, he tackles each problem in order. He sends the violent patient to the psychiatric unit for observation. He calms the blind man and makes an appointment with his lawyer to talk about dropping the threat of legal action. He gets the nurse to back off the union talk by promising to increase night security on the unit and discuss other issues within the next two weeks. He calls Fawcett and satisfies him the situation is under control. He listens to the risk manager's fantasies of litigation and sends her away with the promise to keep in touch, and intercepts the director of nursing and suggests she meet with his charge nurse when she returns in the evening for her next shift. All this before 9:15.

His troubles continue with an advising session with one of the new therapists who is having trouble maintaining distance from an emotionally-devastated, co-dependent family; with a difficult meeting with the risk manager, the blind man, and the twerp who is representing him, who wants to sue the hospital for $8.5 million; with a handful of intake interviews; and with a meeting with a representative of Kolata Construction, Inc., who wants to talk to him and the vice president in charge of building services about a prospective remodeling for the clinic, which Robert badly wants done but not by Kolata. "Why do we have to use this guy," he asks. The veep for building services shrugs eloquently.

He also gets a call from Debby Saunders, which his secretary fails to screen.

"Hi," Debby says. "How are you?"

"So frazzled you wouldn't believe. I can't describe what's going on here today. What's with you?"

"Doing better than you are, sounds like. Just wondering when I'll get to see you again."

"Let me look at my calendar."

"How about tonight?"

"Can't," he says, for no reason other than he's not in the mood for her. "This weekend is better. Why don't we plan on Friday? We'll talk again during the day and we'll get together at night."

"Sounds good," she says. "I had a nice time the other night."

"Me, too."

He is relieved to say goodbye. She is perfectly pleasant. But he's not sure this relationship has much of a future.

2

T. Moneybags is all pinks and pastels and billowing, nostalgic art deco curves on the bar and bannisters and partitions. The same curves find their way onto the salad bowls in the form of huge clam shells, in cut-outs on the menus, in stand-up cards on the tables.

Brooke and Robert meet in the foyer. They shake hands. He stifles the urge to hug her. Well, he is getting older, and self-control is a trait sometimes learned late. This woman, he suspects, was born with it.

They are seated at once and handed enormous pink and pastel billowing menus that require both hands to hold. "Oh my," says Robert at their heft.

"Aren't these awful?"

"I'd say so."

"The worst part is, I designed them," Brooke admits. "Don't worry. I'm the first to admit they're hideous. The owner wanted them. I tried to talk him out of it, then said fine when I realized he wasn't going to change his mind."

"Customer is always right."

"Ugliest menus in town."

"Spare no expense. Only the worst will do."

He finds it hard to take his eyes from her as she talks. The attention thrills and unnerves her. She decides to return the fire. She takes off her red-rimmed glasses and lays them upside down on the table. Gives him the full searchlight treatment with her green eyes, forthright and engaging. Gotcha. There could as well be a bubble around their table, so little does the world around them intrude.

After they order, he says, "Shall we get the business out of the way so we can enjoy the food?"

"Sure."

"I'm the incoming editor of something called the *Journal of Alcoholism and Other Drug Abuse Prevention*, which is put out, as you might expect, for people in the field of alcohol and other drug abuse. Both practitioners and researchers. It's a revolving position. Each editor has the job for a year. I'd like to make some lasting changes. I want somebody to take a look at the journal and shape it up visually. Make it more attractive. Bring it up to date. Now it looks too much like it comes from the Soviet Union in the 1950s. I'd like you to take it on."

"Harry has some great artists on his staff. They do things like this all the time. Why don't you just use them?"

"Frankly I haven't been impressed with the work he's shown me."

He holds a hand up to stop the protest that she is gathering herself to make. "He's okay on the brochures and newspaper ads and like that, which is mostly what my campaign is going to be. The artists' work is okay, and under the right circumstances it could be good. But it isn't first-rate."

"I don't agree with you."

"You're being loyal."

"No," she says, but knows he is right. Harry hires only kids just out of school, with little in the way of developed technique. As soon as they get some experience they move to a bigger agency or they move out of town. She plunges ahead anyway with what she knows is also the truth. "It's some of the best work in town."

"I don't doubt that. But look, there's a built-in problem with ad agencies. There are so many people involved in the development of the campaigns, the final products are usually a mishmash of everyone's mistakes. The client has what he mistakenly believes is a good idea, and that's interpreted by the account executive, and that's interpreted by the art director, and that's further interpreted by the artist and the copywriter. And then the piece has to make its way back up the chain before it goes out to the client.

"I don't want a whole crew of people interpreting my ideas. For my own project, I want to be able to sit down with the artist and say, 'Design me the ugliest, godawful menus in the world because that's what I want.'"

This makes her smile. She smooths her pink napkin across her lap. "So how did you pick me for this?"

"I liked your work."

"When did you see it?"

"The other night at your house. There were copies of your magazine on the coffee table. I looked them over while you were in the kitchen. I think your stuff is terrific."

She shakes her head modestly while she explodes with joy inside.

"I want you to work on my journal for me."

She can't contain her brightest smile. "How can I say no?"

"I was hoping you wouldn't be able to."

"It's a deal." They shake on it. Something more is starting here than a business arrangement.

"I assume you want to get started on it right away?"

He nods. "It's a quarterly journal," he says. "I'd like to come out with a new design for the Spring issue. I still have to get the design through the editorial committee, but that should be no problem."

"I need to look the present design over first. And I need to know your budget and the printing arrangements."

"I can get it all for you tomorrow. Can you come around to my office? We'll have more privacy. I'll show you some back issues, and we can go over the costs for the last one. I wouldn't mind increasing the budget—but we can talk about that tomorrow."

They agree this will be mutually fine.

Driving back to her office, Brooke begins to look forward to seeing him again, a meeting that feels illicit in a private setting that is paradoxically entirely sanctioned by the social powers. It is the best of both worlds.

3

The Sebrings, Kelly and Jack, Harry's friends, greet them in the foyer of the Scotch and Sirloin restaurant. Jack is the scion of a local family who started out with a small rent-a-car outlet that grew into a franchise that has expanded to include auto-body repair shops and a fleet of busses they lease to schools. Like Harry, he is a handsome man who is settling into an extremely comfortable early middle age of money, power, and personal influence in the town's best society.

"Oh, Brooke," Kelly says. She is petite, dressed in her regular uniform, like a preppie teenager with tartan plaid skirt and crisp blazer over a silk blouse with a huge bow. She could be 13 instead of 31, if you didn't look too closely at the wrinkles around her eyes and on her neck. A diamond tennis racquet pin is attached to her blazer lapel. It is her signature; she wears it on all her clothes. "Before I forget. Next month we're having a winter hat show to raise money for the new EEG Lab at the hospital. We're looking for models. Interested?"

Kelly, like many of the wives of these men, is bright and energetic with no outlet for her energy besides her children, the Junior League, and the hospital auxiliary, of which she is vice president. She is forever after Brooke to join, showering her with arguments that leave Brooke feeling as if she is betraying her duty to her class by not taking part in the luncheons and social events with which these women, aging girl scouts and cheerleaders, occupy their time. So far Brooke has refused.

"What's an EEG Lab?"

"A way of measuring blood flow through the vessels. It's quite a new thing. Quite high-tech. We'd be the first hospital in the area to have one. And it's going to be expensive to start up. It's one of our major winter projects, raising money for it. We're giving all the proceeds of the hat show to it. What do you say? I bet you look super in hats."

"I hardly ever wear them."

"Oh, come on. It'll be fun!"

"I'd love to, Kelly, but I just don't think I can find the time."

Kelly pouts prettily. Overgrown boys with money, aging adolescent girls with families and social responsibilities: Where does Brooke fit into this scheme?

After dinner, when the men light up cigars and put their heads together about something (she has never gotten used to seeing Harry smoke a cigar, which is just beginning to shed its working-class associations as it's being adopted by the middle classes), Kelly asks her again about the hat show. Well, she is in too good a mood right now, with her belly full of sole Oscar, in the afterglow of her meeting with Robert, and she knows it. But she relents. Slightly, it is true, and not wholeheartedly, but relents nevertheless. "I guess it might be fun."

"You'll do it?"

"Sure. Why not."

"Great!" Kelly claps her hands in girlish glee. She has brought off a major coup: she has recruited Brooke McGuire. "It'll be soooo much fun," she says. "You won't believe it. Now listen: We're having our first meeting tomorrow night. I know it's short notice—

but can you make it? I really think you should."

"Oh," says Brooke, "tomorrow—I don't know. I don't think so. I have—"

"What's going on tomorrow?" says Harry, who would pick this moment to tune into her conversation.

"We're having a meeting of the models for our winter hat show, and your wife"—she rests a hand on Brooke's forearm, an unpleasantly possessive gesture—"is going to be one of the models."

"Mmm," says Harry, mid-puff, big stogie stuck in his face. He flashes his eyes, nods his approval.

"It's going to mean a lot to us," Kelly says.

Brooke smiles weakly. She is already sorry she has become part of this.

"I don't mind telling you, we've wanted to get you involved for a long time," Kelly says.

"I know."

"You're quite a feather in my cap."

Harry puts an arm around his wife and kisses her cheek. His breath stinks of panatela. "That's my girl," he says.

"The first meeting is eight o'clock tomorrow night at my house," Kelly tells her. "Don't be late!"

"Tomorrow night will be good," Harry says on the way home. "I'll be late at the bar again."

"How unusual."

Amazing, how concerned he can be when he wants to. He has urged her to become a part of something like this for a while, not because he feels strongly about their goals, but because he has long wanted her to be a part of something more than just her work and his family.

"Actually, I do have something for tomorrow night. I have an appointment to talk about a freelance job."

"Oh yeah? I thought you weren't taking them anymore. Who's it with?"

"Robert Fitzgerald, actually."

"Robert Fitzgerald? My client Robert Fitzgerald?"

"The very one."

"What kind of a freelance job does he want you to do? I don't understand."

"He wants me to do some design consultation for him."

"Hold the phone, Brooke. What the hell kind of joke is this? This guy is *my* client. Why on earth would he want to talk to you? And why would you want to talk to him?"

"I asked him why he didn't have you do what he wants, Harry. He said he didn't want to work with an agency on this. It's a personal job."

"That's a scream," Harry says. "My client doesn't want an advertising agency, so he hires my wife. That's screamy."

"Harry," says Brooke lightly, "you can't have all the jobs in town, you know. Some people might want something an ad agency can't give them."

"Yeah? Like what?"

"Like me. He likes my magazine work."

"Oh, that's great. My client likes your magazine work so he hires *you*."

"Harry, please. You're being unreasonable about this."

"I don't think I'm being unreasonable at all. In fact, I think I'm being particularly reasonable. I think it's a reasonable question to ask why my wife is doing a freelance design job for *my* client. Don't you realize you're in competition with me?"

"It's not for the hospital. That's your client. The job I'm going to do is for the editor of a professional journal who wants a new look for his publication. And I'm a publication designer, and nobody on your staff is."

"I guess I thought you were a consultant for my staff."

"Harry, he saw my stuff when he was over the other night, and he thinks I can do a good job for him. That's all. I'm not stealing your client. Or food out of our mouths. This is something completely different from your job."

Harry drives on in silence.

By the time he turns into their driveway he has regained his composure. He now sees the benefits that will reflect back upon him by this turn of events, he explains to her as they get ready for bed. Between himself and his wife he now has a complete lock on this client. Whatever Fitzgerald wants now, sooner or later he will want more than Brooke can give him. And sooner or later, the work at the hospital will grow, too. Harry knows that work makes more work. Besides, he likes the idea that after his shop, his wife is the next best choice for art work in this town.

The more he thinks about this, the more his vanity is tickled.

"Anyway," Brooke says, "that's why I can't make Kelly's meeting tomorrow night. I have a client meeting."

"That's an acceptable excuse," Harry allows. "I guess I should know that better than anyone."

4

Brooke expects Robert's office to be deserted when she appears for their meeting and is surprised when it isn't. She has not realized that he works in an inpatient unit staffed around the clock until she gets there at seven-thirty and finds a nurse on duty at the nurses' station across from a meeting room where a group session is taking place. A dozen or so people sit around tables. At the table nearest the door, people listen closely to one woman, a drawn middle-aged housewife-type, describe her pattern of drinking. Brooke hears only a snippet of it and is reminded of her mother, whose problem isn't drinking but who is nevertheless impacting the entire family.

The nurse asks her business and writes out a visitor's pass and directs her toward the end of the hall. Brooke walks by rooms with numbingly boring draperies, industrial strength beige carpeting, and sparse particle board budget motel furnishings. Can people really recover from alcoholism in such a depressing environment?

Through the open doorway to his office, she sees Robert Fitzgerald sitting at a PC. His office is as small as one of the patient rooms and outfitted as sparsely, with a desk piled high with folders, two chairs, a worktable with the computer, and a steel file cabinet. On his wall is a poster with that prayer about serenity and acceptance.

He looks up when she knocks on the door frame. He is wearing a wrinkled white cotton shirt and a gray wool tie undone at his neck. His hair is tousled with gray highlights and he has an end-of-the-day stubble. There are black semicircles under his eyes behind Ben Franklin glasses halfway down his nose.

He brightens at the sight of her. "Hi."

"Hi."

"Welcome to my cubby-hole. Come in. He stands. They shake hands.

"It's so small! Don't you get claustrophobic?"

"Claustrophobia clinic's down the hall," he says. She rewards his wit with a smile.

She takes off her coat, folds it carefully over the back of the only other chair in the tiny room, and sits down. She has brought a large portfolio with her. She is wearing a silky royal blue print dress with a high collar and pearls at her neck. She wears opalescent stockings. Her legs are strong and shapely and right under his nose in this tiny space. He tries not to stare.

"I do have a view," he says. He nods toward the window behind his computer workstation. He tosses his glasses on the rubble on his desk and parts the drapes. "At certain times of the day." Nothing in the night outside is visible. The window throws back their reflections.

"That's important," she says.

"Of course, it looks out on a parking lot. When you can see out of it. Uninspiring, maybe. But good enough for me. My needs are small. Any trouble getting away?"

"No, my husband's used to me having client meetings. Or used to be. I haven't done any freelance work in a while. I did have a last-minute engagement, but I'll survive without it."

"Good. So where do we start?"

She opens her portfolio. "I brought some samples of different kinds of publications I've done."

He thumbs through the plastic sheets of her binder quickly, unfolding some of the larger pieces. She is better even than he thought. "These are wonderful," he says.

"Thank you."

Another smile. Her lips glisten with dusky rose lipstick under his fluorescents. He looks through the portfolio, acutely conscious of her scent, tart and light and perfectly suited to her.

"You're very talented."

"Thank you."

"You ought to go into business for yourself."

"I was, once."

"What happened?"

"The job at the insurance company opened up and I had wanted to be someplace where I had access to more resources."

"Well, I hope they appreciate you there."

"I'm not sure they do. But thanks."

He tells her what he has in mind: not only the redesign of the journal, but brochures, journal ads, flyers for conferences. He is actually quite sophisticated in this area for someone not in the field. Listening to him, she can see where he might not be as cowed by Harry's confident line of bullshit as some around town. The engineering types were particularly susceptible, proud that they understood few things apart from their incredibly obscure technical knowledge, especially something as trivial as advertising.

He has budgets and printing requests for past issues, but not, as he had thought, the issues themselves. They must be back home somewhere, he says. For close to an hour they go over the budgets and his ideas, and conclude by deciding she will go ahead and work up a design. He will get her the copy after he chooses it with his steering committee. First he will get her some recent back issues so she can get a sense of the amount of material they use, and how far they can push the design. Then she will call him when her stuff is ready and they will meet again. She assures him she is a fast worker.

Though they have spoken of nothing other than the job that is immediately before them, Robert feels they are as sympatico as if they have just agreed upon everything in a much wider-ranging conversation. He walks her out of the unit, then down the elevator to the entrance. He fills her in on what his association does and stands for, then what his plans for his unit are. Then their discussion opens up to include Harry's current limited competition in the advertising field in town, the advantages and disadvantages of the town itself, and, finally, the weather, using it as a transition not into the conversation, as ice-breaker, but out of it, the strategy seized upon by both of them at once, it seems, to give her a means of exiting gracefully from a conversation that could go on and on. After a half-hour more of talk standing by the front doors, they hit on this as a practical way to get her to button her coat and get going. Which, clearly, neither of them particularly wants to happen. The weather is too cold to allow him to walk her to the parking lot in his shirtsleeves, which he would certainly do if he didn't think he would catch pneumonia (pee-nomia, his daughter the reader used to call it, when he was still around) while they stood outside her car continuing their talk.

Talk, talk. On her way home, she is surprised she found it so easy to talk to him, and that she had so much to say. With Harry, with Joyce, with her other acquaintances, talk is difficult, a process that requires her first of all to pierce through the layer of gauze that sometimes seems to surround her, which is perhaps harder than actually making conversation. She is used to keeping herself in, receiving more information from the outside world than she sends. This is a conscious choice she made years ago; that way, she figured, when she started to go crazy no one would notice. As someone with hereditary coronary disease becomes an exercise fanatic to confound fate, Brooke hopes in her own way to keep herself appearing sane for more years than her mother could.

Brooke is dozing in bed when Harry comes home from the bar. He undresses and slips his furry smell under the covers beside her.

He presses against her until she stirs.

"How was your client meeting?"

"Mmm. Good."

"Did you find out what he wants you to do?" She explains what he needs.

"And for that he didn't want an agency? Doesn't he know I used to be an editor on a trade organ on Madison Avenue?"

"Guess not."

"Did you tell him?"

"He didn't ask about you. I told you, he doesn't want to go with an agency."

"No problem," Harry says, settling in, pressing his cold knees against the back of her warm legs. "One way or the other, he's going to get the best in town."

Robert sits by himself in the darkened living room. Upstairs all is quiet in his housemates' rooms, except for Gene's snoring. Outside the weather is changing; a harsh wind slams against the back of the house, sending periodic shivers through the old structure.

His mood surprises him. When Brooke McGuire left and he closed up his office and came home to the House of Grins, he was exhilarated at the connection they had made. The meeting went as well as it could have; she seemed comfortable with him and they chatted back and forth like friends who had known each other for years. But thinking back on her as he lay in bed, sleepless and staring at the ceiling, his mood darkened. Together they were copacetic. This could turn into something; this could be serious. Was that really what he wanted? To be drawn back into the messy, helter-skelter world of emotional entanglement?

And if it was—and he suspected it *was* something he wanted with this woman—was that what *she* wanted? No longer could Robert enter into another woman's life simply because he wanted to; now he realized the implications of it, and realized that the woman herself had to want it, too, and he had to grant her equivalent center of self. Not like the old days when he could overwhelm someone like Maureen, she of the couchus-interruptus episode. Catherine Keane and Andrea had taught him that: it wasn't all about what he wanted; no longer could he blithely toy with other people; sometimes other people, and life itself, bit back.

After the exhilaration of the aftermath of his meeting with Brooke, he felt the contrary urge to take a step back and consider this situation more seriously.

CHAPTER NINE

1

Friday the town wakes to the season's first serious snowfall. It is a heavy, wet snow that Gene Anderson says Robert better get used to. Blown in by the winds of the previous night, it falls gravely and clings to the bare branches of the lilac bush outside the kitchen window and piles up three inches high on the back steps. Robert and his housemates stand in the kitchen before going their separate ways to work, looking out the window at the grim, damp, iron-gray day that has not so much dawned as grown less dark. "But it's only October," Robert protests.

"Welcome to winter," Martina says. "It's going to be like this until May."

Robert is edgy. The kitchen is well-lit, and his household is together to greet this new development in their communal lives, this change of season; snow brings us together, somehow, where rain drives us apart. But the sound of the plows scraping the streets already grates his nerves.

Today is the day he said he would call Debby Saunders. In the old days, when he had a chance with an attractive, willing woman, he would have gone to any lengths to see her. But this is a different, older Robert, one who doesn't get around much anymore, and doesn't even want to. In fact, not counting the time he has spent with Brooke McGuire, this will be his first real date since the whole thing with Catherine. Now, watching the fat flakes of snow falling, still in the grip of the agitation of the night before, he is not so enthusiastic.

Still, he said he would call her, and does, from the office later on. He even gets up for the task, moderately, by telling himself that she is earthy and available, and maybe she would take his mind off of Brooke McGuire. And he did say he would call her . . .

Duty is the last refuge of—well, of Robert, anymore.

"Shall we do it up right?" Debby asks. "Dinner and movie?"

"Actually," Robert says, determined to enjoy himself now that he has committed his night to her, "I've never been to the Cider Mill Playhouse. Have you?"

"Yes. It's wonderful."

"Have you seen the thing that's on now? *The Cherry Orchard*?"

"No, but I'm up for it if you are."

They go through all the motions. He picks her up at her condo in a new development on a hill in the town of Vestal, as suburb of Buckingham. She keeps him waiting in her living room, which is decorated in glass and chrome and white leather, while she finishes getting herself pink and perfumed. She fusses with the flowers he has brought. They have dinner at Moko's, a restaurant on the Vestal Parkway with the largest salad bar and the worst decor Robert has ever seen. He pours over the huge menu for signs of Brooke McGuire's handiwork, which he finds after Debby tells him that Moko's and T. Moneybags are owned by the same man, a local underworld type named Vito. The menus are as ugly as the ones at T. Moneybags, but because this is a finer restaurant (meaning the prices are higher and the portions smaller), the ugliness is on an even grander, more meretricious scale.

The play is put on inside a converted barn that houses both a small thrust stage and a cider mill and bakery. The production is sweetly redolent of apples, passable and pleasant, the work of the local university's Theatre Department augmented by some especially hammy locals. After the sound of the axe dies away at play's end and the actors have milked their third curtain call, Debby and Robert stop off at a bar that features late-night live music (eleven o'clock considered late night for their age group in this town), a dim cave where a group of what look like young computer engineers from IBM play loud and mediocre fusion.

He takes her home to her condo and she invites him in for a nightcap. He sees all the moves laid out like the transcription of a chess match . . . the trail of clothes through the unit to her bedroom, her powerful body twisting and thrashing under him, pressing against her afterwards, clinging to the faint sour odor of perspiration under her perfume, the acrid cigarette smoke from the bar in her hair under the strawberry smell of shampoo, rolling out of her bed in the middle of the night . . .

"Thanks," he says, "but no."

She stares at him. "I thought we had a good time tonight?"

"We did. But I'm going to have to leave it here."

She continues to stare at him as though she can't believe anyone would turn down what she's offering him. Finally she breaks away and gets out of the car. She slams the door on this night, on him, and on the evening she had planned.

The drive home over icy streets clears his head. He goes carefully down Vestal Parkway, over the bridge on the Susquehanna River, and around the rolling curves of Riverside Drive to his neighborhood on the west side of town. He breathes heavily, fogging the car windows, proud of his virtue at turning down the woman's full and fragrant body. Gradually the vessel of his thoughts fills up not with the woman he has just left, but the last woman he slept with. Catherine Keane. Almost two years ago it was. The last time they made love was the night before Andrea died. Her little daughter.

His thoughts are pricked with the needles of sadness, of love lost forever, of his powerlessness in the family tragedy he tried to take part in and the accompanying rage of his own unmet needs, the primary one of which was to join their family unit. Catherine denied him the possibility. Tonight he drives along on the empty roads in the clear cold darkness knowing that this is really what has caused him so much anxiety about seeing Debby Saunders, and why he turned her down . . . because in the sex with her he knew would ensue, he would be brought back to that Victorian farmhouse outside Seattle, to the damp weather that has been very like what he's found here so far. To his last happy night with Catherine. The next day would be Andrea's last. From Catherine's bed to the space-age equipment of an ICU, to the brutish yellow cemetery backhoe, all within the space of four days. His relationship died with Andrea; they buried it in her casket. He had seen death before but still couldn't believe that little girl would never open her eyes, wouldn't jump laughing out of the coffin, and they would all have the picnic she had been cheated out of by the grotesque accident that sprang, ironically, from her mother's love for her.

Instead they planted her in the ground that day under a ton of wet black earth. There goes Andrea. And Catherine. And, incidentally, Robert too. Funny, the day they buried her was so sunny, after so much rain. Even the weather mocked them.

And now he was almost back—to the celebration of physical love, at least. From there it would be a journey up the spinal column to something more. But Debby Saunders is not the woman he wants to make that trip with. Now, freed by the hour and his sense of being alone on the planet and his need to hold himself in check, he admits that the woman whom he wants as company for that journey is Brooke McGuire—who, at this moment, he imagines lying in bed beside her husband, deep in sleep, smothered by the proximity of Harry's heavy body, and of all the comforts of her perfect life. Robert sees the bed Brooke lies in not as a source of life and joy and pleasure, but, like Andrea's final place, as a dark box to which Brooke is chained by bonds of love. Though unlike Andrea, Brooke has a way out of her imprisonment. He can help her pull herself out of her casket. If she wants to come.

2

At the bottom of McGuire Marshall Concepts' letterhead, in small print, are listed the cities where the company has branch offices. They are not the major capitals of the world: Greene, New York; Erie, Pennsylvania; Towanda, Pennsylvania; Phillipsburg, New Jersey. In these out-of-the-way spots are the light electronics assemblers and plumbing supply manufacturers and makers of high-tech industrial widgets and pressboard doors and paneling that comprise much of Harry's work, in addition to the IBM and GE jobbers that he handles in his home town. It is to these cities and villages he travels every few weeks to service his accounts, gained through luck and old boy contacts and kept through the political maneuverings of his clients and the hard, slavish work of his staff. Turnover in his agency is high. Young people are continually joining and then leaving his employ after they discover the work is too hard and the pay too paltry while Harry himself wears five-hundred-dollar suits and drives a Seville. Well, Harry tries to keep them happy, but good help in this business is so easy to find that he makes no bones about his shop being a revolving door for designers and copywriters. The university in particular is an excellent source of untried talent who work for McGuire Marshall Concepts for a year or two and then move on. Harry believes he is providing the industry with a necessary service, an advertising farm team of sorts.

What he really loves to do, though, is sweep into these small and smaller towns in his suits and his car and proceed to wine and dine the locals and leave them open-mouthed at his ideas. Because Harry believes he is a great idea man, and great at "making face" with the clients, as client meetings are called. He makes them feel important by appearing important himself. Advertising is a funny business.

At the beginning of their marriage, Harry and Brooke were hardly ever separated. He worked as assistant director of the marketing department of a fork lift manufacturer and kept regular hours. After he started his own business, she grew used to his periodic trips, which rarely lasted more than two days. He stayed overnight in Holiday Inns, which he then considered his local branch offices. Hence the names at the bottom of his stationery. Not world capitals, maybe, but good enough to make him an extremely prosperous man. For this stage of his life, anyway. World capitals would come later.

Just now his partner John sticks his big head into his office doorway. "Fitzgerald just pulled up outside."

"Take him into the conference room and wait there with him. I'll be right in."

Harry gets his thoughts together. Things are not going as well as they should with this client. Fitzgerald seems to need a special kind of touch. He is no dummy, nor is he very friendly. Harry had thought he would be able to melt him a little, what with those invitations to the bar and to his house and his blatant attempts at friendship, including introducing him to Debby Saunders. So far nothing's worked. Harry is not used to failure. He has no doubt he will get Fitzgerald's number sooner or later, though for the time being Harry is uncharacteristically off-balance.

In the conference room John is blabbing away about something in that loud voice of his that Harry automatically tunes out. Fitzgerald sits silently, unamused. "Hello," Harry says. His hand is out and his face is smiling. "Good to see you."

Robert returns the shake. "Got some good stuff for me?" he asks without preliminaries.

On the felt showcase at the front of the room, Harry has already tacked his boards, covered with white paper. Harry likes to reveal things gradually, dramatically. It helps create a narrative in the client meeting, which builds tension, suspense, and the client's sense that something rather significant is going on here.

"This is what we put together," Harry says. He had a whole line for this guy, including a little reference to Brooke. Now he cans it and goes right for the throat.

"What we wanted to do," Harry says, "is work with the concept of helping and caring."

"Right," says Robert, "which is exactly what I asked you to do. Harry, I appreciate the buildup, but I'm running kind of late. And if you don't mind, I'd like to take these back to the hospital and look them over when I have the time."

"Well," Harry says, "we just wanted to walk you through how we arrived at what we're going to show you."

"And I'm sure it would be wonderful and enlightening. But I have conferences waiting for me and a full meeting schedule, and I more or less told you what I wanted in the first place. So if we could get this show on the road?"

"It won't take ten minutes."

"I don't have ten minutes today."

When Harry makes no move to take the boards down, Robert stands—stands! In the middle of Harry's show!—and begins taking the tacks out of them himself.

Harry steps in. "Why don't you wait a minute," he says, testily, "and let me help you with these before we do some damage here."

"Do you have a folder or something I can put them in? I was expecting a little smaller format."

"We'll find you one," Harry says. He quickly recovers his cool. "John, get something to put these in, will you?"

John lumbers off to find a folder. "I'll get them back tomorrow with my comments," says Robert.

"Take your time."

"I don't have any time to take. I need these in the field, Harry. I thought I made my urgency clear. I'm getting a lot of pressure to get this going."

"I know, but I'm going to be out of town for a couple of days on business. So you may as well keep them till Friday."

"Can't your artists get started on them tomorrow if I bring them back?"

"I usually go over the specs with the client before I give it to the Art Department. Just to head off any misunderstandings."

"What about John?"

"John doesn't do this kind of thing."

"So you're telling me you can't get started on these till Friday?"

"I advise you to wait."

John returns with a large portfolio of the kind that Brooke brought to Robert's office.

"Tell you what," Robert says, "I'll bring them back tomorrow so your artists can get started *thinking* about what I want, and I'll talk to you when you get back in town. How does that sound?"

"I'm comfortable with that," Harry says, though he isn't really but wants to keep the peace with this touchy guy.

Robert pauses at the door. "Where are you going? Anyplace fun?"

"I'm making a swing of some clients. Down through Pennsylvania and New Jersey."

"And you'll be away till Friday?"

"Yes."

Robert nods. "Leaving tomorrow?"

"First thing in the morning."

"I'll be in touch."

That night Robert takes a long walk around the snow-covered neighborhood, up and down the undulating sidewalks in a thoughtful saunter past the stately homes with their inviting front porches. He gazes into their brightly lit picture windows like proscenia into the happy plays of his neighbors' lives. The details accumulate as though on one large set created to illustrate happy family life, with shovels and sleds propped against porch railings, sepia and full-color family photos lining the old hand-carved mantelpieces inside, cases crammed with books in the living rooms, Moms and Pops reading in deep cushy chairs by the fires, Juniors and Sisses crossing in front of the windows on their way to the kitchens offstage for late snacks, staircases leading up to the intimate secrets of the second floors in one house after another, street after street. Robert zig-zags over the entire area, tramping in his duck boots over icy walks through the resin smell of wood stoves in the crisp air, and it is the same on every street, small town America buttoned up for the winter night. They remind him of his memories from his own neighborhood as a boy, his own home, sometimes, these scenes infused with what could pass for the family warmth that politicians and advertisers insist is the basis for the nation's values, shining out like the yellow light that cuts through the early evening winter darkness.

Yet where are the disobedient children, the raging fathers? Robert, walking along by himself, not being a fool, knows they are hidden, the troubles that live deep within the hearts of these people's lives. The alcohol abuse striking statistically every tenth adult. The drugs, depression, and despair. The frustrations and fury, many of these problems as it happens arising from people's sense that their lives do not measure up to the ideal as perceived by strangers walking past. Robert takes care of these people in his business, his therapist colleagues care for them in theirs. Happy families are a freak of nature.

No, he is not taken in by the scenes he strolls past, but he is still attracted, seduced even, by the promise they hold out to him of stability, of being part of the human effort to satisfy the need for help and support and company and a place to belong. These are strong drives, learned early and thwarted later. But they hang on. They have brought, he knows, the House of Grins into being. And the House is okay, it's cool, it's working. But it's not enough. Maybe he just needs different people living it. But there is this woman who has been intruded into his life now, this Brooke McGuire person, who seems to hold out to him what is missing in the House, the possibility of personal connection with someone else that is the concrete symbol of being part of something larger than ourselves. Yeah, yeah, she does have a husband. But his close encounter with Debby Saunders has, ironically, reopened a door for him, and against that he has the opportunity to pursue Brooke, to act out his desire for contact, to touch and be touched. And he is, as he tells his clients about their own situations, conflicted. To pursue her or not. Impelling him is her attraction, his needs; restraining him is her situation and, more importantly (his respect for Harry being what it is) the futility of giving in to these needs, learned the hard way through experience that has shown love doesn't work.

Which is the stronger pull?

As he walks along, solitary, needing so much more than he has, than his experiment with the House has thus far been able to give him, than the broken families he tries to help in his work give him, aware of his gaps, he knows that whatever he decides intellectually, he will not be able to resist the possibility of an emotional connection with this woman. He knows himself too well after all these years, and even though he understands beforehand that nothing good will come from this (probably: there is always the miniscule chance), he also knows that he has to try.

3

The next morning, Robert Fitzgerald calls Brooke. He wants to talk a few things over with her. "Your office again?" she asks.

"Actually, I have a late meeting tonight over on your side of town. If it isn't too much trouble, I could stop over your place afterwards."

"That would be fine," she says. "Harry's out of town, so we wouldn't disturb him."

"Ah. What luck."

She smiles when she sees him standing under the porchlight. It seems a bright, open expression of joy at seeing him. He has come to associate it with her, unforced and genuine. It is easy to smile back at her.

"I brought some back issues for you," he says.

"Great. Let's take a look." She stands aside for him to enter and leads him into the living room. He follows the sweet curve of her bottom in tight unfaded blue Levis. This is, he realizes, the first time he has seen her in casual clothes, when she is not at work or being her husband's wife entertaining the client. She is just herself in a pair of jeans and a red and white striped cotton top. She has eased off the public makeup, just a bit of lipstick and mascara, and her hair is casually tied back from her face. Robert likes her better. Robert likes her a lot. Robert watches her lips smile.

She spreads the issues out on the marble octagonal top of her coffee table, three late editions of the journal, each one uglier than the one before, and settles herself on the sofa. The room is as immaculate as it was the night of her party, but does not, as then, smell of food. There is only the lemony-oil tang of furniture polish from the thin wood framed chairs and sofa. A rust and blue oriental rug on the floor draws the pieces together and contrasts pleasantly with the abstract paintings and lithos, some bearing her signature, in silver frames on the walls. Tables are filled with wooden carvings of elephants and giraffes. The entire effect is tasteful and elegant, like the woman herself.

She goes through the samples he has brought, quickly and professionally holding each up, judging its heft, running the paper between thumb and forefinger, evaluating the typestyles and layouts. Her jade green eyes narrow in judgment.

"Are these bad, or what?" he says.

"I've seen worse."

"And you've done better."

"You flatter me too much," she says without looking at him. In profile her features without the makeup are finely etched.

"I don't think so," he says.

She pulls a sketch pad onto her knees and uncaps a black felt-tip. She fires off a few ideas for a cover, a table of contents, a sample inside page, then shakes her head and tosses the pad on the sofa beside her. "Have to work on these for a while."

"How do you go about it, usually?"

"Like this," she says. "Making sketches, trying ideas out. Until something hits me. Then it turns into a process of revision."

"Like some people think aloud. Except you think with a pen in your hand."

"I know some designers who plan out everything in advance. And I mean everything. The first time they put pen to paper is the last time."

"Doesn't seem like that would leave room for any spontaneity."

"I've seen their work. It looks great. Though it's not a way of working I could do."

"You know how you work best. Isn't that more important than having a finished product right off the bat?"

"I think so."

"My father was a sign painter," says Robert. "Which is a kind of designer."

"Sure. Did he specialize in anything?"

"Screen process printing."

"I've always been fascinated with that."

"This was in Detroit. He did a lot of work for the car companies."

"He must have been busy."

"Oh, he was busy, all right."

"Why do you say it that way?"

"My father," Robert says, "was a piece of work."

"I have one of those," she murmurs.

They sit in strained silence. "Would you like some coffee?" she asks.

"I'd love some."

He follows her out to the kitchen. "I like the paintings in the living room."

"Oh, thanks. The ones of mine are old. The others out there I bought at art shows here in town. Most of them are by Benjamin Artaud. Do you know his work? He runs a frame shop downtown. I think he's really talented. He shows in New York more often than he does up here. He's not that interested in this market. Which is why I snap his stuff up when I see it around. It's about a third of what you'd pay in New York."

"Do you get down there a lot?"

"Couple times a year. Not as much as I'd like. It's hard to get away."

"I hear that."

"I don't have much in the way of food to offer you," she says. "I was going to go shopping while Harry was away. Haven't had a chance yet."

"No problem. I ate earlier."

She prepares the coffee in a tall silver percolator, pouring the boiling water through a paper cone filter that fits like a jester's cap atop the carafe. When it is ready, they stand drinking their coffee in the kitchen, she with her back to the sink, he leaning against the counter at her side. Behind him are pine cabinets finished a soft brown. Overhead is a Victorian ceiling fan, all paddles and curlicues. "Nice kitchen," he says.

"Thanks. You should have seen it before we had it done over."

"Who did it?"

"Al Kolata. He's a builder. Good friend of Harry's."

"I know the name."

"He's very good. He's done a lot of work in this area. Do you live here in town?"

"On the west side." He explains his living arrangements.

"You all live together?" she asks in fascination.

"Sure."

"But how does it work? Aren't you all at each other's throats all the time?"

"No. Works just fine. We respect each other's privacy and space."

He flashes on Dennis listening to Martina and Max screwing away on her squeaky bed, on Gene compulsively stacking cartons in the garage. "Most of the time."

"But what happens if you want to have company?" She is imagining a different scene, Robert and Debby Saunders screwing like bunnies on a different squeaky bed in what she imagines to be Robert's room. It is bare and masculine, without the softening touch of a woman, not counting Debby's underthings strewn around.

"No problem. We all have our own rooms, and we can all use the common rooms downstairs whenever we want."

"But what if you want to have someone over? Isn't it really awkward? For everyone?"

"I haven't run into that problem myself," he says. "Though there's a woman in the house who has her friend over all the time, and that gives one of the guys a real problem. I think he's more embarrassed than put out, but still. We have to work that out."

"Just one big happy family."

"You got it."

"Never have a problem bringing women home, eh?" she says playfully.

"Nope."

"So what do you do with all your girlfriends? Go to their places?"

"I don't have any girlfriends," he says with a virtuous hand on his chest.

"Oh, right."

"It's true. Newcomer in town kind of thing."

"What about a certain social worker of our acquaintance?"

"Debby Saunders? I wouldn't call her a girlfriend."

"What would you call her?"

"A friend. Hardly a girlfriend."

"Right."

"You don't believe me?"

"Listen," she says, "I saw the way she was looking at you the night you had dinner here. She was eyeing you like you were dessert."

"Well," he says, "I've seen her since, it's true."

"And you probably talked about great literature all evening."

"As a matter of fact, we saw *The Cherry Orchard* at the Cider Mill Playhouse."

"Uh-huh. Is that what you kids are calling it these days?"

"It's true. We had a nice time, but I doubt I'll see her again."

"You don't have to explain to me."

"Anyway, she's not where my heart lies."

"Where does your heart lie?"

The question surprises them both—she for having let it slip out, he for the challenge it poses.

In the second before answering, he calculates the risk of honesty, decides he does not know her well enough, nor is their connection far enough along to justify it.

He opts instead to further things along with irony. "My heart doesn't lie," he says with a crafty smile.

They share a look, which she cuts short. Before she turns her glance away and sends it into the corner as though in punishment for her thoughts, in her deep green eyes he sees the growing awareness that things are close to getting out of hand here.

He decides to up the ante. "Men my age aren't supposed to get crushes. But I think you'd be very surprised if you knew who's in my thoughts most of the time lately."

"Who?" she says before she can stop herself, but she knows the answer already, he can see that in her eyes too, and now she physically turns away before he can say what she doesn't know if she wants to hear. She splashes the coffee left in her cup into the sink and rinses the cup out and sets it in the sink.

"Want any more?" she asks without looking at him.

"No. Thanks. I still have some here. Listen," he says, "I feel like we're developing a connection. I'd like to see you."

"You're seeing me."

"I mean I'd like you to have dinner with me tomorrow night."

"I teach my class tomorrow night," she says. She is surprised at herself for saying this instead of explaining that she doesn't think it would be a good idea. This tells her something.

"Afterwards."

"It'll be too late."

"Then before."

"I don't think it would be a good idea," she says.

"It's only dinner. You have to eat."

She catches his eye again, and is hooked. He's right, it's perfectly innocent. Suddenly she can't think of a reason to refuse.

"All right."

He places his cup on the counter. "Good. I'll call you tomorrow. We'll set up a time and place."

"Okay."

"I'll leave those back issues for you to look at."

There is a long, scary moment when she fears he is going to put his arms around her, at the same time as she hopes he does. He doesn't. Instead, he raises a hand and is gone.

She remains in the kitchen. "This floor is really dirty," she says to the empty house.

She gets out the mop and floor cleaner and scrubs the blue and tan ceramic tiles until they shine. She'll have to say something about this to her housekeepers.

The next day he calls her a little before noon.

The ringing of the phone breaks the spell she has been living within since the night before, a spell marked more by confusion than anything else. She awakens that morning convinced that she should not see him. She wants to see him; what she does not know is how to see him. She is widely known in this town. There is nowhere she can go in public with this man and not risk running into someone she knows, and more to the point someone who knows Harry, except maybe the town's lone punk-gay bar downtown in the middle of the night. Harry knows everybody. The episode with Lee in the bar is still bright in her mind as an example of what will happen to her; you never know who will be lurking behind you. And while it could easily be explained away as an innocent get-together, just like their business lunch the other day, and her meeting with him at his office after hours, and his coming over last night (even this short list already seems suspicious to guilty Brooke), in her heart she knows that innocence no longer has much to do with this whole thing.

No, by morning the relentless logic of her situation convinces her that she should not see him.

But when he calls, his voice slices through her obscured desires and confused conscience, and (once again, where this particular man is concerned) sweeps her careful logic away. "I had a thought," he says. "Why don't you come for dinner at my house after your class? That way you can see my living arrangements for yourself and draw your own conclusions."

"Oh," she says, stunned at the simplicity of this solution, unable to believe something so obvious could work. But what if his housemates know Harry? How will they explain this? What phony-baloney reason can they possibly cook up for her dining at his house that doesn't make it seem as bad as she thinks it is?

How can they possibly know Harry, she wonders. Then again, how can they not?

"I'll make the dinner," he continues.

"What about the people you live with? Won't they be there?"

"If they are, they can eat too. I told you, it's a casual arrangement."

This seems to take the edge off of what she believes they are embarking on. They will be chaperoned.

She agrees. As she knew she was going to all along, regardless of the arrangements. And she is very excited.

4

The house is warm and inviting with the sweet odors of grapes. "Welcome to the House of Grins," he says, and ushers her inside.

"The house of what?"

"Grins. One of my housemates named it that. Grins. You know, as in good times? Happiness? Did you see that face outside above the door? It's marvelous. Look at it on the way out. May I take Madam's wrap?"

He takes the navy wool poncho Harry bought her at Bloomingdale's on their last trip together to New York. He shuts it up in the closet where it can fling no recriminations at her for what she is doing. She notes with distress there are no curtains on any of the windows. Their get-together is open to the world. Automatically she tries to remember if they know anyone who lives around here and can come up with no one, which does not ease her mind. Harry has friends everywhere. They will jog by the house. They will be driving by and have a flat tire and ring Robert's doorbell for help. They will be collecting house-to-house for a fund drive for muscular dystrophy and catch her here.

He walks her through the downstairs, pointing out work he has done, wood he stripped, wallpaper put up, replastering finished. He describes his plans for breaking through walls, adding skylights, and so on. Grandiose plans that he will probably never get to. Short-range plans and long-term goals. Her surprise at how nice this place is gradually displaces her nervousness. Once when she visited a friend at college, she was appalled by how dirty the house was where the friend lived with five or six others: filthy clothes everywhere, dishes piled high in the sink, even graffiti on the walls. This was what she had in mind for Robert's house. Here, though, things are actually quite elegant. These are not students. Robert is not a young man. His taste is really quite fine, with sand-colored paint on the walls and dramatic iridescent rich peacock-tail-shaped half-moon wallpaper in the dining room.

"Everybody's out," he says, "or I'd introduce you to them. Everybody but Dennis, and he's in his room. I respect his privacy."

"That's thoughtful." So much for being chaperoned. "I wanted to meet them."

"Next time, maybe." The tension that marked their last moments together last night, which had given way to the developing intimacy that comes from seeing where he lives, now returns.

"How was your class?" he asks when they are seated at the dining room table. He has waiting for them two place settings on woven mats in one corner of the large table, a plank of apples and Bosc pears and Jarlsberg to start, beside a bottle of Evian.

"Good," she says. "It's a lot of fun. We only have three meetings left. I'll be sorry to see it end."

"How did you wind up doing it? Try some cheese." He cuts her a wedge of apple and a sliver of Jarlsberg. She is not used to being waited on.

"Thanks. I heard about the opening, and applied. I'd been wanting to do something like this for a long time. I had thought about teaching a course in design at the Arts and Crafts Center, but when this opened up, I jumped at the chance."

She leaves out the labyrinthine story of Harry's involvement in getting her the job: how the managing director of the symphony plays racquetball with Harry; how he happened to bring as his guest one day last August the dean of liberal arts at the community college, who (by way of joining the conversation about the vicissitudes of life that the symphony director began with a story about a cellist who had died of cancer, leaving a hole in the orchestra that had become difficult to fill) let drop in the locker room that a car accident had just put one of his art teachers out of commission for the upcoming semester; how Harry volunteered Brooke as a replacement; how she was accepted on the spot.

"Will you teach it again next semester?" Robert asks.

"Next semester they're offering the next course in the sequence. I asked them to consider me for it, but I won't find out if that class makes until just before the semester starts."

"If it 'makes'?"

"Teacher talk," she says. "If it draws enough students."

Over the chicken and grapes he has prepared, they talk of the joys and failings of teaching, of his dislike for school until he started college after the army, of his work, of his profession's jargon. Small talk. Their real communication takes place subverbally, in the increasing length of time their eyes connect, in the easy laughter that passes between them, in the smiles the other prompts, in the small taps of their fingers on the backs of the other's hands and arms that initially make points but then take on a life of their own and begin to happen for their own sakes as the awareness grows between them that being in the other's company is a pleasurable thing.

It is only after coffee, when his housemates begin drifting in, that reality intrudes. Martina comes in looking pert and in control and pleasantly surprised that Robert has a lady friend in for dinner. Gene shuffles in looking worn out and dazed. They exchange greetings with Brooke, comment on how good the food must have been if the smells are any indication, and disappear upstairs. No one mentions Harry.

The thought of Harry intrudes on their time together and gets her antsy again. He's not home, but what if he calls her and she's not there? She'll have to invent a story for him . . .

"Look what time it is," Brooke says. "After eleven. Gotta go."

She picks up the dishes at her place and takes them into the kitchen. "No," he says, "please. Leave it. I'll take care of all this."

"It's the least I can do, considering the feast you put on."

"It was a pleasure. Please. Don't."

"It's been so long since I ate a meal without cooking it beforehand, I wouldn't know how to leave the plates alone." She rinses the dishes and puts them in the dishwasher while he clears the rest of the table. In truth, there is not much to do. Most of the dirty dishes and pans came from the preparation of the meal, which he cleaned up before she came.

When he places her poncho around her shoulders, she feels as if he were wrapping her up in her old life—until he lets his hands linger on her shoulders, which she allows him to do as she ties her belt around her. She turns to face him in the front hall and his hands drop to his sides, then crawl into his pockets.

"I can't tell you how impressed I am by all this," she says. "The house, the meal, everything."

"I'm glad you liked it."

"How did you learn to cook like that?"

"I never made that dish before in my life."

"No."

"It's true. I just pulled a recipe out of *The Joy of Cooking* and decided to try it on you."

"Showing a reckless disregard for the welfare of your guest."

"Actually," he says, "my regard for you is filled with reck."

At once the hyperawkwardness of the night before returns. Brooke decides this is her cue to go—but before she can turn, he stays her with a hand on her arm. "Don't go yet." His touch nails her to the floor. "I want to talk to you for a second." She says nothing.

"I'm glad we're getting to know each other," he says.

She can bring herself to say only, "Thank you."

He takes a step closer and moves his hands to her shoulders. The moment she has been dreading. She gathers the courage to look him in the eye and shakes her head in a vague attempt to dissuade him from whatever is coming. He moves even closer, and she allows herself to be taken into his arms, and tips her head for the kiss that she knows is on the way. This is why she came here, isn't it?

And it comes. It is light and fast, no soul kiss but no cheerful friendly goodbye peck either. A warmup to something bigger. Much bigger: bigger than she can handle, as she realizes in a panic.

But he places a hand on her cheek and it calms her. She leans her head into it, and they kiss again, longer. The kiss takes her breath away.

They stand there with their arms around each other. He roots through her hair with his nose.

"Robert," she says.

"Mmm?"

"This is not a good idea."

"It can be."

"I've never done anything like this before."

"I know."

He kisses her again and she melts into him. Despite what she has told him, she thinks, I can do this very easily.

"It's going to be all right," he says. "All we have to do is go with it and it'll be fine."

She does not respond.

"Do you want to leave?" he asks.

"I don't know what I want."

"Then I guess you should go."

At once she is struck by the pang of loss. What, lost him already? Has she, with her inexperience, driven away already exactly what she wants and needs? Has she said and done the wrong things yet again in her life? "Robert, I'm sorry," she says. "I don't know what to do. I just don't know."

"It's all right," he says. "We'll talk later."

"I need some time to think. To get used to the idea of this."

"You need more than time," he says. "You need someone who appreciates you. And you don't have that in your life right now. And you know you don't. And you know I have it for you."

This time it is she who throws her arms around him and kisses him. Then she turns away and sweeps out the door and is gone.

5

How easy it is, after all. As easy as meeting him for dinner at one of the diners on the Parkway the next night, as easy as inviting him back to her empty house for coffee, as easy as kissing him again, long and deeply, as easy as drifting up the stairs to her room (not knowing who made the first move, if either of them did, or else they headed in that direction with two minds joined by a single thought), as easy as letting him remove her clothing and then removing his own, as easy as pressing his body against hers and feeling his kisses on her breasts, her arms, her belly, her legs, and finally letting him enter her, opening her body to him and feeling him slide further and further in as smoothly as if he belonged there this whole time, as if he were finally where he was supposed to be, this strange man, home at last. He is slender where Harry is thick, bone and sinew where Harry is muscle, silent where Harry is loud. He is fast where Harry is slow, choppy and thrusting where Harry is silken and long, over where Harry goes on and on. But he is in her and on her and with her while Harry is not, and she is with him, moving and squeezing and holding and tightening and remembering the boys she used to do this with in college when she was wild, not knowing them even as well as she knows this man and not caring for them at all, and not even knowing how much she cares for this one. And finally she is releasing all the accumulated tension of years, first in rhythmical spasms and then in a rush that leaves her calling out in surprise. Immediately afterwards she feels him stir atop her, moving back and forth and tensing and shivering, and she comes again with deep, deep shudders.

Afterwards they lie in each other's arms, their former lives washed away, residing now in a place where things are much more important than they once were.

"I guess this was a good idea after all," she whispers.

"I guess it was."

"My situation . . ."

He doesn't reply, and he doesn't stay. After a while he leaves her in bed and silently steps into his clothing. She watches his body disappear, its glow of skin covered with textures, buttons, zippers. Before he goes, he leans over the disheveled bed to kiss her goodbye. It is, she knows, the last kiss she will have from him. This must never happen again.

He holds her close to him. She smells what they have done; the odor clings to her skin, her sheets.

She gives him time enough to get home, then finds his number from directory assistance and calls his house. The phone rings several times before he answers. "I was hoping you'd pick it up," she says.

"I just got in."

"I just wanted to say good night."

"Good night."

"That was nice," she says.

"I know."

She debates the appropriateness of telling him this must never happen again, decides against it.

"Talk to you tomorrow?" he says.

"Sure."

"You okay?"

"I think so," she says, but knows she isn't.

Welcome back, he thinks. Welcome back to the world of the flesh, to ripeness and surging body fluids. And love's decay. And the mocking isolation in its aftermath. And there is always an aftermath, no matter how lively that familiar world of wet warmth.

But until that happens, we celebrate each other, Robert thinks. What else have we got? If we can't help each other fulfill needs that we equally can't ignore, what can we do for each other? Catherine came to that place where she could neither help nor be helped, and look what happened to her. To us.

Catherine, Catherine. Lying in bed in his own room, staring into darkness, he reaches back to Catherine to tell her he is almost healed. He has been afraid that he had left too much of himself with her, and with her daughter Andrea in the grave. But what had been lost has been restored, almost, and he has now started something else with someone new. Which will undoubtedly leave him as unhappy and dissatisfied as what he had with Catherine. But at least he is back, starting to open again, like a flower, the petals of a peony foaming out. After its hard shell is eaten away by ants.

Of course, all this is happening because he is with another man's wife. But if marriage is a barrier to emotional fulfillment and honesty, should it serve to keep two people apart who could enrich each other's lives otherwise? Even if only for a short time? His marriage never did. Not that his playing around ever had anything to do with emotional fulfillment. Or honesty, for that matter.

A tide of emotion passes over him, catches him up in some liquid sadness that leaves him awash and teary in remembered feeling, losses recollected from years ago, from last year, from earlier this evening. Oh God. He tries to plug it all up again by pressing the heels of his hands to his eyes in the darkness until false fireworks fill his night vision. Finally the tears dry up and he is left with a stuffed up and tingling nose. What have I done to myself this time?

For most of the night, or what remains of it, alone in her own bed Brooke can only lie awake and stare at the ceiling. When she does finally doze off towards dawn, she awakes in a cold sweat. Her dreams of suffocation have returned.

In the morning she changes the sheets and Robert's smell is gone forever.

6

She tells her secretary that she does not want to take any calls all day from anyone except her husband. Who does not call.

Robert calls. He does not get through.

When she gets home after work, she grabs the cordless phone in the living room and before she even changes clothes does what she has been thinking about doing all day: calls him. She tries the clinic first. He is still there.

"Hi," he says. "I tried to get you today, but they told me you weren't available."

"I know. I wasn't taking calls. But I got your message."

"How are you?"

"Not so good."

After a long pause, he says, "I'm sorry to hear that."

"I know."

"I want to see you."

"No."

"We should talk."

"We don't have anything to talk about."

"I think we do. Are you home now?"

"No," she lies. "Anyway, I don't want to see you."

"It's important," he says. "For both of us."

"No, it isn't. Not for me."

She begins to weep. Ever the counselor, he says, "This is very hard for you, I know."

"It is!" she shouts.

The first time he has heard her raise her voice, it surprises him.

"This is harder than anything I've ever done."

"Go slow."

"No. I know myself. I know I can't handle this right now. I feel horrible for Harry. I've betrayed him."

"You haven't done anything to Harry. Nothing happened that you should feel badly for Harry about. It's yourself you should be concerned with."

"Please don't make this any harder than it is. I'm just not built for this. I thought I was, but I'm not."

Her tears come freely now and she is angry with herself that she is losing control over herself because of this man, this stranger whom she barely knows, who has shared her body.

"All right," he says. "If you can't, you can't. But listen: I think what happened last night was important for us both. And it may have been hard for you, but it was worth it. It was hard for me too, and I'm sure it was worth it. And if you decide you want more of what I have to offer you, I'll be here for you. All you have to do is ask and I'm here."

"I won't ask," she says miserably, and hangs up.

She collapses on the sofa, drained of all her animal energy. It is only with the greatest of efforts that she is able to jump up when her stomach gathers itself and begins to rise burning in her throat. She rushes through the kitchen and into the half bath and vomits what feels like the entire contents of her body, guts, inner organs, blood, everything, out into the toilet in a horrible, painful cascade.

When she is finished, sweating and groaning, she props herself against the vanity and stares down into the foul-smelling curds of vomit. Jesus. Does she feel bad.

In a while she is able to clean herself up. She returns to the sofa and lies down with her arm thrown across her eyes. The phone rings. She does not answer it. It is probably Robert Fitzgerald with another line for her. After the fourth ring, the machine in the den picks up the call.

It's from Harry. He says he is coming home tomorrow.

7

Well, that was fast.

Robert sits in the kitchen in the dark with an empty cup in front of him. He meant to put some water on for tea, but somewhere between the intention and the action he lost his purpose.

Martina comes in. "Troubles?" she asks.

"Some."

"Whoa. If you say you have 'some' troubles, there must be some kind of shit hitting the fan somewhere."

"A momentary indisposition."

"Mind if I turn a light on?"

"Be my guest."

She flicks the switch several times. "What's going on?"

"The bulb blew. I didn't have the energy to change it."

"That's what's got you down, the bulb blew?"

"That's it," he says.

"All you have to do to fix it is change the bulb. You'll feel better right away."

"Why didn't I think of that?"

"Men can be so helpless."

She searches under the sink for the bulbs. "How are you doing?" he asks.

"Not much better than you seem, to tell you the truth."

"Well, that cheers me up considerably. At least you hide it better than I do."

"That's just because I can change a goddam light bulb. Don't we have any bulbs?"

"Somewhere."

"This place is going to hell in a handbasket."

"Everybody's a critic."

She finally finds a box of new bulbs and pushes a chair over to stand on. "Careful," he says.

"Don't get up."

"I wasn't going to." He watches her remove the ceiling fixture, screw in the bulb. "This reminds me of an old joke. How many certified alcoholism counselors does it take to screw in a light bulb?"

"Spare me." She steps off the chair and washes a layer of dead bugs out of the ceiling globe at the sink.

"You know," she says when she is finished, "if you want to talk ever, feel free to knock on my door."

"I will. Thanks."

"I won't open it, of course. I'll be too busy fucking like a bunny. But feel free to knock anyway."

"I'll be okay."

"Really?"

"Yeah. Takes more than this to get me down."

"Could have fooled me."

"I'll be okay. Eventually."

"Let me know if I can do anything. Oh, before I forget. Message for you on the machine. Somebody named Debby. She the cause of all this?"

"Not hardly."

"The young lady you were entertaining recently?"

"On the nose."

"Would you like to know the sum total of my knowledge of people and relationships? I don't share this with everybody, but you look like you need to hear it."

"I'm all ears."

"It's knowledge I've gleaned over the years, and it stands me in better stead every day. Ready?"

"The suspense is killing me."

"People can only give you what they have to give. If you're looking for something more, you're SOL."

"Wow. That's heavy."

"I'm serious. You keep that in mind and you'll never go wrong."

"And here I thought you were such a happy chick, with old Max and all."

"Let's just say I've learned that knowledge the hard way. And I live it every day."

"Thank you really a lot for sharing it with me."

"Go to hell," she says, and pats him on the shoulder.

"Yeah, might be a nice change. Heaven is such a drag."

CHAPTER TEN

1

Gene Anderson's ex-wife Leslie swings the door open to his ex-house and a shiver goes down his back. He recognizes the grim look on her face, the set of her boney jaw, the thin lips pressed together, the withering eye, all boding a shitload of unpleasantness, which, knowing her as well as he does, he braces himself to have wash over him.

And it does, before he even sets foot inside. "Do you know what your son did today?" she demands.

"No."

"I didn't do nothing," comes Jason's raw adolescent voice from the living room.

Leslie zooms around the corner, a missile homing in on his denial. "I picked you up at the police station, Jason."

Gene follows her. In the small living room, Jason sits forward on the sofa with his hands between his knees. His greasy hair hangs long over his eyes, which are vague and unfocused.

"Tell your father what happened," Leslie says. She stands by the fireplace with her thin arms crossed over her chest. "Go on. Tell him."

"I don't have to tell him nothing."

"Will somebody please tell me something?" Gene's own voice rises as his anger threatens to skitter out of control. Can't he even pick up his son for an evening out without walking into a scene? "Jason? What's this all about?"

"Nothing."

"Oh, for chrissake. What the hell is going on"

"Your son was arrested today."

"Stop calling him *'my* son.'" Gene sits beside the boy, who ignores him. "Jas, what's this all about? Would you please tell me?"

Jason refuses to say anything.

Leslie says, "I got a call from the police at my office this afternoon. Seems this young man was picked up for speeding today. In my car. Which I left parked in the lot outside my office."

"He took your car without permission?"

"And got caught by the police. They held him at the station until I could come down and pick him up after work. I tried calling you, but of course you were no place to be found."

To his son, Gene says, "What do you have to say about this?"

"I don't have nothing to say about it."

"Why did you take your mother's car? You're only fifteen. You don't even have your license yet."

"I wanted to use it."

"But why?"

"I wanted to go for a ride."

"I figured that out for myself, Jason. My question is why you did something you knew was wrong."

To this, Jason snorts. He looks in fury off to the far side of the room.

"Jason? I'm talking to you."

Jason snorts again. "Ain't the first time I took it."

Leslie darts forward and pulls the boy to his feet by his arms. She shakes him and pushes him toward the stairway. "Go to your room!" He lets himself be pushed part of the way across the living room before loping up the steps two at a time under his own power.

"And stay there until you learn how to act!" she shouts after him.

"Did you see his eyes?" Leslie asks. "Can't you tell he's on something?"

"Like what?"

"I've been finding bongs and roach clips in his room over the last couple weeks. Who knows what else he's doing?"

"Since when?"

"Since the semester began."

"Have you talked with him?"

"Does he look like somebody you could have a reasonable conversation with?"

"Maybe not the way he is now. But I can talk with him later, I'm sure."

"Right. Gene the hero."

"No, I can. I'll take him out and we'll have a man-to-man talk."

"Oh, great. Who are you going to get to be the man?"

"I'm not going to get in a fight with you about this."

"Good, because you're not going to take him out, either."

"But this is my night."

"This is a crisis, in case you haven't noticed. He's grounded. He's not going out of the house."

"How can you ground him on the one night a week I have to see him?"

"If you want to see him, go upstairs and spend some time with him in his room. You don't always have to take him out and play the sugar daddy."

"I resent this. Goddammit, I resent this so much. I have the right to take my son out to dinner if I want to."

"He's my day-to-day responsibility, and I make the decisions as far as his activities are concerned. And based on what he's done today, I decided he's not going out of the house, and that's the decision I expect you to respect."

"I swear to God, Leslie."

"Oh, you swear to God," she shouts. "Maybe if you took some responsibility for disciplining this boy instead of sweeping in here like a prince every week, he wouldn't act this way."

"So this is my fault?"

"It sure isn't my fault. I never taught him to do things like this."

"And I did?"

"I don't know what you teach him. I know I'm not the one who used drugs in this house."

"I never used drugs, so don't pin that on me. Did you ever stop to think he may have picked them up at school?"

"No, Gene, I never stop to think about anything! I'm just your ignorant ex-wife, remember?"

He goes up the stairs. He knocks on Jason's door. When there is no response, he turns the knob and pokes his head inside the room. The lights are off. The air is foul with the smell of sweat socks. Posters of androgynous rock stars in spandex and lipstick fill the walls. They pose with guitars pointing up like outlandish phalluses. "Okay if I come in?" he asks.

Jason is lying on his bed facing the wall.

"Jas?" Gene says softly.

When he realizes his son will not acknowledge him, he closes the door softly and goes lightly down the stairs. He will talk with him some other time. Jason is in no mood to go out with the old man tonight anyway.

His ex is in the kitchen, banging pots and pans as she gets dinner ready.

"Well?" she says sharply. "Did you straighten him out?"

"He was asleep," he lies. "I didn't want to wake him. We'll make it up another time. I'll speak with him then."

"Asleep?" She glares at him. "Asleep or passed out?"

"I don't want you blaming me for this. This kind of behavior is not that unusual for an adolescent boy today. So what should we do about this?"

"What should *we* do? I dunno, Gene, what should *we* do? I thought you were going to save him."

"I just meant we might want to get him some counseling."

"Are you going to arrange it?"

"I can."

"Are you going to pay for it? Because my insurance only pays twenty dollars for mental health visits, and I can't afford to make up the difference week after week. And as we know, you don't have any insurance, even though you're supposed to be responsible for his medical bills. So unless you get one of your buddies at the hospital to give him some counseling for free, I don't know where he's going to get any."

"I'll see what I can do."

"Yeah. You do that."

With great relief he leaves the house and drives away from his ex-wife, son, house, and all their problems. This hasn't worked out quite right. He was supposed to forge on ahead of them, sail away from personal confusion and pain, from his family's bourgeoise concerns like insurance and property and domestic squabbles. And yet here they are threatening to capsize the tiny, spunky craft of his new life, his wife and son's anger and frustrations battering his own aspirations for himself. This former husband, former full-time father, former homeowner, former minister, former member of the conventional classes. Current seeker after freedom and truth and the life of the consciousness-expanded spirit.

Gene has a hard time working up any anger against his son

because the boy may be chasing what Gene himself is after. Jason just doesn't know how to do it, yet.

But then of course, neither does Gene.

2

"Mmm," says Max Masterson.

With tongs Martina places a chicken breast that is rusty with paprika beside the steaming microwaved baked potato and pale succotash on his plate. She has cooked this meal for Max and his two daughters. They sit around the kitchen table at Max's barren townhouse apartment. "My favorite," he says.

"Daddy," says Liz, the younger, "I'm sick of chicken. We have this like every night."

"Mother is like never home to cook anything else any more," says Deirdre.

"Don't talk that way about your mother," Max says.

"What's on this chicken," Deirdre asks.

"Paprika," Martina says.

"It's gross. It looks like dried blood," Deirdre says. This elicits a gale of laughter from Liz. Max lifts a cautionary fork in his large fist and shakes it at his daughters. "Watch it. I'm going to knock you two out, you don't behave."

"Oh Daddy," Deirdre says, "you're wicked funny."

"Not trying to be funny, young lady."

Martina sits in her chair at the opposite end of the table from Max and tears into the crispy skin of the chicken to reveal the steaming white meat underneath. "Martina," says Deirdre, "will you drive me to the library tonight?" She does not bother asking her father, whom she knows beforehand will say no.

"I don't want you kids bothering Martina," Max says. "First you insult her cooking, then you ask her favors. Who taught you kids manners?"

"You did," Liz says.

"Well," Martina begins. She would have preferred that he said nothing and let her handle it, but . . . "I have a meeting at the hospital tonight, but I can drop you off on the way."

"I have to get ready," Deirdre says, and jumps up from the table.

"Just a minute, young lady," says her father. "You come back here and finish your dinner."

"I am finished," Deirdre calls back. "I have to get my homework together."

"Can I have her piece?" Liz asks.

"Finish your own first," Max says sourly to the one still young enough to remain under his control.

Martina bites her tongue. She hates it when he pulls this shit. This is how he thinks fathers should behave, like bullies. She hopes it isn't how he thinks husbands should behave, too. He can be so old-fashioned, the big dope.

They eat in silence. When Liz finishes her meal, she decides that she does not want her sister's uneaten portion after all, and she too disappears upstairs.

"These kids," Max says. "They're like wild animals."

"They're just kids. Don't you remember how you were?"

"Girls were different when I was a kid."

"You ask me, it's a change for the better."

"I don't see it. Girls should be refined. And what about you?"

"What about me?"

"You're spending a lot of extra time at the hospital lately, aren't you?"

"I have a lot of meetings. Lydia left, you know. There's a lot more work for everybody."

"You have to do her work on top of your own?"

"Some of it. Some they're giving to Larry."

"How much longer is this going to last?"

"Till they hire somebody to replace her. Which is going to be soon, I hope." She has told him she has applied for Lydia's job, but it does not seem to have penetrated.

"Who's your meeting with tonight?"

"Nobody. I'm behind on a lot of reports and I don't have time to finish them during the days."

"What time will you be done?"

"Nine-thirty, maybe. Ten o'clock."

He takes a sip from the glass of water he has at each meal. He insists they all drink water, but the girls bring their Cokes to the table anyway. "I hope you don't burn yourself out on this job," he says. Translation: I hope you're planning on being home to cook my dinners once we're married.

She gets up to clear the table, pausing to plant a kiss on his receding hairline. "There, there," she says. "I won't desert you."

"Better not," he says. "I'll knock you out, too."

After she drops Deirdre off at the library—and in the rearview mirror watches her run down the steps and off to meet her friends—Martina continues on to the hospital. A note is waiting for her on her desk. It's from Dr. Gerard. *See me as soon as you get back.*

She has not had much to do with Gerard since their last meeting where he assaulted her. As far as she can see, nothing has basically changed in her prospects. If anything, Larry Kowalski has become even more obnoxious and insufferable, leading Martina to fear that he knows something she doesn't. Which angers her: that's usually what he wants people to think. Can he possibly know about her? Would Gerard have spilled to Larry what happened between them?

She dismisses that thought as too horrible to contemplate.

Gerard is still in his office. He glares at her over the top of his reading glasses. "Martina." His voice is as cold as his eyes.

"You wanted to see me?"

"Come in. Shut the door."

She does as he orders. She sits in the chair opposite him. He finishes a note he is making on a legal pad and pulls his half-glasses off and tosses them onto the desk. "Going over the notes for my next show," he says, rubbing his eyes. He does a five-minute weekly segment on a local news broadcast where he covers topical health related subjects such as treating heat exhaustion in the summer and frostbite in the winter. He likes to think of himself as one of the town's media stars, this homely little frigid man with bad skin and worse teeth.

"What's this one on?"

"Proper conditioning for winter sports."

"Sounds timely."

"I'm taping it tonight. The segment'll air next week. They're down in PT, setting up now. So I don't have long to chat."

"Okay." She feels as though a test she had to take in school has been postponed because the teacher called in sick.

He gets up and comes around to her side of the desk. She wants to shrink from his touch on her arm, but holds herself firm in her chair.

He takes his prescription pad out of his lab coat and dashes off a word and a number. He tears the page off and hands it to her.

"What's this?" she says. "I can't make this word out."

"It says Ramada. Room 215. Here—let me add something else."

He takes the sheet back and writes *12 noon* under the motel name.

She looks at him quizzically.

"Meet me in room 215 of the Ramada Inn tomorrow at noon," he says.

"I can't." She is appalled at the thought of carrying this on in broad daylight. Fending him off at night after hours is one thing; at noon in the middle of her business day makes this part of her real life. "I have meetings. I have patients."

"Put them all aside for an hour and meet me there. It's all arranged already. It'll be a mini-vacation for us both. If you want to remain the leading candidate for Lydia's job," he adds.

He stands and gathers his notes together from this side of the desk. "Have to go," he says with a gruesome little smile. "My public is waiting."

He is gone before she can protest, complain, or voice her profound regret that she has started along this terrible path.

3

Dennis Parker lingers at his desk until big, balding Baumgartner, that boob, sails past Jackie with his usual "Goodnight, sweetheart. Don't do anything I wouldn't do to you." Then Dennis wanders out with a contact report in his hands and asks her, "Oh, the big guy left already?

Thinks, O you are just too devious for words.

"Just left," she says.

"Damn."

"He'll be in first thing in the morning. Can it wait?"

"Guess it'll have to."

"Got something important?"

"No. I'll catch him tomorrow."

"Okay, then."

"How are you doing?"

"Good, and you?"

"Same."

"Great," she says brightly. "Whatcha got planned tonight, anything?"

"No," he says, "just going home and chilling."

"Sounds good to me. I'm wicked tired, myself."

"Busy day?"

"Sort of. Lot of new orders to type up."

But none from Dennis.

"I was wondering," Dennis says, "if you'd like to stop for a beer or something on your way home?"

"Dennis," she says, "I'd love a beer."

While waiting for her to get ready, his heart pounding, terrified he will not know what to say to her, he draws up a list of things to talk about. With shaking hands, he writes on the back of a phone message slip:

1. Where she went to school

2. How long she's worked here

3. What she likes to do outside of work

4. What she wants to do with her life

He folds it up and sticks it in his shirt pocket for surreptitious reference.

She tells him she knows of a bar near the office, and they stop there. It is small and smoky, with aged dusty decorations, Christmas and Halloween, hanging sadly on the walls. A knot of old men sit gathered around the elderly bartender at the bar, while young males in tight jeans and plaid shirts shoot pool and laugh. Heads turn when Jackie walks in. She blithely ignores them. Life is so good, so easy for attractive women; they sail through it like exotic birds.

They sit at a metal luncheonette table in an empty adjoining room. Boisterous shouts from the pool game disturb their peace.

Dennis imagines them mocking him.

"Interesting place," he says.

"I been here a couple times with my friends. It's not much to look at, but the drinks are cheap and nobody rushes you."

She is right about the drinks: ninety cents for a couple of beers, which taste watered down.

"So," she says before he needs to work into his questions. "How've you been?"

Dennis is almost too tongue-tied at the thought of being out with her to reply. He sputters about how badly things are going for him on the job, trying to strike a note of self-deprecation that sounds to himself as whiney. But from that point on he is mostly a bystander anyway as she carries on her own conversation. She talks about Baumgartner, about hating to work around a man who chain smokes, about wanting to look for another job, about jobs she has had in the past (waitress, hairdresser, light electronics assembler, secretary for a kitchen cabinet store), about her mother who works as an LPN at Buckingham General Hospital, about her father who divorced her mother when he fell in love with his own secretary in the small construction company he co-owned, about her consequent strict rules against going out with married men or men who say they are separated, about the difficulties of making it on your own as a single girl living by yourself, about her former boyfriend who was a goalie for the local minor league hockey team, the Whalers, about this, about that . . .

Well, to be frank, after a while Dennis—grateful though he is for not having to draw on his poor social skills to keep up his end of the conversation—kind of spaces out. He concentrates instead on her eyes, great round gray orbs that smile constantly and convey the most wonderful sense of loopy vulnerability as she looks at him while rambling on. He examines them down to the mascara caked on the tips of her lashes and the charming slate-colored circles that surround each iris, and presses even these small details into his memory for later use. Prattle on: it's okay with this boy. He is too happy just to bask in her company, just to wallow (imaginatively) in her hair, to gaze upon her glossy, newly-painted lips and know that she has put on makeup specifically for him. What could be better? Nothing. Except maybe banging her brains out in some sordid motel room somewhere while she screams herself hoarse in primal cries of unrestrained passion in his ear. That could perhaps be better than this, but this is a great start.

Drunk on her, intoxicated by her citrus female smell, Dennis also has a bit too much to drink on an empty stomach. But he holds it well, and the beer is watered anyway, and he doesn't do anything to scandalize her, or himself.

Before he can even wonder with his befuddled judgment whether he should try to make another date with her, she is up and gone in a limey cloud, pulling him in her wake and, turning and giving him a big smile (which he makes a mental snapshot of for all perpetuity, and which is noticed and appreciated by the young rogue males in the poolroom), flounces to her car and drives off. Leaving him behind. His head spins.

This is just the beginning, he tells himself on the careful drive home. Before you can run you have to walk, and before you can walk you have to crawl. This here is crawling.

Well, boy, he tells himself, slightly looped, in the mirror in his room back at the House of Grins, where only Robert is home, spearing some takeout chicken and cashews with chopsticks down in the dining room, you have just started to crawl. She seemed to have a good time, and you know you had a good time. This broke the ice. Next week (he decides with snockered bravado), you are going to ask her out to dinner. That's right—you're going to make some excuses to stop off at the office during the day and talk to her, and during the course of your conversation you're going to casually ask her if she'd like to have dinner with you some night. And you'll make a date with her to have dinner together. Then, maybe, if all the signs are propitious, maybe you can make a stronger pass at her. And then if she accepts that—his mind works up their relationship into a flow chart of events—you can play some serious Hide the Salami with her. Trying to be sharp and scientific even though he is mostly dulled by the beer and his disbelief that any of this has actually happened tonight, he imagines a relationship with her on into the rosy future.

Because that's what it is now, he thinks: a relationship. You have a relationship with this tasty little number. No more masturbatory fantasies for you. Soon it'll be the real thing.

Well, not so fast. There will definitely be more masturbatory fantasies on tap, but there is also the real thing to anticipate.

He is too wired to sleep. He lies awake inventing reasons for her to spurn him. As if the cat could read his mind, Howard crouches, grinning, on his chest.

CHAPTER ELEVEN

1

As if to shield her from the turmoil of the unexpected, unwanted emotions set loose by the whole episode with Robert Fitzgerald, the events of Brooke McGuire's life crowd upon her in November.

On election day Harry's candidate wins as county executive, as everyone knew he would. This takes up a great deal of time and attention and discussion at her work, where her unit's director is the winner's campaign manager. The Republican landslide that sweeps Reagan into his second term as president is barely noticed in the general euphoria over the local election. In the week before Election Day, Harry's agency must prepare last-minute newspaper and radio ads, most of the creative work for which his staff does but which Harry shuttles back and forth to the client's campaign office with great urgency. The night of the election is the victory party, to which Harry and Brooke are grudgingly invited and then treated as hired help. Which, strictly speaking, is all Harry really was.

Immediately following this, before Thanksgiving, The Great White Way of Lights Festival kicks off the long holiday season. The buildings on Main Street downtown are festooned with lights that will remain on through March (creating a rather ghostly effect at night after New Year's, when the blazing lights strung up and down the sides and across the tops of buildings will illuminate only deserted streets). Mayor Schultz, Six-Pack Jimmy, launches the Festival at a lighting-up ceremony in front of City Hall, which continues as the gala Great White Way of Lights Festival Ball at the nearby Holiday Inn. Attending are the political and business luminaries of the area, including Harry, who here plays an important role as spokesman for the Chamber of Commerce. The mayor makes a civic booster speech, various others, including Harry, say a few words, and the evening is given over to dancers and merrymakers. Including Harry, who has a great time. After the ball almost everyone (it seems) jams into Harry and Mike's for a nightcap.

To her distress, Brooke finds herself scanning faces in the crowds for Robert Fitzgerald. Or more accurately to make sure that he is not where she is. She does not find him, of course, because he would neither be invited to nor attend this kind of thing, as she secretly suspects. Still, she looks for him compulsively, and does not know what she would do on the off-chance she were to find him.

After The Great White Way of Lights Festival comes the Many Lands Market, when the American Civic Association sponsors a huge holiday sale of odds and ends from the variety of ethnic groups who live in town, the old reliables from eastern and western Europe who came years ago to work in the shoe factories, as well as the more recently burgeoning population of refugees from southeast Asia. This too occupies much of Brooke's attention, since the insurance company is a key donor and she must work many hours of overtime preparing artwork.

Also filling her time are a large antique show at the armory put on by the Junior League, on which she works without actually joining up; a quick weekend trip to New York City with Harry to reap some of the rewards of his latest deal with his stock-tipper friend Jay; and Thanksgiving, which Brooke spends at Harry's parents' with Michael and Joyce and Maggie.

It is, then, a full month that allows Brooke to plunge back completely into the stuff of her life. She does not hear from Robert, and though she knows she should get in touch with him sooner or later about the design project he has commissioned to her, she can't bring herself to speak with him. Surely he'll understand and find someone else for the project. She comes to see him as a malevolent intruder who tried to woo her away from the comforting and insulating life that she has created around herself, that she is not willing to change. Thinking about him angers her, particularly at his presumption in trying to come between her and her husband and their life and the barriers against the craziness of her family heritage that she has so carefully and successfully erected for herself. She is even able to convince herself that nothing significant passed between them that night they spent together.

With the beginning of December comes the Christmas Tree Festival at the Arts and Crafts Center, which is the traditional start of the season's house and office parties. Brooke and Harry are invited to hundreds, it seems, and attend at least a dozen each week of the month, party-hopping from one house to another on Friday and Saturday nights and all day on Sundays. They go to their friends' houses, to Harry's business contacts, to her office associates. It is wearying. How much mulled cider can she stand? How many hors d'oeuvres? How many Christmas cookies before things get blurry and seasonal cheer turns to bloat?

She reaches her limit early on. Her mood is not helped by the news from India that penetrates her bubble: toxic gas from an industrial accident in a place called Bhopal that kills 2,000 people and injures 150,000. One hundred fifty thousand people—three times the population of her town! Already depressed, she can barely cope with the thought of human suffering on such a horrific scale. She develops an upset stomach during one party that turns into a roaring case of the flu that knocks her out the week before Christmas. It coincides with her period, always a difficult time of the month, and keeps her from going up to Rochester to be with her family on the holiday. On Christmas Eve, she is still too weak even to go to midnight mass with Harry and his parents and his brother's family. She stays home by herself, in bed.

That night on the news she sees Robert Fitzgerald on television, in a feature on avoiding overindulging in alcohol during the holiday season. It makes her feel worse.

She ends the year exhausted, ten pounds lighter, and in a state of depression that grabs hold with the tenacity of a tick. Confining herself to an easy chair at the Kolatas' party on a bone-rattlingly cold New Year's Eve, unable to bring herself to toast the new year with anything stronger than Perrier, Brooke stares disconsolately at the bubbling lights on the Kolatas' gay Christmas tree and yearns for spring.

2

Which will come late, as always.

So Robert Fitzgerald is told. And once it gets here it will only last about a week, everyone at the hospital is more than happy to let him know, and won't show up anyway until just before Memorial Day. The locals take pride in the drabness of their weather.

It has been a long winter of freezing, snowy days landlocked in a frozen valley. Never an outdoorsman, he fills his time away from work with projects around the house. His attempts to celebrate the holidays as a household fall flat; the others have plans for Thanksgiving and he winds up eating the turkey that Debby Saunders cooks for him at her condo instead of cooking a meal himself with the others at his house, which is what he really hoped for. He buys a Christmas tree that Gene and Martina do decorate with him, but they spend their Christmas and New Year's outside the house, as does Dennis, who visits his family for both holidays and returns to his room both times in a stuporous depression. As they said they would be, Robert's children are too busy either to come visit him or to make time if he comes to them. He stays home.

Instead, outside the house he focuses on work, with patients, patients' problems, patients' families, and crazy, stupid fights about resources with the executive vice president, who is now more concerned with, as he says, "running lean," than with expanding Robert's clinic's services. Fawcett has vetoed all of Robert's staff requests, halved his supply budget for next year, and seriously cut back on money appropriated for the campaign to boost the program's census. From the havoc Fawcett wreaks on every other program throughout the hospital, Robert comforts himself that it's not personal.

As it turns out, Harry McGuire is seriously screwing up the development of the ad campaign anyway. Robert is furious with him. It now looks as if things won't get off the ground until summer at the earliest. Which will be, of course, too late to have any real effect. Now they'll have to wait until next fall to begin if it's to have any chance at being effective. Not until then will people be around to read the ads, hear the radio messages, thumb through the brochures that will go out in the mail. By then people will be getting back from their vacations and start resuming their lives, with all the problems they thought the summer would fix. Then, too, maybe in the fall Fawcett will come back to supporting the clinic. Or move on to a new job.

Thus far the problems with the campaign have come from Harry McGuire's inability to listen to Robert's directions. Harry has his own ideas about how the campaign should be shaped, how the copy should read, how the designs should appear. They are not good ideas. Robert has his ideas, too, and while they may not be good ideas either, he knows his business better than Harry. And besides, he's the Client, and has the right to insist on how he wants his job to look. I want the ugliest menus in town!

At every argument with Harry, Robert recalls his lunch with Brooke at T. Moneybags and grows sad, which causes his relationship with the woman's husband to deteriorate further. During February, with the short gray days of winter beginning to lengthen, traveling around the slushy streets of town or the bleak gray and brown snowscape of the valley on long drives to clear his mind, Robert wonders if his days of passion, of emotional connectedness and excitement, may really all be behind him, left back in Detroit and Seattle and points in between, including Brooke's bed on Sweethaven. Of course nothing will ever match the high drama of his relationship with Catherine and its aftermath; he is getting too old to abide it. Yet has he become too cynical in his ability to see the end of things already intrinsic in their beginnings? Is he too inured to the futility of passion to enjoy it while it lasts? So he fears. Winter is a hard season this year.

He hasn't talked with Brooke since that night on the phone. He has written off her contribution to his journal, of course, and feels no urge to call her about it (though he does need back the material he gave her) despite her being so often in the front of his thoughts.

He believes the circles of this small town will turn soon enough to bring them back together to finish what they had started, if this is what they were meant to do.

Till then, over the course of the long winter he hibernates, works on the house by himself mostly, and with his housemates only when he can manage to get them all together at the same time and cajole them into working. This in itself is a feat. They get along well, all of them, even Dennis and Martina now. But they do not cohere as he had once hoped they would. They are four people who live together, cordial with each other, even friendly, but not supportive, nor particularly interested in each other or Robert's great project, the House of Grins. Which from Thanksgiving through the Presidents' birthdays becomes more like an island of mutually independent people than a true community of the kind he had in mind. They keep each other company when they're around, but there is no mutuality, nor does anyone besides Robert seem to want it.

So he makes the kitchen, the heart of the home, his personal project, and replaces the cabinets himself, and the counters, sink, and floor with only intermittent help from the others. Nobody helps with the wallpapering, but he loves the task so he doesn't mind doing it alone. It is all good therapy; the results are tangible.

CHAPTER TWELVE

1

Harry's own machinations bring his wife and Robert back together.

He conceives the first part of the idea that will unite them after dessert at the American Heart Association dinner at the new Sheraton downtown at the end of February. The dinner is winding down, the self-congratulatory speeches are finished, and he is sitting back in his chair, relaxing with his legs crossed at the ankles and wishing he could enjoy an after-dinner cigar (too heart-unhealthy; no smoking here tonight). He talks with Jim Overmiller, the local marketing director for Marine Midland Bank, another young man of Harry's generation, buoyed by a cheerful, brittle wife and the eternally youthful sense of being open to life's possibilities.

"What have you been doing with yourself, you old character?" Jim says. He is well on his way to being drunk. His features melt away from the sharp point of his nose. He sits sideways in his chair, the bowtie of his tuxedo askew. "Haven't seen you at the Y, guy."

"I've been busy," says Harry.

"What with?"

"The business. The bar. Other things going on."

Jim nods seriously. This making a manly living is nothing to sneeze at. "Irons in the fire. Same with me and Christine. Too busy. We never even see old friends anymore."

Harry agrees with a thoughtful pull on his cigar.

"We should get together," Jim insists. "Maybe I'll talk to Christine, eh? We'll have you over? That'll be fun, won't it?"

"Sounds like fun to me."

Jim pulls himself to his feet. "Jesus, guy. At least you got to come to the Y. At least you got to keep in shape."

"Keep smiling," Harry says, and Jim ambles away with his inebriated penguin walk, feet splayed, head wobbling from side to side.

Harry imagines a lingering final drag on his stogy before mentally stubbing it out in the low-fat lemon pudding in front of him. He sits alone at the round table, surrounded by dirty plates. Across the room, the servers start to clear the tables and hurry the guests home.

He scans the room for Brooke. She is off with Kelly Sebring, who is bending her ear about something, probably another try at getting her to join the Junior League. She is weakening, Harry feels. Soon she will join, and a lot of her moodiness will disappear, he believes. The Junior League won't be as good as getting pregnant, of course. Harry thinks this weighs on her mind too. It certainly does on his.

He strolls over to collect her, pausing to exchange words with his network of business associates. The physical act of connecting with people always gives him pleasure. Tonight it convinces him Overmiller is right. We don't keep in touch enough. There is just so much going on that we don't make the time to see the people we like often enough. Crossing the room, Harry decides to throw Brooke a party for her birthday in a little over a month, with twenty or thirty of their closest friends. He is sure this will make her happy; she loves parties. A party will snap her right out of her depression. Speaking strictly for himself, Harry feels better already.

He hatches the second half of his scheme during the next week while going over his agency's hot sheet, the list of projects under way. Robert Fitzgerald's New Directions campaign has taken up permanent residence on the sheet, as it sticks in his craw. Harry is not used to having as much trouble with a client as he is having with this one, nor projects lingering uncompleted this long, And he thought he was going to hit it right off with Robert Fitzgerald, thought Fitzgerald would be his entry into the hospital. He thought after he opened his home to Fitzgerald for dinner they would be friends as well as coworkers. Not so fast; it all only seemed to make his client less tractable.

Time to try again. He makes a quick note to himself to add Fitzgerald's name to the list for Brooke's birthday party. Fitzgerald doesn't really qualify in that he has not made himself a friend to

Harry. He's been a royal pain in the ass, in fact. But Harry is willing to make an exception. There's always room for business. Harry wants to win Fitzgerald over so they can finish up with this campaign and get on to more lucrative jobs for the hospital. There's money in this account, he is sure of it. Somewhere, deep, lots and lots of money. And he wants it. Indeed, he feels he has a right to it.

Robert listens to Harry's invitation with amusement.

He turns it down.

Which catches Harry by surprise. "Well," Harry begins, sputtering into the phone, "I'd really appreciate it if you could come. It'd mean a lot to me. And to Brooke."

Robert smiles. "To Brooke?"

"Sure. She didn't know I was going to ask you, of course. But I know she'd like to see you too."

"She would, huh?"

"Sure. We both would. I know you'd have a good time. You'd meet some good people, have a lot of laughs."

"I dunno, Harry. Sounds more like a personal kind of party than business."

"Come on. They're the same thing! Starts at two o'clock three weeks from Sunday. Be there or be square, hey?"

"Well. You talked me into it."

"Great. You won't regret it."

Robert is not so sure about that.

Later on, Harry forgets to mention to his wife that he has invited his difficult client. When he remembers again, he decides to let it slide. No problem. Robert and Brooke get along, don't they?

2

The McGuires have not had a party like this since he set up a tent in their parklike backyard three years ago for the 4th of July party of all time. It was catered by the Rizzoli Brothers Fish Market, who supplied fresh clams, steamed lobsters, corn on the cob, and tossed salad for a hundred and fifty people. Their friends talked about it for months.

This party is not going to be quite so fancy, will even be intimate by comparison. Brooke has made Harry promise to keep the guest list within reason. (Understanding, of course, that Harry can't do anything within reason.) So when he tells her he has hired a band for the occasion, and is planning on having the affair outside, under a tent, she is not surprised. Nor is she surprised to learn that he is having this one catered by the Riverside Cafe, a new restaurant downtown by the confluence of the Susquehanna and the Chenango Rivers. She is not surprised, and not particularly happy, either—the food will be excellent, she knows, but it will be French, which reminds her sadly of the last time she had French food, that night at Robert Fitzgerald's. Her mistake, as she has now come to think of the episode.

She transmutes her sadness into worry, which gloms onto the high probability of rain in the unpredictable April weather. Of course the day of the party brings the first warm weather of the season. How could it do otherwise, with Harry, fortune's golden-haired boy, in charge of things? By the time the guests start collecting under Al the Tent Man's yellow and white striped canopy in the afternoon, the temperature has climbed to a balmy eighty degrees, a record for the date. The sun shines brightly on Harry McGuire. Even the dogwoods are rushing the season today with their creamy rose blooms.

The guest list, their closest friends, is a collection of this town's best and brightest, smiling and carefree in the first real spring sunlight. Swaying to the 1950s music of the brassy combo that Harry has hired are the Kolatas, Alphonse and Louise, elder statesmen of this predominantly nouveau crowd; and the Sebrings, Kelly wearing her trademark diamond racquet pin on her seersucker blazer and her husband in white ducks and deck shoes, rushing the season; and the Steens, Polly and Lee; and the new County Executive and his wife, not really members of this set but pleased enough for the invitation to want to put in an appearance; and the Tinklepaughs, Herb and Dottie, he the heir to the Tinklepaugh Industrial Conveyance Corporation fortune (forklifts and high-lows, where Harry used to work), she the new treasurer of the Junior League; and the Woolfes, of Woolfe Peacham Brady, the town's largest law firm; and the Jewitts, Bob and Lois, the director of the symphony and his wife, who runs a small but fabulously successful frame shop downtown; and the Overmillers, Jim slightly drunk as usual, his wife Christine outrageous in the briefest of sunsuits that allows Harry to count the moles like chocolate chips on her thighs as she crosses her legs at the table beside him; and the Brewsters, Frank and Betty, he the assistant plant manager of the local IBM, she a teacher of special education for the school district; and the Piercys, Charles the owner of the area's most successful Century 21 real estate office, Liz seated on the school board; and the other dozen or so who are invited but whose own party schedules on this delightful spring day are too crowded for anything more than a brief stop-in.

And, of course, Robert Fitzgerald.

Who slips into the backyard without his hosts seeing him and wanders around holding a plastic cup of Tab from the bartender, his eye out for Brooke. This is definitely not his crowd. He keeps to the fringes of it, and when he spots Brooke across the yard, he tracks her going about her hostessing with Robert Fitzgerald the absolutely last thing on her mind (or so he thinks, not realizing that she has rarely stopped thinking about him since their night together, and that he has in fact taken on mythic proportions in her mind, and that even now, at her own party, she automatically has an eye out for his face, which she knows she will never see here of all places in the world and which he is careful not to show her yet in any event). Brooke circulates with a huge magnum of champagne from one of the many cases they have stockpiled for the occasion, filling glasses. She accepts kisses and hugs with a broad smile, gracious, moving from one group to another, attentive, the picture of social amiability. This is the same role she played as hostess of the open house for Harry's bar. This is her role as Harry's wife: giving, attending.

She is a different person from the woman Robert came to know last fall. Even from across the yard in the lambent spring sun, she looks gaunt beneath her makeup. She has lost weight, cut her hair shorter, tinted its highlights brighter than he remembers. She seems to labor under a forced cheeriness, her smile too fixed, her shoulders too stiffly held back.

Robert matches his moves to hers, triangulating the point at which they will meet but for the time being keeping himself from it, not sure now, here at the party, watching her, if this is such a good idea, not certain even why he is really here. Brooke laughing, Brooke listening with interest, Brooke resting her hand on the arm of a man whose open-collared lilac Ralph Lauren Polo shirt reveals a twisted gold chain buried in curly black chest hair—this Brooke is not going to be glad to see him, Robert is suddenly certain.

He feels a prickle on his neck and looks away from her. Harry is watching him, as intently as Robert watches Brooke, to judge from his hooded eyes and vulpine grin. Caught? No. Harry raises his hand, and his grin turns to the brilliant Harry McGuire Memorial Charm School smile. Robert raises his own hand in greeting—and his gesture catches Brooke's eye.

She stands facing him, separated by a knot of people and about twenty yards. She stares at him in (by turns) disbelief, outrage, and finally cold terror. She has looked for him at so many different occasions that now, when she actually does see him in her own back yard, she cannot believe it. The eye contact they make is so riveting that she breaks it only when dragged away by a Junior Leaguer.

With Robert still watching her, she is pulled into a group of women. Abruptly she disengages and runs into the house.

Robert glances around. He's come this far, why not go the rest of the way?

Satisfied that Harry is safely tied up for the moment, he eases across the yard and through the back door of the house. He hears muffled steps running up the carpeted stairway to the second floor. He follows, remembering the last time he did this in here, only with an expectation of much more pleasure. In the short term anyway.

He finds her hugging herself on the bed. She looks up. Gay voices from the crowd outside tap on the window. "What are you doing here?" she hisses.

"Your husband invited me."

"What?!"

"Didn't he tell you?"

"No, he didn't tell me. This is a party for our friends."

"I told him I wasn't interested. He insisted I come."

"I don't believe it."

"I figured he wanted to butter me up so I wouldn't give him such a hard time on my project."

"How could you come here?"

"I wanted to see you."

"But I don't want to see you!" Her tone makes it less a rejection than a plea for understanding. "I told you that."

He takes a step closer and she shrinks from him. "What's the matter with you?" she says in a crazy whisper. She rises and begins to pace. "Are you crazy? Get out of my bedroom. Harry'll see you up here. What'll I tell him?"

"Tell him the truth. Tell him we're friends."

"We're not friends."

She turns away to collect herself, then faces him again. "Robert," she says, struggling to sound calm, "I thought we had an understanding."

"We do," he says. "And I respect it."

"Then why are you here?"

"Your husband invited me to come over today."

"But he doesn't know what happened—."

She can't bring herself to finish the sentence.

"I couldn't pass up this chance. I wanted to see you again. In spite of what you think, there is something special between us, whether you want to admit it or not. We don't have to do anything about it, but it seems ridiculous to me to pretend it isn't there. It was only a matter of time before we met again anyway. This town is too small."

"But in my own house? In my *bedroom*?"

"As well here as anywhere."

"Robert," she moans, "please don't do this to me. Please. Go."

"Look, I'm not going to embarrass you in front of your husband and your friends. I'm not that big a jerk. I just wanted to see you again. And say hello. And find out how you are. And tell you I still think of you. Now I'm starting to get the hint: You want me to leave, right? Is that your general drift? Fine. I'll see you around."

He walks out of the room, down the stairs, out of the house, and away from the party. And back into her life with a vengeance. She stands rooted to the oriental rug in the center of her bedroom and covers her face with both hands.

He sits in his car for a long time. The key is in the ignition but he can't bring himself to turn on the motor. He can't bring himself to leave, to re-enter the world that is now changed because Brooke is back in it. He missed her during their time apart. Seeing her again reminds him how much she moves him, how strong their connection is.

He has made this move, coming to see her, reopening the channel of communication. If she wants to further their connection, the next move should be hers.

In the middle of the following week, she makes it. She calls him from a pay phone in a far corner of the lobby of the Holiday Inn downtown. "It's me," she says when he answers. Her voice is low and urgent.

At the sound of his voice, her legs grow weak. She leans against the wall of the phone booth.

"Where are you?" he asks. He is calm, reassuring. He uses his counselor's voice. Who knows what crisis she is interrupting?

"There's a luncheon at the Holiday Inn to talk about the Junior League Spring Fashion Show."

"Are you in the Junior League now?"

"No. I'm just helping them with the show."

"With the ladies who lunch. Are you going to be in it?"

"I'm going to be a model. I have to wear a spring dress and a hat."

"I bet you'll be beautiful in it."

"I won't." She laughs and begins to cry. She chokes it off.

"I'm glad you called," he says.

"I shouldn't be doing this."

"I'm glad you did. I wish I could be there."

"I do, too." It is a great relief to say so.

"Can I see you?"

"I don't know."

"Have lunch with me tomorrow." She says no. He asks her again and she agrees.

3

Things are a little too serious between them to meet at T. Moneybags in town, she believes. She suggests the Peking House, a Chinese place on the outskirts. Robert, with more experience in these matters, knows what seems suspicious downtown looks even worse in the suburbs. But he acquiesces and suggests they meet late, after the lunch crowd empties out. When they get there, she does not eat a thing, a bad sign. He reaches a hand across the table. She takes it in both of hers and squeezes. Her eyes mist up. She is on the edge.

They wind up back at the House of Grins, which at this hour of the midafternoon is empty. In short order it becomes the House of Hugs, the House of Kisses, the House of Clothes Hurriedly Unbuttoned, the House of Condoms, then the House of Moans, of Shouts, of Tears, of Soft Curses, of Wild Thighs Thrashing.

Afterwards it is the House of Tristesse. Lying together, she wraps her arms tightly around his neck. He examines the fine lines of skin around her mouth, the green specks in her eyes, the gritty black lines of mascara on her lashes. He cups this face in both his hands and kisses it with all the tenderness he can muster, which is considerable.

They dress in silence, coconspirators. She wriggles into her pantyhose, lets herself fall heavily onto the bed. "Christ," she says. "I don't want to leave."

He sits beside her. "We have to go and do grownup things. Go back to work and stuff."

"I've never done anything like this before."

"With me you have."

"What'll I do if Harry calls me at the office while I'm gone?"

"Tell him you were discussing a project with a client."

"That would be a lie."

"Oh, right. Then I guess you better tell him the truth."

"I don't think so."

"Haven't you ever lied to your husband before?"

She shakes her head wanly, knowing she has, over and over. That's why she can do this now, in the middle of the day, with this man. Who she's also lying to.

"Do you do this a lot?" she asks.

"No. I used to be a lustful man in my day. The sun seems to have set on my day for quite some time. I'd sworn off sex completely, for a long time."

"Why?"

"It's a long story. I'll tell you when we have more time."

"I don't know when that'll ever be."

He shakes his head. "Stolen moments."

"Quickies at lunchtime."

"I like 'stolen moments' better."

"You're a romantic after all."

"Never said I wasn't."

"That's what I'm afraid this whole thing is going to turn into. Stolen moments."

"What is life if not one long stolen moment?"

"That was profound."

"Listen, the people I counsel are used to stealing moments."

"So what do you tell them?"

"I don't tell them anything. What I try to do is help them clarify what kind of moments they're stealing, and what they get out of the experience. If the experience is negative, which it usually is, I try to get them to either give up the need to steal those moments, or else get the same need satisfied in some more positive way. When will I see you again?"

"I need some time to process this."

"Can I call you?"

"It doesn't seem like last fall, does it," she asks distractedly, avoiding the question. "The last time we saw each other. It seems like it's been much longer."

She gets up and starts to make the bed with quick, practiced swipes at the sheet. "Stop that," he says.

"I'm just straightening up."

"I know. But I don't want you to. Check that impulse at the door."

She is not, as she suspected she might be, racked with guilt. Instead, she marvels again at how easy it was. Robert was right, way back then. All she had to do was let it happen, and it did, easily and sweetly. How simple. If she had known it would be like this, would she have avoided a lot of aggravation, not only with Robert, but before, with the other men who had made passes at her that she turned down or pretended not to notice, men she was attracted to? Lost chances. Some moments are stolen, some opportunities are lost. How much better to steal a moment, Brooke McGuire now thinks in the fading afterglow of sex with Robert, than to regret opportunities unclaimed.

No, she is not riven with guilt. It felt too good for that. She does, however, dread her first confrontation with Harry, wondering, on the way home from the office (where there had been no message from him), how she will face him, how she will dissemble, how pretend that she did not make love with another man this afternoon. How she will toss off his inevitable "How was your day?" And what if he wants to make love tonight? What will she say, how will she perform with Harry, who will be the second man inside her body today? Getting kind of crowded in here. Will he notice? Will she?

When she pulls into the empty driveway, she remembers with relief that he had said he would be at the bar tonight meeting some salesman. By the time he gets home she will be asleep. Good. She can face him better in the morning. Tomorrow is another day.

She takes a long hot bath, enjoying the feel of the water, the time to herself.

She towels off. I am determined to stay cool about this, no matter what, she tells herself. Plenty of married women go through this and don't even have feelings for the men they sleep with. I, on the other hand may well be in love with this guy. Though whether this is the truth or simply a lie she is trying to make herself believe to justify what she did today, she cannot as yet say.

Robert stays late at the hospital, finishing reports and charts and the miscellaneous paperwork that piles up around him daily. He calls home to say he won't be around for dinner and has a quick, unsettling chat with Dennis, who is as voluble as Robert has ever heard him, euphoric, almost, which makes Robert nervous. Why is he so happy? Happy like he's in his right mind, Robert's father used to say of Robert's high spirits with such deliberate meanness.

After he hangs up, he wanders down to the cafeteria for some dinner with the night shift of nurses and housekeeping staff. Things are calmer, less crowded at night down here. The staff is younger, the newer nurses stuck with this less desirable shift. He eats by himself, ostensibly reading the newspaper but really thinking about what happened today, replaying everything, his thoughts unfocused.

Barry Reinhardt comes over holding his tray before him like an offering. "Mind if I sit down?"

"Be my guest."

Reinhardt is the director of Biomedical Engineering, the

department that fixes medical equipment throughout the hospital. Robert met him last month when he came up to New Directions when the intercoms all went out. He is skinny and manic, Robert's age with a headful of gray hair and wild eyes, wearing Levis and a red and black buffalo plaid shirt with a black cotton tie.

"Sure you don't mind?

"Not at all."

"Got those squawk boxes working all right?"

"Right as rain," Robert says. He automatically adopts Reinhardt's breezy put-on manner.

"Awright." Reinhardt begins to eat rapidly, shoveling in his broiled chicken and baked potato and peas as if someone were coming to take it all away. "Here pretty late," he says.

"Yeah. Getting some work done. Eating. Thinking."

"All three at once? That's awesome."

"What are you doing here?"

"Same. Except for the thinking part. This is the best time of the day to work. Nobody bothers you, no interruptions, none of those clucks who work for me hanging around screwing things up. Can't beat it."

"Hear that."

"You married?"

"Divorced."

"Me, too. Friggin' women, ha? Can't live with 'em, can't shoot 'em in the head. Got any kids?"

"Two."

"Live with your ex?"

"No, they're grown. Out on their own."

"Good for them. I got three kids. One of each. Hah. Live in Scranton with their mother. Never get to see the little shits, either, only when she wants me to. It's intense, man, I'm telling you."

"Sounds like it."

Barry is already finished with his meal. He throws his knife and fork down and begins an elaborate routine of wiping his hands and fingers and the areas in between his fingers with a stack of napkins. "Any lady friends?"

Robert says, "Maybe."

"Maybe? You don't know?"

"No."

"I don't know about you, man. Don't even know if you have a

girlfriend. And you're supposed to help those drunks in that unit? Who's watching out for you?"

"I just started something. Dunno what's going to happen."

"I'll tell you what's going to happen. She's going to break your heart and kick the shit out of it. That's what's going to happen."

"I don't think so. Maybe once. Not this time."

"That's what always happens. I've been seeing this chick myself. Got some kids of her own. Yours got any kids?"

"Nope."

"Too bad. Good thing to have, kids. I miss mine sometimes so much I can't think of anything else but. But it's cool. I give to Barb's kids some of what I can't give to my own, you know?"

"Yeah. That's good for them."

"Good for me, too. I tell you, man, I miss being married. I really do. I hated my old lady like poison, but I sure miss being married."

"So get married again."

"I asked her. She don't want to marry me. Says I'm too irresponsible. Can you believe that? Me?"

"Women."

"So this chick of yours, you going to marry her?"

"I seriously doubt it."

"What's the matter with her?"

"She's already married."

"For real?"

"For really real."

"Whoa. My estimation of you just went up a notch there, chief."

"No big thing."

"You know, some guys think porking another man's wife is pretty low. No offense. Not me. I don't think it's anything to be proud of, necessarily. But my feeling is, people have to try and get what they need, and sometimes you get it, and most times you don't. But you still got to try. And if messing around with another guy's wife is going to do it for you, I salute you. People don't control each other. Anyway, if your wife runs around, I say it's probably your fault somewhere along the line."

"How'd you like a job counseling alcoholics?"

"No thanks. I'm having enough trouble living my own life. Besides, I'm a Friend of Bill myself. I couldn't stand to hear other drunks' problems all day long. I'd go off the deep end for sure."

He wipes his mouth with his napkin and tosses the crumpled

ball into his chicken bones. "Robert, it's been real. Gotta go. Let's hang out sometime, okay? You're a pretty cool guy."

"You're kind of awesome yourself."

"I try."

"How was your day?" Harry asks.

She is lounging in front of the television in the family room, not trying to stay awake for him, just not sleepy. She had planned on going to bed without waiting up for him, but she couldn't sleep; her thoughts were too jumbled. Maybe this is good, too. Now she has the chance to get this over with so she can get on with other things, with stealing more moments, to take one extremely probable example.

She also makes a mental note not to overdo the attention she pays Harry. Remember to act normally, striking a balance between not enough and too much. Sneaking around is a real performance art.

He stands in the middle of the room, slowly loosening his necktie, unbuttoning his shirt, airing his monkey fur. Everything is changed, and nothing is. Harry, of course, has no reason to suspect anything (she hopes), though her universe has been fundamentally jolted. Which is somewhat distressing. She almost wishes he could tell.

He flops into a chair. "Boy, am I tired."

"You should go to sleep."

"I will. So should you. Busy day?"

"Kind of." Then: "Get done what you needed to at the bar?"

"Yeah. Had a couple of drinks with Michael and came home."

He yawns, bites off the end with a growl. "Guess I'll go up to bed."

"I'm going to watch the end of the news and I'll be up."

He trudges off. She has passed her first test. Did she think she wouldn't? Did she really think she'd freak and confess to her new secret life?

But don't think it isn't scary either. How much easier it would be if Harry took one look at her and read her secret in her eyes and told her she must never see this man again. And forgave her immediately, of course; that has to be part of the deal. She knows Harry will never do this, because then he wouldn't be Harry.

Fortune's honey boy would never consider that his wife would take a lover unless she hit him over the head with a chair while telling him. He will definitely not be the problem here. She will be her own problem. Unless she does something to stop it, the sky's going to be the limit on this one.

Which is the scariest thing of all.

4

"Tell me why you swore off sex," Brooke says, and attacks her sandwich. Excess tuna oozes out the sides of the rye.

They sit at a picnic table in Otsiningo Park, a small, kidney-shaped recreation area on the edge of the downtown near the interstate. He has brought tuna sandwiches for their lunch, thick juicy goodies on rye wrapped in wax paper. At this time of year, the only other people in the park are retirees who come to walk the circumference, young mothers taking their children for a stroll, and teenagers skipping school. Set beside a river, the park is tranquil.

"I'm glad your appetite is back," Robert says.

"Don't change the subject."

"You're sure you want to know?"

"Yes."

"It has to do with a woman."

"I sorta figured that."

"Before I moved here, I lived with a woman in Seattle. Her name was Catherine Keene. She had a little girl named Andrea. Who had an accident and died."

"I'm sorry."

"It was pretty awful."

"Were you the father?"

"No. But her father was sort of crazy. He and Catherine were divorced, and he was living with another woman. But he used to call her on the phone all the time, and I mean all hours, and beg her to let him come over, crying over the phone, threatening to kill himself if she didn't let him come."

"What was his problem?"

"Drugs. I'm talking a major-league polydrug problem.

Catherine left him because it was out of control. Which was ironic, considering what I did for a living."

"Sounds crazy to me."

"No question about that. So Catherine went out of her way with Andrea to try and counter his craziness," Robert continues. "Catherine had a thing about keeping her word no matter what. As you might imagine, Andrea's father disappointed her pretty much constantly. So one day Catherine told Andrea we were going to go on a picnic on the weekend. Andrea spent the whole week planning it out. Where we'd go, what we'd eat, what we'd do . . ."

"That's an organized little girl."

"She was compulsive like you've never seen compulsion. Well, the picnic was supposed to be for this one Sunday. Sunday comes, and it's pouring down rain. Seattle, right? It lets up a little in the afternoon, but it's still raining, a heavy drizzle, like. Andrea is having a heart attack because her plans are ruined, and Catherine decides a deal is a deal, rain or no rain we're going to go on this picnic. So we start out with picnic baskets, blankets, Raid, and raincoats and umbrellas. When we get to the park it's raining too hard to put a blanket down on the grass, so we eat in the back of Catherine's station wagon.

"Andrea was antsy to get out of the car and play in the rain, so she took my baseball glove and a softball and jumped out. Catherine took her umbrella and followed her. It was one of those big golf umbrellas. I stayed in the car while they walked around for a while, and all of a sudden the rain stopped. They were the only ones in the whole park. Brooke folded up the umbrella and Andrea wanted to play catch. She threw the ball to Catherine and Catherine threw it to her. Then Catherine took the umbrella and squared off with it like a baseball bat. They were only about ten feet apart. Andrea threw the ball, and Catherine took this enormous swing. She missed the ball by a mile but the shaft of the umbrella separated from the handle and flew out directly at Andrea. The steel point hit her right here."

Robert indicates a point on his cheek just below his right eye. "Right on the bone. Knocked her out cold. When we got her to the hospital, she was awake but groggy and her speech was slurred. By the time a doctor looked at her in the emergency room she'd lost consciousness again. The whole side of her face swelled up. Later on a doctor told us the handle probably hit her with the force of a bullet."

"How horrible."

"Freak accident."

"What happened to her?"

"She never came out of it. She had a cerebral hemorrhage. She was dead by midnight. Catherine blamed herself, of course. As did her crazy ex-husband. He started calling her and screaming at her about how she'd killed his daughter. I tried to talk to her and get her to get some help, but she didn't want any part of it. What she did want was to punish herself. She asked her ex to get her some phenobarbital, which the crazy fuck was only too happy to do, and one day she took about eight hundred of them. Her sister found her. They pumped her stomach and she survived. Notice I don't say lived. Part of her died with Andrea, and another part of her died when she took the pills. What was left of her future. I tried to help her as best I could, but she didn't want any part of me anymore. She withdrew more and more, till finally she told me to leave. Said the only way she could cope with what happened was on her own, without the emotional demands I made on her. I tried not to make any demands, but just being around her was more than she could deal with. And look, I was grieving for Andrea, too. I'd only lived with them for a year, but I loved her. I loved them both. I was in pain, too. But she became completely inaccessible to me. I felt totally powerless. There didn't seem to be anything I could do or say to anybody.

"I thought she'd pull out of it after a time but she didn't. I hung around Seattle but it got to the point where I started calling her and screaming at her to snap out of it, just like her ex-husband. That's how bad off I was. Then finally I just freaked and said I couldn't take it anymore and moved out."

"Oh, Robert. That's so sad."

"I spent the rest of that year in a daze. Then get this: Catherine's ex started to call *me*. When she took the pills he gave her, he split for parts unknown. Then he surfaced by way of a series of midnight phone calls to me. He blamed me for all of it."

"Where was he?"

"I never did find out. Which was okay, because I'm sure if I'd known I would've found him and killed him. Finally I just wanted to leave Seattle, the Northwest, and preferably my entire adult life and accumulated history behind and start over again somewhere else."

"So you came here."

"And started my new life. Where the swearing-off-sex part comes in is the way I felt after all of it. I was just unable to even consider another emotional involvement. And without that, sex seemed beside the point."

"So why me? You could have had all you wanted with Debby Saunders, I'm sure."

He shakes his head. "Sex without emotional connection is all hydraulics. I didn't feel a connection with her. I do with you."

"But why?"

"I think people who have suffered in life can identify other people who've suffered in the same way."

She is silent. She can't bring herself to talk about her family to this man . . . not yet. If ever.

Instead, she says, "You sure don't sound like the other men I've known."

"After Catherine, I felt as if I'd seen through everything, as if my ego strength had collapsed and I didn't have the energy or the desire to try and connect. I started to see the male-female connection in terms of the male's urge to dominate. Raging testosterone without much joy."

"It must have been so hard."

"It's been interesting. You probably have some amazing stories yourself."

"I do have some amazing stories," Brooke says, gazing off into the bright yellow bells of the forsythia growing by the river's edge beside heavy clotted mud tracks from a tractor that has been moving earth.

"I'd like to hear about them."

"Not today."

After a while she says, "I better get back." They walk to their cars, parked side by side. She gets into hers and turns the key to lower the window. He bends his head down and they kiss. "It's hard to say goodbye to you," he says.

"I know. And it's hard for me to relax with you, still, when we're together. It's hard to get excited over something you're so ambivalent about."

The words hit him like a punch to the gut.

5

Stolen moments:
"Robert," she says, "I'm falling in love with you."
"Ditto."
"I feel like I'm walking around with my insides hanging out or something."
"Maybe they like it out in the fresh air."
"They can't stay out."
"Try it."
"No. It's my life. I know what I'm talking about."

"My husband's a good man," she says to him out of the blue.
"If you say so."
"No. He is."
"Maybe."
"What do you mean?"
"The Harry McGuire I've seen is different."
"How?"
"I don't really want to talk about your husband."
"I want to know how you see him."
"As a manipulative, acquisitive man who doesn't know how lucky he is to have you."
She doesn't know how to respond. Sometimes—she has to admit to herself—she feels the same way about Harry.

"Do you have any children?" she asks.
He tells her.
"Do you ever see them?"
"Not very often. They've never quite forgiven me for what I did to their mother. So they don't care much for seeing me."
"What did you do to their mother?"
"I made her extremely unhappy."
"How?"
"By being selfish and unstable."
"Are you still?"

"Sometimes."

"Do you miss them?"

"I do. I regret the family life I botched for them. Jesus, I was so bad at it. But as I've gotten older, I've started to see how important it is. Family life, I mean. I seem to need one so badly. Once upon a time I thought families had outlived their evolutionary usefulness. But what else do we really have?"

"You had a family in Seattle, didn't you?"

"I tried. I thought Andrea was my second chance to be a good man. What about your family?" he asks.

"What about them?"

"Tell me about them."

"It's no Holy Family," she says. She refuses to say more.

"What do you want from me?" she asks.

"Why do I have to want something from you?"

"Did I get you to swear back onto sex?"

"You helped me heal."

"I don't know how."

"Why did you pursue me?"

"You're an attractive woman. It was chemical. Besides, you flirted openly with me."

"I did not."

"You did."

"Not."

"Did. Anyway, that's not the only reason. I've been at such loose ends for so long. I'm attracted by your stability. I find you extremely compelling and special."

"I don't know if that makes me feel good or not."

"Do you like it here?" she asks.

"Right here? Now? Yes."

"The town, I mean."

"I like my house. I like my housemates. The job is okay. Nothing special. The town itself is too insular for me. Too complacent. Too in-bred. I'm too much of an outsider to fit in, or want to fit in.

Everybody knows everybody else's business. And their grandfather's business."

"Tell me about it."

"Do you like it here?"

"Yes," she says at once. "I like my life here. A lot."

"You can't like it that much."

"I do. It's not perfect, of course," she says, and shuts up. She has said too much.

"What can I give you?" he asks, but she does not answer or say any more, except "I better get going."

6

Saturday night. Brooke and Harry go to a party at the house of Ron Selby, vice president for communications at Brooke's company. And her boss. Harry knows him well; they worked together on the County Executive's campaign. Harry is not here tonight as hired help but as one of the town's top businessmen. Likewise, because this is not a company party, Brooke is here not as Selby's employee, but as his social equal.

When they arrive, she searches the place to make sure two people in particular are not here: Robert Fitzgerald and Edith Markowitz. Not to worry. This is another of the occasions that neither would be invited to, much as Edith would love to be. She is not part of things. An outsider, as Robert takes pride in being.

The gathering is a very quiet, very civilized occasion, a summer cocktail party where everyone stands and chats while holding a beverage glass. The men are all in sportscoats and ties and pastel slacks, the women in blazers over cotton dresses with shoulder pads. Harry mingles with the men:

"I told him, I said I've already thrown enough money away on advertising and promotion, I want to see some results."

"The Steelers can't hit from the outside this year, I dunno what it is but they can't."

"He shouldn't even be worrying about it. I told him. I said put twenty percent down, they'll never even check your references. Then, I said, if you want to, you can borrow against it and sink the money into another house. The market's gangbusters."

Brooke mingles with the women:

"Last semester Marlene's teachers said she's going to need a reading tutor twice a week after school. I said, is this going to catch her up with her age? Because if it isn't, I don't see where it's worth it."

"My Emily wants to take soccer and ballet lessons."

"We better start on the Auxiliary Autumn Dance as soon as we can. October'll be here before we know it."

Brooke detaches herself from the group to fill a plate with chopped broccoli and cauliflower and a dollop of peppery dip. Kelly Sebring follows.

"How do you feel about doing some volunteer work for our dance in the fall?"

"What kind of work?" Brooke asks.

"We're going to need a lot of help. You could work on decorations, maybe, with all your talent."

They are joined by Edie Albrecht. "Well," says Brooke, "I don't know if I can put in a lot of time this summer."

"What's taking up all your time?" asks Edie.

"I'm a busy woman," Brooke insists with comic fussiness to throw these sharks off the scent of her blood.

"Well," says Kelly, "you were so helpful with the Fashion Show and the Antique Show, I just know we can count on you for this one, too."

"As much as you can give," Edie says, "we'll take."

Brooke laughs along with them. The story of her life. "I'll do what I can," she says, and excuses herself to get another glass of wine from the bartender whom her boss has hired for the evening. He is a gravely serious black man in a short white waiter's coat. "Isn't he wonderful?" says an older woman who passes by Brooke. "He reminds me of the houseman who used to work for my husband and me when my husband was still alive. These people can be such hard workers when they want to."

Brooke flees.

She drifts from room to room, passing by the group of men that Harry is attached to. She hears him telling the joke about the pig and the wheelbarrow. She's heard that joke a hundred times. She continues through the house. From the other room she hears the laughter attending the punchline.

The guests here tonight are the town's successful entrepreneurs, the wheeler-dealers, the professionals and merchants and sons of merchants, the latter of whom, by and large, comprise Brooke and Harry's social circle. Men and women Harry grew up with and who, the men anyway, graduated from college with majors in business administration and accounting, worked for other entrepreneurs or for their parents for a few years after college before starting out on their own and making it almost immediately. Which is just what Harry did. The times are good, prosperous and ripe with possibilities.

Yet they still give the impression of being overgrown boys in grownup clothes, these men whose toys may be more expensive, whose games may have higher stakes, but whose juvenile petulance and willfulness are never far from the surface.

There are other groups represented here, and she passes by them, too. They are the managers, the men and, lately, women, who work for the big local corporations, IBM and General Electric and Singer-Link and the others. Mostly middle-aged, but there are some younger ones too, like their elders well-educated technocrats, no risk takers, content with a career path for themselves and all the money they need for the same grownup toys the young wheeler-dealers collect, toys with initials, VCRs, PCs, CDs. The main difference between the two groups, besides the temperamental and intellectual gaps that separate them, is that the young entrepreneurs are usually born and raised in this town or else married to women who were, while the young technocrats almost always come in from out of town, touching down for a year or two or five before moving on in their ambitious climbs up their corporate ladders, or else staying, captivated like Brooke by the valley's staid charms. There is some commerce between the two groups, such as at these parties, but not much; each keeps to its own.

Also here tonight is Old Money, with more wealth than Brooke would have believed possible until Harry showed her a secret list of the wealthiest residents that he got his hands on as part of his volunteer fund-raising chores for the Symphony. There are literally scores of millionaires, older entrepreneurs, men and wealthy widows whose fortunes came from real estate or insurance, or else old-line managers or their widows who had the good fortune to have been in on the ground floor of IBM or Endicott Johnson, who grew old and prospered as the stocks that were part of their original benefits packages matured beyond their dreams.

It is this older group that mainly supports the Downtown Club and the Country Club. As the young wheeler-dealers make it, they join the town's exclusive society. The young technocrats never bother. They know they aren't going to be around long enough to make joining worthwhile, or they don't care to associate with doddering old farts (Harry excepted, Brooke quickly thinks). Anyway, their employers give them their own clubs and recreation.

There are other groups in town, too, Brooke knows, but they are not invited tonight. One is connected with the university. They scorn the bourgeoise pastimes and occupations of the town as they concentrate on their own academic careers at what they flatter themselves to be the flagship institution of the state university system. They accumulate grants and tenure, and fix up their houses and gardens with every bit as much concern for property values as those on whom they look down. And there is a lower class, too, Brooke knows them well, the people who work in the blue-collar jobs at the large corporations, who drive the trucks and pack the cartons for the entrepreneurs. They make up the bulk of the population of this little town; it is the previous generation of blue-collar workers that spawned many of today's young entrepreneurs, like Harry. In America everyone moves up.

Just then Harry approaches where she stands in the breakfast nook, gazing into her boss's darkened acreage. "What's up," he asks. "What are you doing back here by yourself?"

"Just thinking."

"Do you want to go home?"

"Not unless you do."

"No. Herb Tinklepaugh's balloon is in the Balloon Rally next week. He asked us if we wanted to go for a ride in it."

"What did you tell him?"

"I said of course. Why, don't you want to go?"

"Absolutely not, I'm petrified of those things."

"You don't mind if I go, do you?"

"As long as your insurance is paid up."

"Oh, Brooke," Harry says. "You never do anything adventuresome."

7

The balloon is fully inflated. It wavers in the warm breeze, a huge and graceful inverted teardrop, quilted checks of blue, green, yellow, red, and lavender. It is one of about two dozen multicolored elephantine party decorations, some already floating above the valley, some poised on the dark green grass of the field and ready to go with their crews aboard, some half-inflated, limp Dali sculptures. This is one of the town's summer traditions, a mass cookout and balloon fest. Hundreds of people mill around in billed caps and paunchy tank tops watching those few wealthy enough to own balloons prepare to entertain them in a rally. Which is kind of boring, really. The balloons get inflated, they go up, they float around for a while, and they disappear over a line of trees. Big deal. Pass the brew.

Brooke stands beside Harry in a small group around the Tinklepaughs, making the final adjustments to their balloon. Harry is happy and relaxed, as always. Life is so good for Harry, Brooke thinks.

"Be careful!" she calls to him as he climbs into the tiny basket. Herb and Dottie are with him. As the balloon floats upward, Herb's brother-in-law runs to the chase vehicle, a Toyota pickup, and takes off across the field to the road, down which he will race to follow the balloon's course. It will land miles from here, in a spot already picked out and ready for these strange conveyances.

Soon it is a hundred feet up. Harry leans over and waves. Fire roars out of the heater onboard, and after several seconds the balloon rises gravely. It takes its place with the others that are already sailing over the trees on the sides of the hills that surround the park.

It is, in fact, a majestic sight. She can imagine being in the balloon, looking down over the fecund fields and trees, a hawk's eye view, caught in the transpiration of wind in the crystalline sky.

When Harry drifts away, she walks back to her car and drives to Robert's.

His housemates are out, he says, for several hours. They retire to his bedroom. It is cool and dark, with the curtains fluttering in a cross breeze from the open windows. When Robert atop her begins his pounding groaning orgasm, she turns her head and bites her tongue so she will not scream and through his second-story window sees a flock of gaily-colored balloons overhanging the distant hills.

Afterwards the breeze cools the perspiration on her skin. Robert lies beside her. She runs a hand over his hard body, letting it pause on his genitals, damp with their mingled fluids. She comes with Harry too, but not like this. This is too different. With Robert she feels freed from the constraints of familiarity. By now she has all of Harry's moves down pat. She is still learning Robert's. Which is part of the attraction, though by no means the only one. The fascination she felt for Robert initially has not deteriorated, has in fact grown as a result of the strange story he told her the other day. She feels as if his are the real grownup problems while hers are petty, of no more lasting import than a pimple on a teenager's chin. She feels as if she has not lived, has in fact avoided life out of fear of winding up like her mother, crazed by it. But this relationship is taking her closer to life as it is lived. Still she feels as if she has a long way to go to catch up with this man next to her. He has suffered, and survived. And touched her so deeply.

She can't stay. Harry will be dropped off at their house after the balloon touches down, she says, and the chase truck picks them up and they get the balloon packed into the back and drive down from the rural community where they have landed.

Leaning against one of the pillars on his front porch, Robert watches her drive away, back to her husband, her home, their life. Gone so soon. After sex she spent the rest of the hour sitting up in bed so she wouldn't have to explain the creases in her face from the rumpled sheets and pillowcases. So she said. Then her formulaic end to their time together, "I better get going." Like the way he ends his counseling sessions: 'We do have to stop now."

As always, he feels bereft when she goes. Left alone, he bends down to snap off dried leaves from the potted geraniums that line the porch. Takes a small tour of his front yard, sniffs the air. Rain on the way. Maybe he can cut the ankle-length lawn before it gets here.

When she gets home Harry is not there yet. The red light on the answering machine is blinking. She has a frisson of fear.

The call is from her father. As soon as she hears the faraway sound in his voice, she knows there is trouble. "Your mother's in the hospital," he says. "But don't come up. Everything's all right. Everything's fine. Don't worry. Don't come."

How like him, how like his double messages. We need you, but don't come.

CHAPTER THIRTEEN

1

"My respite care worker didn't show," says Crystal Williams. "I'm going to have to stick around tonight."

"Isn't there somebody else you can call? Isn't there an emergency number?"

"There is, but this isn't an emergency."

"No," Gene has to agree. "But I mean isn't there a backup for when something like this happens?"

"Only in an emergency," Crystal explains patiently. "Like I said, this isn't an emergency. I don't have to go to work, and Derrick isn't sick."

Gene is silent. He and Crystal sit on plastic webbed chairs in the fading sunlight in her backyard, holding chipped mugs of coffee in their laps. It is a small yard, outlined by a cyclone fence, overgrown with bushes that need pruning and weeds that need pulling. Derrick sits in his bright blue plastic Tumble Form chair in an oversized stroller beside his mother. He intertwines his long slender fingers. Every so often he brings them to his mouth and sticks them in. He is perfectly content, which puts him ahead of Gene.

No, there is no emergency tonight, but they did have plans, he and Crystal. She does not have to work, and the respite care worker was due to relieve her for a few hours. He thought they would go out to dinner, a rare enough occasion for them. He is proud of her; she is a beautiful woman with a dark garden of colors in her face, and he loves it when heads turn in this ignorant little town when they go anywhere. But what can he do? The respite care worker is only a special ed student at the university, without the sense of obligation she needs for a job like this. She didn't show? Change of plans, that's all.

Yet Gene is nonplussed. He was looking forward to this evening. Now they have to stay home, and while the evening would end the same way, he was certain—in bed, Gene marveling at the rounded curves of her belly and thighs, the sleek ripe red-brown of her skin, literally night to the pale sparse pink day of his own body—he is put off by the wrinkle in their plans.

"Sun feels good," Crystal says. She holds her head back and gathers in the final rays on her broad face, her full lips that he loves to feast upon.

He says nothing in reply. Soon she says, "I'm sorry, baby. I can't leave Derrick. You know that."

"I know."

"Besides, I wanted to do some housework. Here's my chance."

This too rubs him the wrong way. "What kind of work?" he asks, trying and failing to keep the annoyance out of his voice. Even housework is more important than he is?

"I need to wash the floor in the kitchen. My feet are sticking to it. And I need to wash the bathroom. And Derrick's room's a mess. I have to do something with it."

"Why do you have to do it tonight?"

"Because I haven't had a chance over the last month. Between singing and working days and seeing you, I've let a lot of things slide around here. I don't like to let it go like this. I can't stand this place when it's a mess."

"I could give you a hand."

"You could," she says. She wouldn't think of asking him outright (it is her house, she should take care of it), though it would be nice if he pitched in. She wouldn't turn his help down. Thus far she hasn't had the chance. He's good with Derrick, but he doesn't offer to do anything around her house. And it's an old house, there's much to do.

Gene reconsiders, put off by her lack of enthusiasm. "It doesn't look so bad to me," he grouses. This time it is she who doesn't answer.

They sit for a while, until the light disappears. "Getting cool," she says, and leans over to give Derrick a juicy kiss on the cheek. She wipes away the excess juice with her hand and he responds with a beaming smile that transforms his whole face into a sun of pure joy.

"Time to go inside, sugar," she says.

Gene folds up the chairs and helps her roll the boy in. She settles him in front of the television in the living room and turns on a rerun of "Hill Street Blues" on cable. Derrick squeals with joy at the commotion from the set. It is his favorite show.

She goes out to the kitchen to rinse the cups and Gene wanders in there with her. "I guess I'll get going," he says.

It catches her by surprise. "Sure? Won't take me more than a couple hours to do what I have to. You can watch TV with Derrick."

"Don't think so."

"Okay then."

"This isn't quite what I had in mind for tonight."

"I know, baby. Told you I was sorry. You could stay anyway."

He shakes his head.

She takes his arm and walks him to the door. He is tense: still upset. On the front porch she kisses and hugs him, and he is distant from her.

"Is something else wrong?" she asks.

"I don't know."

"Yes you do. Something's bothering you."

"I feel—."

He searches around the porch as if his answer could be found in the peeling paint on the slats on the walls and ceiling, the uneven pile of wood under a bench, partly covered with cloudy, torn plastic sheeting left over from the winter.

"I feel constrained," he decides.

"By Derrick?"

"Partly," he admits.

She draws away and retreats into defensiveness. "You knew about Derrick. He was no surprise. I never tried to hide him."

"I know."

"You always knew he was going to take up a lot of my time."

"I know that."

"He's my baby. He needs my attention. Gene, honey, do you think I'm holding you back from something?"

"I feel like I have to rein myself in whenever I come over here. Like I could run and jump if I let myself go. That's not how it was in the beginning. You made me feel so—so free."

"Maybe you shouldn't come over so much."

"I want to," he says, backpedaling. "I want to see you. I look forward to seeing Derrick. I'm really fond of the little guy."

"Then I don't know what you're trying to say to me."

"I'm not sure I do, either."

"Maybe we should try again some other night."

He is silent.

"And maybe you should try and figure out what you want. For me and for you."

They kiss again, and she pats his chest with her slender hand. Watching the red lights of his car disappear around the corner, Crystal smiles despite herself. How come these men are so stupid?

Then she steps back inside the house and turns off the overhead light and the tattered porch falls into darkness.

On his way home, Gene detours into the neighborhood where Sharon Krasner lives. Sharon has children too, except hers are normal and therefore less trouble, with a father and grandparents to take them off her hands every so often. Derrick has a grandmother and she watches him occasionally, but he is too big for her to haul around. Derrick will always need help, always need his mother to support him, physically, emotionally, and financially. Crystal will never be his the way Sharon could be.

He decides to stop at her house. It is dark. She does not answer the bell. Okay. This is probably a bad idea anyway. He continues back to his place. But not before resolving to give her a call in the morning. This idea cheers him up at once.

2

Martina meets Max at the offices of TV Channel 12, where he is advertising sales manager. They drive over to the Midtown Mall, a new downtown shopping center that is already dying a slow death. There they have a late dinner in the empty restaurant before going on to the Antique Exchange, open late tonight, where Martina wants to look for some furnishings for his new house, which is supposed to be ready later in the fall.

Max follows her docilely around the lower level of the store, an old Victorian house cluttered from floor to ceiling with every type of antique imaginable from the town's bygone days. She finds nothing she thinks would be suitable for Max's house, just huge overpriced butler's desks and photographs of stern old pioneers and cupboards overflowing with Depression glass and mismatched cups and saucers and stinky cigar boxes and moth-eaten quilts and ratty oriental rugs and yellowed embroidered cloths and horrible little glass animals and aged iron cooking utensils and hats with sweeping brims and fragile ruby earrings that Martina imagines some desiccated old lady in town used to wear when she was young and gay. All very cluttered and Junior League-y, like Dottie or Betsy or Meg or Babs or whatever the woman calls herself who produces the bone mirror in which Martina admires herself trying on an earring and holding her hair back from her handsome sloe-eyed reflection. Pretty enough, she thinks of the jewelry, but they are the clip-on type, which she does not wear on her pierced ears.

"What room are those for?" Max asks with what passes for his wit.

"Closing," Dottie/Betsy/Meg/Babs sings.

Walking to the car parked across the street, Max says, "Coming into the home stretch now."

"Did you talk to the builder today?"

"He wasn't there. I left a message."

"You don't think he's avoiding you, do you?"

"I'm sure he isn't. Al wouldn't do me wrong." His home is being built by Al Kolata.

"I want to go to one more place tonight," Martina says. "The carpet remnant store."

"It's closed, isn't it? It's after nine."

"They're open till ten. We can still make it."

She settles back in his Blazer and watches the dark houses flash by along Riverside Drive. "Going to be a nice little house, once we get finished decorating it," he says.

"Yepper."

"Shame I'll be living there by myself."

"Mmm."

"Course, if we got married, I wouldn't be there by myself, would I?"

"Guess not."

"Well? Whadaya say? Want to get married?"

"Max, I've told you four hundred times: I'm not ready yet. I wish you'd stop asking me."

"When are you going to be ready?"

"If I knew, I'd be ready."

The logic here is too much for him. He shakes it off like a pitcher shaking off a catcher's faulty sign. "I think you're as ready as you'll ever be," he says.

She closes her eyes. In that case she'll never be ready. Max is a nice man, and she probably loves him. He is not the smartest guy she knows, but he is not the dumbest either. She knows that of such compromises are life made. Maybe she is ready after all.

The next day Dr. Gerard's secretary calls her. He wants to see her. Sighing, she leaves the draft binder of her revision of the newest nursing treatment protocol open on her desk and goes down the hall to his office, steeling herself as always for him.

"I have some news for you," he says. "This is strictly confidential. You have to promise not to tell a soul."

"My lips are sealed."

"There's going to be a management shakeup soon."

She says nothing, waiting for him to continue.

"On the vice presidential level. It's going to have ripples all the way down the line."

"What kind of ripples?"

"Big ones. Don't tell a soul," he says again.

"I won't."

"If I hear this information got out to anyone on this floor, I'll know where it came from. McCarthy's out."

McCarthy is the vice president for ambulatory services, a universally disliked martinet. This has long been rumored to be in the works. "When?"

"End of the month."

"How did you find this out?"

"I got it all from Fawcett. I'm going to be tapped to fill McCarthy's chair."

Martina says nothing.

Then she makes herself ask, "Who's going to fill your job?"

"They're going to recruit from outside the hospital."

"And in the meantime?"

"I suggested you be appointed interim director, in the continuing absence of an assistant director. But I was overruled.

Fawcett wants somebody in here with more administrative experience."

"But I have administrative experience."

"I told them. Larry's going to be acting director until a new director is appointed."

"Oh shit."

"Once a new director is found, Fawcett wants Larry to stay on as permanent assistant director to ease the transition. I'm sorry, Martina," says Gerard. "But it was out of my hands."

He rises from his desk and comes around to her side. Oh God. He can't, not now. Not any more. She thought she made that clear.

"Sorry," Gerard says. He sits in the chair beside her. "I know how much this meant to you."

"Excuse me," she says, standing. "I feel sick."

3

The big man scowls at the figures Dennis Parker has written out for him. They are sitting in his kitchen underneath a slowly revolving ceiling fan that channels the smoke from the man's endless cigarettes directly into Dennis's face. The man is wearing a worn yellow Kool's tee shirt that bulges over his belly. He shakes his head, blinks, rubs a hand across his eyes. His wife, a demurely pretty middle-aged strawberry blonde, smiles helpfully at Dennis.

"Christ, I been working so long I can't even see straight," the man says in a gravelly smoker's voice. "I got the late shift over to the job this week and I can't even focus my eyes. S'posed to get off at eleven. Last night the machines went down and they kept us till three in the morning. Then they got the boy working nights over with the city and he's here trying to sleep during the day too and between the two of us . . ."

He shakes his head. "Christ!"

Dennis forces a weak smile. Ever since he set foot in this house this man has done nothing but complain about being too tired to concentrate because of his revolving shift work. He works at one of the local factories making film for medical x-rays, spending most of his time, as near as Dennis can make out, knee-deep in chemicals.

Which perhaps better explains his inability to think clearly than any changes in shifts.

"Well, Mr. Korotki," Dennis says, "maybe I can just leave these figures here with you."

"Yeah, Dennis, can you do that? I can't even tell the difference between a two and a five right now. Can't even focus my eyes."

"You can look at them when you have a chance, and let me know what you decide."

"I don't even know what shift I'm supposed to work till the day before."

"Just give me a call if you decide to have these installed."

Dennis gathers his papers and stuffs them into his briefcase. He starts moving for the door before everything is even inside.

"Dennis, you got your phone number on here somewhere?"

"Right at the top of the page."

"Oh yeah, there it is."

"Just give me a call when you make your decision."

"'Say, Dennis, can you do anything for me on these prices? These're kind of steep for windows, don't you think? Yeah, I was sick there awhile back, and spent damn near all the savings. Couldn't work. Dunno if I can put my hands on all this money. Unless I hit the lottery! Huh-huh! Yeah, I was sick there, and then come back to work to find I'd been laid off!"

"I can maybe talk with my sales manager. If you're really interested."

"Yeah," Korotki says, "because these prices are kind of steep for windows. Unless they're made of gold! Huh-huh! I won't be able to afford them. Unless I win the lottery. Huh-huh! Unless I'm not reading it right—which could be, Dennis, I only got three hours sleep last night."

"Mr. Korotki," Dennis says, "Mrs. Korotki, thanks for your time."

Mrs. Korotki stands with Dennis to show him out. Her husband remains seated, puzzling over the estimates.

Outside Dennis makes a beeline for his car to carry him away from this house as fast as it can. Another unsatisfied noncustomer. For a minute there he was afraid this guy was actually going to buy some windows, and there Dennis would be with a sale on his hands. Fortunately, Chester Korotki didn't let him down. Bless his big, dumb, stupid heart. Huh-huh!

Jackie's chair is empty when he returns to the office, though her desk light is on and her typewriter is humming and contracts are scattered over her desktop. She's still in.

Unfortunately, so is Baumgartner. He sits in his office with one foot up on an open drawer, his high pants cuff showing a cadaverously white hairless leg. The sales manager Catalpa is in with him. They each have a can of Genesee open in front of them.

"Parker," Baumgartner calls through the doorway.

Dennis sticks his head inside the office.

"Parker, what the hell's going on with you?" Baumgartner asks. "Make any sales tonight?"

"I may have. I have a good lead."

"Don't bullshit a bullshitter, Parker, that's all you ever got is good leads. Don't you ever make any good sales?"

"I try."

"Yeah, you're very trying," says Baumgartner. Catalpa guffaws.

"Hey, Parker," Baumgartner says. "What are you snooping around our girl's desk for?"

"Just wanted to ask her a question."

"Yeah? What kind of question?"

"About a form, that's all."

"Yeah? What kinda form? Long and skinny? That the kinda form you got for our little lady?"

When Dennis does not reply, Baumgartner says to Catalpa, "Gus, I think old Parker here's got the hots for little Jackie. What do you think?"

"Looks like it to me," says ass-kisser Catalpa.

"How do you think little Jackie feels about him?"

"Got me."

"We could ask her."

Baumgartner kicks in the drawer his foot is propped on. "Parker, how'd you like me to put in a good word for you with this girl?"

"Mr. Baumgartner, I definitely wouldn't like that."

"Why not? You got a thing for her, don't you?"

"No sir."

"You're not the only guy around here with a hard-on for that gal. Listen. I'm going to do you a favor. Why you deserve one, I dunno. But I'll tell you what. I'll put in a good word for you with

Jackie if you go out and try to sell some windows. How's that? Sounds like a good deal to me, eh Gus? All you got to do is try and sell some windows. For a change."

"I do try, Mr. Baumgartner. And please don't tell Jackie anything about me, all right?"

"Why not?"

"Please," Dennis says, "just don't, please? I really—really—wish you wouldn't."

Baumgartner pulls at his nose hairs a few times, says, "Parker, you're a constant disappointment. Here I was going to set you up with some prime pussy, and I'm talking pussy that's hotter'an anything I can guarantee you've ever had, and all you can do is say, 'Please don't, Mr. Baumgartner, please please don't.'" His mimicry of Dennis is cruel and precise.

"I just don't want to put her on the spot, that's all."

"Come in here, sparky."

Dennis moves inside the room. "You haven't sold shit since you've been here, have you?" Baumgartner's voice is low and serious now.

"I've made some sales."

"No, you haven't made more than enough to squeak by with. I'll tell you what. No bullshit now. I'm giving you another month. If you don't bring in something more than this nickel and dime shit you pull in, I'm going to have to let you go. Understand that?"

"Yes sir."

"I've carried you for long enough. It's time you pulled your own weight. Instead of your johnson."

"I understand."

"I hope you do. All right, now go do something with your life. Hey, Parker," Baumgartner calls after him. "You should have taken my deal when you had the chance, son." Catalpa snorts.

Dennis returns to his desk in the other room fearing more that Baumgartner will actually say something to Jackie than that he will lose his job. Though this threat is not good news either. If Jackie hears anything from anyone, Dennis doesn't want it to be from Baumgartner. He wants to tell her himself, and he is nowhere near ready.

He cleans his desk, throws away the unread sales memos that have accumulated over the past few weeks, makes piles of blank sales contracts, turns his light off, and waits until he hears a commotion out front that he takes as Baumgartner's goodnights. He edges out to the front room and ducks back as he sees Baumgartner's broad back and bald pate at Jackie's desk.

"Parker gone yet?" Dennis hears him say.

"Haven't seen him," says Jackie. Please, please, Dennis silently pleads, in the same whiney way that Baumgartner mocked so well, don't say anything to her. Please.

"Our boy Dennis has a thing for you, young lady," Baumgartner says. Dennis's heart dissolves in his chest.

Things quickly get worse. "I know," she says. "He's such a doofus."

"Listen, he's the asshole of all time. He came snooping around your desk when he got back from his last call. Empty handed, as usual."

"He asked me out a couple times."

"He's pitiful. What'd you. tell him?"

"I kept putting him off, until he asked me the last time. I wasn't busy, and he looked so sad, I said yes. We went out for a drink at this place I know. I felt so sorry for him."

"Well, 'sorry' isn't what he feels for you."

"I know. I hope he doesn't ask me again. Otherwise, I'll have to tell him about Dave."

"Our Dave? Back in Installation?"

"Yeah. We're going out. I tried not to tell Dennis about it. But if he asks me out again, I'm gonna have to let him know there's somebody else."

"If I were you, I'd tell him there was somebody else even if there isn't."

"Oh, Mr. B."

"So, sweetheart. Tell me about you and Dave," Baumgartner says. "Is it serious?"

"Wicked serious."

Dennis slinks away to the back of his office where he can't hear them except for their laughter. He sits at his desk and stares at the stapler and Scotch tape dispenser.

Baumgartner leaves after a while. Dennis waits until he hears Jackie go out the back, where, Dennis now realizes, Dave will be waiting for her and they will begin their night.

He gives them time enough to drive off before he slinks out the front door.

CHAPTER FOURTEEN

1

In an unnaturally bright cubicle in the ICU at Strong Memorial Hospital in Rochester, New York, Brooke's mother lies with her head bandaged and her left arm wrapped in a cast from the shoulder to the wrist. Her free arm is connected to an IV line and a monitor that sends spikes of heart activity and jagged waves of respiration rolling erratically across a screen above her bed. A cannula taped to her nose infuses her with oxygen. On her big toe is a little clip that shines a red light through the nail. Her mother looks 105 years old, with a gray face and sunken mouth where they have taken out her false teeth.

"Hi, ma," Brooke says. Her mother does not reply. The medical waveforms do not change their herky-jerky travel.

"Can she hear us?" she asks her father standing beside her, peering over the bars on the bed.

He shrugs. He too looks old and sad beyond his years, grim around the mouth, sallow complected, hair tousled. "She's sleeping," he says. "They gave her something to relax her." His eyes fill with impotent tears as he looks down on her.

Brooke lightly squeezes her mother's free arm. "Ma," she says, "I'm here. Daddy's here."

"Everything's going to be all right," Brooke's father says, all appearances to the contrary.

They can only visit for ten minutes each hour. When their time is up, they return to the waiting room where others maintain rumpled vigils for their own loved ones. "She's going to be all right," her father tells her. "She'll come through this. She's strong."

"She looks bad."

"It's the bandage," he says. "And all that crap they got her hooked up to. It always looks worse than it is."

She puts an arm around his stiff shoulders. "Who found her?"

"Easter. She was going down the basement to do some wash and found her at the foot of the steps. In a pool of blood. She thought she was dead. She called me right away. I called 911 and rushed home. The ambulance was there and they were working on her."

"How did it happen?"

"Can't figure that out. She never goes down the basement. Easter didn't hear her scream or fall."

He shakes his head, unable to approach the alternative to slipping: that his wife jumped, took a dive off the bottom landing of the back stairs, launched herself into space for who knew what reason and plummeted head-first to the concrete floor. Is her mother that sick? A wave of nausea passes over her at the thought of it.

"She's going to be all right. I know she will. She's going to come through this just like she came through all the others."

"The others were never like this."

"She's going to pull through," he insists.

"Does Lenny know?"

"No."

"Why not?"

"I don't want him involved with this."

"But why?"

"He's back on drugs."

"How do you know?"

"I know. He was on drugs when he was here the last time with you."

"How do you know that?"

"I found drugs in his room. I found pills. I don't want to talk about him," he says, shaking his head tensely. "I don't want him here and that's that. We have enough trouble in this family without him."

2

Brooke tries to get her father to come home for some rest, but he refuses. Characteristically, he insists that she go instead. Characteristically, she does as he says.

The house is empty, except for the housekeeper Easter, asleep in her room upstairs. It is 2:45 a.m. by the clock on the microwave in the kitchen. After she called her father from her house in Buckingham, she threw a suitcase together, waited for Harry to come home from his balloon ride, turned away his offer to go with her, and jumped in her car for the three-hour drive. She thought of calling Robert Fitzgerald from the road, but decided against it. This is her own family life, and she must face it by herself.

Now, walking around the huge darkened split level, she thinks back to all the bad times her mother has caused the family, and she feels herself sink into the hopelessness that is so familiar, that she has tried so hard to escape throughout her life, most recently (and successfully) through her marriage to sunny, optimistic Harry, Harry of the charmed life, opposite in every way from her family, her darkly claustrophobic, secretive family, ashamed, squirming in the grasping talons of the demons of her mother's condition.

As always, whenever her mother pulls something like this, Brooke is left with the palpable sense that any effort she makes to escape the influence of her home life is doomed to fail. Her mother's deep disturbance, and her father's denials that anything is wrong— and her brother's own life-long reactions to these tensions—leave Brooke unable to function, a victim of her own flesh and blood.

Later, when her mother's episodes would pass, Brooke would regain the control over herself that helped her organize her life so well. It was, in fact, following one of her mother's hospitalizations that she decided to marry Harry. After her initial feelings of hopelessness, she knows even now in the midst of a spell, is an equally strong reaction, a snapping back to attention almost, during which she will lock her negative feelings like barking dogs in a room in the cellar of her mind. If she can keep these dogs under control, she can get on with her life. And, she has always secretly hoped, give her mother an example of how force of will can vanquish depression. It always does for Brooke, never for her mother.

Every room she passes through in this house, every piece of furniture is linked to some past trouble or other. The sofa: once her mother couldn't be urged to leave the sofa in the living room for a month straight; she slept, ate, used a bedpan, submitted to the sponge baths of the nurse her husband was forced to hire. The kitchen range: her mother scalded her own legs once in the kitchen with a pot of boiling water that inexplicably tumbled off the stove one night when she said she felt well enough to cook dinner. The dining room table: scene of many monumental fights, the most memorable one on a Christmas that ended in a screaming match between her mother and Lenny that caused Lenny to leave home for the first time when he was fifteen; today Brooke cannot even recall the reason; she just remembers her father sitting there with his head buried in his hands. And the sofa bed in the den: here is where her father moved permanently after her mother refused to share a room with him anymore, for no good reason he was willing to talk about or Brooke was capable of discovering. These are the shards and shreds of her early life, one family trauma after another, the dissolution of her family's hopes charted across the floor plan of her parents' home.

But her family never did totally dissolve. There were good times, too, as all families have, even the most desperate. Still, when Brooke conjures up her family life she is left not with the glow of happily remembered memories of beaches and amusement parks, but the acid tastes of embarrassment from when she was young and constant disappointment when she grew older. They rise corrosive in her throat.

She is drawn downstairs, to the basement. She turns on the light at the top of the stairs and peers down and around the landing as though something were waiting for her down there.

Holding tight to the railing, she steps down carefully, watching the carpet beneath her feet for any sign—grease, maybe, a dark telltale spot—of what might have caused her mother to slip. Could there have been a section of newspaper that Easter had failed to pick up? A bag of rubbish that her mother tripped over?

Evidence cleared away immediately by Easter, lest she be blamed for this latest catastrophe?

No, this is unfair. Easter is not that sneaky. Had this been in any way her fault, she would have accepted responsibility for it at once. And then quit in remorse.

Brooke stands at the landing, in the spot she imagines her mother stood before she fell. Or jumped. How could she have fallen and hit her head so hard? It is only five steps down. Had she simply collapsed? If so, holding the railing, as her mother almost certainly would have, she would not have been able to make it as far as the basement floor.

Back upstairs, in the den, she lets herself be sucked into the Barcalounger. At home in Buckingham now, Harry would be sleeping his usual sleep of the comfortable and confident. She hopes; what if he is out doing with a woman what she does with Robert Fitzgerald? Her spirits sink even further, and she forces the thought out of her mind at once. Tonight, in the throes of this family crisis, she cannot afford to think of that. Or of Robert, or his attractions, or how he makes her feel or what he makes her feel, or what he holds out to her, or what she does with him. Because even these are more curse than blessing. He threatens the one refuge she has been able to create and hold onto in her life.

With Robert Fitzgerald trapped behind a closed door with all the barking dogs of her past and current lives shut up in the basement, she drifts off in the lounge chair to a sleep troubled by dreams of herself as a lost, lonely child chased by a crone down endless forest paths.

3

When she gets to the hospital in the morning, Brooke sees her father curled up on a couch in the waiting room. He is covered with a white hospital blanket, just as she had awakened in the morning on the lounger to find herself covered with a blanket offered in kindness by Easter. We must really be pitiful, Brooke thinks. We need so much taking care of by those around us.

She goes into the ICU. None of the nurses bustling around pays her any attention. Her mother is still asleep. When a nurse comes over to take some vital signs, Brooke asks her, "How is she?"

"Your mom's doing good today," the nurse says. "She had a restful night." Her name, Brooke reads from the badge on her robin's egg blue smock, is Lexie Schmidt. She straightens the blankets around the woman on the bed and pauses with a hand on the sideguard.

"Is she doing any better?"

"Kinda early to tell. She was in real bad shape when she came in. Her vital signs are stable now, but she took a bad hit on the head."

"What does that mean, she was in bad shape?"

"Have you talked to the doctor?"

"No. I just got here from out of town last night."

"Maybe you should talk to the doctor. He can tell you more than I can."

"Where is he?"

"He usually makes his rounds in the morning and at night. He's been in to see your mom already, so he won't be in again till later on."

"Well, can't you tell me what you mean, she took a bad hit on the head?"

"With head injuries, it's touch and go in the beginning. Her spine and all's in good shape. She's going to go down for another CAT scan later on. We'll just have to wait and see what happens when she comes out of it."

"When she comes out of it? I don't understand. Are you saying she's in a coma?"

"You really should talk to Dr. Zimmerman. I'll send him over if I see him around again." She turns and hustles back to the nurses' station.

When her ten minutes are up, Brooke goes out to sit with her father. As soon as he wakes up, stretches, rubs his head, smacks his lips, she says, "Daddy, why didn't you tell me the real problem with Mom?

Her father blinks a few times without comprehending.

"She's in a coma, Daddy. Didn't they tell you that?"

"I figured there'd be time to talk about things."

"What things? Like she's in a coma and might never wake up?"

"I don't believe that," her father says angrily, turning from her. "Did somebody tell you that? I don't believe it. The doctor told me most people wake up from their comas. People only stay in comas in horror movies and soap operas."

"I wish you'd have told me the truth." For once in my life, she almost adds.

"She's going to be all right," he insists. "She's going to be fine.

Did you go in to see her?"

"Yeah."

"How is she?"

"I don't know. The nurse said she had a restful night."

"That's a plus."

"I wish you'd told me the truth last night," she tells the exasperating man.

Her father pats her arm. "I didn't want to worry you, sweetie." Then, "I'm glad you came," he says.

4

She spends the next night at home by herself again. In the morning she goes searching through her parents' house one more time. In an address book in the drum table under the phone in the living room she discovers the long list of numbers and towns penciled in under Lenny's name and canceled with a line drawn through all but the last. The list stretches so far back in time that the early entries are now mostly blurs of pencil lead. The legible entries trace Lenny's wanderings over the past decade, through the underground railroad of the counterculture: from the latest (which surprised her), Susquehanna, Pennsylvania, not that far from where Brooke herself lives, to the earliest, and every stop in between, New York City, Ithaca, Denver, San Francisco, Seattle (no—she looks again—yes, it's true, he was probably there around the same time as Robert), Laramie, Hoboken. She had no idea he was so close nowadays. Nor that her father kept such close tabs on his son's whereabouts. How odd, for a man who claims to despise his son, to know his exact whereabouts for almost twenty years.

Brooke does not know what her brother does for a living nowadays. Once, she knew, he sold drugs to pay his way. She also has a vague remembrance that he worked construction, painting houses or installing drywall. Once upon a time he wanted to be an artist. He was talented when he was younger, especially with watercolors. In this he was Brooke's first role model and the inspiration for her later studies, which she, characteristically enough, made practical through a degree in graphic design.

This remembrance, this tendril of connection, along with her father's careful log of Lenny's moves, makes her believe she is doing the right thing. She awoke this morning to the realization that her brother deserves to know what has happened. This involves his mother too, and just because they are not a typical family doesn't mean Lenny shouldn't take part in this if he wants to. He has to have that option. It is, she feels, a good decision, a mature, adult thing to do. She is proud of herself.

She tells Easter what she is going to do. Easter tells her that her father will be upset when he finds out. Easter herself is not thrilled, either.

When she places the call to Susquehanna, there is much confusion on the other end of the line. She hears a gaggle of male and female voices yelling, children crying, the sound of a game show on television in the background. She talks to a woman with a young, breathy voice. Brooke imagines her as an earthy eighteen-year-old hippy princess with hairy armpits and legs. "Who are you calling for?" the woman says.

"Lenny Cooper."

"Oh," the woman on the other end of the line says. Brooke hears the squeak of a hand covering the mouthpiece of the receiver, then the other woman returning, saying, "Lenny can't come to the phone now."

"Would you tell him it's his sister, please."

"His sister?'

"Yes. It's very important. Our mother is in the hospital and I need to talk to him."

Again Brooke hears a hand covering the phone—imperfectly, because she hears the woman saying, "Does Lenny have a sister?" and a man's voice screaming something in reply in the background. She cannot tell if it is Lenny.

"What's the matter with his mother?" the woman asks when she returns.

"She had a serious accident."

"Is she going to die?"

"I don't know. She's in a coma."

"Look, Lenny really can't come to the phone. But I'll tell him you called."

"Would you ask him to call his parents' house in Rochester? That's where I am."

"I'll tell him."

Brooke replaces the receiver slowly. At least she tried. And even if she didn't get through, she made the gesture. Maybe this is all it will take, one member of this family reaching out, saying it's time to forgive and forget, time to let go of the resentments and anger . . .

Right. As if that would help. As if that would be sufficient to undo whatever caused her mother to throw herself off the back stairway in the first place. If that's what she did.

On the way to the hospital, her new familial impulses waver. She thinks maybe it is really better after all if Lenny doesn't come. Judging by the background noise on the telephone, his life sounds too disorganized already. A trip to Rochester would only make things worse. Maybe her father was right.

The friends and neighbors gather at the hospital during the day to shore up her father, then leave in obvious relief. Brooke's mother's sister and brother and their spouses, her father's brother, the relatives, all live out of town. They will not be notified of this unless the worst happens. Her father bears up under it all exceptionally well, putting on exactly the face everyone hopes he will: everything's going to be fine, he says. She'll pull through this one like she pulled through all the others.

Among the visitors, the neighbors are gladdest to see Brooke. The Krumms who live next door take her downstairs to the cafeteria for lunch. From them she learns that her mother has been especially despondent lately, though over what they couldn't guess. From them she gets the unmistakable impression that her mother has once again done this damage to herself.

When they roll her mother out for a CAT scan, Brooke and her father follow the gurney down in the elevator, her father struggling back tears and Brooke patting her good arm and murmuring such words of encouragement as she can muster. She lacks her father's ability to cast everything in a good light. She expects her mother to expire at any moment, here in the elevator where no one can run up to her and pound on her chest and do all the other things they must do to save her life.

Late in the long day, it seems as if her father's refusal to give in to bad news will pay off. The word that trickles out from the nurses in the ICU during their ten-minute visits grows more promising each hour. Her mother's vital signs are getting stronger, and while everyone is too busy to explain exactly why that's happening, Brooke and her father know it is a happy development.

Finally, when she returns from the cafeteria after taking a dinner break around seven, her father is sobbing by himself in the waiting room.

Fearing the worst, she rushes up to him. "Daddy—what happened?"

He raises his tear-stained face. "She opened her eyes," he says. "She's going to be all right."

She only stayed awake for five minutes, but this is an excellent sign, the nurses say.

Her mother has a slight setback during the evening, but the doctor, when they corral him, insists this is a natural happening as night slows down the body's rhythms. Her father opts to stay in the waiting room again to be close to his wife, despite his daughter's entreaties that he go home and at least get cleaned up. Again, he insists she go, which she does.

Exhausted, emotionally drained, Brooke still cannot bring herself to sleep in her old room. She spends yet another night on the lounge chair in the den.

She wakes being shaken by Easter. The older woman is too distraught to speak. There is a great commotion coming from the front of the house. Brooke throws the blanket around her shoulders and follows Easter's bent back.

Lenny and a woman are at the front door. Lenny is pounding on the door, which Easter has refused to open, and the woman is trying to restrain him. Behind them, Brooke sees a banged-up Chevrolet parked in deep ruts diagonally across the front lawn.

"Where is she," Lenny demands when Brooke opens the door. He is wild-eyed and flying on something.

"At the hospital," Brooke says, and Lenny turns and runs down the steps to the car.

"Lenny! Lenny!" His companion takes off after him. He gets in the car but can't start it. He pounds the steering wheel in frustration, throws himself out of the car and pounds the hood once with his big fist. Again his companion tugs on his arm, this time to keep him from hurting himself. He doubles over and puts his head on top of his fists. His friend pats him until he is calm, then approaches Brooke, who has been watching in horror the violence of this scene, which she believes she has unleashed.

Lenny's friend has long tangled red hair and an angular, lined face, sharply pretty but for the deep circles under her eyes and the boney jaw. She wears dirty Levis torn at the knee and a University of Pittsburgh tee shirt that is thin from washing. Her breasts are small and clearly outlined against the fabric. She seems older than Lenny by a good ten years.

"Are you Lenny's sister?" Hers is a husky voice, not the breathy hippy princess Brooke expected.

"Yes. Brooke."

"I'm Grace. I'm a friend of Lenny's."

"Is he all right?"

"He's in a state. Sorry about the lawn. I knew something like this would happen, but he wouldn't let me drive. At least it's just the lawn. How's his mother?"

"Getting better."

"He'll be glad to hear that. He didn't get home until late last night. When I told him about his mother, he went sort of crazy. You know what he's like, I'm sure. Well, maybe you don't. Anyway, he jumped in the car and was ready to tear up here in the middle of the night. I told him I wouldn't let him go unless I could come along and take care of him."

They walk together down the lawn to where Lenny is still leaning against the pinging car. Lenny picks his head up with a shock. "Lenny," says Grace, "it's all right, man. It's cool. Your old lady's going to be all right."

"No," Lenny shouts. He brings his fists down hard on the hood and Grace grabs onto his arm.

"Lenny, it's cool, it's cool!"

Lenny tries to shake Grace off his arm and Brooke tries to get hold of his other arm and he pulls her off her feet and around in a circle and slams her against the fender. He is big and strong, but tires quickly. Together the two women wrestle him to the ground. His body odor is foul, as usual. Close to Grace, Brooke notices hers is too.

"Lenny!" Grace shouts. "Come on, man. Snap out of it!" Gradually Lenny calms down.

"I told you she was going to be all right," Grace says to him.

After she catches her breath, Brooke says, "Why did he come?"

Grace looks at her strangely. Brooke will remember this look. "Because you asked him to," she says.

Lenny sleeps it off in the spare bedroom upstairs. They are just able to get him into bed before he collapses.

Easter makes Grace scrambled eggs and coffee. "You look like you haven't slept either," says Brooke.

"If you were driving with him, would you sleep?"

"I guess not."

"I thought he'd crash much earlier. I thought he'd pull over and I could lay him out in the back seat. But he kept on going all the way. Till he got here and parked it on the lawn." She smiles. She has long white teeth and thin lips. In the clear light she looks about forty-five years old.

"Has he been doing a lot of dope again?"

"He has his moments."

"I'm sorry I called him," Brooke says.

Grace shrugs. "What else could you do? He's your brother. And she's his mother."

Her father, of course, forbids Lenny to come to the hospital.

"Daddy, he wants to see her," Brooke says.

"She doesn't want to see him."

"You don't know that."

"She doesn't want to see him, believe me. I don't want to see him, either."

"She's his mother too."

"I don't want him at this hospital."

She calls Lenny and asks him not to come down. "Not just yet," she says. "He'll want to see you. Give him time."

"Honey," Lenny says, "nobody has that much time."

Lenny shows up, of course. He looks awful stomping down the hall, hair long and stringy and belly hanging over his Levis. Grace trails behind him.

Mr. Cooper is furious. From the waiting room he sees the bearish figure of his son and he takes off to intercept him. "No," the older man says, holding his hands up. "No. No, no, no. I told her I didn't want to see you."

"Dad," says Lenny. He tries to throw his thick arms around his father but the older man stiff-arms him and backs away.

"I came all the way up here to see her."

"You're not in any condition to look at your mother."

"What kind of condition do I have to be in?"

"I don't want her to see you."

"That's a different thing."

"No it isn't. Go away. Go back where you came from. And stay there."

The old man turns his back on his son and walks away.

"What's the big deal, you old prick," Lenny calls after him. "She's not going to give a shit anyway. She's out to fucking lunch. As usual."

His father stops, turns, yells, "You son of a bitch! [n] and rushes back to where his son is standing and pushes him into a utility cart that clatters into the wall. The commotion draws the attention of a pair of nurses from down the hall. "How I hate you," the old man cries. Lenny holds his arms up to block the older man's feeble swipes. "You did this to her. You made her this way."

"Dad," Brooke pleads.

The old man waves her off. "Go away," he says to his son. "I never want to see you again."

Brooke holds his arm. "Daddy, please."

"No. Go away!"

Grace stands behind Lenny, Brooke behind her father, holding back these men. Lenny stands sneering at his father with his hands on his hips, then spits, "Fuck you. I hope she dies." He stalks off.

When she gets her father calmed down—no easy task, as he spends the next hour storming up and down the halls—Brooke goes off to look for Lenny. He is nowhere, not the cafeteria, the coffee shop, the main lobby, or the visitor's parking lot.

She drives home to look there. His car is gone from the front of the house, leaving the ruts in the center of the lawn. On her hands and knees in the living room, Easter says Lenny and Grace came back to get their things and then took off again. He said he wasn't coming back, ever.

Before he left, he heaved a table lamp into the huge mirror over the mantle in the living room. Easter is picking up the shattered pieces with a pair of Playtex gloves. "Seven *more* years bad luck for this family," she murmurs.

Brooke sits on the sofa and buries her face in her hands. It is not long before she is sobbing hard into her palms, without even the presence of mind to think: Jesus. Now *I'm* losing it.

That evening her mother wakes again. She looks around, connects with her husband, and turns away vacantly to examine the flower arrangements that line the window ledge. She stays awake for several hours. Her husband cries. Brooke smiles weakly. She has no more tears to shed.

She makes plans to leave.

CHAPTER FIFTEEN

1

And do you know the worst of it?" Martina says. "The absolute worst?"

"No."

"The lousy bastard kept leading me on, even after I told him I wasn't going to put out for him. He told me to meet him at a motel, and even after I said I couldn't do that, he still kept telling me I was the leading candidate."

They stroll along the shaded walk behind the hospital. Robert bumped into her on the way to the cafeteria and invited her to have lunch with him. When he asked her why she looked so down, she told him she had been passed over for her promotion. He had said, "That's always hard to handle."

"You don't know the worst of it," she said, and began the whole story.

They gravitate to a redwood table with benches under a gaily striped umbrella in the open space between two wings of the hospital. The Auxiliary has funded a handful of tables and chairs for the staff to use during their breaks. It is past the main lunch hour now, so only one other table is occupied, by a trio of nurses having a last cigarette before returning to their unit.

"What do you think I should do?" Martina asks him.

"Have you thought about filing a grievance for sexual harassment? He's the one who took advantage of his position over you. You were doing what he made it clear you'd have to do to advance in your job."

"I don't know."

A maintenance man riding by on a mower waves. After he passes and the clattering of the machine fades, she says, "That may be true, what you said. But I feel I'm as much to blame as he is. I couldn't bear to bring it out into the open. Can you imagine the things he'd say about me? I wish I could go back in time and do everything differently. When I was young, you know, I thought you worked hard, you did a good job, and you were rewarded."

"Boy, were you naive."

"God, Robert, I feel so dumb. And dirty."

"Your part in this notwithstanding, the eleventh commandment for an administrator is, 'Thou Shalt Not Take Advantage of Those Over Whom You Have Absolute Control.'"

"I feel so incredibly stupid."

Two nurses wander by and sit at another table. They lick ice cream cones from a Mr. Softee truck in front of the hospital.

Robert eyes them. "Wait right here."

He returns with a melting sugar cone in each hand. "You're a nice man," she says.

"I know," he sighs. "Sometimes I'm just so darn nice I could puke."

When he returns to his unit after walking her back to the elevator, he closes his office door and gives Brooke a call. It is Wednesday; he has not heard from her since the balloon fest the previous weekend. Something's up.

Her secretary says she has been called out of town by a family emergency.

"When do you expect her back?" He is told Mrs. McGuire is expected to be away for at least the entire week.

He hangs up and stares out the window at the parking lot below. He knows little about her family. Though he did ask. What was it she said about them? They're no holy family. She has never talked about her mother, or her father, or any siblings beyond that line. He knows she comes from suburban Rochester, but the only thing he knows about her life before college is that she was a cheerleader in high school. Listening to her, you would think that her life started only once she met Harry. Not that she talks about herself very much. She questions Robert mostly, about what he thinks and has done in the fifteen years that is the approximate gap between their ages.

Sometimes she does not want to talk at all. She seems to need to reconnect with much in her life.

"Anybody call?" he asks from Dennis's doorway. Dennis, lying on the bed, staring at the ceiling, shakes his head.

"Everything okay?"

"Dunky-hory."

"Had dinner?"

"Not hungry."

"I'm starved."

"Bon appetite."

"Can I make you anything?"

Dennis shakes his head.

"Dennis?"

"Mmm?"

"If there's anything you want to talk about, I hope you know you can talk to me. I'm careful, confidential, and reliable."

"I'll keep that in mind."

"Everything okay?"

"Why wouldn't everything be okay?"

"Because you look like you're prostrate in the face of life's vicissitudes."

"Leave my prostrate out of this, if you don't mind. I'm fine."

"You don't look fine, big guy."

"I am fine. Trust me on this one."

Reluctantly, Robert goes downstairs to make himself an aluminum tumbler of iced coffee. He sits with it in the living room. He places it on a coaster on the table beside his chair. Even the metal sweats.

He notices with dismay a crack up in the corner of the wall. He is about to pull himself up to examine it close up when he hears a car door slam out front, then the sound of feet on the front porch. They are heavy-heeled and determined. They stop at the front door, where they are replaced by the sound of the bell, which rings back in the kitchen.

Robert heaves himself to his feet and goes to the door. Through the flimsy curtain over the glass he sees the top of the dark brown head of a woman who is staring down at the ground. Her head snaps up when he opens the door. Her brown eyes are burning. They pierce the middle of his forehead and feel strong enough to sear through his skull and into the rest of the house like laser beams.

"Oh," she says, "hi." She mitigates the force of her stare. She wears no makeup on her olive skin, though her brows are finely shaped above a long nose and fleshy cheeks. "Gene home?"

"Sorry," says Robert, "he's out."

"Do you know when he'll be back?"

"Nope."

She grimaces.

"Want to leave a message for him?"

"Yes," she says, "if I could."

"Sure," Robert says, and waits for her to give it to him.

"Actually, if I could just come in, I could leave him a note."

"Oh, sure," Robert says, and steps away from the doorway. "Where are my manners?"

She sits on the living room couch and pulls a notebook from her purse.

"Won't be a minute."

"Take your time."

She begins writing quickly and angrily. She hunches over with narrow shoulders.

"Can I get you something to drink?" Robert asks.

"No, thanks. I'm not going to be here that long." But she continues writing and writing, shaking her head at what she is saying.

"Look," says Robert, "you really look thirsty. Why don't you let me get you some iced coffee or tea?"

"I'd prefer iced tea. If it's not too much trouble."

"Instant okay?"

"Fine."

"Lemon?"

"Sure."

Today he is a helper of women in distress. He goes back into the kitchen and she is still writing when he returns with her drink. "Thanks," she says. "I'm just about done."

He is silent for another five minutes. Her note stretches out to cover four sheets of notepad, back and front.

"Done," she says, and folds the bunch of paper in half. She scrawls Gene's name across one half and then caps her pen and shoves it back into the depths of her purse.

Robert says, "That's some note."

She lifts the aluminum tumbler. "Cheers."

"Cheers."

She takes a long drink.

"'It is when I struggle to be brief that I become obscure,'" he quotes. "Horace."

"Are you with the university?"

"No. I read that once on a Post-It note."

"I was definitely not obscure," she says. "Not that he'll understand any of it anyway."

"At least you probably feel better for writing it down."

"No. But I've said what I needed to say."

"Just as good. I'm Robert Fitzgerald."

"I know. Sharon Krasner. We've met before."

"Sure, I remember. At a party at this house. A long time ago."

"It was only a year. Not even."

"Seems longer."

"I suppose. Lot of water under the bridge, I guess."

"Not that it's any of my business, but Gene's told me a little about what's gone on between you."

"I see his mouth continues to be too large for his brain. What's he been doing, bragging about it?"

"Not at all. He was concerned."

"Concerned, but not sorry?"

"Concerned."

"That's about right. For all his touchy-feely personal freedom bullshit, he's a real jerk."

"If it's any consolation, just between the two of us, things aren't so great with him and his new friend."

"I figured that out," Sharon says. "He's been leaving calls for me on my machine. He says he wants to get together again. Thinks he can dump me and then pick up right where he left off. What's the matter with you men?"

"Can't live with 'em, can't shoot 'em in the head. Guy I know said that."

"He's not worth shooting. It's enough to tell him how wrong he is."

"At great length."

"Listen, he deserves everything in that note. And more."

"I'm sure he does."

She takes another long drink, forces herself to calm down. "Gene actually mentioned you a couple times with admiration," she says. "When he wasn't talking about how his kid doesn't love him anymore or how he's getting old. Or how his options are narrowing. Or any of his other bullshit midlife crises. How are things going around here?"

"Like many great ideas, my experiment's lost something in the translation to reality. I don't know how much Gene talked about what I wanted to do here."

"A bit."

"I thought things would work themselves out over time. We never really have whipped up much of a family feeling."

"Pardon my saying so, but with people like Gene as part of it, you were sort of doomed to fail. His problem is he's too self-centered. Maybe he was different once. He fundamentally doesn't care about other people, and it sounds like that's what you really needed here if this was to work."

"Sounds right."

"Not that you could have been expected to know that about him. He fooled me too."

She finishes her drink and stands. He follows. "I guess I better get going," she says. "I've taken enough of your time complaining about my problems."

"It was nice to see you again."

"Likewise. I guess life doesn't end when somebody dumps you."

"No, it doesn't."

She reaches out a hand and he shakes it. "Will you make sure he gets that note?"

"Absolutely."

Out on the porch, she says, "Thanks for your hospitality."

"No trouble at all. I'm in the middle of a relationship that's sort of dying on the vine myself."

'Yeah, lot of that going around. I hope everything works out."

"Thanks. For you, too."

"Bye."

"Take care."

"I'll try," she calls back over her shoulder with a weary smile.

2

Dennis watches the pre-dawn light creep over the dresser in his room. It picks out the details, plain but increasingly distinct, of the brass handles, the round wooden sunburst between the two rows of four drawers, the helter-skelter on the dresser top of empty deodorant pushup cylinders, half a Bugs Bunny glass of flat Coke, mismatched socks, used and crumpled tissues from his pants pockets, assorted change, a pair of sunglasses, receipts, overstuffed wallet, half roll of Tums, Robert's Seahawks cap, opened bottle of generic extra-strength non-aspirin pain reliever. The detritus of his life. As the digital numbers of his radio alarm measure off the minutes—5:17, 5:18, 5:19—the mirror over the dresser reflects the changing bare wall across from it, its color lightening from dark charcoal of deepest night to soiled eraser gray to dirty cream, which is its color when Dennis finally brings himself to sit upright in bed.

In the back yard sparrows chatter in the black walnut tree. They started an hour ago. Dennis was still up, having never fallen asleep this night.

He rises from the bed, still wearing his Levis and polo shirt from the night before, and looks out the window. The world outside is the same hue as his room. Quietly, he unlocks the screen and slides it up in its track. You would not have to do this with WonderWindows. With WonderWindows, all you would have to do is move two little gizmos with your thumb and the screen would drop open at an angle. Easy to clean. Ensure security with a flip of the thumb.

WonderWindows also would not accommodate a shape the size of the human body, as these ordinary double-hung windows could. An extra safety feature. But not much use to Dennis Parker this morning.

Though, as it turns out, it doesn't matter. From his window, Dennis, on the second floor of the rear of the house, looks down upon the smooth blanket of lawn below him. Howard the Cat is in his usual position, beneath the black walnut, eyeing the birds beyond his reach. Of all the times he has looked out this window, this is the first time Dennis has viewed the backyard with disappointment. Funny, he never realized how soft a landing the yard beneath his window would make.

He leaves his room for the last time, pausing outside the door. The others' doors are closed. From Robert's room comes only the regular buzz of snoring. Gene's and Martina's rooms issue only imposing silence.

He tiptoes barefoot down the stairs. Conscientious Robert has long since fixed the annoying squeaks in these things. Dennis's descent is soundless.

He moves ghostlike through the downstairs in a circuitous route to the mud porch. From one of the cupboards he extracts a new bundle of rope, perfectly white, tightly wound, stiff hemp.

In the backyard Howard sees him and scampers over with tail high. Dennis bends down and gives him a scratch on his sleek head and the cat humps his back, rubs his body against Dennis's leg. Dennis steps over him to the black walnut tree and rips the plastic wrap from the rope. He balls it up and tosses it away. Howard attacks it and soccer kicks the wad across the yard.

Dennis unknots the rope, plays out several feet over the grass, and tosses the thick core into the air. He has to do this three times before it sails over the lowest, thickest branch of the tree, which is about ten feet off the ground. He makes a slip knot in one end of the rope and works the knot up to the branch so that the rope is secure. He returns to the mud porch to retrieve a stepladder. Under the tree again he stands on the top step and winds the rope around his neck and, with difficulty, makes a knot in the unyielding cord close to his skin. It is a tight uncomfortable knot. At once he feels his head begin to throb. From this point on, things must happen quickly. He gazes up through the branches of the black walnut. They interlace in a thick network of wood and leaves. Hanging down in pairs are small lime-green walnuts in their casings. Farther up toward the top of the tree he sees the rapid movements of birds. Their noise has increased with his intrusion. All the way up are dappled patches of lightening sky.

Dennis takes one last look around. Across the yard Howard is standing still as a sphynx, glaring with disapproval at his friend standing on a stepladder with a rope tied around his neck.

"See you," says Dennis to his one friend in the world. He takes a deep breath and kicks the stepladder away and sways in a tiny circle in midair, struggling despite his desire for death against the sudden unexpected bodily panic that comes of suffocation. He claws automatically at the noose, makes small gagging noises, swings, twists around, the branch above him creaking and dipping but finally holding firm. A wash of red blurs Dennis's vision as if the blood vessels in his eyes have all burst and carry him struggling out of this world in a wave of crimson.

Martina Vitale eases her car door closed silently and then leans a hip against it to shut it all the way. The sound dies in the early morning street. She is, she believes, the only one up at this ungodly hour. Fortunately, for she is a mess. Her hair is uncombed, her face is blowsy, her clothes don't fit her right, the laces on her Reeboks are untied and dangling. At the first sign of dawn she had dashed out of Max's bed, where she had not planned on staying last night, and thrown on whatever was handy for the ride home. Now she can take a shower and get dressed properly before going in to her early morning staff meeting.

She tiptoes up the stairs. Dennis's door is open. This is unusual; her eyes are drawn inside. No Dennis. The bed is rumpled but not slept in. An open window overlooks the backyard. Through it she notes the sparrows who live in the black walnut tree are putting up a furious twittering. Thinking perhaps the cat has finally mustered the courage to climb the tree and is slaughtering as many birds as he can, she enters the sweat-smelly room and crosses to the window to see what the problem is.

She sees Dennis's limp body twisting slowly in the morning air.

She stops just long enough to burst into Robert's room and cry, "Dennis hung himself outside!" Robert is up and on his feet in an instant, as if he has, at some level of awareness, been expecting this.

Martina flies down the stairs shouting, "Come on, come on!" Out the back door, without so much as pausing for thought, she stands the stepladder back up and climbs on it and grabs Dennis's inert body and holds him up so the rope is slack. She tries to undo the knot at his neck but she cannot get it with one hand while trying to hold his body with the other.

"Get a knife!" she shouts to Robert, who is stumbling through the back door wearing only his red bikini underpants. He races back inside for a breadknife, which he hands up to Martina. He holds Dennis as she cuts him down. To Gene, who is now lumbering in his turn through the back door, Robert yells, "Call an ambulance!" Gene stops dead and rushes back inside.

When they get him down on the ground, Martina slices the noose off Dennis's neck, nicking the skin and drawing blood. She positions his head back to free his airway. "I don't feel anything," she says, placing her fingertips against where the pulse should be on his neck and leaning her face close to his. She manipulates his jaw to begin CPR. Robert moves in and the two of them alternately blow and pump life back into Dennis Parker's body.

Which is breathing on its own by the time the ambulance crew arrives, a long twenty minutes later.

Robert tosses on some clothes and in his own car follows Martina in the ambulance with Dennis. As Dennis is being ministered to in their hospital's ER, Robert calls Gene to let him know their housemate has survived. "It's a question of how much damage was done before she got to him," Robert says. "They won't know that for a while yet."

"Thank God," says Gene. "Thank God for Martina."

3

That night they gather around Dennis's hospital bed. That they all work in this place is not lost on Robert, who once upon a time worried that too many of the residents of his house would be connected with the hospital.

Dennis is sleeping a deep, sedated sleep. Bruises and cruel red welts ring his neck. There is a bandage just below his jaw where Martina cut him with the knife. An oxygen bag burbles.

Back home after the night charge nurse chases them away, Robert, Gene, and Martina sit together in the living room, subdued. Martina elaborates on the dangers that Dennis faces: brain damage from lack of oxygen, psychological trauma, further inability to live a life that is not maladjusted.

"If you hadn't have come home exactly when you did," Gene says, "we wouldn't have found him until too late."

"The funny thing is, I popped awake at Max's out of a sound sleep. Just as if a bell had gone off letting me know it was time to get moving."

"It's like you knew," says Robert, shaking his head.

"This seems as good a time as any to say this," Gene says. "I was going to tell you all sooner or later. I've decided to leave."

"You're moving out?" Robert asks.

Gene nods. "Leaving town. I thought I'd go out and visit my older son in California for a while. See if there are any roots I could put down out there."

"Where in California?" Martina asks.

"Outside San Diego. I've stayed with him before. He's got a great place with a big huge yard. I could find work in San Diego, I'm sure."

"What made you decide?"

"Oh, things haven't been going so well for me lately. I thought I'd try my luck out there for a while. And now this thing with Dennis . . . it's very upsetting."

Robert says, "I'll be sorry to see you go."

"And I'll be sorry to leave. I enjoyed living here. I really did."

"When do you think you might be going?" Robert asks.

"I'm hoping to leave by the end of the month."

"Soon."

"Not soon enough."

After Martina excuses herself for bed, Robert and Gene sit together in silence.

"I've been to San Diego a couple of times," says Robert.

"Pretty country."

"What's your son do out there?"

"He runs a landscaping company. I thought I'd work with him while I tried to get hooked up with a hospital or social service agency."

"Shouldn't have any problem doing that, I wouldn't think."

"Yeah," says Gene, "things have been getting a little tight for me around here."

Robert says nothing.

"I feel . . . blocked. Plugged up. Can't seem to think freely, breathe freely, can't talk freely, can't even screw freely." He pulls at his ear. "I need some open spaces."

"What makes you think you'll find them in San Diego if you can't find them here?"

"Mostly because it's not here."

"One way to look at it."

"You probably think I'm leaving because I've ruined my life here beyond correction."

"Is that what you think?"

"No," Gene says. "Not beyond correction, anyway. I just need to clear my head of a few things. After I'm out there for a year, maybe I'll be ready to come back. My younger son can come out and visit. Might be good for him to get away, too."

"After you're out there that long, will there be anything here to come back to?"

"Dunno the answer to that either," says Gene with a crooked smile. "The only thing I do know with any conviction is how anxious I am to get away."

CHAPTER SIXTEEN

1

Her eyes still adjusted to the dim light of her family visit, Brooke walks back into her grown-up life, which now seems suffused with painful light. She has been away a week.

She gets home on Friday around eight o'clock. Harry is at the bar. There are dirty glasses in the sink but no dishes. He probably never made a meal for himself. She finds newspapers scattered over the floor of the family room downstairs and dirty clothes at the foot of the bed in the bedroom. His dirty shirts are in a pile on the ironing board in the spare room; he did not even look for a plastic shopping bag to stuff them into. Automatically she tidies up.

She calls him at the bar and tells him she made the drive okay, hears him say he will be home early. She calls Joyce, tersely describes the trip as a nightmare, makes plans to meet her for lunch the next day. There is one more call she should make but cannot bring herself to do it, even though she is alone in the house with all the privacy she could wish for. Why does she find it so hard to get in touch with him all the time?

Tonight it is her own house she wanders through, her grown-up haven, set up to counteract the effects of the house in which she has just spent the last week. It is bright and airy, as different as possible, she now realizes, from the home of her first eighteen years and many of the next four. She has kept the furniture to a minimum because her father thought a well-appointed house was one piled high with heavy tables and chairs and sofas and highboys. She favors wispy, lacey curtains that fill the rooms with diffuse sun because her mother never cared for light and tried to shut it out of her life with layers of heavy draperies. Only now does Brooke notice this, with the sense of discovery of a traveler who, returning home, finds domestic habits that she once paid no attention to now scream with significance.

Harry, too, she sees clear-eyed when he gets home. She remembers why she married him, sees him for what he is, the archetypal good provider, steady, stable, handsome, industrious, rich beyond either of their dreams . . . What more could a woman want?

What more could *she* want?

2

Have you ever had an affair?" she asks Joyce. They sit in T. Moneybags, dawdling over coffee, the tale of her trip told, even now fading, reinterpreted in the telling, taking its place as yet another horror story of her family life.

To her surprise, Joyce replies, "Once."

"Joyce!"

"It's true."

'When?"

"Couple years ago."

"Was I around?"

"I think it was before your time."

"Wow. Joyce."

"It was more of a heavy flirtation than an affair, really."

"What happened?"

"He was an old boyfriend from school. He called me up out of the blue one day. I hadn't seen him for years. Turns out he was living in Syracuse. He asked me to meet him for lunch."

"He came all the way from Syracuse to see you?"

"We met halfway, in Cortland. The first time. The second time I dropped Maggie off at Mom's and drove up to Syracuse on one of my days off. We slept together a couple times, but we just didn't have that much to keep us together. Which was exactly why it fizzled out when we were in school."

"Sounds like more than a heavy flirtation to me."

Joyce shrugs. "Maybe it was."

"Why did you do it?"

Joyce stirs her coffee thoughtfully, taps the spoon against the cup, lays it delicately in the saucer. "I think partly I was flattered some guy from my past thought enough of me to track me down."

"Were you a bored housewife?"

"Not bored, I don't think. As much as wondering if everything was already over. It was just after I had Maggie. I loved her and I loved being a mother. But I was feeling kind of trapped for the rest of my life. And then here was this guy making grand romantic gestures. It was hard to resist."

"Did Mike ever find out?"

"If he did he never said anything."

"Has he ever had an affair?"

"If he has, I don't want to know about it."

"What would you do if you knew?"

"I'd be hurt. Angry."

"Would you forgive him?"

She thinks about that one. "I would've wanted him to forgive me for mine, so yeah. What I did was so reckless. It was definitely not worth wrecking my marriage over. I think if I was going to do something like that again, it'd have to be for somebody I thought was worth the risk, not just because my head was turned or whatever."

Brooke is silent.

"So what's this all about?" Joyce says. "Which one of you is playing around?"

"Why does one of us have to be playing around? Can't I ask a simple question?"

"Sure. So what's his name, or don't you want to tell me?"

"What makes you think it's me?"

"Honey, please. You're red as a beet!"

"I am not."

"Anybody I know?"

"No."

"How long has it been going on?"

"Not very long."

"Wow. Brooke. Does Harry know?"

Brooke shakes her head. "Don't tell him, okay?"

"Wouldn't dream of it. Is it, like, mad passionate love?"

Brooke shakes her head again, and smiles guiltily, which Joyce shares. It is only with this last answer, which is the real lie, that Brooke admits to herself it is finished with Robert. Finished, and already in the process of being reconstituted in her own mind, like her trip home. All she must now decide is how to tell him.

3

Kelly Sebring and Edie Albrecht have the McGuires over for brunch the next day with some other couples. The women are interested in her trip. They are caretakers of elderly parents themselves. Brooke finds them sympathetic and understanding of all she has gone through in a way that Harry is not. (Though he tries, she has to give him that. He does try. It's just that his sympathies don't extend much beyond himself.)

After she describes her visit, while the men discuss their work and President Reagan's latest shenanigans and Kelly serves up their chicken and radicchio with vinaigrette, Kelly and Edie catch Brooke up on the local news earnestly, as if she were one of their intimate circle, which in fact they are trying to make her. They tell her who is making a play to take over the Junior League, whose physician husband is taking in another partner, who saw Dr. Gerard (the best cancer man in the city, they agree) for a lump in her breast that turned out to be malignant. Listening to them she realizes (with no little surprise) that she cares more than she used to about them and the people they are discussing. This is my life, she grasps as never before, here with these women who understand me and try to include me in their own lives. My life is not somewhere else, with someone other than my husband. It is here, with them, discussing the milestones of our middle-class days. I worked hard to get here; these women signify my arrival.

Standing in the doorway on her way out, Edie fills Brooke in on what's happening at the hospital where Kelly and Edie volunteer. "And oh," Edie says, "I heard that friend of yours is having some trouble with the Administration."

"What friend?"

"You know, that one who runs the alcohol treatment program. What's his name? Harry's client?"

"Robert Fitzgerald?" Kelly supplies the name helpfully.

Brooke's heart stops.

"That's him," Edie says. "I heard he had a run-in with Fawcett."

"That's a tough program," Kelly says. "Tough to get clients for. There's so much denial around alcoholism."

"And Fawcett is a tough customer," Edie agrees.

Brooke asks, coolly, "What makes you think we're friends?"

"Well, I don't know, exactly," Edie says. "But Bruce"—her husband, the head of OB/GYN—"told me he saw you two talking together once at the hospital a couple months ago. I guess I just always made the connection. Maybe because he's Harry's client. I assumed you were all friends."

"I was just doing a freelance job for him."

"Harry's so friendly to everyone," Edie says.

"He sure is," Kelly agrees. "Didn't Harry invite him to the bar opening?"

Brooke says, "I think so."

"Yeah," says Kelly. "I'm sure I saw him there. Talking with you, as a matter of fact. I thought I also saw him at your birthday party."

Brooke feels their eyes on her. "He was there, now that you mention it."

From out front, Harry saves her. "Brooke. Let's go!"

"Well," she says, "I better get going. We're on our way to dinner at his parents'. Then we have a reception for the Y Board of Directors."

"Busy, busy," Kelly chirps.

"Is Harry still on that Board?" Edie asks. "My Bruce had to resign. Not enough time for everything, is there?"

4

On Monday morning after his staff meeting, Robert shuts himself in his office and calls Brooke. To his surprise he gets through right away.

"Brooke McGuire."

"Hey. It's Robert."

"Oh. Hey."

She is distant. Disconnected.

"How are you?" he asks.

"Okay. I was out of town."

"I know. I called your office and your secretary told me. Family emergency?"

"My mother was sick. Well, she wasn't sick, really. She had an accident."

"How is she?"

"Better. It was pretty serious. She was in a coma for a couple days. They think she'll be coming home soon."

"I'm glad to hear that."

"Yeah. My father's been a wreck. He didn't get any sleep at all when I was down there. I'm sure he still hasn't slept much, even though she's going to be all right. He spent every night in the hospital with her."

"How have you been holding up?"

"I'm sort of exhausted. But I'm all right."

"I'm glad to hear that."

Silence. She won't ask him how he is.

"I've been good," he says.

"That's good."

"Busy around here."

"Keeps you out of trouble," she says automatically.

More silence.

"Listen," he says. "I think we should talk."

Even more silence.

"We should," she agrees at last.

"How about lunch today?"

He hears the sound of pages flipping on her desk calendar.

"Today is okay. But I have to be back for a meeting at two."

"Okay. Peking Dragon okay?"

"Fine."

She doesn't offer him her cheek or hand. Things are terribly awkward. She picks up the menu as soon as the waiter puts it down. She has nothing to say. She looks drawn and pained.

The good therapist, he talks about how hard it is to go home as an adult, about the problems of having aged parents. Then about the buffet of Chinese food, about any number of other things. She is more like a polite stranger with whom he has wound up sharing his table at an airport restaurant than his one-time lover. She nods at what he says, feigning the least interest. Mostly she looks like she wishes she were elsewhere.

Robert is careful not to engage in any overtly affectionate behavior. No touching, no engaged smiles, no flitting of his gaze over her face and hair that bespeaks attention to something other than their meaningless small talk. It is not hard to be distant from her. She rarely meets his eye, gazing instead across the restaurant, twirling a curl of her hair with her long, ink-stained fingers, or else gazing down at her hands intertwined on the glass tabletop.

How different she is from the woman who flirted with him last year. He has definitely worn out his welcome with her. And, he has to admit, she with him.

It is only when the waiter whisks the check onto the table under two fortune cookies that Robert believes it is time to get serious. Because clearly it is up to him to bring the conversation around to serious matters.

They open their fortune cookies. His: Children around you will contribute to your happiness. Hers: You don't miss the water till the well runs dry.

"So," he says. "I haven't heard from you for a while." Tries to make it friendly, nonconfrontational. It's hard. To his own ears, his words sound accusatory.

"I told you. I was out of town. "

"That's okay. Only I was worried."

"It didn't occur to me you'd be interested in my mother."

The words come out harshly. He wonders if she means them that way. "I'm interested in you," he says, voice lowered.

"I'm sorry," she says, softening. "I was going to call you. I did think of it. I just—didn't know what to say."

For the first time she screws up her courage enough to look him in the eye though she still has to turn her head, as if she can't bear to look at him straight on. "This trip up there was hard for me. My mother's . . .always been a problem. I had a lot of things to sort out. My relationship with you was one of them. I didn't call you when I got back because I wasn't ready to talk about it yet. I would have called you. Eventually."

Eventually. When she got around to it. Another gut punch.

"What would you have said?"

"I would have said . . . that what we have has been very special to me. It really has," she adds, to add force to this cliche. "But my marriage is very special to me, too. For a bunch of good reasons. Going home made me realize that."

He nods, scowling not in anger but concern, sympathy. Understanding.

His therapist's face.

Momentarily her green eyes flash in anger as she thinks: you're so understanding, aren't you?

This makes it easier for her to continue. She takes a breath and plunges ahead, staring at her hands, which are now clenched on the table top. "I don't think we should see each other again."

"You know, Brooke, that's no newsflash. I figured that out when I didn't hear from you for three weeks. I'm not stupid."

"I didn't know how to tell you."

"It was pretty clear that what you wanted to do with me, you'd already done."

"Is there anything you don't understand," she spits.

Her anger takes them both by surprise. "Plenty," he says. "I don't understand why you didn't bother to talk to me about any of this. I don't understand why you didn't think we were close enough so you could be honest with me. And I don't understand why you didn't have the consideration to give me a call and tell me things were up in the air. I don't understand any of that."

Instead of easing things, this just makes her angrier. "You know, Robert, you didn't have that much to give me, so don't try and come off like you could have taken me to the stars or something. You never stopped to ask yourself what I needed from this relationship."

"I told you in the beginning what I thought you needed. And I told you I thought I could give it to you. And you obviously agreed with me. At least at that point."

"No, you just thought you knew what I needed. You didn't really have any idea. You still don't."

"Did you ever give me a hint? I asked you pointblank what you wanted from me and you never gave me an answer."

"Did it ever occur to you I was too confused to know?"

"Of course. That's why I didn't force the issue. I assumed we'd work things out between us."

"And now I guess we have. Let me ask you a question. What did you expect me to do about my husband? Did you expect me to leave him for you? Would you have wanted me to leave my husband for you?"

"Would you have wanted to?"

"Don't turn my question around."

"To be honest, I didn't think that far ahead. I didn't think in terms of leaving or not leaving. I thought in terms of what we could be to each other now. In a way that accommodated your situation."

How far apart our worlds are, he thinks, how different our expectations of love and connectedness. How badly I misjudged this whole thing.

She's right, he realizes. How little I really have understood. Again.

She shakes her head as if in reply, holds up her hands in surrender. "I don't want to talk about this anymore."

"Fine. Look. I want to say one more thing to you, before we say goodbye forever."

"You mean before I settle back in my husband's cozy life again? That life means a lot to me."

"I know it does. Oops, there I go understanding things again."

"No, you don't understand anything."

"I was going to say one more thing about how it felt to be treated the way you've treated me after you felt compelled to tell me you were falling in love with me, and after everything else we've been through in the last couple months. But I think I'm just going to skip it. It's not going to mean much now anyway. Take care of yourself."

He takes the check off the table. He leaves her behind to glare in silent fury at the four broken crescents of fortune cookies on the glass tabletop.

5

Dennis is awake. He looks horrible, of course, as you would expect of someone who tried to kill himself. There are deep, deep circles under his eyes and a gauze bandage around his throat. His hair is oily and unwashed. He has a four-day growth of beard.

"How are you doing?" Robert says. He stands at Dennis's side and holds the younger man's hand tightly.

Dennis shakes his head in a depression in the pillow. At the foot of his bed an aerator burbles. "Almost bought the big one," he says. His voice is croaky.

"You know who saved you, don't you?"

"She came to see me. She told me all about it."

"Did she tell you how she happened to be up at five in the morning?"

"She told me."

"I always said screwing has its uses."

"I just never got the chance to prove it personally."

Robert is silent.

"I was so dumb," Dennis says. He begins to cry. Robert bends down and cradles his head.

When the spell passes, Robert says, "You were lucky, my friend."

"I really could have fucked myself up."

"You sure tried. You're going to be all right. It'll take some time, but you'll be okay."

"Physically, anyway."

"And emotionally. You'll heal that way, too. Listen," Robert says, "I have to say this. I'm really sorry, Dennis. I should have been there for you."

"You were when it counted."

"No. I was part of the problem. I should have known, I should have helped. I shouldn't have let things get that far."

"You tried, man. I wouldn't let you. Hey, you want me to say I forgive you?" Dennis moves his hand in a weak approximation of a priestly blessing. "If it wasn't for you, I wouldn't be here now."

Dennis starts to laugh. It turns to a sob, which he tries unsuccessfully to stifle. Robert bends over again and folds him into his shoulder.

When this passes, Robert says, "I'm going to split. You need some rest."

"I almost got more rest there than I wanted."

"That'll come soon enough. No reason to speed it up."

"Guess not."

"Come home soon. We'll keep the light on in your room for you."

"Just don't expect me to kick in for the electric bill."

On his way down the hall, Robert runs into a tall thin woman. "Excuse me, doctor," she says to him, "but you just came out of my son's room."

"I'm not a doctor. Your son lives in my house." He introduces himself.

"Oh, Mr. Fitzgerald. It's such a pleasure to meet you. Dennis has spoken so highly of you." She shakes his hand with enthusiasm. "I'm Gloria Parker. Dennis's mother."

"It's a pleasure. Please, call me Robert."

"I wonder if I could talk with you for a minute, if I could just impose?"

"Sure."

Robert leads her down to the lounge at the end of the hall.

"My husband and me, we want you to know how much we appreciate everything you've done for Dennis."

"I like Dennis a lot. I'm glad I was there at the right time. I'm just sorry I missed the signs."

"Dennis hides his feelings a lot. Sometimes it's hard to know what's really going on with him."

"He's a sensitive guy. It's not an easy way to be."

"Well," she says, as if she can't figure out if this is a compliment or not, "I don't know where he gets that from. I do know he gets the part about hiding his feelings from his father." Nervously she tucks a limp length of fine hair behind her ear. "What I wanted to ask you was your opinion on something."

"Sure."

"I want to talk to Dennis's psychologist about this too. But first I thought I'd ask you. When Dennis gets out of the hospital, I thought he might be better off if he comes home with us for a while."

"Okay."

"I know he's happy at your house and all," she says, wringing her hands. "But where he's so troubled, I was thinking he might be better off at home, where we can take care of him. And keep an eye on him, too."

"Well, Mrs. Parker—."

"Gloria."

"Gloria, first of all, this is something you and your husband and

Dennis have to work out together."

"I know, I know. But where you're so close to him, and he's been living in your house and all, I just thought you might be able to give me some advice about what might be best for him."

"I agree he's pretty fragile right now. I do know his independence is very important to him. And I think his ability to function on his own is going to be an important part of the process of healing from this."

"I know that," she says. "That's why I didn't know whether he is in good enough shape to be on his own right now. I'm just afraid it's going to be a matter of time before he tries it again. I think I can keep him from doing it if he's home with us."

Her concern touches him. "You might be right."

"I think I am," she says. She seems a kind and generous woman.

"Not knowing what Dennis's home life was like, I can't really make the decision for you. My sense of him is that he needs to be on his own again as soon as possible, even if he goes back with you now. I'd be perfectly happy to have him come back to my house, as I just told him. But really my best advice is first talk all this over with Dennis and his therapist. And whatever decision he comes to, he'll need support for it. He'll have mine, and so will you."

"I understand."

In the elevator on the way down to the lobby something strange happens. Something overcomes him, some smothering hand that seems to slide across his mouth and clamp his jaws closed and make it impossible to breathe. He leans against the wall and grips the side railing with both hands. He fights a panic that makes his belly flutter and his chest heave, stifles a cry. People in the crowded car, lingering after visiting hours and now on their way home, watch him oddly, give him room.

One older man lends an arm to help him to the lobby, where Robert falls heavily into a chair and waves away an offer of further aid. He leans forward and tucks his head between his knees to keep from blacking out from lack of oxygen. Some portion of his mind thinks, "How extraordinary!" He covers his face with both hands and with an act of will forces his chest to rise and fall, tries to draw air down into his lungs and push it out again to expel the poisons of his mistakes out of his body and his life. He hears a raw, ripping sound and realizes it is himself, gasping.

After what seems like a long time, he feels a hand on his

shoulder and then a cold wet rough paper towel scrapes across his forehead and down his cheeks and over the back of his neck. Icy water dribbles inside his shirt. He jerks his head up abruptly—and sees Sharon Krasner bending over him, wiping his hair from his damp forehead.

She cools his skin until his brain clears and his pulse slows. He sits back and takes a deep, cleansing breath. "Are you okay?" she asks, and pats him on the shoulder.

"I think so."

"What happened?"

"I think I just had your basic anxiety attack."

"Just sit still for another few minutes."

"Not that I'm complaining, but what are you doing here?"

"My sister's in the postpartum unit. She just had a little girl. I was on my way out and saw you. You looked like you could use some help."

"Your sister's timing is impeccable."

"What are you doing here so late, besides hyperventilating?"

He tells her briefly about Dennis. "I think the last couple of days—or years—just caught up with me."

He grips the arms of the chair and shakily pushes himself up.

"Easy," she says. She stands along with him and wraps a steadying arm around his.

"I'm okay now," he says. "You came along at exactly the right time."

"Are you sure you're okay? You look a little green."

"I'm fine. My blood sugar's kind of low, on top of everything else."

"Look, I was just on my way to grab something to eat," she says. "Want to join me?"

"That's the best offer I've had all day."

6

Over guacamole at El Cholo's, the Tex-Mex place near the mall, he discovers she is a nurse, a maternal child health clinical specialist at St. Vincent's Hospital, the town's chief rival of Robert's own hospital. She was a surgical nurse in the army in Viet Nam. When she got out, she retrained in maternal and child health to be able to help on the beginning of life instead of the end of it. She has three little girls. She shows him their photos in her wallet; they are miniature versions of her.

Through the meal, and afterwards over endless refills of coffee in the emptying restaurant, they talk about their lives. She has been divorced for several years, since her husband left her for another woman. She never saw it coming. To make matters worse, right after he left she came down with a kidney infection that put her in the hospital, and when she got out she discovered he'd moved out half of the furniture, including things that would be helpful for a woman just out of the hospital with young children, like their bed. Between the mental and emotional pain and her run-down physical condition, she skirted the edges of a breakdown. She was able to pull herself back only by the thought of her children, how much she loved them and how much they needed her.

She recovered enough to resume her life, though since her husband left she has gone through a short series of increasingly bizarre relationships with men. She had seen Gene the longest of anyone since her husband, and Gene lasted only because she realized early on she was never going to get what she needed from him. He was able to give her almost nothing in the way of comfort and support, but what he did provide her with was another outlet for her most satisfactory source of emotional connection with others: her maternal concern. She was mother and lover to him, and (rarely) friend. But where she was getting ready to make a commitment to a man again, Gene was at a different place entirely, preparing for a middle age of adolescent exploration and play, not involvement. The timing would never be right.

Their thoughts turn to Dennis. He gives her the full story. "I'm never going to forget the sight of him hanging from that tree," he says. "That poor guy. I let him down so badly. I felt responsible for him. It was my house, my living arrangement. This whole thing was my idea."

"So? You're not responsible for his life."

"But I'm a counselor. I knew he was fragile. There has to be more I could have done."

"Maybe," she allows. "But people are allowed to make mistakes. And so are you. I'm sorry you feel so bad, but you can't act like this was your fault."

"You're doing a damn sight more for me than I did for Dennis. Or Catherine," he continues. "Or Andrea."

"Who are they?"

"Or Jeannie. Or Maureen. Or Brian or Nora. Or Gordon. Or any of the others in the whole messy business of my life outside the counselor's office."

"Whoa. You're losing it here, pal. Come back to Planet Earth."

"The other thing is, remember that relationship I mentioned when we talked at the house? It finally melted all the way down."

"Just what you needed."

"Well, it was no big surprise. Today was just the finish."

"Are you devastated?"

"No. I'm not overjoyed, of course. It was a really difficult ending. There was a lot of anger between us. A lot of anger in me, and not entirely toward her. I guess we each expected something the other couldn't deliver."

"That's always hard."

He tells her the woman he was seeing is married. She clucks her tongue, asks him if he really expected it to work.

"I don't know what I expected," he says. "I thought I had what she needed. And she had what I needed. I guess I was wrong on both counts."

"Did you love her?" When he does not respond immediately, she puts a hand on his and says, "I'm sorry. That was a presumptuous question."

He turns his palm up and grabs her hand with a small squeeze. "I wish I knew the answer," he says. She returns the pressure.

The next day he picks her up at St. Vincent's and they go for lunch at the Tallye-Ho Diner. The day after that they have dinner again, and the day after that Robert takes her and her daughters out for McDonalds. The girls' names are Shelly, Donna—and Andrea, this one an impish brunette. They tell him they are wild about speidies, a local specialty like shish kabob minus the skewers that Robert cannot stand. Nevertheless, the next night he brings over takeout speidies from Lupo's Char Pit, which the nurses on his unit tell him has the best speidie takeout in town (if not the most appetizing name).

Late that night the Tallye-Ho burns down. A seventeen-year-old who breaks in to rob it douses the place with gasoline and sets a match to it. He is caught in the act, but the diner is a total loss. "Oh, man!" says Robert the next morning when he reads about it in the paper.

"I loved that place," Sharon says when he sees her the next night.

"Me, too," he says. But they already know this about each other. It is going on one in the morning. and they have been talking for hours at her house. He has told her everything about himself that he can remember, including about Catherine and Andrea. He feels as if he knows everything about her; he wanted to reciprocate.

"'Life is short,'" she says, "'the art long, opportunity fleeting, experience treacherous, judgment difficult.'"

"Where's that from?"

"Hippocrates. I read it once when I was in nursing school."

"It's even better than my Post-It note quotations."

"That wouldn't be hard."

"You are a rare find," he says, and hugs her as they stand in her narrow front hallway.

CHAPTER SEVENTEEN

1

In a room on the sixth floor of the St. Moritz Hotel in New York City, Brooke McGuire stares at herself in the mirror as she adjusts a string of pearls around her neck. She approves of what she sees.

She steps back to take in the whole picture: face, hair, pearls, slinky silken black dress showing off her curves. Tonight is a special night. They are celebrating her new job, among other things. At the new Performing Arts Center back home in Buckingham, the university is going to launch several series of events for the coming year. The producer who is handling it all has asked her to become his Advertising Director, to create the promotions and showbills for each event. It is at a much higher salary than she makes at the insurance company, with much more responsibility and room for creativity. She accepted the offer at once. Harry suggested she apply after he found out about the job from the producer during an afternoon golf match one day last week. The final details worked themselves out quickly, and she gave her notice at the insurance company the day before.

Now she turns from the mirror to the window. She parts the curtains and looks out over the vista of Central Park that extends from the hotel across Central Park South, an oasis in the middle of this shining city. To the left she sees the line of buildings bordering the park on the upper west side like sentinels, and beyond them the blue haze of advancing twilight in deepest New Jersey. To the right she can see the Metropolitan Museum at the edge of the park, and the modernist corkscrew of the Guggenheim, both of which she will visit tomorrow while Harry is off making money with his friend Jay. This time it will be Harry making Jay an offer he can't refuse, a huge venture to join Harry and Al Kolata in Al's scheme to buy the abandoned courthouse downtown in Buckingham and turn it into the first of a series of luxury hotels along the east coast that they will run themselves, a scheme so big that its potential financial rewards scare even Harry.

Life, continuous and chaotic, goes on below her, on the sidewalks crammed with people, hundreds and hundreds of people everywhere she looks, completely oblivious of her. New York, New York! At this late hour of the afternoon, the sidewalk across the street is jammed with men in suits and attaché cases, women in business clothes and sneakers striding with determination down the street. Against the low retaining wall of the park a trio of bums lie in clothes stiff with dirt, so filthy she can almost smell them all the way up in her room behind the double panes of glass that separate her from the outside. They shout after whomever walks by them, she presumes for money. Two big cops stroll in conversation down the sidewalk. A little further up the street toward Fifth Avenue, an exhibit of some kind of art propped against the low wall draws crowds of passers-by.

The rush-hour traffic at this moment is congealed in a mass in front of the hotel. People on bicycles blow whistles and zip in and out among the stalled cars and taxis and busses. In the curb lane, Hansom cab horses wait patiently for things to get moving again, only to clip-clop a few paces down the street, oblivious to the activity around them, until traffic stops again. In the back seat of one cab down there drawn by a sturdy bay is a couple from Iowa or somewhere, the man in a beige sweater with a camera around his neck and his legs in khakis stretched out on the seat across from him, and the woman beside him in long sweatshirt that covers her black jogging pants and her face obscured by a blue Mets cap. The driver, a lean woman in a top hat and leather vest, turns back in her seat to point something out to them on Brooke's side of the street. They attend, as Brooke does, to the constant pulsing of this city's energy.

Harry comes out of the bathroom grimacing. He is tugging at the wings of his new bowtie. "Babe," he says, "how's this look?"

"Looks great," she says, and crosses the tiny room to straighten the tie. "Very chic."

"Really? Doesn't look dumb?"

"Not at all."

"Feels dumb. I suppose I'll get used to it."

Waiting for the elevator to carry them downstairs, she says, 'Why did you buy a bowtie if you're afraid to wear it?" She speaks low and with urgency, though there is no one nearby to overhear.

The swank surroundings themselves compel her to lower her voice. "I'm not afraid," Harry says. "I'm just not used to it."

When the elevator comes and they step inside, Harry, to her surprise, says, "Lance," and extends his hand to a strikingly handsome man who looms over them.

"Oh," the man says, "hello. Harry, isn't it? Nice to see you again." He has the bluest eyes and the squarest jaw Brooke has ever seen, and precisely clipped gray hair combed back from his patrician forehead.

In the lobby she grabs Harry's arm and hangs onto it as they make their way to the front doors. "Who was that?" she asks.

"Guy named Lance Weaver. He's an actor. I think he's in something on Broadway."

"How do you know him?"

"I met him with Jay the last time I was here."

"You didn't tell me."

"Slipped my mind. Sorry."

"How does he remember you?"

"I must have made a good impression," he says with his grin. Outside they step into the warm fall day and foul air and cacophony of the city. The doorman at the curb raises his hand and out of the molasses of traffic a cab appears. Harry presses some money into the doorman's hand and the cab moves two feet with them inside before they are stopped in traffic. Tonight Jay has gotten tickets for *Phantom of the Opera*. They are going to meet him for dinner first, at a new Cajun place he recommended in the Village, the Blackened Fish.

Harry immediately strikes up a conversation with the driver, who replies in the lilting English of the Caribbean. Out of the crowd in the street she picks out Lance Weaver's tall back. He walks briskly, with great dignity, head up, shoulders back. An actor, off to his night's work.

No, she thinks, settling herself on the seat, there was no way she could have thrown all this away. Not that there was ever any question of that. But it is still much easier to enjoy everything like this, these privileges, without feeling torn and disloyal. She was much too uncomfortable thinking about being with someone else when she was with Harry. Brooke does not like to be coaxed into doing anything. And that was the real problem with her little episode, wasn't it? That he kept trying to coax her into taking part in something he insisted was more than it was.

No, best it's over and done with. Now she can be her husband's full-time wife.

As well as the mother of his children. Because Brooke is finally, gloriously, pregnant. This is the other thing they are celebrating tonight. Earlier today, before Harry left on what was to be his solitary business trip, she got the report back from Dr. El-hakim. Success! She called Harry immediately, and he was so excited he suggested she come with him this weekend so they could make an occasion out of it. She jumped at the chance to go to the biggest, brightest city in the world and celebrate, amidst its teeming life, the infinitesimally small life that she herself is creating now within her. Her baby. Harry's.

Beside her Harry sits relaxed and confident, chatting about city traffic with the Trinidadian at the wheel, holding the world, as always, in the palm of his hand. Brooke knows this baby, as Harry's child, will be the most beautiful, healthiest, sanest little boy or girl in the entire world. Baby-to-be will have all the good luck and happiness that is the birthright of any child of Harry's. And their child will be smart, too, with a rich wisdom that will keep it from making the same mistakes Brooke has made. A wise child, greatly loved.

Starting now. As the cab cuts out into traffic and they speed through a red light, Brooke, happy and secure at last, rubs a hand over her belly in a gesture of protection and reverence. Bless you, baby, she thinks. You took your sweet time, but you're finally here. Bless you. Bless us all.

2

Counselor, heal thyself.

"This your new bed?" Robert asks.

"Yeah," Sharon says. "Except it's not so new anymore."

"New to me."

They lie entwined on it in her room. In the light from the corner lamp, everything appears in shades of violet: the walls are dark, the woodwork is darker, the headboard is darker still. Only the blades of the ceiling fan that cool their bare skin are a beige shade of rattan.

"I like this room," he says. "It feels like we're underwater. It's nice. It's revivifying."

"Revivifying. I like that word."

"I like you, Krasner."

"I'm kind of in like with you too, Fitzgerald." It draws a smile from him. "I have to say, though, it worries me, knowing you were seeing a married woman."

"It's over."

"I understand. But it seemed like you were doing to another man's family what another woman did to mine. It makes it difficult to trust you. And the fact that you took up with me the day you broke up with her makes me even more uncomfortable. It makes me feel like this is a rebound and you're an opportunist."

"Is that how you see me?"

"It's what I'm worried about you being."

"Did you ever hear the saying, 'It is better to travel hopefully than to arrive'?"

"Get that off a Post-It Note?"

"I read it in a book. For a long time there, after Andrea died and Catherine and I split up, I was afraid I'd never travel hopefully again."

"Well, Robert, my God: her daughter just died. You needed to give her some time to grieve. And you needed to give yourself some time, too."

"Now I see that. Then, I thought my mistake was not giving her enough space. So I thought if I backed off with Dennis and gave him some breathing room, I'd be doing the right thing with him. And it was the wrong thing to do with him, too."

"I guess you're just a jerk."

"I love to fish for compliments."

"You know," she says, "your friends' lives are not about you. You have to learn to let go."

"Let go and let God," he says. "You'd think I of all people would know that."

They lie quietly beside each other.

Then she says, "Now my trip with Gene—that was never very hopeful travel. Trying to get simple human warmth from him was like trying to get blood from a geode."

"Not every trip is hopeful. Not every movement is growth. Besides, maybe Gene was one stage in a longer journey."

"Oh please. Now you're sounding like him."

"Did you ever hear the story about the Chinese farmer and his horse?"

"No, I missed that one."

"Once upon a time there was a Chinese farmer who lost his only horse when the horse kicked down its stall and ran away. 'How unlucky for you,' his neighbors said. 'How do you know that?' the man said. The next day the horse came back with a whole galloping herd of wild horses. 'Lucky guy,' his neighbors said. 'How do you know that?' the man said. The next day his only son broke his leg while trying to ride one of the wild horses and couldn't work in the fields. 'How unlucky for you,' the neighbors said. 'How do you know that?' the man said. The next day the local prince came through the town and took away all the able-bodied young men to fight in the army and certain death. Naturally, the man got to keep his son because his leg was broken."

"Where'd you get that one? Little long for a fortune cookie."

"I also read it in a book."

"Same book as the travel hopefully?"

"Different book. Know what the moral of that story is?"

"Yeah, yeah. If it wasn't for my tortured relationship with Gene, we never would have met."

"And if it wasn't for my tortured relationship with everybody else in my life, I wouldn't have been ready for you."

"While it doesn't make me feel terrific about Gene, it has occurred to me that this might be the best thing to come out of the whole sick mess with him."

"Which proves my point exactly. Now if I could only earn your trust . . ."

"I think this may be the beginning of a beautiful friendship."

"Speaking strictly for myself, it couldn't have come at a better time."

CHAPTER EIGHTEEN

1

Gene heaves the last box of books aboard the U-Haul trailer and slams the gate. "That everything?" Robert asks. Gene, out of breath and red-faced, nods yes. Dennis, to appear helpful, pounds a box in the front of the trailer. Mostly he has just been standing around watching Robert and Gene bring his things down from his room and up from the basement. He did take the initiative in packing up, however, this being something the others could not do for him.

"That's it, then," Robert tells him. "All packed and ready to go."

"More here than I thought there would be," Gene says.

"Not me. I knew we'd need a trailer. I've moved enough times in my life to judge a big load when I see one."

"You were right."

Dennis walks around the trailer hitched to the back of Robert's Cutlass. Robert has persuaded him that his old Pinto wouldn't be up for the trip, short as it is.

Not that it took much persuading. Since he got out of the hospital two weeks ago, Dennis has been more tentative in his ways than ever. More confused than usual, too, in general but mostly about the smaller questions like what to have for breakfast and when to have it, the large questions like what to wear being entirely too much to handle. As a result, he has worn the same clothes, his Levis and Shit Happens tee shirt, every day. He is getting pretty gamey, among all his other problems.

His parents are trying hard not to show their concern. Though he was discharged to their house, as though into their custody, he has spent almost every evening of his last two weeks at the House of Grins, ostensibly to pack up his belongings to move home, but actually spending as much time as he can with his friends and his independent life before being reabsorbed into his family.

Robert took the opportunity to talk with Dennis and help him clarify what he wanted for himself and how he might achieve it, and what might be the effects of going back to his family. He wanted to come back, he said, but it was clear to Robert that even the vision of an independent life at his house could not counter the pull of his parents. Finally, there was no substitute for his own family for Dennis. The memory of his blood ultimately called him back home. Just as Brooke had been called by her family back to her wifely role.

Still smarting from his failure with her as well as with Dennis, Robert had tried to help Dennis as a friend and not a counselor, convinced as he was in the end that Dennis needed to go back home, and so should. Home for Dennis was where he hung his head, where the tensions and conflicts he must deal with originated, and where he must deal with them. Dennis is in charge now, not Robert. From this point on, what will happen, will happen. Shit happens, but so does lots of other stuff.

Now, under the hot sun, the three men stand around the small trailer loaded with Dennis's things, awaiting what is the most difficult thing for him to do, say goodbye to the house, and his friends, and, temporarily at least, his grownup life.

At the end, it is Gene who hurries things along. "Well," he says, "I don't mean to rush you, but I'm going to need to be finished up by two o'clock." It is now twelve.

"Okay," says Dennis. "No problem." He tugs a box once more and says, "I'll just go inside and make sure I have everything."

Robert and Gene watch him trudge up the front walk. "Poor guy," Gene says. "Going home like this. Breaks my heart."

"His, too."

Inside Dennis goes up the stairs slowly, takes a last look around his room, and is about to go back down when Martina comes up.

"I wanted to say goodbye before you left," she says. "And wish you good luck."

"Thank you," Dennis says. He sticks his hand out and she takes it and kisses him on the cheek. She gives him a big hug.

Her body is warm and strong and her breasts are conspicuous against him. "Take good care of yourself," she says.

He is too befuddled to say anything, so he just nods into her shoulder and she pulls away to arm's length. She brushes her hair back from her forehead with her hand. "There's always going to be a place here for you, you know that, right?"

Dennis nods.

"When you're ready to come back, Robert will have your room for you."

"I know."

"Listen. Take care, all right?"

"I never really thanked you for what you did for me."

"Consider me thanked."

"I just wanted to say—how sorry I am for all the trouble I caused you."

"Forget it. You just get better, and come back to give me some more trouble."

She hugs him again and sends him downstairs in a fog.

At his parents' home, his younger brother helps Robert and Gene unload. Robert is glad to see Dennis take a more active role in this part of the move. He stations himself in his old room and directs them where to put his clothes, his bookcase, his bed, his boxes of stuff. Howard the cat has already reestablished this room as his own and has begun a campaign of terror against the Parkers' dog.

Now Dennis even begins to unpack the boxes. It seems as if he is forcing himself to be active, but that's good too. At least he is not beginning his stay at his parents' house passively. Maybe the things he had around him during his independent life will inspire him to become independent again.

When the trailer is empty, Dennis goes with Robert and Gene to return it to the U-Haul downtown. The Tallye-Ho having burnt down, they stop at another diner for lunch, and then drop him off at his parents'.

Dennis lingers outside the car. "Come back and see us," says Robert.

"I will."

"Why don't you come for dinner a week from Wednesday?"

Dennis smiles nervously and says he will come. They part with good feelings and the expectation of seeing each other again soon.

Sharon is waiting on the porch when they return to the House of Grins. Her children are walking around in comical circles on the front sidewalk, three little brown-haired girls, miniatures of their mother. They return Robert's greeting with giggles like the chirping of birds.

"Hi," Gene says to Sharon. He and Robert pause on the front stoop.

"Hi," Sharon says. Awkward moment. Gene looks at Sharon, who looks at Robert, who smiles at her and squints into the late summer sunlight. Gene sees the look that passes between them. He says, "You didn't come to see me, did you?"

Sharon shakes her head. Robert keeps squinting.

"Oh," Gene says. "Well. I'll just get on inside. Nice to see you again," he tells her, and takes the three steps up to the porch in one long stride and disappears into the house. "Hi, squinty," Sharon says. "That your Clint Eastwood imitation?"

"Yup." Laconic. Eastwoodian.

He sits next to her on one of the three white rockers on the porch and puts his feet up on the railing with a grunt of comfort. "I think Gene just smelled the coffee."

"I hope so."

"Is that what I owe the honor of this visit to? Sweet revenge?"

"Sort of. I wanted to see you. And I thought if that got Gene to eat his heart out a little, well, that's gravy."

"You're a tough cookie."

"You noticed how he greeted my children with such warmth and tenderness."

"Why are they walking around so obsessive-compulsively?"

"Because they're weird. I heard Gene and his new girlfriend are definitely on the outs. How she more or less kicked his ass more or less out the door. I wanted to more or less gloat with my new squeeze."

"Did you also hear he's leaving town?"

"Yeah."

"You must have great sources."

"The best. Turns out his ex-wife and I have mutual friends in the mother's network. I hear things."

"Any other interesting things?"

"He tells his son a lot in some misguided attempt to get into his good graces. His son is turning into a real troubled kid. Anyway, the son tells the mother, who tells other mothers, who tell me."

"Small towns. Gotta love 'em."

"Did you get Dennis moved?"

"We did."

"How was it?"

"He was kind of spacy while we were loading the trailer. But he perked up when we got to his parents'. He even took charge of things, sort of."

"Had lunch yet?"

"I got a bite with Dennis and Gene."

"Aw, the boys got to say goodbye to each other. Nice."

"Male unbonding."

"You look tired."

"I'm exhausted. I'm clearly not as young as I used to be."

"The troops are hungry so we're going to get some lunch. Want to join us? You can have dessert."

"Love to." He stands and stretches his body, which is growing stiffer by the minute. "Got time for me to grab a quick shower so I won't be quite so funky?"

"Please do."

"In the meantime, see if you can get those children to stop that neurotic behavior. The neighbors'll talk. We've already given them enough to talk about." He goes inside.

Shortly Gene comes out and sits on the railing in front of her. He smiles so he won't appear threatening. Or, God forbid, jealous. "So you and Robert are an item now?"

"We're friends. Does that make us an item?"

"Depends on how close your friendship is."

She lets a silence divide them further. Then she says, "We're pretty close."

"That's what I thought. Is that why you didn't return my calls?"

"No. You are."

"I'm leaving town," Gene says. When she does not reply, he says, "Thought I'd go stay with my son in San Diego, see what might be out there for me. But you probably knew that."

"I did. I hope you find what you're looking for out there."

"Thanks."

A half-dozen pre-teenage boys with tie-dyed tee shirts and skateboards and buzz cuts walk down the street, laughing loudly and artificially for a reason that is not apparent to Gene or Sharon, though Sharon's daughters crack up when the boys pass.

Gene says, "Robert's okay."

"I'm glad you approve."

"His little community here's dwindling down to a precious few, though. You heard about Dennis?"

"Of course."

"Maybe you can come out and visit me in California. You and Robert, I mean."

"I don't think so."

"No. I guess you wouldn't want to. I understand."

"I don't think that's necessarily true, either."

"I guess not."

Neither says anything else.

"Kids," she says, "get in the car. We're leaving soon." Amazingly, they obey.

When Robert comes back out, Gene stands and says, "Well, if I don't see you again, best of luck, Sharon." He bends down to kiss her cheek. She turns her head away.

Gene is still sitting on the porch when Robert gets home. It is near dusk, cool and with a hint of the season change in the air. "Beautiful weather," Gene says. "I'm going to miss this part of the country. Especially this time of year."

Robert sits beside him. "I can't say I've gotten all that fond of this place. I need a little more sun than you get around here. Too much like Seattle. The winters are too long. Too dreary. Though this hasn't been a boring year, I'll say that."

"I wouldn't say it's been boring at all. In fact, it's been more exciting than usual, since you hit town. I'll miss it. I'll miss you."

"Myself, I need water. This is a pretty area, but there's not enough water. The rivers are okay, but they're always moving. And they're straight, mostly. Give me an ocean, or at the least a lake that's round and stable. You can meditate on a lake."

"Still, there are some beautiful little lakes out in the country. Seems like there's a nice little lake around every curve, glittering in the sun. My thing is mountains. I just love mountains. These are little hills around here, compared with what you find out west."

"Then you're moving to the right place."

They are silent until Gene says, "You're seeing Sharon now."

"I am."

"That's good. It's good for her. I could tell this afternoon. I was never good for her. Never could give her what she wanted. Or needed. And vice versa. Just one more reason to leave."

"Gene, I feel duty-bound to point out that it was you who dumped Sharon. Pretty goddamn hard. What she does now really isn't your concern anymore."

"You're right, of course. I was rotten to her. If I feel bad, it's just what I deserve."

Robert sighs. "I guess it's your karma then."

Gene does not disagree.

2

They all show up for Dennis's dinner: Robert and Sharon, her three girls, Martina and Max, and Gene.

Dennis receives their hugs with a relaxed and natural smile, a fine contrast to the limp and anxious young man he had been the last time they saw him. He even laughs and claps his hands when Robert brings out the main dish on a huge tray under a gunmetal gray cover. He removes it with a flourish to reveal a saucepan filled to the brim with tuna noodle casserole with cream of mushroom soup and peas.

"My all-purpose meal!" Dennis shouts.

"What else?" says Robert. "You were expecting something fancy? And a sturdy dish it is. Your four basic food groups, your pasta, the meal of marathoners, your protein, your legumes. But look: who says this isn't fancy—I've garnished it with parsley."

"A significant source of potassium," Martina points out. "Just the thing for depression."

Dennis snaps up the sprig and gobbles it down to applause.

"I hope this is up to your usual quality," Robert says as he dishes out the grub.

It is a noisy meal, with Sharon's daughters happily chattering nonstop and everyone else talking at once—except for Dennis and Robert, who each slip into silence once the food is served. Dennis remembers meals past, mostly eaten alone in front of the television in the living room, and how miserable he generally was, and how much he misses it all now.

Robert's silence, too, is elegiac. This dinner is a transitional event. Seated around the table are what will soon be his house's past—Dennis, Gene—and its near future—Sharon, Martina, children. Dennis, though he may heal, will never return as a resident, Robert knows. The place will be here for him when he is ready to come back; he will be different. Gene is leaving at the end of the month, and despite what he may say will never return either. And Robert would not want him back, as he would take Dennis back if Dennis were capable of returning. Past and future meld into the present for the duration of the meal, and, once finished, will separate into their own channels once more, the past receding, the future approaching.

Once they have all helped themselves to dessert (again, Dennis's favorite, hot fudge sundaes with Smucker's hot fudge and Häagen-Dazs), Robert and Sharon clear the table as the others retire to the living room with their coffee and conversations, which now, as if they had picked up the tenor of Robert's own thoughts about transition, eddy around discussions of all the places each has lived and the problems adjusting. Robert leaves them to slip out the back door and fills his lungs with the full crisp night air.

It is clear out, the stars as visible as they can be in the reflected glow from the lights of this small town. Outside the town limits, not fifteen minutes away, the sky will fairly sparkle. Maybe he should explore the country areas Gene mentioned earlier. The thought of perfect, contained lakes with houses lining the edges is an attractive one. Maybe that would be an area to consider moving to. He could sell this place and begin again, fresh start number three. Third time's the charm.

Fiendish Howard darts out of the shadows across his feet and Robert tumbles into the lawn headfirst. Hot on Howard's heels is little Andrea, Sharon's youngest, who crashes into Robert's fallen thigh and dives over his back. He turns, asks, "Are you okay?" She giggles maniacally in response, and he, equally uncontrolled, laughs and grabs her skinny ribs and tickles her until she screams in glee. "Tickled to death!" he cries, "what a horrible way to go!"

He lifts her squirming in snaggle-toothed happiness into the air and holds her against the night sky before letting her fall back into his arms. He hugs her, wraps his arms around her for all of the ones he can't reach now, inhales her sweet little girl smell and feels her tiny heart go rat-a-tat in her chest as she returns his embrace. He lets her go and she darts off again after the cat.

Breathing hard, smiling broadly, he slaps at the occasional late season bugs that bother his face, and he wanders out front. The street is quiet. His is the brightest house on the block. Every light is on in every window of all three stories.

The House of Grins. Tonight, once more, the name fits. There is much grinning going on. He can see them all through the picture window, sitting around the living room. For the time being they have put aside the bad feelings that had settled in after the initial period of grace. All is forgiven: the depressions, the sexual jealousies, the frustrations, all the woes of their lives. Forgiven, or at least displaced for tonight. No deaths of children, no suicide attempts, no heat and passion, no fruitless searches for the free and spiritual life, no pernicious ambition, no rejections, no dejections. Just grins and good feelings. Hugs and tickles.

This is a breather, he thinks, from the events of the past year. We are all pausing before we leap into the next phases of our lives, where the struggles will be as hard. Dennis will have a long road to travel to extricate himself from his parents' house and from the sense of failure he gives off like body odor. Gene will travel out to San Diego to meet himself waiting at his son's. Martina will have to come to terms with the lengths to which her ambition drove her—as well as her loneliness, Robert firmly believes, though she would probably not agree with that. Sharon will come to terms with what Gene did to her, and with this new relationship with Robert, and with whatever other things Robert is not even aware of yet. Her kids (he hopes) have all their lives ahead of them, including whatever he will be able to bring to them.

And what of Robert himself? He has come out of this year with more losses than wins. Another failed relationship. To the list of Catherine, Andrea, Jeannie, his own children, and Maureen, among the many others, including of course Dennis, now add Brooke. Will Sharon join that list? Can he handle Sharon, handle a woman who is not emotionally inaccessible? Can she handle him? Can he handle the end of the House of Grins and all it represented?

He hunkers down on the curb and picks up a twig from the maple tree that covers the front of his house. The stick is long and skinny and gnarled, and the two huge lobed leaves that hang off it are dry and papery already. Harbingers of what's to come, when they will be knee-deep in fallen leaves.

He crumples them in his fingers and lets the crackling pieces fall into the street between his feet. Brushes his hands clean, takes a deep breath. Looks up and down the block. Yes. He can handle her. Wants to. Is ready to. Looks forward to. Is maybe not confident about his ability to, exactly, but knows he needs to.

Because the House of Grins has just about collapsed, more like a House of Cards in the end. Over, like the long phase of his life that he now sees it was the culmination of. His great vision, his great experiment was, he now realizes, not a way to overcome the pain of Andrea and Catherine, and, truth to tell, all the rest, all the connections with people he's ruined over the course of his life. No, it was a way to return to it all before moving on. He thought he would be helping usher in a new era in his life, a new way of living, an era of neo-family living, helpful and supportive and without the stresses of traditional families. But he missed it by a mile. It was the people he chose and their lack of stability and commitment to each other, but it was also Robert himself and his stubborn selfishness. He tried to control it all, and of course he couldn't. He tried to base this new iteration of his family upon independence instead of interdependence. His misguided attempts to understand without being involved that so infuriated Brooke, to control without caring that almost lost Dennis, to assume responsibility without the skill or wisdom to meld its components, duty and love for the others, into something larger than themselves—all these meant the family he created in this house was just as bad as, and in many ways worse than, every other family he'd ever been a part of. And, as in all the others, the problem was with him.

Silently Martina sits beside him on the curb. He starts; she places a quieting hand on his arm. "Sorry," she says.

"How's it going in there?"

"It's a love feast. Everybody's on their best behavior. For Dennis's sake."

"Good. About time. How are you doing?"

"Pretty good." Then she says, "Max's house is going to be ready next month."

"Great. Has he asked you to marry him lately?"

"Of course. Within the last few hours, as a matter of fact."

"Still said no?"

"I still said no. I did say I'd move in with him, though. And if that worked . . . Then we'd talk."

"So you're leaving too."

"Afraid so. I'm sorry. I was the last one."

"I was just sitting here thinking things are pretty much coasting to a stop anyway."

"What are you going to do by yourself in this big old thing?"

"I think I'm going to enjoy it for a while."

"Not going to bring in a new group?"

"You make it sound like camp."

"Sometimes that's what it felt like. Could you stand not being a house father?"

"I could not only stand it, I yearn for it."

"Maybe you'll have some company."

"What do you mean?"

"Sharon seems like she's going to be good for you."

"Don't look for her to move in any time soon."

"I never did meet the woman you were in such a funk about. But I think you and Sharon are good together."

"Not as good as Max and you, of course."

"Before it's said and done, I probably will give wifehood a try with that big lug. And motherhood. Or at least stepmotherhood."

"That's good," he says. "After all that's happened this year, I still think people belong together."

"I'll let you know."

"You better."

"Nice night," she says. "You can smell fall in the air."

"Hard to believe it's going to be snowing before we know it."

"Winter comes early around here," Martina says. "As you now know."

"It's true. And spring comes late."

ABOUT THE AUTHOR

Donald Levin is an award-winning fiction writer and poet. He is the author of the Detroit Quartet, including *Savage City*, a historical novel set in 1932 Detroit, *The Arsenal of Deceit*, a historical novel set in 1941, and *The Ghosts of Detroit* a historical novel set in 1955. He is at work on the fourth book in the series. He has also written seven Martin Preuss mystery novels; three books of poetry, *Are You Listening* (West Vine Press, 2024), *In Praise of Old Photographs* (Little Poem Press, 2005), and *New Year's Tangerine* (Pudding House Press, 2007); *The Exile* (Poison Toe Press, 2020), a dystopian novella; and co-author of *Postcards from the Future: A Triptych on Humanity's End* (Whistlebox Press and Quitt and Quinn Publishers, 2019). He lives in Ferndale, Michigan.

To learn more about Donald and his works, visit his website, www.donaldlevin.com, and follow him on Instagram at donald_levin_author.

If you enjoyed this book, please post a review on Goodreads, Amazon, or your favorite book review site.

ALSO BY DONALD LEVIN

The first three books in the Detroit Quartet

Detroit, 1932. The fates of four people converge during a violent week of labor unrest in the bleakest year of the Great Depression. Against the backdrop of the bloody Ford Hunger March, events hurl these four into the center of a political storm that will change them—and their city—forever.

Detroit, 1941. With the nation on the brink of war, four people unite against the subversive forces that threaten Detroit, America's "arsenal of democracy." *The Arsenal of Deceit* recreates a rich historical period with chilling parallels to our own time.

Detroit, 1955. Factory closings. The Red Scare. Racial hatred. Four shattered characters take an unforgettable journey through these forces that shaped mid-century America.

The Martin Preuss Mystery Series

One cold November night, police detective Martin Preuss joins a frantic search for a seven-year-old girl with epilepsy who has disappeared from the streets of his suburban Detroit community. Probing deep into the anguished lives of all those who came into contact with the missing girl, Preuss must summon all his skills and resources to solve the many crimes of love he uncovers.

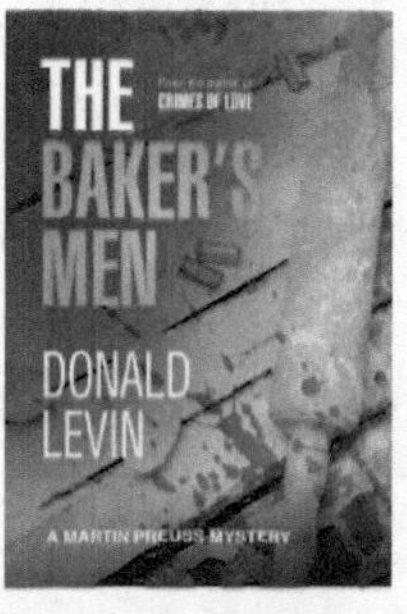

Easter, 2009. Ferndale Police detective Martin Preuss is spending a quiet evening with his son Toby when he's called out to investigate an after-hours shooting at a bakery in his suburban Detroit community. Struggling with the dizzying uncertainties of the case and hindered by the treachery of his own colleagues who scheme against him, Preuss is drawn into a whirlwind of greed, violence, and revenge spanning generations.

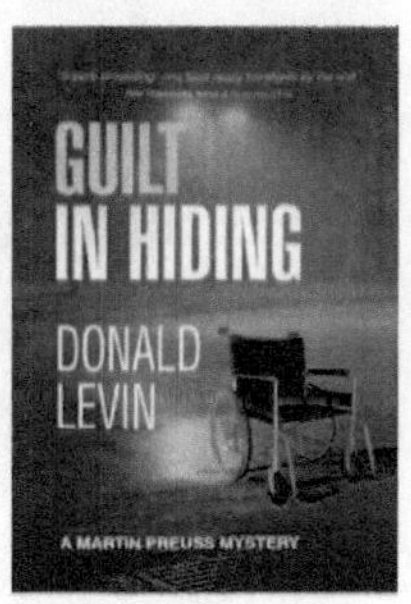

Preuss is called out to search for a van that has disappeared along with the woman who was driving and her passenger, a handicapped young man. Working through layer upon layer of secrets, Preuss exposes a multitude of contemporary crimes with roots in the twentieth century's darkest period.

When a friend asks newly retired detective Martin Preuss to look for a boy who disappeared forty years ago, the former investigator gradually becomes consumed with finding the forgotten child. Preuss revisits the countercultural fervor of Detroit in the 1970s—and plunges into hidden worlds of guilty secrets and dark crimes that won't stay buried.

Twenty years have passed since Raymond Douglas went to prison for the kidnapping and murder of a local businessman's wife. Now Douglas's daughter has hired private investigator Martin Preuss to track down a previously-unknown accomplice to the crime—who may or may not even exist.

A young man takes a walk on the wild side and ends up clinging to life in a suburban Detroit motel. When private investigator Martin Preuss searches for the reason, he plunges into the young man's dark world of secrets and lies.

When the police investigation into the murder of a retired professor stalls, friends of the dead man plead with PI Martin Preuss to learn what happened. The twisting tale leads him across Detroit into a treacherous world of long-buried family secrets . . . where the painful relations between parents and children meet the deadly gathering storm of domestic terrorism.